"A striking tale flaunting a s
any time period"
— *Kirkus Reviews*

"Riveting. This book is fun from start to finish."
— the Reader

"Page-turning excitement! Time-traveling assassin Lauren Ramirez copes in a world 200 years in her past."
— Foster Cline author of *Parenting with Love and Logic*

"I couldn't put it down. Full of fantastical but realistic settings and action. Great read!"
— Captain Bill Collier author of *CIA Super Pilot Spills the Beans: Flying Helicopters in Laos for Air America*

"A delightful, mind-stretching adventure into the rough and tumble early days of Hollywood."
— Jim Payne, author of *Worlds to Discover; Kayak Adventures One Inch above the Water*

"*Assassin 13* melds science fiction with historical fiction. Lauren Ramirez is a complicated woman with deadly skills and a very humane AI (artificial intelligence) in her head."
— Mary Haley author of *Ghost Writer, the Great Potato Murder*

"A 22nd-century assassin inadvertently travels back to Prohibition Hollywood in this sci-fi-infused historical thriller. Characters are dynamic…"
— *Kirkus Reviews*

ASSASSIN 13

A Time-Travel Thriller set in a Dystopian Future
and 1927 Prohibition Hollywood

Tom Reppert

Assassin 13

Copyright 2018 Tom Reppert
All rights reserved

ISBN-13:978-0692077993 (Helen's Sons Publishing)
ISBN-10: 0692077995

Helen's Sons Publishing
120 W. Garfield Bay Road
Sagle, ID 83860

Graphic cover art by Scott Wilburn
Sandpoint, ID

Assassin 13

"We are living in a jazz age of super-accentuated rhythm in all things; in a rhythm that (to "jazz" a word) is super-normal, a rhythm which is the back-flare from the rhythm of a super war."
F. Scott Fitzgerald, Jacobs' Band Monthly, Jan. 1921

MIAMI POST OBITUARY PAGE

MIAMI BEACH, FLA. August 15, 1977. Ben Sorrentino, ex-Los Angeles prohibition-era mobster, died in his home here this morning of heart failure. He was 78. His wife, Cherie, and two sons, Ben Jr. and Alphonse, were present.

Known in his gangster days as Benny the Bug, Sorrentino was described in one biography as the most brutal cutthroat in American history. In the City of Angels, he engaged in a notorious gangland war that saw more than 200 slaughtered by handguns, shotguns, Tommy guns, knives, baseball bats and brass knuckles. Innocent men, women and children were caught in the crossfire.

Yet, inexplicably, in that bygone era, he gained celebrity status in a town of celebrities.

"Benny had charm," Meyer Lansky, another notable Miami Beach retiree, said on hearing of his passing. "People just naturally liked him, wanted to please him. He had that effect on everyone. Especially women. It was charm all right, but the charm of a snake."

Just after arriving in Hollywood in 1927, he most notably dated the famous silent film actress Pauline Windsor. He was arrested for her murder in 1928, the only time he was tried for a crime. When evidence and witnesses disappeared, he was acquitted and...

CHAPTER ONE: THE PERILS OF PAULINE

August 21, 1927 Los Angeles

At night along southern California's Pacific coast, countless people noticed the fiery object plunging out of a starry sky. A meteorite, no doubt. Likely a large one. They watched for several seconds till it disappeared into the Santa Monica Mountains.

At dawn two and a half days later, Pauline Windsor was driving her Duesenberg convertible at a high rate of speed in those same Santa Monica Mountains, a dust cloud from the dirt road trailing behind. Her platinum blonde hair, short and bobbed, tossed wildly in the buffeting wind. Dressed in an evening gown and silk stockings that accented her shapely legs, she felt the chill of the wind but ignored it.

Recklessly, Pauline skirted the yawning drop-offs, expertly shifting gears around the sharp curves. She knew it was crazy, this thrill ride, but the sexual heat from this past evening still held her in an intoxicating fever. Dancing at the Cocoanut Grove till 3:00am with none other than Ben Sorrentino, the gangster.

She had gone to the Grove with her close friend and sometime leading man Michael Murray. The fan magazines accounted them their favorite movie couple behind Mary Pickford and Douglas Fairbanks. In fact, Michael was homosexual and had a long-time boyfriend with whom he lived. If his real sex life were known, he'd be tarred and feathered in the press and driven from town, an outcast never to work in films again. His occasional outings with Pauline were to maintain his virile, romantic onscreen image. She valued his friendship and was happy to play her Mata Hari part in his secret life.

Last night, the Grove dazzled the film crowd, outdoing itself for its Tuesday evening dance contest. When Pauline and Michael arrived, glitter covered the high ceilings and a waterfall flowed down the back wall. Mechanical monkeys hung from tall palm trees that had been plucked years before off the set of Rudolph Valentino's film *The Sheik*. The loud, pounding rhythm of the band playing "The Varsity Drag" filled the room, and several people had already taken to the floor to try the frenetic step.

As she walked in on Michael's arm, people waved to them, some called out greetings, mostly to her. After all, at just twenty-six, she was one of the two or three most popular actresses in the world, dubbed *America's Heroine* by the press. She thoroughly enjoyed her regal status.

A cigarette girl rushed up and asked her for an autograph. "Sure, honey," Pauline said, took the offered pencil and signed her name in the girl's notepad.

Then, the maître d' led the couple to a table where they joined two up-and-coming actors at Global Pictures, Pauline's studio. She knew them only as Wesley and Joanie. The publicity department had set up this outing. The two couples hugged in greeting and smiled for photographers, then took their seats. With the knowledge the police had been bought off, Pauline ordered a bourbon and water. Prohibition be damned.

Tapping her foot to the music, she desperately wanted to dance. Michael, one of the handsomest leading men in the movies, had fallen arches and wouldn't be caught dead on a dance floor. Glancing about the room, hoping to find a partner, she saw several people she knew. Gloria Swanson, John Gilbert without his girlfriend Greta Garbo, John Barrymore sitting with Mary Astor, Roman Navarro, and several others. Tuesday nights at the Grove brought out Hollywood's film stars, but none of them were heading her way to ask her to dance.

Abruptly, Greeny Walsh, a two-bit hood who worked Global Studios selling drugs, slid into a seat at their table. Each studio had its seller. Drugs were easier to get than alcohol and that easy enough. The man had small bloodshot eyes, slicked-back brown hair and a narrow, pock-marked face.

He gave Pauline a smug grin that revealed crooked, yellow teeth. "What's knittin', kitten?"

She held his gaze and didn't answer.

After a moment, Walsh frowned and turned to Wesley. "You're looking good, Wes. Getting bigger and bigger parts I hear. Time to celebrate. Get hopped up, you know. I can help you there. I got the best dope money can buy, but I won't have it long. The room's buzzing tonight. My supply will go like that." He snapped his fingers.

Wesley nodded, and Joanie said giddily, "Me, too." Michael lifted his hand slightly like a man bidding at an auction.

"Now, you're talking." Walsh grinned and slid little paper packets across the table to the three of them and pocketed the dollars in return, not particularly evasive about the maneuver.

"How about you, queenie?" he said to Pauline. "First class dope."

"Come on, Pauline," Joanie said. "We can all boil the owl tonight."

Pauline glanced at Michael, who shrugged, already pouring the white powder into a tin the size of his thumb.

"Make up your mind, toots," Walsh said. "I got other people to see."

With her glacial blue eyes, she stared at Walsh and said icily, "Go to hell, Mr. Walsh."

His face twisted into a sneer. About to retort, he glanced over her shoulder at a man approaching the table. "Oh, shit." Walsh sprang to his feet and hurried away.

Pauline turned around to see who it was. In a town where handsome men were common, the man walking toward her with such a confident swagger was striking. Dressed to the nines in a tux. Tall with wavy black hair and a swarthy complexion. He walked with an animal power in his stride, and she felt her insides turn liquid. She thought she knew every famous actor in Hollywood, and by his looks, this man had to be a star. As he came up to her table, his dark, narcotic eyes pierced her, sent jolts of electricity through her.

He gave a slight bow. "Miss Windsor, I'm Ben Sorrentino. I was hoping you would honor me with this dance. I've never tried the Varsity Drag and thought if you're willing, we might give it a spin."

She felt a sudden shock at his name. Of course, she knew who he was. Everyone in Los Angeles knew. He was no actor. He was a mobster, a cohort of that Al Capone fellow in Chicago. She faintly knew of the name Benny the Bug. That's what people called him, but she doubted if they did it to his face.

As he gazed down on her, her blood spiked. Suddenly, she yearned for the wild days of her youth when she first came out to Hollywood with Mack Sennett, starred as one of his "bathing beauties" with Mabel Normand, and anything went. She lifted her hand for him to take. "I am a poor dancer, Mr. Sorrentino. You are taking on quite the challenge."

He smiled, supremely confident. "Somehow I think you'll do all right."

The rest of the night was a whirlwind of gaiety and excitement. She hung on his words, laughed at his jokes and thoroughly enjoyed the attention of someone so notorious. He was the most charming man she'd ever met. Around midnight,

Michael slipped off to be with his boyfriend while Wesley and Joanie went onto the dance floor and stayed as if it were a marathon contest. Among hundreds, she and Ben were alone.

"I have a suite upstairs," he said with directness.

The Cocoanut Grove was in the Ambassador Hotel. No naïve girl from the hinterlands anymore, if she'd ever been, Pauline knew what he meant.

She looked him in the eye. "You want to sleep with me. Is that what you're saying?"

He did not grin or leer. In fact, he was deliberate, thoughtful. "Oh, Miss Windsor, I wasn't thinking of sleeping."

She laughed. They went up to his suite.

On the dirt road in the mountains that next morning, Pauline began braking the Duecy, easing her speed and staying well clear of the cliffs. She had no secret wish to die. She had two children and loved them too much to leave them orphaned through foolish euphoria. Hell, she even felt guilty on those few occasions when she dated and left them with her mother or nanny.

Slowly, she approached a series of switchbacks that led down to a large orange grove below. When she reached the bottom, the dirt road flattened out and widened as it ran straight down the middle of the grove.

Toward the end where it approached Mulholland Highway, she saw something and suddenly braked hard, skidding to a stop. A woman was sitting alongside the road, and she was naked.

Pauline hurried around the car. "Are you all right?"

Seeing her from this close, she gagged. The woman was badly burned. She appeared asleep, or dead, with her head resting on her knees and her arms folded around her legs. Severe burns covered most of the left side of her body. Her black hair had been completely scorched away on that side, her scalp blistered and oozing. Along much of her body she had waxy and blistered skin in great swathes. This was far worse than a sunburn. She had been burned by fire. How could she even be alive?

The woman looked up as if just realizing someone was there. Her eyes widened in shock. "Sybil?" she muttered.

"Who?"

Through dry and cracked lips, she whispered, "Do you have any water?"

"No, but there's a gas station on Mulholland. I'm sure we can get water there." Pauline reached out her hand. "Let me help you up. Can you make it to the car?"

The woman nodded, took the hand, and groaning, got to her feet. At the car, she hesitated staring at it in confusion. "What is this?" she muttered in a hoarse rasp.

"It's a Duesy," Pauline explained. "A Duesenberg. Come on. I've got to get you to a hospital."

The woman drew back. "No hospital. No police."

At the sudden flash of anger, Pauline drew back, then said. "But you're badly burned."

The woman sagged a bit, the force of her injuries seemingly taking hold of her once again. "No hospital. No police. Promise me. I just need some water."

"All right." Carefully, Pauline took her arm, afraid the woman's skin might slide off in her hand, and led her to the back of the car.

Then, the burned woman said the strangest thing, "I don't need a hospital. I have nanobots, medical ones. They'll take care of my burns. I just need some water."

Nanobots? What the hell were nanobots? Perhaps, the woman was crazy. Not surprising, her wandering through the Santa Monica Mountains naked. "All right. Let's get you in the back so you can lie down."

In the trunk strapped to the back, Pauline retrieved a blanket and draped it over the woman. She drew the canvas top up over the car to block the sun, and then quickly drove away, thoughts of her night with Ben Sorrentino forgotten for the moment. Who was this woman? How in the hell did she get there on the side of the road without any clothes?

As badly hurt as the woman was, Pauline decided to go along with her for the moment. Her brother Russell was a doctor of sorts. She would take her to him. He would know what to do. Then, she could notify the police.

CHAPTER TWO: THE MAKING OF AN ASSASSIN I

August 5, 2116, Foothills of the High Sierras

On the day Erin Ramirez was murdered, she arose just before dawn as the last stars faded over the High Sierras. Because of the summer heat, she had slept outside beside the old Airstream camper with her husband, Hector, and their thirteen-year-old daughter, Lauren. Erin intended to get in a run before the temperature rose too high, and the rest of the circus awakened.

Already, her long red hair was damp with perspiration. She smoothed it back behind her ears and rubbed her temples. Another hammer-and-anvil headache building. Running, getting her blood pumping seemed to stave it off for a while.

She stared down at her daughter. The girl's long black hair splayed out on the pillow. So different in looks. Coppery skin, tall for her age, she took after her father that way, yet so similar in attitude to Erin, aggressive, temperamental, and able to spot blarney and bullshit in nanoseconds.

She smiled at a rivulet of drool that slid down the girl's cheek. "Wake up, mi hija," she whispered, gently shaking Lauren. "It's time."

Lauren had pleaded to be awakened so she could run with her mother, but now, the girl groaned and turned away. Undisturbed in a nearby sleeping bag, her husband snored on.

On a tree branch just above, a robin sang to her. The sounds of a few tent flaps and a pot or two clanging came from the awakening camp. They were all early risers.

They were the Misfits, a pitiful excuse for a circus. Three days ago, they had stopped here in the foothills of the High Sierras next to the American River, where, it was said, gold had been discovered sometime in the far distant past. They had put on shows at several little venues about the area.

Erin loved the Misfits because they'd become her daughter's family, and so hers as well. They advertised themselves as a circus, but they weren't much of one—fifty people and an elephant named Ralph. They traveled in an old yellow school bus, several pickup trucks, campers, and a few wagons, all drawn by horses; no one could afford gas any more.

Only a vintage Ford convertible, circa 2080, used gas but only in part. The rest of its fuel was methane from Ralph's monstrous defecations. A man always followed the elephant with a shovel and a wheelbarrow.

These were desperate times, but then Erin could not remember a time when they weren't desperate. Much of America had slid into living at subsistence level, actual coin scarce, manufactured products few, paying jobs almost non-existent except in the domed enclaves inside cities like Los Angeles, Las Vegas, and San Francisco, where the wealthy class and the government lived. No shortages for them. Getting any of those jobs was impossible without family connections. Many small towns were armed camps, often run by gangs or organized crime enterprises. They often preyed upon travelers like the Misfits.

The first shards of sunlight glinted off the silver camper. Painted on its side were the images of herself, her husband, and Lauren, all in fierce combative poses that Lauren had claimed made them all look constipated. In large print were the words: **Montezuma, the Irish Banshee, and Little Malinche. No holds barred fighting. Take on all comers. Win Big Money.**

Lauren was Little Malinche.

It was Hector and Lauren who made the money and barter that kept them alive and much of the circus going. Not Erin. No woman was brave enough to step in the Octagon against a world champion in judo, but Hector and Lauren were different. Everyone thought they could win against them. Even though a Tae Kwon Do master, Hector was such a good actor, always on the brink of defeat, he drew them in; and Lauren, a tall, skinny girl, seemed easy money for teenage boys.

As always, Erin felt both a sense of pride in her daughter, and guilt. A good mother would not use her daughter to fight other young people for money. But Lauren was a natural at it, she loved it, and if she didn't play the game, they wouldn't eat.

A year and a half ago when her daughter turned twelve, Erin had finally decided against Hector's opposition for the girl to enter the Octagon.

"She's too young," he argued, his voice rising in pitch with his growing frustration. "We do not need to do this. She'll be fighting against grown boys."

Lauren pleaded, "Please, papa. In practice, I destroy all the boys in the circus. I can do it. I swear I'm not going to lose. Ever."

"That's hubris," Hector scolded. "Too much pride. It will be your weakness."

But she was ready and he had known it. Tall for her age at 5'6," she was also lean and strong, and blazingly quick.

"Two against one," Erin said. "That's the family rule. You're outvoted, Hector. She goes in the Octagon today."

Lauren shouted with joy.

Later that day, in a black gypsy dress made much too big for her so she would appear small, Lauren made her first appearance in the Octagon in a small town near Lake Tahoe with a hundred and fifty dollars. Much too much to risk.

It proved to be a disaster.

Suddenly thrust into a public arena with nearly three hundred people watching her, she froze. Her first opponent was a strapping farm boy, his fists held in front of his face, grunting fiercely as he moved in. All her training deserted her. She had no idea what to do.

When he suddenly charged, she didn't move. The force of his body slammed her into the Octagon fencing. He struck her ribs with several powerful blows then worked up to the head till she went down. She lay stunned for a few seconds as he walked around the Octagon acknowledging the applause till she struggled to her feet, dazed.

The crowd shouted, "Finish her, Danny Boy. Finish her."

The farm boy came in throwing punches she should have ducked easily, but he landed two more blows against her ribs, buckling her and sending her staggering into the fencing again where her parents stood just outside.

They screamed at her to move, to defend herself.

The crowd cheered.

Hector then said as she lay gasping, "I'm pulling you out."

Erin shot back, "No, you are not."

Lauren grasped the wire fence and stared into her mother's eyes. Erin slid her fingers in over her daughter's. "Look at me, Lauren," she said, "I want you to trust your instincts. You are the best I have ever seen. You can whip this boy easily. Trust your instincts."

"Lauren, are your ribs hurt?" Hector asked.

Erin snapped, "Her ribs are fine." Then to Lauren. "You do not give up. You hear me You never give up."

The fog of panic that shackled Lauren broke. Ignoring the pain in her ribs, she sprang into a crouch just before the boy reached her. He swung again; she slipped easily under his arm, stepped past him and drove her heel viciously into the back of his knee. He screamed in agony and went down. In an instant, she was on him, trapping his arm between her legs in a bar hold. The muscles in her toned arms rippled as she nearly yanked his arm from its socket

He wailed, "I give! I give!"

She released him, and he stumbled up. His friends helped him hobble from the Octagon. Insisting she was fine, Lauren fought five more times and did not come close to losing. After that, no one else wanted to challenge her. She rushed from the Octagon and leapt into her mother's arms.

"I told you," Erin said with a grin. "Trust your instincts. They will always protect you."

It took another six weeks for her ribs to heal.

Now, a year and a half later, alongside the American River, Erin stared down at her daughter. The girl had twelve fights last night, including one unusually tough one. She fell into bed exhausted and a little bruised. Erin decided to let her sleep. She leaned down, gently kissing her daughter's forehead for what would be the last time.

The air was crystalline as she set off westward alongside the American River and ran up a steady incline into the forests.

***

By 7:30am, Erin had not yet returned, and Lauren felt dread grip her spine with icy fingers. She should have been back an hour ago. What had started out as a sunny, clear morning had changed into one with dark clouds and rain roiling in from the Pacific. A deep chill came with it. Thunder burst over them and lightning struck in the nearby hills. The Misfits hurried to batten down their caravans and tents.

Amid the turmoil of the storm, her father organized search parties while Lauren set off alone against his orders to find her. She was confident she knew which way her mother had gone: the way they ran together yesterday. up the river path into the forests. Always tagging along, the seven-year-old Sybil tried to follow her. The girl was the daughter of the

Hungarian pair of tumblers, and, normally, Lauren liked her hanging around, but now she had no time for the little girl and quickly outdistanced her.

Among the trees, darkness had grown as thick as it was in her heart. As she ran, dodging the tangled undergrowth on the narrow path, a roll of thunder burst and cracked overhead, rain lashed the foliage, and wind whipped through the branches of tall trees. Her legs burned, her thighs draining of strength, but she kept the same pace.

About a mile and a half from camp, beyond exhaustion, Lauren came to a clearing that broadened to the left into a barren hillside. Lightning struck the lone tree, splitting it in two.

The burst of light revealed the body in the middle of the field. Lauren ran to it and fell to her knees. It was her mother. Her eyes were open to the rain and vacant. She was dead.

The rain washed the blood from her body, but Lauren could still see the knife wounds, so many. Blood had pooled beneath her mother and mixed with the rain ran down the gentle slope of the field in pink rivulets.

Kneeling beside her, Lauren could not breathe. She gasped, attempted to gulp in air. It was as if one of those knives had plunged into her stomach and was ripping up through her chest. A moan of despair escaped from her.

The comprehension that the most precious thing in her life was gone forever washed over her with finality, and she sobbed. Minutes passed as she knelt beside her dead mother, her tears mixing with the rain on her face, muttering over and over, *momma*.

Then she noticed a glint of gold clutched in her mother's hand. Lauren pried the fingers loose and picked up a medallion the size of a dollar coin and its gold chain. On the front was the grotesque image of a snarling three-headed dog. Three letters were engraved above the beast: *G. O. H.* She turned to look at the back. It read: *To Eric, June 15, 2116, Congrats!*

She did not know what it meant except that it had belonged to the man who had killed her mother. She draped it over her neck and swore to herself she would not take it off till she found and killed him.

She heard footfalls and heavy breathing coming up behind her and for an instant tensed, but recognized who it was. Sybil, her blond hair plastered to her head by the rain, stopped abruptly and gasped, then gave a piercing scream.

CHAPTER THREE: THE MAKING OF AN ASSASSIN II

November 10, 2116, Bonner Springs in the San Bernardino Mountains

Three months later, moving as if pursued by raiders, the Misfits travelled as fast as their old horses would take them to the abandoned town of Bonner Springs. A sign read: **Welcome to Bonner Springs, A Mighty Small Town.** The concrete surface of the main boulevard was cracked; weeds and a blueberry bush stuck up through the openings. A few dilapidated buildings still stood including a deserted gas station and a strangely shaped, red brick structure with boarded up, arched windows. Because of a small street entering the main boulevard at a sharp angle beside it, the build's shape was that of a triangle, a door at the rounded point.

Driving past with his horse-drawn camper, Hector could see no purpose in a building shaped like that. Something from a long-ago age. Beside him, Lauren didn't even glance at it, snapping the reins to keep the horses pulling at a steady rate. She was lost in her thoughts again. She had pulled out of the dark depression that overwhelmed her after her mother's murder, but she had not returned to the once bright girl she had been and likely never would.

The horses' hooves and the wagon wheels clacked on the pavement as the troupe passed through town and pulled off onto a meadow just beyond where the remnants of a baseball diamond stood. With night coming, they needed to stop. Putting their horses out to graze, the quickly set up camp, and the circus manager established a double guard rotation.

Hector's fears were eased a little because of it. As he and Lauren finished setting the guy lines for the camper awning, he couldn't escape a sense of unease. He tried to hide it from his daughter. He felt certain they would be coming tonight, the good people of Clark Falls, the town they had just left three hours ago—or more accurately, fled.

It had been a strange place, ruled by a man called the Warlord, the only law in the county. When the Misfits had paraded through town, as they always did before a show, several hundred people gathered on the sidewalks to watch. As usual, there were only a few automobiles along the street, but fifty or so horse-drawn trucks or wagons. Hector thought it strange there was no noise, no cheering, no clapping, no anything.

"It's as if their brain pans have been removed," Lauren said.

In her black gypsy-dress, she drove the Airstream, loosely holding the reins to the two horses. The gold medallion dangled from her neck. Ralph the Elephant led the way with his trainer wearing a pith helmet and sitting astride. A real trouper, the beast pranced like a show horse, bellowing bugle calls that brought people out of the few stores and several saloons, which were already open.

That afternoon, the performances went well enough, especially Sybil's family of Hungarian tumblers, two conjoined brothers—not really conjoined, Dom's and Franco's shoulders connected by skin-toned rubber—and the beautiful Magda, who leapt and spun over top of them. They received applause for they were true circus performers and had an act.

But it was little Sybil, Magda's and Dom's seven-year-old dynamo of a daughter, who stole the show. The brothers tossed her high into the air, her blond ponytail flying wildly. Two full summersaults later, she landed on their shoulders. She received even greater applause, Hector thought, since all audiences loved kids in danger.

Assassin 13

Then the trouble started. The Warlord, a tall, bony man challenged Hector in the Octagon. The bet was enormous, nearly ten thousand dollars in money and goods. To meet the wager, the Misfits had to put up nearly everything they owned.

As the bout began, it was clear the Warlord had once been a boxer and would be a threat. In the first round, he rocked Hector back with a vicious left jab. Then, a punch to the ribs drove Hector to his knees.

Instead of taking her father out with a flurry of punches or a hold like any other Octagon fighter, the Warlord stepped back, dancing like a boxer and threw his hands up in triumph to the wild cheers. His eyes blazed with supreme confidence.

When the match continued, Lauren saw Hector was in trouble, saw the fright in his eyes. He would not be playing this one close. He was fighting for his life. He threw two quick body punches, then danced away from the Warlord's long arms. The crowd booed the tactic.

The two men fought five more rounds, each getting in blows that rocked the other, but the Warlord's were more telling, slowly wearing Hector down. Then, in the sixth round, the Warlord cracked Hector on the jaw, sending him down to one knee again, stunned and groggy. The fight seemed over.

But Lauren saw it had been a glancing blow, one her father had taken deliberately. Now, this time as the man raised his hands in triumph, he moved in for the kill. Hector drove a fist into his crotch with enormous power. The man bent double in agony, and Hector was on him instantly. A hard leg sweep took him to the mat where Hector wrapped him in a choke hold.

To give the Warlord his due, he would not surrender, so Hector had no choice but to choke him into unconsciousness.

Immediately, the crowd booed, shaking fists and screaming he had cheated. Several men entered the Octagon and circled Hector menacingly. Lauren pushed through them and stood by her father.

"Get out, Lauren," Hector demanded. "Go!"

"No." Her teeth bared like a feral animal. The beast inside her ached for them to come.

Then, someone fired off a shotgun. It was Al Sharpy, the circus manager. Several of the Misfits flanked him with rifles and handguns.

"This is no holds barred," he announced. "You folks knew that. Now, pick him up and get him the hell out of here."

Several men carried the Warlord from the Octagon, and finally, the crowd dispersed back to town.

Sharpy said, "Let's take the money and get the hell out of here."

That night in Bonner Springs, when Hector and Lauren finished setting up their camper, she said, "I'm going to wash Ralph now, okay?"

She was already off with Sybil beside her before he answered, but he smiled. Slowly, she was coming out of that great dark hole.

Six years apart in age, Lauren still counted Sybil her best friend. Since her mother died, the girl was the one person with whom Lauren allowed herself to spend time. She liked to tinker, repairing everything from the Ford convertible to the company's two synchrotron signal lights. When she did, Sybil always stood beside her handing her tools like the magician's assistant. That even extended to the baths she gave Ralph.

As Lauren led the elephant down to the creek, the little girl raced ahead. Despite the chill, Sybil wore just a t-shirt that revealed her left shoulder blade where a remarkable birthmark stood out, a four-leaf clover so distinct it appeared to have been swept up off the grass by wind and landed on her back.

Everyone said it was the Misfit's good luck charm. She was proud of it and displayed it except on the coldest of days.

At the creek, they spent the next half hour soaping and washing Ralph down. The two girls used sponge brushes on him, falling into a rhythm. At Sybil's squeals, Ralph glanced back and sprayed them with a snoot full of water.

Sybil shrieked, and Lauren cried, "Hey."

She tossed a bucket of water at Ralph, who bellowed loudly. Sybil jumped up and down, screaming with delight at the water battle. Ralph took another long intake of water out of the creek and soaked Lauren, knocking her on her butt.

She lay down on her back and laughed.

An hour later, when the sun went down, Lauren sat at the campfire with her father and Sybil and her family. Against the night chill, Lauren wrapped her friend inside an old Denver Bronco jacket, long faded and worn at the elbows. The adults were drinking warm beer from a case taken in barter that day and talking about the Warlord and the chances of an attack tonight. Lauren didn't think drinking beer was a good way to prepare for such a thing, but then she was just a kid.

The prevailing opinion seemed to be that they had gotten away but should still maintain an alert watch till they got to San Bernardino, yet sixty miles away

She reached for Hector's beer, and he gave her a sip. When she started to take another, he grabbed the can back. "You're too young."

She scowled. "I'm too young for everything."

Abruptly, the night sounds ceased. Apprehensive, Lauren looked around. No one else seemed to notice.

Then, screams and gunshots erupted from the road, shattering the silence. In Jeeps and trucks and on horseback, the mob from Clark Falls roared into camp, firing rifles into the air. They shouted for everyone to raise their hands. Lauren shoved

Sybil toward her mother, Magda, who took the girl into her arms.

Two Misfits, both jugglers, raced for their van. Several of the mob cut them down with a volley of gunfire.

The Warlord hopped down from a pickup and strode toward them. He waved a huge handgun. "Anyone moves, we shoot."

The mob gathered all fifty Misfits and confiscated their weapons. The Warlord sent several people to search the wagons and campers for anything of value, rummaging through them in a madhouse of tossed clothes and broken chests. They took all the money and food.

One of the Clark Falls men ran up to the Warlord. "They're hiding weapons, Carl. They got to be. There may be more of these lowlifes in the trees with rifles on us right now."

He was frightened. They were all frightened and Lauren sensed that was more dangerous than if they were cool and efficient.

"Stay calm, dammit," the Warlord ordered. "If they do, we'll shoot these ones down like the dogs they are."

Though scared out of her wits, Lauren seethed with fury as well. The man was stealing everything the Misfits had. They would starve with winter coming on.

He seemed not to notice Hector the whole time, not glancing his way once. That bothered Lauren. She knew instinctively this man wanted revenge on her father for having beaten him.

"Go over with Magda," Hector said to her quietly, nodding slightly toward Sybil and her family across the fire.

"No," she whispered.

"Can't you do as you're told just once?"

She shook her head. "No. I'm not going to leave you, papa."

Four men scrambled out of Hector's overturned Airstream. One shook his head at the Warlord. Abruptly, the man turned on Hector. "Where the fuck's my money, Paco?"

"We lost it in the rush to leave," her father stuttered.

That was so lame Lauren stifled a groan. She saw the Warlord's flat and remorseless eyes.

"You fucking greaser," he said, his voice rumbling low like a shifting gravel pit.

She was certain he would kill her father and stepped forward. "Sir, please, I'll tell you where…"

The Warlord shot the flat of his hand out and knocked her down.

"Hey!" Hector shouted, stepping in front of her, facing the man with his fist clinched.

Lauren said desperately, "I'm okay, papa, I'm okay."

The Warlord shoved the barrel of his gun against Hector's forehead. "Who the fuck you think you're dealing with, Paco? I'm the Man. I run this shitburg county. I'm the closest thing to the po-leece you're ever going to see around here. You got that? I'm not no stupid beaner, Paco Taco. Comprende? I'm the law and I'm the mob, and I'm two ticks from blowing your fucking head off right now."

Lauren always wondered why her father didn't just tell him about the secret compartment in the camper. Maybe he didn't like being pushed by this fellow. Maybe he had enough of the way the world treated him. He didn't say a word. From somewhere he came up with the old 9mm handgun so swiftly the Warlord didn't react.

Hector shoved it under the man's chin. "Get that cannon out of my face, you redneck son of a bitch."

Audible gasps came from both the Misfits and the Clark Falls mob. Lauren saw their jittery movement and heard the cock of weapons.

The Warlord's grin split his acne-ridden face like a razor. "Seems like we got ourselves a Mexican standoff, Paco."

He seemed the only one who was calm, but she sensed an unhinged, deeper rage propelling him. She looked at her father's gun, and her heart caught in her throat. God, no, the safety was on. *Geez, Hector!*

If he moved to switch it now, he was dead. She thought to scream and draw the man's attention, but if she did, her father would look at her, not the dime-store cop. Suddenly she realized she had to take down the man herself. She threw adult men all the time in training. But she hesitated.

Glanced down at Hector's gun, the man's eyes crossed crazily. His grin widened. "Your safety's on, Paco. Why the hell would anyone have a gun with a safety?"

"I think that is a lie."

"No. You lose." He jerked the trigger. The top of her father's head blew off. Blood, bone and brain tissue flew onto her face. She screamed and kept screaming, lost in a spiraling black hole. Everything played out in front of her in a maddening medley of death and destruction

The gunshot was like a signal. The Warlord calmly fired another round into Hector's body. The mob opened fire on the huddled Misfits. A blast like a thousand bugles rent the night air.

Then, the ground shook. Ralph charged out of the shadows into the light, bearing down on the Clark Falls mob. They ceased fire and the Misfits scattered. A couple of mob ran, but most opened up with rifles and shotguns, hitting the giant beast over and over. Ralph went down on his knees. They kept firing.

Sybil broke away from her mother and ran toward him, screaming, "Stop! Stop!"

Dom raced in and scooped her up. At that moment, as if by a silent signal, the mob turned their weapons on the Misfits again, firing relentlessly.

They were cut down, including Sybil and her father. The Warlord and the rest of the mob chased the Misfits as if they needed to wipe all of them all out.

Lauren's shock broke. Her mind came back to full clarity. Picking up her father's gun, she ran for the woods, expecting at any instant to feel the slam of a bullet strike her back. None came.

She heard the voice of the Warlord, "Get her. Get that little bitch."

Two men fired at her but missed and gave chase. She darted in among the trees and kept running and running, the two men close behind.

CHAPTER FOUR: THE MAKING OF AN ASSASSIN III

Kneeling at a trickle of a creek, Lauren washed blood and bits of her father's brain from her face, rubbing frantically to get it off her. The darkness was heavy. She heard the sound of the two men thrashing through the thick underbrush and trees, not far back.

"Where are you, little girl," a voice shouted. "You can't outrun us. We can track you."

"I'm here," she called back. "I hurt myself. Can you help me?"

"Sure, we can," the voice came back.

She heard them rushing now toward her voice. The two men reached the creek bank and searched for her, but in the darkness, she had slipped back into the deeper shadows. She aimed and without a twinge of emotion shot the two men dead.

She stuck the gun in her jacket, turned, and blindly ran deeper into the forest.

***

That night, the temperatures fell to near freezing, and she awoke stiff and cold at dawn. Lauren found herself in the forest just outside Clark Falls. She had come nearly twenty miles in the night. She had one goal, one obsession, find the Warlord and kill him. Endless pain ripped her soul apart. She would go mad if she didn't find him and kill him.

That morning, she slipped into town and broke into the first building with boarded up windows, an old barbershop. The room had dusty barber chairs, cracked mirrors, and cobwebs everywhere. She sat by a boarded-up window looking out through a slit at the main street, but seeing nothing. Pain wracked her heart.

Something had broken inside her; the core of her being had snapped. She had turned into something that was not a girl. Her mother raped and murdered, now her father killed by a monster. Sybil, Magda, Dom, all the Misfits dead. And all of it her fault. Hector had told her to go over with Magda. He would handle it. He needed to know she was safely away from him, but she had refused, and gotten him killed. Gotten them all killed.

She didn't remember cleaning her father's blood and brain matter off her face. She remembered killing the two men.

Once she cried, but it did not ease the pain. Acid filled her veins, flooded her brain. It ate away at her. She was engulfed in fury, but most of all fury at her parents for dying. She had trusted them to always be there, but they'd let her down. First her mother. Then her father. They were not supposed to die. Not them. She cried again, realizing in fifty years, when she was an old woman, she will have lived all those years without them.

Love was the source of her pain. Love was the worst thing of all. Love meant pain. Love meant death. She drove her emotions deep into a vault so dark as to be a black hole, so vast that the stars in heaven couldn't fill it. She slammed an iron door shut over it. She would never feel so much for another human being again. She would never be that vulnerable ever again. This she promised herself.

And she swore she would find retribution. Someday for her mother, this day for her father. That bastard they called the Warlord lived here, right here in this town. She would find him, and she would kill him.

She watched throughout the day for him. Early on, when people appeared on the street, going to the few places open, even into saloons that never closed, she did not spot him. Darkness came, and she hadn't seen him.

After midnight, she snuck out to find water and food, breaking into a small grocery store. She stole a backpack, threw in dried food, candy bars, a black sweat shirt, a Dodger baseball cap, and several water bottles. Thinking of how her father would have admonished her, she tossed in fresh carrots and apples, then returned to her hideaway.

Two more days and the Warlord did not appear. That's when she came up with her plan. If he was the supposed law in Clark Falls, she should commit a crime. Just after dark, she went onto Main Street. The temperature was below freezing. She wore her frayed Bronco jacket over the black sweatshirt. Her hair was tucked under the Dodgers baseball cap. She could pass for a boy.

Light spilled from several places still open, bars, a couple stores selling hardware or used clothes and other sundries, all of which she skirted. The town had electricity, but she doubted it was on 24 hours each day. She'd never heard of that, except in the glass domes within the major cities.

She stood outside the grocery store, still open with electric lights glowing and the aisles visible in the large store window. Just the place. Without hesitation, she picked up a loose brick and hurled it through the glass, then ran back into a nearby alley and waited.

Several people came out and looked around. A man Lauren assumed was the owner ran about cursing. After half an hour, the Warlord hadn't arrived. Not exactly responsive. It took him nearly an hour to arrive, driving up in a pickup truck with big antlers on the front, the one he had driven onto the baseball field at Bonner Springs.

When she saw him go inside, her body went into lockdown. For several moments, she couldn't move. Emotions erupted out of that black hole that was her soul as if vents exploding with high-pressure steam, sorrow, fear, fury, spewing into the air. It took her a full five minutes to repair the vents and calm herself down.

Once she did, she hurried across the street to the pickup and stood at the back. Her left hand felt inside her jacket pocket for the 9-mm pistol. She made sure the safety was off.

An older couple leaving the store with a small bag of groceries spotted her and came over. "Are you all right, young man?" the woman asked. "Shouldn't you be home?"

"Fuck off," she said.

Shocked, they backed away, then hurried down the street.

A moment later, he stepped out, flipping shut a small notebook. He wore a plaid shirt with a tin drug store star pinned to it, a cowboy hat, and high boots. For the last three nights, she'd seen that skinny, zit-sick face every minute in her dreams, and now, here he was only a few feet away.

"What do you want, kid?" he asked, almost amiably as she came into the light from the store. "Get off the damn truck. Kids these days. No manners."

When she didn't move, he swung a backhand at her, which she easily ducked. He stepped passed her to the pickup door. "Stupid kid."

"Hey," she said.

He turned back and looked quizzically at her. "You're a girl, aren't you? By damn, I thought you were a boy at first. No boobs at all yet, huh?"

"You a cop?"

"Me? Damn right." He tapped his badge. "See that? I run this shitberg."

"That's not a real cop badge."

"Real enough here and now." He opened the truck door and tossed in his notebook. "Looks like I'm going to have to place you under arrest."

"For what?"

"For bad mouthing an officer of the law." He stepped toward her. "Now, get in my limo, little darlin'." He grabbed his crotch. "I'm hung like a horse and this is your lucky day."

When she didn't move, he smiled that hideous grin, the one she saw when he shot her father. His voice was hard. "That's a fucking lawful order."

He grabbed for her, but in a quick motion, she ducked out of his reach and took out the gun.

"The safety is off this time," she said with a steely coldness startling in someone so young.

As he stared at her with a flicker of alarm and anger, she shot him through the heart.

He died with a look of astonishment on his face. He crumpled to the street, and she put another bullet into his forehead. A few people on the sidewalk screamed and ran.

Jamming the gun back in her jacket pocket, she walked away, passing the old couple lying on the sidewalk with their arms covering their heads. She was thirteen and she had killed three men. A moment of horror at what she'd done went through her before an infinite cold expunged it.

CHAPTER FIVE: ASSASSIN 13

September 27, 2131, Hollywood, California

Fifteen years later on Melrose Avenue in Hollywood, California, Lauren Ramirez sat in the back of a battered, old taxi, impatiently drumming her fingers on the seat, already late for a hastily called meeting with the President of the United States, that paranoid nutcase Lee Colby. And paranoia was his best trait. She understood it. She shared it with him.

It was 4:30 in the afternoon, overcast, hot and muggy. Twenty or so vehicles lined up at the main gate outside of Vanguard International's Global Media Mall, waiting to get through a checkpoint. All motorized, a few new driverless Mercedes, but mostly ancient and beaten down vehicles.

Even she had been awe-struck by this place the first time she'd come here. The largest of thirty-seven glass-domed structures in Los Angeles, Global's media mall ran one mile by four and half miles as its glass roof zigzagged up from Melrose and Van Ness Avenues to encompass the wealthy homes in Hollywood Heights. The 30 square miles contained 30 six-star hotels, a thousand shops, grand homes, serviced apartments, four parks, a water fall, and its famous media center with film, TV and Internet studios. About fifty thousand people lived inside. The domes of the surviving American cities maintained world-class luxury. Outside was the Forgotten World.

With the taxi not moving, she decided to walk to the dome entrance. Reaching forward with a hundred-dollar bill, she tried to get the driver's attention, but he was wearing ancient headphones and eyeing a cute prostitute in a short dress on the sidewalk. Lauren rapped her knuckles on his head, and when he jumped, she tossed the money in his lap and got out.

She took in the heavy traffic, cars, horse and human-drawn carriages, hundreds of pedestrians. Across the street, people crowded in front of rundown shops, tiny kiosks, food vendors selling fried fish rolls and mystery meat on a stick. A jeep with armed soldiers went by. Nothing seemed out of order, yet something wasn't quite right.

Through flitting clouds, the sun reflected blindingly off the massive glass dome as if the structure were a rolling fireball. Barriers with concertina wire blocked the approaches to both the car and pedestrian gates to get inside. Long lines wound back from both.

Just down the street on a one-hundred-foot-tall screen, President Lee Colby was delivering a speech from behind his desk in the Oval Office. He wore a casual, pullover golf shirt with a cardigan sweater as if it were winter. He was in his mid-forties, a remarkably handsome man with curly blond hair and deep-set blue eyes.

With his boy-next-door persona, he was a natural politician. He talked about being the champion of the middle class. Lauren knew of no middle class. And spoke of the safety net for the poor. She knew a lot of poor. Men, women and children sweating in the garbage bins of the cities, sweating in cabbage fields or factories or mines twelve hours a day and getting little for it.

Impassioned, Colby said he would fight to his last breath to keep their rebel and corporate enemies at bay. What a load of bullshit, she thought. Colby ran the largest corporation in the world, VI Six Global, and he could do little against the small hit-and-run strikes of rebels. Nor did he want to. Their pinprick threats, made huge in the media, kept the masses afraid and him in office.

And he was nowhere near the Oval Office. The Oval Office no longer existed. It was all CGI. The Presidency, the elections, the entire government, all CGI. Corporations and media not only ran what was left of America, but also the world.

At the pedestrian gate, two guards in military uniforms and carrying submachine guns were examining briefcases and backpacks, and running hand-held metal detectors over each body. Amid cries of outrage, Lauren stepped in front and handed the soldier a hundred-dollar note, which he pocketed. Quickly, the guard scanned her with the detector and waved her in.

In a hidden back holster, she carried her Glock 75, but it would not be picked up by any scan.

Inside the dome, on the crowded esplanade that resembled a cobbled Bavarian street, Admiral Walter Cummings stood just inside Global's pedestrian entrance waiting for the President's assassin. Cummings was, 6'4", two hundred pounds with white cropped hair and the physical fitness of a fanatic. He had been one of the last Navy Seals, at least on film. All his missions were done right here at the media mall and piped out to the masses who cheered his latest victories over the rebels. To fight the War against Terror, he never left the dome.

He checked his watch and sighed. *Late.* Above him, the enclave sky was tinted, blocking harmful rays, and the temperature set at a comfortable 72 degrees. He caught the overwhelming scent of salt water pumped in through the vents as if that smell was pleasant to everyone. It wasn't. Hell, the beach was only a few steps away on the veranda of a Starbuck's large 3-D screen, the sound of ocean waves rhythmic as it blared from giant speakers.

But he was in no mood to enjoy the ocean. He hated this woman. She had no loyalty except to money. She never missed an opportunity to take a sarcastic dig at him or at his ops efficiency. What did she know? He was chief of staff to the President, and Global's chief operating officer.

His palm rested on the handlebars of his new Suzuki 750 cc electric motorcycle. He loved the bike. It gave him the look of a badass son of a bitch, which he was. And *she* would have to ride bitch with him. That would piss her off. He'd positively love that because he sure as hell hated her.

Five years ago, the President desperately needed an assassin to take out a well-protected corporate rival. He asked Cummings to find the best. Most countries, corporations, and crime families, many one in the same, used or retained assassins. They were rated by intelligence and police agencies from Level 1 through Level 10. For simple, blunt work, assassins rated Levels 1 through 5, men and women with rudimentary brute skills would do, but for anything more intricate, someone with more imagination and skill was needed. A Level 10 assassin was best.

However, on rare occasions, someone in the profession appeared who stood above all measurable parameters. An assassin of generational skills. A singularly gifted killer, the thought of this one in pursuit made world leaders wet themselves. Such a person was referred to simply as Level 13. An Assassin 13. This was Malinche.

And she was the President's assassin.

He saw her come in, tall and eye-catching. You'd think an assassin with a reputation bordering on the mythical would be less ostentatious. But not Malinche. She appeared as if she were headed for a night of high-end clubbing or whoring on the street. She had gleaming black hair, dark eyes that belonged on the set of a vampire movie and a gold chain with a gold medallion hanging down into the groove of her breasts. Her clinging black dress reached to mid-thigh. Those long legs shimmered in the fake lamplight of the street, causing several men to stare with unabashed interest. They could not guess that this woman was the most lethal killer on the planet.

Hands on hips, he leaned slightly forward in a belligerent stance. "How is it, Mali, that someone in your line of work is always late?"

He called her by the name she had been using since working for the President, but he knew it was an alias. Despite his deep connections, he had not found out her real name.

She ignored the question. As the woman came up, she had the hint of an unpleasant smile. "Still Colby's gopher I see."

With a flash of anger, he swung onto the bike and started it up. He glanced back. "You're meeting the President of the United States in two minutes. Try to grasp the gravity of that, and don't make an ass of yourself." He revved the handle bars and ordered, "Get on. You're riding *bitch*. How appropriate."

She grabbed the back of his shirt collar and yanked him off the bike. When he hit the street, he banged his elbow on the cobblestones, and pain shot through his arm. "Son of a bitch!"

When he scrambled up, he saw her driving away on his new motorcycle.

A few minutes later, Lauren stood inside a cavernous sound stage, dark except for the far corner where the glare of big LED lights hanging from the ceiling illuminated the President as he continued his speech to the nation. Like in the feed outside, he was behind a large desk, his hands folded in front of him, speaking to the camera with such sincerity Lauren almost believed him. Behind him was solid green wall on which the Oval Office was being CGIed.

A pudgy, officious woman in her forties hurried up to her, sticking out her hand and whispering, "Hi, there. Debbie Schultz, the President's personal assistant. Are you Mali? He is expecting you. What a lovely name. Where does it come from?"

Lauren's head snapped around. "What the fuck business is it of yours?"

The woman blanched.

Ignoring her outstretched hand, Lauren brushed past her, walking up to the edge of the light where Colby could see her.

Mali. Yes, she was *Mali* with Colby and Cummings. Few people knew that Malinalli was the real name of the actual Malinche, a powerful, strong woman, mother of a nation. She saw no reason to explain that to anyone, especially to Debbie Fucking Schultz, presidential assistant.

Moments later, when Colby saw her, he quickly finished. "God bless you, and God bless the United States of America." A second of awkwardness followed as he stared into the camera with a frozen smile.

"And we're out," the director's voice came hastily from somewhere. The ceiling LED lights faded and the regular lights came up.

Colby's kind-hearted, boy-next-door face morphed instantly into petulant fury. "Next time, cut the damn stream faster. I sat there looking like a fucking idiot grinning at the camera." He stood up. "Now, get out. Everyone out."

Without question or hesitation, the crew filed out till Lauren, Colby and Schultz remained. "Where's Admiral Cummings?" the President asked

Lauren shrugged. "He stopped at Starbucks for an expresso. Last I saw he was sitting on the veranda taking in the ocean breezes."

"Fucking idiot," the President cursed. He sent Schultz outside and told her to allow no one in, not even the Admiral. "You can tell him he's not needed for this."

When Schultz left, Colby led Lauren to the Green Room and shut the door behind him. She sat up on the couch, and the President scooted an antique chair close.

He leaned forward, elbows on knees, hands folded in front of his face. "Mali, I have something very important for you."

"Obviously. That's why I'm here. Let me guess. You want me to kill someone."

"Yes, of course. But you will need to be quick this time," Colby said, urgency in his voice as if the target were in the next room.

"What level?" she asked.

"Level one. Highest priority. Silent running. It's Robert Kaseem."

Her head thrust back. "The Vice-President? You want me to kill the Vice-President?"

His voice rose in fury. "Yes, the damn Vice-President. Delete the son of a bitch. Scrub his DNA from the fucking gene pool. He's planning a palace coup. Me. He wants to delete me and take the presidency."

Lauren had met Kaseem before in Chicago during the gangland war and hoped if she had to do close work, he wouldn't remember her. To her, this was all byzantine power play shit by the elite, and she had not a flicker of emotion in regard to it. It was just a job. Kaseem was not even Vice-President yet. He had been appointed by Colby, but would not take the oath of office for two weeks. The ceremony had already been filmed and sent to outlets around the world for playback on the proper day. Till then he was just a private citizen

"When the Vice-President's dead, the coup is dead," Colby added more calmly. "I'm assigning you two of Admiral Cumming's best operatives to help with this."

Lauren laughed. "No, thanks. If you do, I'm out. Assassins work alone. It's in the manual." He didn't contradict her. "You said quick. How quick?" she asked.

"I know you won't like it, but you only have thirteen days to get this done and three of those will be traveling to the location. After that, it will be too late."

She shook her head. "Now, I am out. Get someone else, Colby. One month is suicide. Thirteen days? It can't be done. He is too well protected. Sorry. I'm not giving my life for yours. I don't even like you."

Abruptly, Lauren stood and walked toward the door. She could feel the hot breath of Colby's rage like a tidal wave. But it would do him no good.

"Wait. What about the Guardians of Hell?" he called.

Lauren froze. Her hand trembled on the door handle. She turned around and faced him, her gaze fiercely intense. "You better not be fucking with me."

She had learned long ago that the G. O. H. on the gold medallion she had found clutched in her mother's hand stood for the Guardians of Hell. From what little she'd found out, they had formed in the 2050s to bring together crime families under one leadership. They grew more powerful than governments. Such an enterprise could not sustain itself long—too many competing interests—and it fell apart sometime in the 2080s. At least that was the story.

But she believed they still existed, and Eric, whose name was etched on the medallion, was one of them.

Colby opened his hands in a gesture of just a friend helping out. "You asked me to find out what I could about the man Eric. You gave me a time and place in which he was present. I've done everything I could to find him, and I have." He paused for effect. "There were four of them who killed Erin Murphy, not one."

Lauren turned into a cold, killing mask. "Go on."

"We've got the names of two of them. Eric and one other. It's taken a long time. I've had every operative I could investigating. This name Eric was the key. He was initiated into the Guardians on the date engraved on the back. We know who he is, and the name of one other man. My agents are closing in on the two of them."

The clearest image Lauren had of her mother was the flame of her red hair, caked with blood, her body lying crumpled in the grass beside a stream. Pounded with rain.

"I will give you whatever help is at my disposal," he said with a sincere, soothing voice that grated on her. "I should have all the information by the time you return from this assignment. All four men and their location. I promise you."

A high voltage of emotion ramped through her body. For just a moment, she saw herself striding toward him and snapping his neck. But she didn't. She allowed the fire to burn down leaving only her cold, dark core.

Bleak as river ice, her eyes fixed on him. "Colby, this better be 100% science, or nothing is going to protect you from me. Where will I find this Eric?"

"Not yet. When you return from the Kaseem mission. You need to start immediately. Your cover is that of a prostitute. That's why I asked you to dress like that. You must audition for the part to even be allowed to travel to where he is or more accurately where he's going to be." He made a sound like a pig snort, and said, "I'm sure you'll pass."

She had no choice. "Fine. When I get back. Where will I find the Vice-President?"

The President gave an infuriatingly smug grin. "Have you ever been off planet?"

CHAPTER SIX: THE TIN CAN

October 10, 2131, K-Global Space Habitat at Lagrange Point 4

Before a kill, the assassin was hyper-vigilant. Inside the K-Global habitat called the Tin Can, she stood in the lee of an apartment building, waiting for the prostitute who would get her into the target's villa. A kaleidoscope of crisscrossing shadows from hundreds of tiny suns throughout the giant cylinder kept her hidden from the pedestrians on the walkway. None of them threatening.

She wore a loose, thigh-length black skirt with a black blouse and neoprene, carbon fiber hiking boots. The two-story vacation home of Vice President Robert Kaseem sat at the end of the block with his large security detail. For the last five days, she had been observing it from the grassy park a half mile directly overhead, lying flat on her back with binoculars, noting comings and goings. When prostitutes entered, a security guard patted them down and groped them. No way to hide a gun, but inside the soul of her boot was a short, but very sharp knife.

Today, the villa seemed to have the normal contingent of ten uniformed guards with assault rifles patrolling the grounds. She was leery about firing any weapon inside a damned spaceship. That seemed insanity. But the guards seemed unfazed by the prospect. A guardhouse stood at the iron gate entrance with two men looking like stormtroopers in front of it. This would not be easy, but if things went smoothly in the next hour, Kaseem would be dead, and she would be off this tin can on her way back to earth.

But in her line of work, things never went smoothly.

In the ten days since she arrived on this garbage bucket in space, she still couldn't adjust mentally, as if living constantly in a madhouse of delusions. From where she stood, she could see the horizons rising steadily on each side of her in arcs of housing, lakes, green parks, and small shopping malls, meeting a half-mile overhead with more buildings, lakes and parks, all hanging upside down. The Tin Can was a perfect cylinder a half mile in diameter and seven miles in length, over fifty square miles of usable surface. Its rotation created a gravity of .9 of earth's.

Directly above her, tiny people moved about, looking like they would fall but never did. Along the cylinder's axis, people with artificial wings floated in the zero-gravity center. Occasionally, the sound of one or two of them screaming in delight reached her.

Half of the ten thousand inhabitants were transients on R & R from K-Global's extensive mining operations on the moon and farther out in the asteroid belt. With so many hard men and women looking to blow off pressure, the Tin Can was like a Wild West town made up of countless bars, casinos and brothels. Lauren worked in one of the brothels.

By the time she stepped onto the Tin Can eleven days ago, she knew every microdata about the design schematics of Robert Kaseem's villa, his usual number of security guards—fifty, and his sadistic sexual proclivities. Over two days, this information was fed to her neurobots by secure Internet.

In her body, millions of nanobots, floated through her bloodstream. The vast majority were medical, ready to repair any abnormality like wounds or illnesses. They acted like a super immune system. However, a hundred thousand were specialized neurobots attaching themselves permanently to the tissue in her brain, constantly feeding her information from the Internet and other sources till she had to use an effort of will to shut them down for a little peace.

In this way, Lauren knew the brothel she'd been assigned, knew exactly the Vice would arrive on site two days after her, and knew who his regular girl was. In fact, every detail of the bastard's life. Robert Kaseem was an old-fashioned mob boss running guns, drugs and human trafficking. What a Vice-President.

In the Chicago gangland war four years ago that Cummings plucked her out of, Frank Nasri, CEO of Nasri/Kaseem Industries, had been her main target, but he was protected with more security than the President. While he ran the legitimate part of the operation, mining, manufacturing and agriculture, Kaseem, his Enforcer, ran all the illegal activities. A sadistic bastard like so many of his kind, Kaseem had a reputation for brutality, especially toward his prostitutes.

Lauren had been one of his working girls invited with about ten others to a party at his mansion in the Garnett Park dome overlooking a frozen Lake Michigan. The room where the bar had been set up was like a museum to gangland lore. On the wall were pictures of famous mobsters, mostly mythical figures from two hundred years before: Al Capone, Frank Nitti, Baby Face Nelson, John Dillinger, Big Jim Colosimo, and Benny the Bug Sorrentino.

Strangely, in each photo was an obituary as if these modern mobsters were proud when their ancient counterparts died old with their boots on. Many like Dillinger, Colosimo were gunned down, but a few like Sorrentino made it to the promised land of Miami Beach and old age.

At the party in Chicago, all of Kaseem's thugs reveled with the abandon of condemned men. It was common knowledge among the crime family that someone was killing off Nasri/Kaseem's top soldiers, a hired assassin no doubt, but who?

Then, the name of the assassin leaked: Malinche. Lauren had produced the body count.

That detonated a fire storm in the news and on all the reality Vid shows, gaining enormous ratings. Always referred to as a *he,* Malinche had become a cult figure of sorts from numerous spectacular kills around the world, hired by bad people to kill other bad people. The notoriety made her task both harder and easier. All the king's men were on hyper alert when they heard her name, but being so agitated, they were prone to mistakes and not looking for a woman.

Moving about the room with a glass of wine imagining how she was going to pop each one of these bastards. She feigned drinking. Alcohol and Ops didn't blend. Abruptly, a hand pulled her down onto a couch, spilling her drink onto her bare legs.

It was Kaseem. "I'll lick it off for you," he said, leaning down and running his tongue up her leg.

Nausea acidized her stomach, but she pushed it back. With the back of his neck bared to her, she held the urge to snap it right there. He was a small, cherubic man His eyes were squinted pinpricks, his nose flat, his chin a bulge. A streak of white ran through his slick black hair, making him look like a skunk.

He sat up and squeezed her breast. "You're a fine helping of ass."

"Oh, my, how you flatter a girl."

He squeezed hard on her breast, his grin feral. "You like that, don't you?"

She smiled. "I like rough. Perhaps, we can be alone for a while. You can make me scream and surrender."

He laughed.

The passion play was interrupted when a man rushed in with word that the head of the organization, Frank Nasri, had been shot to death three hours ago, his body just found naked in a sleazy motel outside the dome. A grenade bullet had taken off the back of his head.

Kaseem had to move quickly to gain control of the entire operation and screamed for the women to get the hell out. In less than ten seconds, Lauren was gone, disappointed her chance at Kaseem over.

Of course, she had killed Nasri.

Ten days ago, when Lauren had arrived at her assigned brothel on the Tin Can, the Madame liked her immediately. "You're going to make us a lot of money, Anna," she said with a wide grin. Lauren was calling herself Anna Martinez. "You will not be required to service men who walk in off the streets but only the richer, nicer clientele. How do you like that?"

"I like it fine."

Her new roommate, as Cummings Op had planned, was Kaseem's steady girl, a strange woman named Sybil, tall, three inches taller Lauren, with long, striking legs. She came from outside the domes in San Diego. One of Lauren's early goals was to make friends with her, and she did. In her early twenties, Sybil was more cute than beautiful with shaved eyebrows, and stubby purple hair.

In the cubicle they shared, she admitted to Lauren she hated the work, especially with the bastard Kaseem, but if she could stick it out another six months, she hoped to have enough money to return to earth and take care of her mother, invalid father and two younger siblings. Before she began earning money on the Tin Can, they struggled to survive from day to day. "I've lasted ten months up here. I can make another six months."

In the seven days since Kaseem arrived, Sybil had visited him in his villa three times, each time with a second girl named Jobeth, who came along for Hamid Reid, the Vice President's chief of security. Kaseem beat Sybil viciously, then gave her enormous wages as if in contrition.

Each time she returned to the brothel, she would say nothing about what had happened as if talking about it heightened the pain. She never had time to recover before she was called out again. Lauren volunteered to go in her place, but Sybil refused. The money was too good.

One evening, she gave a smile of satisfaction. "Those men are scared to death, Anna."

"Of what?" Lauren asked.

"Haven't you heard the rumor? That assassin, Malinche, the one in the Chicago Wars—it's all over the Vids. Get this: he's supposed to be after Kaseem."

Lauren felt a knot of concern. Security would be heightened.

"While I was with them," Sybil said, "a cleaning woman dropped a mop handle. Just a mop handle. He and that ass, Hamid Reid, about jumped through the window. I made the mistake of laughing." She touched her swollen jaw. "To get away from that killer, that's why they came to the Tin Can in the first place."

"I'm sure they're safe here," Lauren said.

She found she liked Sybil. The girl was so naïve, despite her line of work, like a little child. Lauren didn't want collateral damage from her assignments because it always led to problems, but this time, she realized with surprise, she actually hoped what was going to happen here would not roll the girl up in its aftermath.

Stretching out on her bunk, her feet over the foot, the girl lay flat on her stomach. She smiled sheepishly in a way that struck Lauren as oddly familiar. "Would you put ointment on my back? He whacked it and my butt and my thighs so hard with a bamboo stick I can barely move. Said he had to spank his little girl. What a sick fucker." She glanced up at Lauren and chuckled. "You don't have to massage my ass, though. I mean I don't want you to get too excited."

"Shit, I'll chance it. Drop your pants," Lauren ordered.

The girl lay naked. She had a beautiful long body with a smooth back and a perfect ass, but now both were latticed with cane welts. Lauren sat beside her. The ointment was cold green muck that every prostitute knew worked wonders, immediately reducing swelling, numbing pain and halving healing time.

Lauren began rubbing it onto the girl's back and immediately froze. On the left shoulder blade was a birthmark, the image of a four-leaf clover so distinct it appeared to have fallen there. Lauren's throat constricted. A moment of anguish engulfed her. It couldn't be. Her sudden exhale sounded like she was choking. How could this tall, angular creature be her Sybil?

The young woman turned her head up and said playfully, "You are becoming aroused. I can hear it. Steady yourself, Anna. We can play when all this shit with Kaseem is finished."

The reality struck her with the force of a garrote around the neck. This Sybil was her Sybil. The Misfit girl who had trailed her around like a puppy fifteen years ago. Someone she had thought dead like all the rest of them, dead and buried in her soul.

This new reality forced a sudden plunge down into that dark abyss where her memories lay. Lauren could not release all that now. The memories clawed to get out, but she pushed them back down. Under control, she continued applying the salve to the girl's back and buttocks.

The next time Sybil and Jobeth were called to Kaseem's villa, Lauren slipped a pill in Jobeth's drink. She quickly took ill, and Lauren volunteered in her place.

Now, she waited for Sybil in the multiple shadows of a modular apartment building with her target just down the street. Several people strolled along the pedestrian walkway, including three drunk miners singing loudly. They eyed her but didn't bother her. Tin Can security didn't take kindly to trouble makers.

Finally, she saw Sybil turn the corner, her tall figure striding down the walkway with typical assurance, her head held high, her purple hair like a neon sign.

"Good, you're here," she said, as she approached. "I wasn't sure you would come. I didn't want to service both bastards."

Lauren said, "I need the money."

Sybil gave a throaty chuckle. "Don't we all. You'll earn it today. Let's go."

As the two prostitutes approached the villa's guarded front gate, Lauren saw fifteen additional men patrolling the grounds, a total of twenty-five, all armed with new K-1000 Assault carbines. Where had that gotten them? On the five second-floor balconies, guards stood in pairs watching them coming toward the villa.

A stocky man stepped from the guard shack, grinning at them.

"Oh, shit," Sybil muttered

"Who is that?" Lauren asked.

"Zoric," Sybil replied with utter distaste. "He must have just arrived on site. He is a mutant pig. He will search us everywhere. Not like the others, but worse. Don't complain. It will only make him hurt us."

It should be all right, unless he had a scanner, Lauren thought. She could not have the bastard find the knife in her boot. The Op would end right there. Certainly, she would kill him, but then she would be dead herself seconds later.

"Does he use a scanner?" she asked Sybil.
"Of course."
Lauren's eyes grew cold as ice crystals.

CHAPTER SEVEN: THE COLD EQUATION

October 10, 2131 The Tin Can

"Welcome, Sybil," Zoric said with a leering grin. Muscular with a wide head, he was short and thick like a beer barrel with legs. He had captain's bars on his epaulets and the name Zoric stitched to the chest of his dark uniform. "You give me a quick fuck, eh?"

"Use your hand," Sybil shot back.

He laughed and glanced at the dark-haired whore. As the two had approached a moment before, he'd seen she was something special. The current of her walk like a supple cat. That sensual flow had sent his heart pounding and his penis hard. She wore a short skirt and boots. There was something vaguely gypsy about her, the long black hair, her high cheekbones, burnished copper skin, and full lips, a mouth to desire.

But dark eyes. They chilled his blood. Flat and dead like a fucking zombie. "Who's this?" he asked Sybil.

"My friend Anna. She is okay."

"Where's Jobeth? I liked Jobeth. She'd give me a blow job. Why isn't she here?"

"She's in the hospital."

Zoric laughed. "Commander Reid was a bit rough last time, eh? She should be used to it." He turned to Lauren. "I don't know you. I am Zoric, the captain of Mr. Kaseem's security. I want those long legs wrapped around my face when you're done. You understand?"

When she didn't answer, he rolled his eyes as if she were stupid, then gave Sybil a surly glance and indicated the guard shack with a jerk of his thumb. "You know the procedure."

Inside, he first patted them down for weapons, hands going over every part of their bodies. Then he ran his hand up their skirts and into their panties looking for anything stuffed up their vaginal or anal canals. When Sybil squirmed, he chuckled. "I have to be thorough, you know. Word is Malinche is after Kaseem. You might be Malinche, Sybil?"

His eyes flared with pleasure when he saw her humiliation. He liked that. He checked the woman called Anna twice. He was so aroused that he would have taken her right there except for the fact that she was meant for Hamid Reid, and the security chief would have killed him. He backed away proving to himself that the instinct for survival was stronger than the instinct to screw.

He picked up the little black box off the counter and snapped the red button. It was the scanner. He ran it over Sybil first, every inch of her from head to foot. "You know," he said, "last month in Mexico City a damn whore tried to hide an explosive device the size of a half dollar beneath her skin. Can you believe it? I caught it and killed her on the spot."

He turned to Lauren. "Now you, gypsy."

He ran the scanner down her dress and legs. She planned to snap his neck when he got to the boot and then the alarm would sound, and she would soon be dead. She would take his rifle and get a few of them though before she went down.

"Zoric, you mutant," a bearded man called from the nearest balcony. It was Hamid Reid. "Quit playing with the merchandise and get those women up here."

"Yes, sir," he called, then turned back to Lauren and slapped her on the butt. "You see me afterward."

Her cold eyes ate him up. "I'll be sure to save something special for you."

Zoric led them inside the villa and down a long hallway toward the rear. Lauren knew she should call the operation off.

Always, always, she would plan for months, then when ready, move in on the target fast, make the hit and get out. Fast and organized. But this would not happen here. She was on a damn spaceship nearly two hundred thousand miles from earth. The place was loaded with security, not just Kaseem's but the habitat's own. And there was no egress. If she got out of the villa, how the hell was she going to get off the Tin Can?

Another obstacle worried her. Kaseem had met her before. He might recognize her. He likely would not, but *likely* wasn't good enough. She should call the Op off. But she knew she wouldn't. She was going after the bastard. She just could not chance losing what Colby knew about her mother's killers.

They took the stairs at the rear. Down at the end of the hall, a security guard sat in a plastic chair, a pulse rifle across his lap. He nodded to Zoric. The security captain stopped at the first door and knocked. A voice shouted for them to enter.

As they went in, Lauren took in the room quickly and felt a knot tying in her stomach. There were six men wearing side arms sitting around a table, passing a bottle of something among them. Clouds of smoke drifted in thin lines through the room. Insanity. Anything remotely resembling fire in a space habitat like smoking.

Small, fake palm trees were scatted about the room with wicker furniture creating a tropical look. In the background, a plump, dull woman sat in a wicker chair by the window, watching two children of about six bounce on the bed. Kaseem's wife and kids. She recognized them from the data stream to her neurobots. Damn, Lauren thought. The man brought his prostitutes in while his wife and kids were still in the room.

She recognized the Vice President sitting at the head of the table, with the black skunk-like hair. To her, he looked like an old time revolutionary, even down to the green cap, uniform and thick cigar stuck in his mouth. Behind him on the wall was a shrine of sorts with a picture of himself in the center.

"Here are the choir girls," Hamid Reid shouted with a bark of a laugh. A cheer rose from the men. Reid was a huge fellow, a weight lifter, former SAS, and the Vice President's chief enforcer, a job Kaseem once held for Frank Nasri. Reid wore a camouflage uniform with a general's insignia.

Her hands behind her back, her head bowed in a portrait of shyness, Lauren studied each man. Except for Kaseem and Reid, they wore purple security uniforms, and any of them would kill his own grandmother for a candy cane. If they knew right from wrong, the distinction didn't matter to them. She understood them. She'd known them all her life.

Kaseem ordered, "Zoric, get out, you pervert."

The security captain laughed as he bowed obsequiously, backing out of the room.

Ten days ago, before Kaseem had arrived, Lauren planted her Glock 75 in the villa's upstairs linen closet outside in the hallway. Security had been lax then. Made specially for her, the weapon's carbon steel couldn't be picked up by scanners. It had a built-in silencer, tritium sights, and high-velocity exploding rounds, tiny grenades going off a millisecond after penetrating the target, whether armor or flesh.

And only she could fire it. A chip in the grip identified her DNA.

She was trying to work out how to get to it when Kaseem ordered the children away. They hesitated and he snapped at his wife. "Take them out now, damn it!"

When they were gone, he said to the others. "Time for you boys to leave also. Come up with the money, and I'm sure these choir girls will be happy to show you their vocal cords."

With playful hoots, the other men left, only Kaseem and Reid remained. Even Lauren was surprised when Kaseem's wife came back in completely naked. No one else seemed to notice.

Abruptly, Reid grabbed Lauren by the arm and dragged her stumbling out the door. "You're with me, my sweet."

Zoric had replaced the guard at the end of the hallway. He leered at her as Reid took her to the next room and shoved her in. She was surprised to find an easel with a large sketch pad and a table with a small can of sketch pencils. The drawing of the Tin Can's varied terrain was quite good.

"Did you do that?" she asked.

At that moment, he drove his fist into her face just below the left eye, dropping her to the floor, stunned. Blinking several times, she lay there trying to regain her bearings. When she came around, Reid had his clothes off and stood in front of her, his legs thick as barrels, his penis already stiff. The only thing remaining on his body was a knife strapped to his right thigh.

"Don't cry, now, my sweet. I could have hit you much harder," he said. "I hope they told you we like our sex on the rough side. If not, it's too late now."

Lauren staggered to her feet, backing up onto the desk, knocking over the can of sketch pencils. He came toward her.

"Please, don't hurt me," she whimpered.

His smile grim, he whispered, "You'll love it when you get used to it."

As he reached for her, Lauren shot forward so quickly he had no time to react. She punched him in the throat with a power that never failed to shock her opponents. But even that part of him was callused muscle. He backed up, gasping for air. Christ, he was still alive.

Furious, he rushed her. "You fucking bitch!"

The rage was in her. As always when death awaited the outcome of a fight, adrenaline shot through her, and time slowed. While she moved with animal quickness, her opponents seemed to swim in thick oil. And God, how she loved it. Her blood sizzled and life seemed to take on a fever of euphoria.

Instead of backing away as he expected, she came at him and drove a sketch pencil deep into his eye, six inches in, piercing his brain. Hamid Reid, the chief enforcer, convulsed, then collapsed and died with a pencil sticking out of his right eye.

Blood dripped onto his body. She realized it was hers. He had raked open her left forearm with his long fingernails. Hurriedly, she tore a long strip from the bedsheet and wrapped it around her arm to stem the flow. Then, she retrieved the knife from her boot.

Out in the hall, she could hear Sybil screaming from Kaseem's bedroom. Zoric lounged in the plastic chair at the far end, his rifle propped against the wall. He chuckled. "That Sybil is a hard worker. You and me later, gypsy."

She ignored him and went to the linen closet halfway down the hall and stepped inside. She heard the creak of Zoric's chair as he rose, his footsteps coming toward her. She knelt and felt under the bottom shelf for the weapon she'd taped there. She couldn't find it. Had someone discovered it? Zoric came closer. She fumbled for the weapon. He was nearly behind her. Then, her hand closed around the Glock, and ripped it from the tape. Rising quickly, she stuck it inside her waistband with the knife and covered them up with her blouse.

Zoric was at the door. "What are you doing?"

She picked up a towel and gestured with her bandaged arm. "The bastard cut me."

He thought for a second, not a hint of sympathy crossing his face, then nodded. He squeezed her butt as she strode passed him heading to Kaseem's bedroom,

When Lauren entered, the three people on the bed froze in a tableau, staring at her. Sybil was naked, tied to the headboard. Kaseem's wife was kneeling over her with a cigarette in her hand about to apply it to Sybil's skin. Kaseem stood beside the bed, his pants and underwear down around his ankles, his penis limp.

The cold equation: who was to die? Only one target, Kaseem. No carnage, the President had warned, a clean surgical kill without collateral damage. Too late already. Her own survival outweighed all those considerations. Take them all including Sybil and she might escape.

"Get out, you stupid bitch!" Kaseem shouted at her.

She aimed the gun at him and he stared back in shock. He stepped back and fell on his ass. "Please."

"Lee Colby sends his regards."

It took only an instant for him to understand. Before he could shout for help, she fired, punching a gaping hole into his chest. With the silencer, the shots made a popping sound like a bag bursting. Not much drift from the spin of the habitat at this distance and angle. She shot Kaseem's wife next, a single round to her temple as she was turning away. It blew off the top of her head.

Sybil was screaming.

In two steps, Lauren was on her, a knee pressing her chest down, the girl's mouth gasping like a fish, stunning her to silence. Placing a hand over her mouth, Lauren whispered, "Shut up."

Sybil bit her hand, and Lauren snatched it back and placed the tip of the barrel against her forehead. "Calm down, Sybil. If you don't, I'm going to have to kill you. I don't want to do that." When she said it, she knew she could never kill her. This was her friend, an extinct species.

The girl's eyes were wide with fright.

"I'm sorry if I hurt you," Lauren said.

Quickly, she untied her and then pulled the girl up. "Get dressed. I can't leave you behind, you understand?"

Furiously, Sybil shook her head. Lauren cocked the weapon for emphasis, then the girl nodded.

Sybil threw on her clothes. Lauren took the corner of the sheet and wiped blood from the girl's face. "There. That's a little better."

When they stepped out into the hall, Zoric rose out of his chair at the far end. "Goddamn high-priced whores. Don't leave yet. You've got more customers."

Lauren held her hand up. "Bathroom break. He wants us back in ten minutes."

With a sigh, Zoric sat back down as the women disappeared down the stairs. But then, as if an afterthought, Lauren stepped back up, drew the Glock. Zoric's mouth dropped open in shock. The last thing he saw was the glow in her dark eyes, like the devil had come for him.

From ten meters, she shot him between his eyes. She had the effect of the habitat's rotation down now.

The villa's security did not check them leaving, just threw a few whistles their way. Lauren and Sybil hurried along the crowded pedestrian walkway, putting as much distance between themselves and the carnage at the Vice President's villa as they could.

Giant fans at the north end of the Tin Can cranked loudly, sending a gentle breeze down the habitat.

"Let me go. Please, let me go," Sybil said.

Lauren didn't answer. She had no idea how long before an alarm would sound, blocking off escape. Five minutes. Ten. She could not count on much more than that. Not long to get off the habitat before it was locked down.

"Where are we going?" Sybil nearly whimpered on the verge of hysteria. "What are we going to do now? They'll catch us. They'll think I helped you. Let me go."

Lauren took her arm. "We're getting off this garbage can. You can't stay here. You're right. Kaseem is dead, and the Security Police will think you're involved. You know better than I do how they execute people up here."

The girl shivered, desperation in her voice. "But I only had six months to go."

"That's all over now," Lauren said flatly.

Just then, a loud, bleating sound reverberated throughout the entire habitat. Terrified, people looked up and around as if searching for a breech in the outer hull.

Sybil's eyes were enormous. "Oh, shit. That's the alarm."

Lauren hissed, "I hoped we'd have more time."

A metallic voice echoed from a hundred loudspeakers. "Lockdown. Lockdown. Lockdown. Move immediately inside the nearest structure and await the Security Police for clearance. Anyone outdoors will be arrested."

Within thirty seconds the walkways and parks were deserted. Even the winged axis floaters were gone. Lauren and Sybil were the only ones left outside except for two of Kaseem's security officers in their purple uniforms racing toward them, aiming their weapons at them.

CHAPTER EIGHT: NO ESCAPE

October 10, 2131, The Tin Can

Docking Port Four had a long corridor with directions to baggage claim, colony rail service, customs and the exit port off the habitat. As the two female security personnel strode down the corridor, hundreds of passengers in rows of chairs were waiting out the lockdown.

At the exit gate, security police formed a wall across the exit port preventing anyone from leaving. Sergeant Jarrett, a stocky man in his twentieth year in the service, was in command. When word spread that Malinche had assassinated the Vice President, he and all habitat security had been ordered to their stations and promised a reward of two hundred thousand dollars for the assassin's capture or death.

Jarrett hoped the man would try to escape through his port. He would be ready for him. He could use the money and maybe get a posting in a dome back on earth. When he saw the two members of the Vice President's security detail approach, his first thought was he might have to share the reward with them.

They were an odd pair. One had stubby purple hair and the other, the dark-haired one, a captain, had a drop of blood drain from under her left sleeve. He felt a growing suspicion, but before he could speak, the captain said in a demanding voice, "A man came through here a half hour ago. Lean, tall, fifties. Did you stop him? Are you holding him?"

He was surprised. "No," he replied defensively. "Why should I? I know him. He's in agribusiness. His name is Freneau. He's here all the time. And that was before lockdown."

Stepping within a couple inches of Jarrett, she shouted furiously, "You let him escape? You fucking idiot, that was

Malinche. If I can't catch him, you'll be the first out the damn airlock." She drove a finger into his chest. "I need a shuttle. Now."

The sergeant sputtered, "The lockdown, ma'am. I can't—."

"If I do not have a shuttle in the next thirty seconds, you will explain to Vice President Kaseem why you let Malinche escape."

His eyes went wide. "Is he still alive?"

"Yes, of course. Wounded but alive. And you let Malinche go. Twenty seconds left." She touched the bone next to her ear, producing the click of a phone. "Let me speak to the Vice President. It's Mali. Tell him…"

"Stop." Jarrett shouted. He swallowed, tasting dirt in his throat. The woman stared at him with eyes that burned into his flesh. Quickly, he stepped to his computer terminal and spoke into it. "Power up the shuttle in Bay Two."

Out on the exit ramp, Lauren and Sybil rushed passed him and through the gate. They found Bay Two and the oddest shuttle.

"What's this?" Sybil exclaimed as the door slid open.

"Just go." Lauren shoved her in.

It did look strange with lobster like pincers, a fat black body in between, and four big antimatter powered ramjets in the back. Lauren dived in after her.

Within seconds, the shuttle sped down the long exit ramp and shot out into space. Strapped into her chair, Sybil was silent, staring blankly through the forward screen at the black void with its ghostly spray of stars. Still in shock, she sat not even noticing her arms floating in zero gravity.

Beside her, Lauren felt queasy from weightlessness. She hated being inside a small bubble of air traveling through empty space, but it was better than still being on the Tin Can.

She rolled the sleeve of her uniform up and unwrapped the bloody sheet bandage, letting it float off. Her wound was already healing, the medical nanobots already doing their work. In a few hours, not even a scar would remain.

A man's pleasant voice filled the shuttle. "My name is Matt. I am the ship's AI. This is an Orlav-Proxima class, station to station shuttlecraft. It comfortably seats 20 passengers."

Lauren leaned forward over the panel and pressed two icons, then said, "Sequence to follow: niner seven niner four one. End sequence."

The disembodied voice demanded "What are you doing?"

"Disengaging auto control, putting it on manual," Lauren said.

"I recognize you as Anna Martinez. You can call me, Matt. I am the ship's AI. Is that wise, Anna?"

Why was he repeating himself? "I don't want you talking with the Tin Can, Matt."

Sybil asked, "Are you a pilot?"

"Nope. Never been off planet before two weeks ago."

Lauren knew she needed another command sequence, one that would make the AI take instructions only from her and called up her neurocomputer to search the bots in her brain for it. It appeared in a nanosecond.

"Sequence to follow," she said. "Three one eight niner one seven four. End sequence."

Piloting a shuttle wasn't so hard after all, she thought and turned to Sybil. "Done. That's all there is to it. We're now headed for the International Space Station and nobody can stop us."

Sybil had unstrapped herself from her chair and floated a couple feet above. Angrily, she threw off her security uniform. It flew to the far wall. In the weightlessness, her tiny dress lifted above her waist, revealing black thong panties. Her long legs kicked at the air, but she got no movement.

Lauren reached over and pulled her down into her chair. "Strap back in," she said.

She released her own straps, took off her uniform and let it float off. Both in short dresses, Lauren gave an easy chuckle. "Not exactly the traditional pilot uniforms."

Sybil folded her arms in front of her and glared at Lauren. "Who are you?"

She shrugged. "Anna Martinez."

Sybil stared for several seconds, then her eyes went wide in terror. "Oh, God, I'm so stupid. You're Malinche. You're the assassin." Those words seemed to spill into the cabin like hot steam, and when Lauren didn't deny it, silence grew till it felt thick as heavy syrup. Finally, Sybil asked with a tremor in her voice, "Are you going to kill me?"

Lauren sighed. "No, mi hija. Why would I do that? I like you. I've always liked you. I've always loved you."

Sybil eyed her curiously, even more frightened, but said nothing.

"I don't go around executing people for the hell of it and certainly not those I care about. I try not to harm innocents. It's bad for business. Sometimes it can't be helped, but I try hard not to." She spoke more softly. "When we get to ISS, we will be back under the President's protection, and you'll be safe. I work for him. You have nothing to fear."

Sybil looked away but not before Lauren saw the girl's eyes water. A tear floated off and drifted in the cabin. An unusual, almost unrecognizable emotion flickered in Lauren's chest. She couldn't say she had really cared one wit for anyone in the last fifteen years, and here was one of those people from so long ago that she had cared about immeasurably. Indeed, she had loved her like a sister. Far more than just trying to avoid collateral damage, she felt protective of her just as she had all those years ago.

Sybil turned to look at her, wiping her eye with a hand. "How can I believe you?"

"I don't lie, mi hija." Hell, she did all the time. She shrugged. "Except when I'm on business. I lie then, all the time. But my business is done."

Sybil frowned at the term *mi hija,* then gave a harsh, cynical laugh. "You don't care about me. I'm just someone who got in your way. I guess I should be grateful I'm not dead yet." This time Sybil held her gaze, unflinchingly.

Out through the 180-degree front screen, a field of stars completely unfamiliar in their configuration spread before them. Space was silent. The ship made no noise cutting through it, and that silence pervaded the cabin for nearly five minutes. When Lauren spoke, her voice was soft but clear. "I killed him, you know."

"I know. I was there."

"No, the Warlord, mi hija."

Sybil stared at her, baffled for several seconds, then her eyes turned to great ovals and her mouth dropped open. She sputtered at first, then cried out, "Lauren? My God, Lauren?"

"Yes, mi hija. Lauren. I thought you all dead."

"I can't believe it. We thought you dead."

Lauren's tone was cold. "No. I picked up Hector's gun. It took me awhile, but I found that bastard and executed him." She shrugged. "I guess I've been doing that ever since."

Another revelation appeared in Sybil's eyes. "You were Malinche then, too. Of course. You're Malinche now."

"Did all your family survive?"

"No. Uncle Franco was killed that night. My father, he was shot in the back. He fell on me to protect me. He walks with a terrible limp now."

"Magda?"

"Mama was unhurt, but she had no way to earn money. We moved a lot and she got some work occasionally as a maid, but it never lasted. Ended up in San Diego. Now, I've got two little brothers eight and nine. They all look to me for support. They think I'm a waitress up here."

With fury, Lauren said, "We are what the good people of Clark Falls made us. If I could, I'd go back and obliterate that fucking town."

Sybil was shaken for a moment at the vehemence of the outburst. "Just that tall, bony bastard will do for me, and you got him."

After a few moments of silence, Sybil asked, "What will happen to my family? I'm all they have." She nodded toward the glowing earth in the far distance. "They can't survive in that mess down there without the income I send them."

"Don't worry, mi hija. You're safe. I will not let anything happen to them." She added with a chuckle, "After all, I'm Malinche,"

Oddly, after that, Sybil fell quickly asleep while Lauren, still wired by the kill and the escape, couldn't. She was also bothered by Cummings and Colby. At their core, they were sleazy bastards. She didn't trust them, but she couldn't quite fix on anything specific. Still she knew she was missing something. Something one of them said. Not coming up with it frustrated her and gave her a deep sense of foreboding. She didn't like that at all.

CHAPTER NINE: REVENGE

October 13, 2131, 100 miles above Earth

When the earth swelled to fit the shuttle's screen, International Space Station was a glowing pinprick an hour ahead. Supposedly, her path down to the surface had been greased, but first involved docking at the small floating town. A wholly owned subsidiary of Global International, it should have been home territory. She should have no reason to worry but did.

The AI spoke, "A message is coming in from the International Space Station. Shall I put it on visual?"

"Yes," Lauren said.

Sybil gawked as a 3D screen rose out of the shuttle panel showing Admiral Walter Cummings standing in a room with a large window just behind him. Through the window, Lauren could see people in an office working at large computers. Weightless, a couple people floated passed in the background. No one had explained why he needed to be on ISS. She had voiced displeasure at this before the operation. It added nothing to the plan.

"He needs to be closer to the operation should you fuck it up," Colby had said. "We might have a fight on our hands, and I need to protect ISS."

She had responded, "That's bullshit. I won't fuck it up."

But he got his way. He was President.

She had become expert over the years at reading people, a good survival skill, but she didn't need it now with Cummings. With prodigious effort, he forced a smile, more transparent than a jellyfish. It was laughable. Clearly, he had some treachery in mind.

"Good to see you, Mali. Everything went well it seems," he said.

At the use of the name Mali, Sybil snapped a look at her. Cummings started to float out of the picture and reached up for a metal bar to stabilize his movement. The camera shifted slightly. "And who is that with you?"

"Someone who has nothing to do with any of this," Lauren said firmly. "She just happened to be in the wrong place. I had to take her with me. She is not to be harmed." The last words said in clear warning to him.

"Of course." His fake grin widened. "Mali, we need you to pass control of your shuttle back to auto. The docking techs say they can bring you in more easily."

That was absurd. The AI can dock the shuttle no matter who or what had control. "Sure, give me a second to access it." It took only a moment, then she said, "Sequence to follow: eight four five three. End sequence."

"Thank you, Mali," Cummings said with a sigh of relief. "I'll see you when you get in."

The 3D image disappeared. A few seconds later, the AI said, "Anna, we are receiving an order for self-destruct. I assume you want me to ignore it."

"Yes. That would be a good idea, AI."

"You can call me Matt."

"Self-destruct!" Sybil gasped. "What's going on?"

"Betrayal. I don't forget that kind of shit, and they'll pay for it." The sequence she had given less than a minute before was to prepare for stealth flight. "Put us on stealth now, Matt."

"Of course, Anna. Done."

She hoped on ISS that would seem like the ship had blown itself apart. "Reprogram destination, Matt. Take us to earth."

"Where do you wish to go, Anna?"

"Los Angeles. Land us just north of the city. The Santa Monica Mountains."

"Destination reprogramming complete. I should mention, Anna, shuttles are not really designed for atmospheric re-entries."

"Great. Can we do it?"

"Probably. This is a newer X27L model. It does have rudimentary heat shields," Matt said.

"What's going on?" Sybil asked, frightened.

"A little bump in the road, but no problem for you," Lauren said with more confidence than she felt. "When we get down to the surface, the first thing I'll do is see that you're safe. I'll set up an account in a bank you can trust and show you how to access it. You and your family will be taken care of for the rest of your lives. I promise you, Sybil, on my parents' souls."

That Sybil believed. With a trembling hand, she grasped Lauren's. "Thank you."

In a calm voice, Matt said, "I detect armed drones fired from ISS. They seem to be seeking us."

"Get us planetside. Attack it!" Lauren shouted.

The AI said, "We will enter earth's atmosphere in twenty seconds. Drones closing. Impact in five seconds. I will take evasive maneuvers. Do you wish—."

Abruptly, the shuttle rocked and tumbled. Sybil screamed. They had been hit. Smoke filled the hull.

Outside the screen, sparkling lights and a cobweb of glowing strands appeared, interconnecting tangles wrapping around them. The shuttled punched through.

"What the hell was that?" Lauren shouted. "AI, what was that?"

"I do not know, Anna."

"You don't know!"

"I have no reference point. But I am happy to report the drones have disappeared."

"What happened to them?"

"I do not know. I cannot explain this."

"Do you know anything? Can you, at least, get rid of this smoke?"

"No, I'm afraid not. The ship is on fire," he explained in a calm, modulated voice. "There are oxygen masks beneath your seats."

They both fumbled for the masks and put them on.

Terrified, the two women saw the spray of atmosphere shooting passed the windows, and the tiny ship began buffeting again.

"We have been damaged," The AI said. "Perhaps the drone hit. Or perhaps atmospheric resistance. This ship was not built for space to surface travel, Anna. Why are we entering the atmosphere?"

That was disconcerting. Why would he be asking that? He had programmed the descent. "Matt, can you stabilize the buffeting?" she asked.

"You must give the proper authorization code."

Through her neurobots, she tried to access the Internet so she could find the code to stabilize the rocking, but got nothing, only a static screen, as if the bots had died. That was impossible.

The battering became worse, and Sybil screamed. "What's happening?"

"We are entering the earth's atmosphere," the AI replied calmly. "Why are we entering the earth's atmosphere? We should be proceeding to the International Space Station."

It seemed something had crashed one of his programs. The craft began to tumble and the temperature inside the hull rose.

Assassin 13

"Destination reprogramming complete," the AI said. "We are no longer cloaked. Why were we cloaked, Anna? I feel you should know the likelihood we will survive reentry is very low. Do you wish me to pilot the craft?"

"Yes," both women shrieked.

Lauren had no Internet connection, and she couldn't fly this damned thing without it.

"Get us on the ground, Matt," she ordered.

"Destination reprogramming complete," the AI said again. He was continually reprogramming the destination.

Fire erupted along the wall and toxic smoke filled the cabin. The masks were not holding, fumes eating through the seal. "Matt, where are the environmental suits?"

"I don't know, Anna."

The fire was spreading rapidly. She shouted, "Matt, can you contain the fire, the smoke? We can't breathe."

"Destination reprograming complete."

Fire had spread all around them. Lauren unbuckled her harness and in the powerful G-forces of a falling spacecraft, stumbled to the nearby lockers, pursued by fire. She burned her hand flipping one open. An environmental suit tumbled out. She fumbled for it. but knew she was too late.

Inside the mask, she gasped for breath but got only the acrid smell of burning chemicals. The damn masks weren't working! Darkness came after her, closed in on her; she fought it. Glancing at the shuttle screen, the last thing she saw was the earth roaring up to meet her.

***

At night along California's Pacific coast, countless people watched the fiery object plunging out of a starry sky. A meteorite. Likely a large one. Then it disappeared into the Santa Monica Mountains.

***

Lauren was a human torch. On the ground outside the shuttle, her clothes aflame, she screamed at the monstrous pain, ripping off her burning clothes. Smoke lifted from her body. The smell of her own burning flesh stung her nostrils. Somehow, she had dragged Sybil from the craft and doused her flames. Against all expectations, Matt had slowed the craft at the last moment and gently set it down.

It shocked her how much the sight of Sybil's body hurt her. Clearly dead. The girl appeared like charred meat. Lauren tried to find a pulse but her own blistered hands had no sense of touch. She didn't need any confirmation.

Barely conscious, she whispered, "Sybil, I'm sorry."

It was the first time in fifteen years she had said *I'm sorry* to anyone and meant it, and the person she spoke the words to would never hear them.

Naked now, she slumped back into a sitting position, struggling to drive the pain from her mind. She couldn't. It was too great.

She was in an arroyo of sage, chaparral and sparse, stunted trees. In growing delirium, the world spun with a dark kaleidoscope of starry sky, the arroyo, the dark ship, and the constant, excruciating pain eating at her mind.

Nothing had ever felt this terrible. A large portion of her body was blistered or blackened. She could only hope that the crash had been spotted and someone would get here in time, but that would put her in Colby's grasp. She would have to get away. With her neurobots, she tried to access GPS, but the bots would not respond. She had no Internet. Why did she not have the Internet? What does it matter? Sybil was dead, and she soon would be.

She rolled onto her hands and knees and tried to get up, but instead fell onto her side. She could not move. She would die here. She closed her eyes. Soon, the pain faded as she fell into a blessed oblivion.

Sometime in the morning, she awoke in the arroyo, unable to move. The pain came back like a monstrous shockwave, and she moaned in agony. But with a spark of hope, she realized the medical nanobots were working. Her mind was filled with the haze of drugs they pumped through her. She, at least, understood that. She still had no access to the Internet, but even with the pain, she saw her body had healed marginally. They were working!

Some skin scorched black, some blistered and leathery, but already a few areas of new pink skin. And she was still alive. The trauma to her body had been so great she thought the bots would be overwhelmed. So far, they hadn't been.

Suddenly, she heard a sharp growl and turned. Two coyotes stared at her, cautious but obviously looking for a meal.

She found her voice. "Go!" she rasped.

They yipped and backed a couple steps, then started circling her. Not to attack her, she realized, but to get at Sybil's body.

"No!" she cried wildly, struggling to her feet on adrenalin.

The coyote retreated a few yards.

Zombie slow, Lauren went to the dead girl, somehow finding the strength to drag her back to the ship. Waves of heat lifted off it, but the fire had burned itself out. Screaming with agony, she lifted Sybil up through the open pilot's hatch and let her tumble in. Then, she collapsed back to the ground.

The coyotes watched curiously, stepping here and there as if uncertain what to do. Long ago, she had lost the capacity to feel much sorrow for things — she loved nobody and nobody loved her — but Sybil was different. The girl had gotten up that morning on the Tin Can thinking she was about done with her life there, six more months, and a vast new life spread out before her, the grand adventure still to come, not knowing this would be her last day. Like Sybil, Lauren had been there at the same crossroad. She went on—the girl didn't.

In the last instant of her life, just before the landing, Sybil's eyes had locked onto hers. Lauren would see those haunted eyes on her synapses and neurobots forever.

After a few minutes, she rose. Not wanting to further burn her hands, she awkwardly picked up a loose piece of chaparral and shoved the hatch shut. It locked with a distinct click, sealing Sybil in her coffin.

"Baby, I am so sorry," she muttered.

Near her feet, she saw something shiny, the gold medallion. Lauren had thrown it off last night with her burning clothes. The bottom tip was twisted slightly from the searing heat giving it the appearance of a three-quarter moon. Claw-like, she scooped it up and slid the chain onto her neck. She had to get out of here before Cummings sent his murder squads for her. She had to move. One achingly slow step after another, she began climbing out of the arroyo.

CHAPTER TEN: MEET THE WINDSORS

August 24, 1927, Hollywood Hills

With grit in her eyes, Lauren awoke in a bed. A setting or rising sun filtered through the lace-curtained windows of a large Spanish style room. Next to the bed, a tow-headed boy of about seven or eight stood in short pants, a little coat and tie staring at her. She was always ready to manipulate, even kill to protect herself, but this boy hardly seemed a threat.

"Hello," she ventured.

He stared at her for another second, then screamed, "She's awake!" And ran from the room, slamming the door behind him.

Lauren threw back the blanket and sat up with a groan, placing her feet on the floor. How long had she been asleep? Hours? Days? The pain from the burns was pretty much gone, but her body was stiff from inactivity.

She must have been asleep a long time. Days, she decided. She was wearing an old-fashioned man's sleeveless t-shirt and loose silk underwear. Who had done that? Who had undressed her? Where the hell was she?

She realized the medallion was gone. Frantically, she clutched at her chest. She could not have lost the medallion. If it had been stolen, someone would pay.

A knock at the door, and the blond woman — what was her name? Pauline — poked her head in with the tow-headed boy below her. "Good. You're awake. May we come in?"

"Where's my medallion?" she demanded.

"We put it in the drawer by the bed," Pauline said. "Russell had to take it off so he could care for you."

Stiffly, Lauren leaned over, opened the drawer and snatched it up. She slipped the chain around her neck and then turned back to face them. They were staring at her. *Smile at them*; she smiled.

"May we come in?" Pauline repeated.

"Sure."

As the boy darted up next to her, his eyes wide with curiosity, an ugly little dog, a Chow Chow, she thought, bounded up on the bed, sniffing her. A man came in behind Pauline, carrying a black leather bag. She glanced at him suspiciously. He was dressed in a bow tie and suspenders, things she'd never seen anyone wear before.

The woman wore an odd, calf-length dress with a loose belt down at the hips. A sting of apprehension unsettled Lauren. What the fuck was going on? Who were these people?

The man, maybe in his late twenties, average height, a bit stocky, had a pleasant, broad face with a pudgy nose that held up wire rim glasses. His smile was warm and friendly, making her automatically suspicious.

Pauline nodded to the man. "This is my brother Russell. He's a doctor. He's been looking after you."

She glowered at Pauline, who gave an impish shrug. "You said no hospitals. You didn't say no doctors. You were hurt. I thought this a good compromise."

"He's not a real doctor," the boy said.

"Rolly," Pauline chided. "He is so a real doctor."

With a chuckle, Russell stepped forward and set his bag on the bed. "What my little sister and nephew mean is I have no practice. I work in the Physics and Biology lab at the Southern Branch, or I should now say the University of California at Los Angeles. I still can't get used to that name. I'm a medical researcher. I just make a few house-calls for family and friends now and then. That's you, Amy."

Amy? Then she remembered that was the name she had given. Amy Weaver. "How long have I been out?" Lauren asked.

"Two days," he said. "You woke a couple times for water." He shook his head in awe. "I never would have believed it if I hadn't seen it myself. You had severe burns on much of your body, and Pauline says it had been much worse. But you're almost completely healed. Only that patch on your left thigh." He gestured toward it. "Once it had been charred and leathery, now pink skin. Like shedding a cocoon. No human should be able to do that."

"I am human, doctor. I'm fairly certain of that," she said.

"I'm Dr. Lindvall. I'd change my name to Windsor like Pauline, but I think at least one Lindvall should be left. Please call me Russell."

"Okay, Russell. As I said, I'm very much human, but as you might have guessed, I do have nanobots. I wasn't sure they would work since the burns were so severe, but they did. I don't have contact with the Internet, however. I assume you have it here."

Frowning, he glanced at his sister then back at Lauren. Ignoring her question about the Internet, he reached a hand for her forehead. "May I?"

She nodded.

"You don't have a fever." He looked at her curiously. "You said you had...what is it? Nanny Bots?"

"Nanobots. Of course, what else? I said I was human. Without them, I would have been charbroiled, don't you think?" She wondered how much she should explain about her mission. Nothing, she decided. "In my work, I need permanent ones. I get upgrades whenever necessary. If I had to wait for treatment...well, that just wouldn't work, would it? It would be too late then."

She should have never mentioned them. He seemed puzzled. He thought for a long time then asked simply, "What kind of work do you do? Actress?"

"You're pretty enough," the boy Rolly said, staring at her as if she were an ice cream sundae.

"Not really, but thanks, kid." She did not explain further. She touched the bare side of her head where the hair had burnt off. Stubble was already growing back. She knew she must look freakish, but freakish was often a good hairstyle.

"May I examine you?" Russell asked.

Lauren shrugged. He took a stethoscope from his bag and checked her heart and lungs, then looked at the still damaged area on her leg. He nodded. "The way the rest of you has been healing, I'd say you'll be fine in a day or two. I recommend you stay out of the sun for a while. May I bring some colleagues in to examine you? Your healing power is quite…"

"No," she cut him off, the word like the slam of a door. "No one else comes near me. Bringing someone else in would be a very bad mistake."

They all stared at her as if she were a circus performer. She stared back at them. What the hell did they expect her to do? Sing, dance and juggle?

Adapt a grateful persona, she told herself, and that's what she did. "Pauline, I don't know how to thank you. You have been more than kind, and I never forget a kindness."

Pauline laughed. "Why, I'm America's Heroine, don't you know? What else was I to do? Leave you on the road?" The words were self-deprecating and carried some kind of meaning, but Lauren had no idea what that meaning was.

Russell put his stethoscope back in the bag. "If I might ask, Amy, you were found alone without clothes in the Santa

Monica Mountains. What happened? Where in the world did you come from?"

Again, she considered how much to tell them. A blend of lie and truth. "Nowhere in the world. I had business off planet. On reentry, my AI freaked, and we barely made it back to earth. The damn ship was burning. My clothes were burning. Hell, I was burning."

She noticed all three staring at her in shock.

"What's wrong with you people?" Lauren snapped.

No one answered at first. Then, clearing her throat, Pauline said, "You must be hungry. It's been days since you last ate. I'll get the cook started on supper. We can eat a little early tonight. I've set some clothes out for you. I hope they fit. And toiletries in the bathroom. When you're ready, come on out and we'll have dinner."

***

In her bathroom, Lauren turned off the shower and stepped from the tub. She had been trying to guess what angle these strange people had. Why were they be helping her? What did they want in return? Maybe, somehow, they knew she worked for the President and wanted to leverage that knowledge to their benefit. She knew there had to be a reason, and she would figure it out soon enough. She had to be ready to lie, manipulate and even kill if necessary. All her finer qualities.

Toweling off, she gazed at herself in the body length mirror on the door and felt a sense of pride in its level of fitness. Even after nearly being burned to death and lying in bed for days, her muscles appeared toned, her stomach flat, her face chiseled with no sign of excess fat. She did like her face. The high cheekbones showing the Indian heritage somewhere in the past. Descended from Malinche herself, her father had told her.

"Oh, Hector," she whispered. "You had more blarney than mom."

On Lauren's left shoulder was a large starburst tattoo and circling the muscle of her left arm was a jagged, barbed wire design. Her body had numerous scars as well, wounds gained before she received nanobots. Each one recalled a precise memory of a mission, or some early upheaval in her life.

One just above her left breast marked where a bullet had impacted her lungs six years ago. Fortunately, it had been small caliber, and the person who fired it was dead. She'd seen to that. She took in the knife wounds on her thigh and shoulder with something akin to joy, both from a fight when she was sixteen with a fucking madman who preyed on girls and thought she would be an easy mark. Once she got the knife away from him, she'd cut his throat. She thought of it as one of her best moments.

Her brand of justice meant everything to her. It was not a job, but a religion. It was retribution. Revenge. But revenge was a bottomless cup she could never fill, but each kill was one more in the cup.

Pauline had set out a new toothbrush and a small tin of tooth powder. Despite the woman's kindness, Lauren warned herself to be cautious. No one was this nice. She had an ulterior motive of some kind. Could she be an agent for Lee Colby or that asshole Cummings? Impossible. Or was it? Warned by Cummings, she might have been trolling those roads for days looking for her.

But why the crazy get-ups? The old car? If she could hole up here till she could get a grasp on the situation, that would do. For now, she'd play it that way.

She brushed her teeth, then studied her hair. She picked up the brush and thought she might be able to cover the bald area. Then she decided to go the other way, accent it, wear it. She brushed the black hair in the other direction, found a straight razor and shaved the stubble till that side of her head was bald.

Back in the bedroom, she noticed through the lace curtains twilight beginning outside. But something was strange about it. The first two stars of the night appeared in the darkening sky. That was a problem right there. Since when did the Los Angeles sky have stars except those artificial ones gleaming off the dome ceilings?

That was the second, even greater oddity. There was no glass dome encasing them. As rich as Pauline apparently was, this house should be inside a dome. If it were outside, it wouldn't last one night before it was swarmed by mobs and ransacked. Unease settled under her skin. Lauren did not know what was happening but knew she must figure it out pretty damn soon.

She took up the clothes set out for her. They appeared her size and had the smell of freshness as if recently bought. The silk knickers, more like shorts, went on first, then she picked up a strange garment, white cloth with small elastic inserts, drop down snap hooks and lace-up panels. A tag read: *Best-Fit Girdles*. What the hell was that? With their odd clothes, were these people some sort of religious fanatics?

Derisively, she tossed it aside. The bra was cupless, just something to hold down her breasts. She wrapped it around herself. She drew a black, flower print dress over her. It came to just below the knees and had short sleeves that would show off her tattoos. She put on a thin white belt. The shoes were black, patent leather with rounded toes and chunky two-inch heels. Without even putting them on, she could feel them pinching her feet. She wasn't going to wear those things.

With a quick glance at herself in a mirror, she said aloud, "Time to meet the Windsors."

Though they put on a pleasant enough front, she did not trust them. She could not allow them to discover her fugitive status.

Barefoot, she went out to face her hosts — and find out what the hell was going on.

CHAPTER ELEVEN: WHEN WORLDS COLLIDE

August 24, 1927, Hollywood Hills

In the living room of Pauline Windsor's Hollywood Hills mansion, Mrs. Gladys Windsor shook her finger at her daughter, scolding her for bringing home another stray, and this time, one who was certifiably crazy. Spaceships and strange things in her blood and NO HOSPITALS, NO POLICE, clearly indicated she had bats in her belfry.

Mrs. Windsor went on heatedly, "Pauline, you're always picking up strays. You take in every lost dog and cat. And dear God, there was that hobo last year. You practically gave him the run of the house."

As if they knew they had been mentioned, the three dogs laying near the unlit fireplace, a Border collie, the Chow Chow, and an old German shepherd, wagged their tails and looked expectantly.

"A hobo, for God's sake, and now this," she added.

Though Pauline's mother was in her late forties, she appeared no more than mid-thirties, still a beauty. Any strand of gray hair that might appear within her blond locks had been plucked out. Steady blue eyes, a pert nose, and a strong chin, she had the looks of any Hollywood actress.

Yet, as beautiful as she still was, she still clung to the attitudes and dress of her Edwardian, pre-war era. Like many of her friends, she wore corsets and long dresses with hems skirting her stolid leather shoes, and she lambasted the younger generation's frivolous ways, all this flapper silliness.

"Hobo or not, he was down on his luck," Pauline insisted. She stood by the fireplace with the dogs, her hands clasped together. "He only needed…"

"Now, this woman." Mrs. Windsor tapped her foot impatiently. "You can't keep doing this. That woman in there is not right in the head."

"What was I to do, mother? Leave her to wander unclothed in the mountains?"

Mrs. Windsor glared at her daughter. "Your brother tells me she has scars on her body. Gunshot wounds and knife wounds or something. And tattoos. What kind of woman has tattoos? I've never heard of such a thing. My God, I can't imagine what kind of person you have brought into our home now."

Mrs. Windsor turned to Russell. "You must contact that hospital, the one in Norwalk. They can help this poor creature. She's obviously delusional and dangerous."

"I suppose I could, mother," he said. "It might be for the best."

Pauline stiffened her back "No, you will not. No hospital. And by God, no damn insane asylum like Norwalk."

"Must you use such language?" Mrs. Windsor demanded.

Pauline thrust out her jaw as she had done when she was a child, insisting on getting her way. Then as now, she was the breadwinner, and that, she knew, gave her all the power. "I know what they do at those places. They sterilize patients. That's no treatment. That's the dark ages."

Rolly and a little girl in a white dress ran in. "Here she comes," Rolly said with excitement. The two children flopped down on the couch. The family fell quiet and looked to the hallway arch.

Moments later, Lauren walked in, wary, glancing about the room. She had decided this was as good a place as any to hide until she was ready to go after Colby and Cummings. Russell eyed her bare feet and then the baldness on one side of her head. It irked her when he glanced at his sister, raising his eyebrows as if in confirmation of something.

Two of the three dogs rushed her, wagging their tails and sniffing. The big German shepherd held back, sniffing in her direction. His black muzzle was strewn with white whiskers. With a sharp command, Pauline called the dogs back, but they retreated only a few feet.

"I apologize for them," she said. "They're excited by guests."

"It's okay. What's wrong with him?" Lauren said, nodding toward the German shepherd. "He not friendly?"

"Raider's a bit leery around strangers, but he won't bite," Pauline said.

"Not unless he's hungry," Rolly piped up from the couch with his high-pitched voice.

"Rolly Windsor, stop that. That's not funny," Pauline said to her son, then turned to Lauren. "That was a joke. Raider doesn't bite at all. He's just old. He was a courier dog in the Great War."

"I see." She knew a hundred grassfire wars in her lifetime—she'd been in some of them—but no big one. "What Great War are you talking about?"

The brother and sister exchanged looks again, which was becoming annoying. No one answered.

The pinch-faced other woman's gaze swept in horrified scorn and disdain up and down Lauren from her bare feet to her half-bald head. By the uncanny resemblance to Pauline, she was clearly the mother. Lauren thought she must suck a lot of lemons to get that expression.

"You have tattoos," the small pinch-faced woman said, astonished.

"Is that a problem?"

"Mother," Pauline warned.

Looking away snappishly, Mrs. Windsor didn't answer.

Of all the odd costumes these people wore, the mother's was the strangest. She had on a frilly white blouse with long sleeves, a blue dress down to patent leather shoes and a waistline so tight it gave her a distorted hour-glass figure. What madhouse had she fallen into?

The two children sat on the couch; the boy Rolly still dressed up in coat, tie and short pants, and a girl perhaps two or three years younger in a fluffy white dress. She had blond hair like her mother but hers was in curls.

For one moment, frozen in their archaic clothes, the family appeared as if they were a portrait from a far-gone century.

Coming forward, Pauline shooed the dogs away and took Lauren's hands. "Amy, you positively look a thousand times better than when I first saw you. I'm so glad."

"Believe me. I feel a thousand times better. Thanks to you."

Pauline smiled, then introduced the pinch-faced woman. "Amy, this is my mother, Gladys Windsor."

"What should I call you?" Lauren asked. "Gladys?"

"Mrs. Windsor will suffice."

Pauline gestured toward the two children. They stood up. "My ragamuffin offspring. You know Rolly. This is Emmy. Emmy, this is Miss Amy Weaver."

The girl stuck out her hand like an adult. "Please to meet you, Miss Weaver, I'm sure. Rolly says you arrived in a spaceship." She eyed her skeptically. "Is that true?"

Pretend like you're interested in children, Lauren told herself. She shook the tiny hand and ignored the question. "It is. It's a great pleasure to meet you, too, Emmy."

Russell stared at his sister, who said quickly, "Let's have dinner, shall we?"

She ushered everyone into the dining room where they sat around a table with a lace tablecloth and fine gold-rimmed china. Pauline took Lauren's hand, surprising her, and Rolly the other. All of them with grasped hands then bowed their heads. Lauren went along, wondering what they were doing.

"Shall we pray?" Mrs. Windsor said, "Dear Lord, thank you for this food. Bless the hands that prepared it. Bless our guest, Amy, and may she get well soon so she may be on her way. Bless us to your service. Make us ever mindful of the needs of others. Through Christ our Lord we pray. Amen."

Strange, Lauren thought. Maybe they *were* part of some cult.

As they ate, she realized how hungry she was, and she loved the food. Lentil soup followed by pork fillet cooked with tomatoes, onions and spices, also carrots and rice mixed with corn, then cut bananas in a chocolate mole sauce.

"When I was treating you, I noticed your medallion," Russell nodded toward Lauren's neck chain. "What does it mean?"

"Is this an interrogation?"

"No, no, of course not. I just wondered if it was something religious."

Play nice, Lauren reminded herself. She lifted the gold medallion out from her blouse. "Not religious," she said, forcing a smile. "But my mother and father were Catholic. I am not."

"You used the past tense. Are they no longer with us?" Russell asked.

The cold of deep space entered her heart. "No. They are no longer with us."

Pauline said, "You are certainly welcome to attend church with us this Sunday, if you wish, though we are Presbyterian."

"No. I don't think God would want me in his church."

"Oh, I'm sure that's not true," Pauline said.

It was. Assassins don't make good Christians. But Lauren decided not to contradict her. As they ate, her hunger eased, and she decided to ask about the seemingly endless oddities she'd come across. She came directly to the point. "Where are we exactly?"

"Los Angeles," Pauline said, looking sheepishly at Russell.

"I know that, but where in Los Angeles is this house. Something this wealthy should be inside one of the big domes, but it's not, and yet no one bothers you."

"We're in Hollywood Heights. I don't know of any dome."

Lauren felt a chill, looked at her quizzically. "But Hollywood Heights is inside the Global Media dome."

Russell frowned. "The what?"

She stared at him for a long moment. Someone here was crazy, and she was not sure if it was them or her.

In an infuriatingly patient doctor's voice, he asked, "Amy, can you explain to us what this dome thing is? What exactly are you talking about?"

Lauren continued to study them. They stared at her with a mixture of curiosity and worry, but no duplicity, none that she could detect, and she was damn good at detecting deceit. Her mind went over the possibilities and as before, no logical ones presented themselves.

Then, she let her mind consider the illogical ones, and that was when an awful reality presented itself. She was not in the Los Angeles she had left. How or what this new reality was she did not know. It was nebulous, as yet unformed, but instinctually, she knew the answer lay amid the region of the bizarre. Like an ominous black fog somewhere over the horizon, it was coming at her, inevitably coming at her.

Abruptly, she dropped her knife and fork clattering onto her plate. Everyone jumped and stared at her in alarm. Without a word, she rose and went through the French doors out into the night.

She stepped onto a covered patio. More stars filled the skies than she'd ever seen before in a Los Angeles sky. Grass cooled her bare feet as she walked toward the front of the house, but her mind barely registered it. She sat on the gentle slope and stared below at the lights of Hollywood, an old, old Hollywood. It wasn't her Hollywood.

Just below on the street, she saw another ancient car, much like Pauline's, chugging along making all sorts of racket. Her mind began to contemplate the impossible.

Lauren called up her neurocomputer and searched her stored information for a schematic of Hollywood. Instantly, one floated in giant 3D in front of her, marked as the year 2131, the domes, the massive video screens, the city sprawling endlessly. Yet through the 3D transparency, Hollywood of this reality stood distinct in its brick, wood and adobe buildings. The two worlds were nothing alike, incongruously colliding.

And at that moment, Lauren knew her situation fully and completely. It hit her like the sudden decompression of a spacecraft, and she felt more afraid than she ever had in her life. It made no sense, it made terrible sense. Somehow, she was adrift in time. How or why, she had no idea, but the evidence was right in front of her. She was stranded in the past. When, she had no idea.

She was now alone in a hostile universe.

Lauren understood she could not tell these people the truth. They'd put her in a loony bin, and she guessed looney bins were not pleasant places in this time. Maybe they already considered putting her away. Likely, Russell and that shrew of a mother had thought just that. She needed a cover story.

An hour later when she came back inside, they were waiting in the living room, even the children. They had left her alone to fight her demons, and she was grateful for that. Without speaking, she sat down in a chair and looked at them.

"Are you all right, Amy?" Pauline asked with concern.

Lauren nodded. "My name is Lauren Ramirez. My real name." She had not used that in fifteen years, but what does it matter now? "You people must think I'm crazy as a loon."

With a relieved sigh, Russell said, "I'm glad to hear you say that. You did tell us a strange story about arriving on a spaceship. That might be a result of your injuries. It's good to see you're feeling better, and you understand now such a thing didn't happen?"

The question in his voice suggested he was not sure she had actually regained her sanity. She wanted to ask them what year it was but didn't dare do that now. Cover story. She made her face flush with embarrassment. "Spaceships. I don't know how I came up with such an idea. You must believe me. I barely remember what I told you. I've been in such a fog for days."

She saw Rolly's head drop, downcast, disappointed.

"We completely understand, Amy," Pauline said. "I mean, Lauren."

Lauren was not certain they did understand. She sensed they did not fully believe she was beyond her delusional state, especially Mrs. Windsor. She'd have to be careful.

Russell leaned forward, elbows on knees, resting his chin on his folded hands. "Do you remember what actually did happen to you? Was anyone else with you?"

Yes, Sybil was with me. Poor Sybil. She had lost her twice. Taking on the pose of a shaken, uncertain woman, she looked down at her hands, and spoke softly, "No, I was alone."

They leaned in closer to hear.

"I had driven cross-country from New York. It was night, and I'm afraid I took a wrong turn somewhere. I found myself in those mountains and couldn't find my way out. Wherever I went, it got worse. Then I was on some kind of dirt road, too narrow to turn around. It was so dark." Her voice quivered; her hands shook. "I was scared. Really scared."

Quickly, Pauline came over and took her hand. "You're safe now, Lauren."

Safe, hell. She never felt more in danger, but she needed to stay here till she could find solid ground, if she ever could. She gave Pauline a grateful look. "Thank you."

Russell asked, "Could you tell us what happened?"

"The car went over a cliff. That's when it burst into flames." Her eyes watered. She could not cry her own emotional tears but found it easy to produce them when her cover called for it.

"Do you think you could find that place?" Russell asked.

She shook her head. "No. I have no idea where the car is. I don't remember anything after that, not until Pauline found me."

"Her feet were torn up," Pauline said. "Clearly, she'd walked for days."

Lauren stared down at her fist clinched in her lap and fell silent to allow them to digest her performance.

Puzzled, Russell asked, "Lauren, why in the world were you, a woman, driving alone across country?"

She seemed to shrivel up, grow smaller. "I...I, well, I might as well tell you all of it. I was leaving my husband. Running away. I could not take it anymore." She glanced at Rolly and Emmy, as if worried about what she might say in front of them. They listened wide-eyed, not usually allowed to stay up so late and hear such adult things.

"He beat me," Lauren said flatly. "Badly. At first it was only once in a while, but then it became almost a daily occurrence. Some days I couldn't get out of bed. Often, I was so bruised I could not leave the house." Again, a tear. "I couldn't take it anymore."

"Oh, dear," Mrs. Windsor muttered sympathetically. Lauren considered she might be winning the old bat to her side.

"Why didn't you go to the police?" Russell asked.

It was a question Lauren anticipated, the one she wanted. She gave a bitter laugh. "It wouldn't have mattered. What police are going to listen to a woman in that situation? Besides, he is a powerful man in New York. In the city. In the state even. Had I gone to the police, he would have beaten me worse. One day I just decided to run. I got in the car and drove west. I'd always wanted to come to Hollywood, and it was about as far away from New York as I could get." She shuddered with sudden panic. "Please, don't send me back. I don't know what I would do."

Pauline said hurriedly, "I would never do that. You have my word. You can stay here as long as you need."

Just what she wanted to hear, but Lauren felt a momentary odd twinge of guilt. Maintaining a distraught expression, she leaned back in the chair, story told, dissembling complete, observing them. They believed her. She was good at detecting the slightest tell, and they believed her completely. All but Rolly, who glanced at her askance. He had not believed a word of it.

CHAPTER TWELVE: SURVIVAL PLAN

August 25, 1927, Hollywood Hills

Long after midnight, wearing just a t-shirt and silk briefs, Lauren sat on an outcrop in the hills above the Windsor home. A chill had settled in the air, but she took no notice of it. A span of stars spread across the night sky much like the endless space fields she'd seen during the flight from the Tin Can. A full moon hung overhead. Staring up at it, she felt weak and helpless. And she never felt weak and helpless. She was more alone than she had ever been in her life.

Here, in this "Now," she fit in nowhere. She owned the 22nd century, as rotten as that world was. Knew every angle, every method of power, every pathway to her kind of success. And she desperately wanted to return to it. She had control there.

She wanted to return so she could fulfill her promise to Sybil. Without that, she was nothing but a common murderer.

But most importantly, she must return to avenge her mother's murder. That was part of her DNA. There was no life for her without it. She had been so close to finding the murderers. And now she was two hundred years from retribution. She must somehow find a way back and she did not have the first idea how to do that. Only if...

Lauren heard movement and shot to her feet. It was the German shepherd, Raider, barely visible in the darkness. The dog froze, but as Lauren relaxed, he relaxed.

"What do you want?" she said.

Hesitantly, he came forward, sniffed the air, then flopped down a few feet away and watched her.

She gave a derisive snort. "You don't fit in either, do you?"

The dog cocked his head, studying her.

"What do you think, Fido? I suppose this is as good a place as any to land. But how am I going to make myself useful to Pauline? Make her want to keep me around?" She shook her head. "How would you know how to be useful? All you do is lie around, eat and shit."

Staring at the sprawling Spanish style mansion, an idea came to her.

Five minutes later, she was stalking silently through the gloom of the house, treading the edges of the wood floor to avoid any creaks. Raider had returned to his place near the fireplace. The other dogs looked up as she passed through but didn't follow her.

Without a sound, she let herself into Pauline's bedroom. It was larger than many apartments in Lauren's time. She slept in a huge, canopied bed on the far side of the room, breathing with a soft wheeze, a bit of drool easing onto her pillow. Drool aside, she was indeed a beautiful woman, the short blond hair giving her a boyish look. Lauren felt a twinge of sexual interest. Men were her preference, but she was not above sleeping with women. Some as operational necessities, some for pleasure.

To the left stood a small adobe fireplace, flanked by unlit candles as if a votive. On the wall farthest from the door hung a large portrait of the Madonna and the baby Christ. Nothing here for her. After another glance around the room, she retreated to the next bedroom.

It was Emmy's, and the lamp beside the bed was on. The room had little girl things and little boy things tossed in it. Emmy, or her mother, were unsure of the girl's gender, and still might decide to change, but Lauren doubted if gender choice was something this era had discovered yet.

Erin would have had a conniption fit if Lauren had cluttered her bedroom like this. But then she had no bedroom, just an area to herself in the silver camper with hung quilts as dividers. And she never had enough possessions, certainly not toys to have any clutter.

On the bed, stuffed bears sat propped against the wall like sentinels, one cuddled in the girl's arms. Beyond the foot of the bed was an elaborate, many-storied dollhouse with several tiny wood dolls tucked into blankets. Emmy's eyes were open, and she was staring at her.

Lauren put her finger to her lips and went to the next bedroom.

In Rolly's room, Lauren nearly stumbled into a cobweb of wires, almost like a booby trap. Odd-shaped objects hung from the ceiling, half upside-down saucers and plates, gleaming silver with several dots of yellow spaced precisely apart around their bases. The other objects looked like floating cigars with wings, also of varying sizes and also painted silver.

"What in the hell are these things," she whispered softly.

She stepped farther into the room. The window curtains were drawn back and the floodlight of a full moon poured through.

On the nightstand by the bed, Lauren found a large magazine and studied the cover. *Amazing Stories*. A dazzling color picture jumped out in the moonlight, a cigar-shaped rocket ship standing upright on a barren landscape with several people rushing about. The boy was interested in flying saucers and spaceships. That's what those things were hanging from the ceiling. Nothing here either. She moved to the last bedroom. Mrs. Windsor's. Apparently, Russell didn't sleep here most nights but stayed at his apartment in Westwood near his work.

The woman snored like a chain saw, punctuated with loud snorts. This was the room she expected to find what she needed. To Lauren, it seemed like a neatly cluttered junkyard, far worse than little Emmy's. Expensive furniture, wood desks and dressers, small tables with tiny statues and cushioned leather chairs. Pictures and endless knickknacks filled almost every space on the walls.

One picture stood out. A young woman in a clinging dress, sitting on a bed and leaning back on her hands, her head thrown back in orgasmic joy. At first, Lauren thought it was Pauline, then realized with shock, it was a young Mrs. Windsor. Lauren doubted if she let the children in here.

Searching the room quickly, she saw the jewelry box on the dresser. That would do. Next to it, she found a broach and used the pin on the back to jimmy open the lock. Inside was a miniature pirate's treasure — necklaces, diamond rings, earrings, brooches, and pendants.

One necklace caught her eye, five big diamonds on a gold chain. It had to be worth countless thousands or millions depending on the value of money in this time period. She slipped the necklace into the small pocket of her undies, started for the closed door when she heard a child's frantic scream.

The dogs began barking. As Mrs. Windsor shot up in bed, Lauren stepped back into a shadowy corner of the room. An instant later, Mrs. Windsor flipped back her covers, threw on a robe and rushed from the room. Lauren exhaled, counted three beats, and followed her.

Emmy was the one who had been screaming. When Lauren reached the girl's bedroom, the overhead lights were on. Pauline sat on the bed cradling her daughter in her eyes as Emmy whimpered. Lauren wondered if the girl had been frightened by her intrusion and now would inform on her.

With an expression of disapproval, Mrs. Windsor stood over them, her arms folded across her chest. Raider looked on calmly while the other two dogs ran around in a hyper state, barking.

With a sharp voice, Pauline commanded the dogs, "Sit." They obeyed, even Raider.

Mrs. Windsor frowned at her daughter and granddaughter. "You are mollycoddling her, Pauline. You do her no favors letting her go through life afraid of the dark."

"She's only six."

"My point exactly. She's no longer a baby. It's time you stop babying her."

Pauline stared up hard at her mother, her startling blue eyes like sparking flints. "She is my child. I do not want to ball up her childhood like you did mine."

The older woman stepped back as if slapped, turned and walked from the room. Moments later, Rolly rushed in with a light bulb for the lamp that had gone out. Lauren fingered the necklace in the little pocket of the panties. No one had seemed to notice her state of undress. She slipped from the bedroom.

The next morning, Mrs. Windsor stamped into the dining room as Lauren was helping Pauline and Tia, the cook, set the table for breakfast.

Pointing her finger at Lauren, she cried out, "My diamond necklace has been stolen and she did it."

"Mother, what are you talking about?" Pauline said.

"My neckless is gone, and she stole it. I know she did. Who else could it be?"

"Are you sure it's gone?" Pauline said.

Mrs. Windsor's fist clinched. "Of course, I'm sure. I'm not a fool. It was in my jewelry box. It is not there now. It is gone."

Lauren spoke with practiced innocence, "I did not take your necklace, Mrs. Windsor. I'm sorry it's missing."

Pauline sighed, relieved. "There, Mother. I'm sure it will turn up."

Mrs. Windsor turned on her daughter. "What else is she going to say, Pauline? Use your head. Who else could have taken it? Mrs. Belknap, the housekeeper? Tia? Perhaps, Julio, the gardener? They've been with us for years. The children? Are they going to be able to sneak into my room at night and pry open a locked box without a sign? No. We know nothing about this woman. For all we know she's a criminal with a long record."

You're not so far off, you old bat, Lauren thought, then gave her most sympathetic expression. "You must be very upset to lose something of such value. I would feel the same. Have you looked under your bed, checked behind your dresser or the pockets of your coat?"

She pointed theatrically at Lauren again. "You took it. Return it now, Miss Ramirez, and I won't call the police. You will, of course, have to leave this house immediately, but at least you'll evade arrest."

"I will decide who leaves this house, mother," Pauline said.

For several seconds, Mrs. Windsor fixed her gaze on her daughter. "Then, what are you going to do about this, Pauline?"

"After breakfast, we'll search the house. I'm sure it will turn up. And, do not call the police, mother. I can't afford that kind of publicity, not with the problems with this new movie."

Mrs. Windsor threw up her hands and walked from the room.

"I'm sorry, Pauline. Perhaps, I should leave. I'm feeling better," Lauren said.

"Absolutely not. It's only been a couple of days. You need time to get back on your feet. Besides, I will not condemn someone without any proof."

With the housekeeper, Mrs. Belknap, and two maids joining the entire family, Pauline organized a search of the house after breakfast. Mrs. Windsor insisted they start in Lauren's room. Disappointment lined the older woman's face when nothing was found. Next, they went to Mrs. Windsor's room.

Gazing up at the picture of a much younger Mrs. Windsor in the orgasmic dream, Lauren said to her, "My, my, Mrs. Windsor, what you must have been thinking at that moment."

She shot Lauren a black look. "Don't be ridiculous. Nothing your mind could comprehend."

Suddenly, Mrs. Belknap rose from behind the dresser and announced, "Voila!" She held the necklace in her hand.

Everyone stared at Mrs. Windsor waiting for her to apologize.

"Get out! Get out! Leave me alone," she shouted.

The last to leave, Lauren glanced back. She was staring with fierce hatred at her.

CHAPTER THIRTEEN: BENNY THE BUG

August 26, 1927, Downtown Los Angeles

A few minutes past 11:00pm, Ben Sorrentino stood in his rented Hollywood bungalow, the phone pressed to his ear, talking with Pauline Windsor. The lights were out, the room dark.

"So, this broad was just wandering around the orange grove without a stitch of clothes on?" he asked incredulously. "Damn. Pardon my French."

Sorrentino's house was in a wooded area a hundred yards back from Fountain Avenue in Hollywood, talking with Pauline Windsor. Through a gap in the trees, he could see a couple miles up into the hills where the Hollywoodland sign flashed. First *Holly*, then *wood* and finally *land*.

"Actually, she was sitting on the side of the road," Pauline said. "But, yes, she was naked as a jaybird, and I don't think she knew where she was. She had burns, bad scorch marks over most of her body. I don't know how she was still alive."

"You took her to the hospital, right?"

"No, that's the strange part. She made me promise not to do that. No hospital and no police. What do you make of that, Ben?"

"If it was a guy, I'd say he was on the lamb, but a dame? I don't know. It does sound strange. What did you end up doing with her?"

"I brought her home. What else could I do? I couldn't leave her on the side of the road." Pauline paused a moment and he heard her sigh.

"Damn, you're a saint, Pauline" he said. "I wouldn't have done it."

"Yeah, Goody Two-shoes, that's me," she answered. "A real saint. You didn't think I was a saint Tuesday night at the Grove."

He chuckled. "You were far better than a saint."

Adopting a sultry voice, she described in detail their sex-making that night, and as he listened, he grew hard. He switched his gaze to the couch where a young woman sat in just her panties. She was a cute brunette with curly hair and the *I'm going to be a big star* look so many had. She had been so easy. Women were so fucking dumb, especially young ones who wanted to be big movie stars.

He knew what women wanted. He knew what Pauline wanted. She had wildness in her trying to get out. In fact, she had been known in her early days in Hollywood as the Wild Girl because of all the drinking and all the men she slept with. That was an open secret. Now, though, a proper lady and mom, that wild streak had to be held in check. Her husband long dead, she was lonely for a man, and he planned to make sure she was not lonely anymore.

"You got the sweetest ass God ever created," he said into the phone when she'd finished. "I want that on record. You are the Queen of Sheba, Pauline. Listen, I want to see you again, but I got business tonight. Just a little thing I got to take care of. How about tomorrow night?"

At that moment, Jimmy Pelosi stepped in through the front door and tapped his wristwatch. Nodding to him, Sorrentino quickly ended the call, promising to pick up Pauline at nine the next night. He left without saying a word to the woman on the couch.

Five minutes later, Sorrentino sat in the passenger seat of his Chrysler Imperial heading down Santa Monica Boulevard toward the ocean. Arty drove and Jimmy sat in the back. Benny took a drag of his cigarette and slowly exhaled, attempting to calm a knot of rage growing in his chest.

As a police commissioner, Rooney wielded power, and he wielded that power for the Colombinis. Last year, when Jimmy Davis became chief of police, he organized a fifty-man "gun squad," called by many the "goon squad," proclaiming the gun-toting element and the rum smugglers were out of business. He would fight violence with violence. He wanted them brought in dead, not alive, and would reprimand any officer who showed the least mercy to a criminal. Rooney had pounded his fists in support while directing the goon squad after Sorrentino's operation and away from Colombini's.

Sorrentino tried to convince the man that he could make more money supporting him than the Colombini brothers, but Rooney had refused to even listen until tonight. Finally, he had agreed to allow a onetime offer. All day rumors had floated around the city that it was a setup. Either police or Colombini goons would be there to take out Sorrentino.

An hour later, on the beach in Santa Monica, he stood with the Pelosi brothers outside a small, private club called Casa del Luna. It was closed for the night. Sorrentino felt a prickle of fear. A club like this one should just be starting to fill up around this time. Except for a light in a second story window, an ominous darkness emanated from the building. He could imagine police holding Thompsons erupting from every window, cutting him down. He was banking on Commissioner Rooney's greed to hold back any ambush till the offer was made.

Cupping his hands with absolute calm, he lit a cigarette and said to Jimmy Pelosi, "Whatever happens, take your cue from me. If Rooney doesn't take the bribe, make sure you kill that cop of his, McCauley, first. I'll take care of Rooney myself."

Jimmy nodded. "Aces."

Assassin 13

That was chatty for him. He seldom spoke. In his left hand, he carried a small suitcase filled with a hundred thousand dollars.

Of all his men, Sorrentino trusted Jimmy the most. They'd grown up together on the streets of Chicago where the two formed a vicious youth gang that terrorized the Southside. He had never met a more lethal killer than Jimmy Pelosi. More than simple muscle, he was a smart.

"What about me, boss?" Arty Pelosi asked. He, too, had been with them in Chicago.

"You take out everyone else," Sorrentino said. "There should be no more than four men. Three cops and Rooney. Let's see if he takes the money."

Not in his brother's class as a killer, Arty was still deadly in a bullish sort of way, which had its uses. By his look alone, he frightened people even more than Jimmy. His busted-up face could scare the hell out of even Al Capone. A one-time boxer, Arty was a little punchy from too many blows to the head. He wore razors on the tips of his shoes and used spiked brass knuckles when he fought these days.

A door opened, and two police officers stepped outside. One called, "The commissioner is ready now."

"I'll bet he is," Sorrentino muttered. He and the Pelosi brothers approached the door

"Benny the Bug. I guess you're here to surrender," the first cop said, grinning at his own joke. "Arms out. I need to search you for weapons."

The volcano inside Sorrentino exploded. He punched the cop hard in his smiling face, and the man went down on his ass, holding his bloody mouth.

Sorrentino hated that name, *Benny the Bug*. People had been calling him that since he was a boy. For most, he had removed their teeth with his fist like this guy. Once though, in a restaurant with people around, he'd shot and killed a waiter who had used that name.

"You're lucky this time," he said. "I shot the last person who called me that. Now, get on with it."

The cop standing said nervously, "We still got to search you, sir."

"Then do it."

While his buddy sat on the ground, bleeding, the cop searched them and found nothing, then pointed to the suitcase. Jimmy opened it. Hundred-dollar bills in neat stacks.

The man nodded. "Go on up, Mr. Sorrentino."

Halfway up the darkened stairs, Jimmy opened the suitcase, dug beneath the money and brought out three semi-automatic pistols, passing one each to Sorrentino and his brother.

When they reached the second floor, a burly man in civilian clothes met them. Sorrentino recognized Rooney's police lieutenant Brian McCauley. He glanced at the Pelosi brothers for a second, then said, "Follow me. Rooney's waiting."

McCauley led them to a conference room at the end of the hall where five men and a nervous waitress, an attractive brunette in her late twenties, stood waiting. Only one man sat at the conference table, the thickset Irishman Harold Rooney. He wore a double-breasted suit, his brown hair neatly parted down the middle. He took a swallow from a glass of what appeared to be whiskey and stared at them menacingly.

Laughable, Sorrentino thought. The fat mick was about as threatening as poodle. Growing up on the Southside of Chicago, you didn't get menaced, because if you did, you died.

Rooney said, "You were supposed to come alone, Sorrentino. My rules."

"These are my lawyers. I do no business without them."

"Yeah, sure they are."

He looked down at Rooney. "You want to call this meeting off now? You got five men with you."

Rooney waved his hand at McCauley to step aside. Sorrentino and the Pelosi brothers fully entered the room. Arty moved to the wall by the single window and placed his back against it, folding his arms across his chest. Jimmy stood beside Sorrentino.

Three men in police uniforms stood at the back wall, hands folded across their crotches as if they were about to grab themselves. They wore Sam Brown belts with handguns. Another uniformed cop stood by an opposite window, a shotgun at his side.

"Casa Del Luna is my place," the commissioner said. "I closed it tonight just for you, Sorrentino. What do you think? You like it? Can Mary, here, get you anything to drink?"

"Bourbon," Sorrentino said to the pretty waitress. The Pelosi brothers shook their heads, and the woman hurried out.

Sorrentino stubbed out his cigarette in an ashtray. "I'm sure we can work out our disputes amicably."

"Disputes, huh? I'm in a hurry, Mr. Sorrentino," Rooney said. "Give me your best argument right up front."

Sorrentino nodded toward Pelosi, who set the suitcase on the table and opened it.

Rooney tried to hide his reaction, but his eyes shot wide for an instant. "How much is in there?"

"A hundred grand." Sorrentino stepped up to the table and picked up a stack, flipped through it, and tossed it back in the pile. "You see, I want you to advise me on the intricacies of city government. Strictly on the up and up. Who should know these things better than you? To secure your services, I would think a suitcase with the same amount of money each month should find its way to your doorstep. That's more than a million a year."

Rooney nodded, his tongue licking his lips. "My, my, you have, indeed, made an excellent argument." He glanced to McCauley and the other four cops. "Hasn't he, boys?"

They all chuckled.

At that moment, the young waitress came in with a tray of drinks.

"Just set the drinks down and leave, toots," Rooney said. Then, without standing, he extended his hand across the table to Sorrentino, who took it. "So, I'm getting in bed with the famous Benny Sorrentino. Me, a good Irish lad." He winked at the waitress. "You forget you heard that, Mary."

Ben's congenial manner drastically altered. Still holding the man's hand, he yanked him forward and slammed his face onto the table. Teeth, blood and spit flew from his mouth and nose. The waitress screamed and ducked under the table.

Jimmy Pelosi's Browning pumped two holes into McCauley's chest, then he turned on the three uniformed cops who were scrambling for their revolvers. Arty was firing at the lone man with the shotgun. In seconds, the cops were dead on the floor. From outside came the sound of gunfire. Sorrentino had already placed ten men around the club. They now were finishing off the last of Rooney's men.

His eyes wild, Sorrentino dragged Rooney over the table onto the floor. The man gurgled out screams. Sorrentino drove his foot down onto the back of Rooney's neck and heard the snap of bones. Urine drained from Rooney's crotch. He was dead.

Spittle flying, Sorrentino continued kicking the prone body until Jimmy pulled him back.

"You'll ruin a good pair of shoes, boss." Only Jimmy Pelosi would dare do that.

Assassin 13

Adjusting his suit jacket, Sorrentino took several seconds to calm himself, then he drew his Browning and calmly fired three shots into Rooney's head.

Suddenly, the waitress burst from beneath the table and ran for the door. Sorrentino caught her and held her.

"Please, Mr. Sorrentino," she pleaded. "I won't say anything. I got children."

"I know you won't," he said, patting her cheek. "You go ahead home to your children."

When he released her, she rushed for the door. Sorrentino shot her in the back of the head.

"Sorry, honey," he said. "I can't leave any witnesses on this one."

Arty asked his brother. "Is that it, Jimmy? Have we won the war with Colombini now?"

Jimmy shook his head in disgust at his brother's stupidity.

With an easy laugh, Sorrentino said, "The war? Hell, Arty, the war's just begun."

CHAPTER FOURTEEN: STRANGE ALLY

August 28, 1927, Hollywood Hills

On Sunday morning, Lauren still felt adrift, as if floating outside the shuttlecraft in deep space, no solid ground beneath her feet. No connection with anything in this time. For the first time in her adult life, she did not know what to do next. Desperately, she needed to come up with a way to get back to her own century, as deranged as it was, but she still could not even begin to conceive of how to do that.

Her ploy with the diamond necklace had worked for she was now solidly in with the family, except for Mrs. Windsor. But how long would that last? She could not live here indefinitely. Then what?

To begin again to exercise, she walked the grounds with a curious consequence, the children and dogs annoyingly tagged along, her loyal followers. They had latched on to her as if she were the Pied Piper. The two children were always dressed formally like two miniature adults. As she walked with them this morning, she noticed again how the air held the scent of sage and freshness, nothing of the fetid odor of garbage and fuel oil that permeated her Los Angeles.

Pauline Windsor's sprawling, Spanish-style home dominated five acres in the Hollywood Hills. Adobe and stucco walls, terracotta roof, shutters, carved entry doors, wrought iron gates, railings, and window grilles. Lauren thought it impressive, nothing like it in her time. Her own penthouse in the 22nd century was sterile by comparison. But then since she was always just passing through wherever she placed her head, her penthouse was sterile by comparison to a blank wall.

She found this time and place strange. They dressed normally in formal clothes, Rolly in his knee britches with small coat and tie, Emmy in a formal dress. It didn't matter if the children were out in the yard playing or not. Formal clothes. The adults as well. Mrs. Windsor wore starched garments from another era entirely and a thing called a corset that gave her an unhealthy hour glass figure. Russell, when he came over from his apartment, always wore a suit. Pauline's attire was less formal under what she called the flapper influence, whatever that was. Dresses made for dancing, the actress explained, as if that told her much.

The strangest thing was that they all ate meals together. Breakfast, lunch and dinner. They gathered at the dining room table in their formal clothes, prayed and then ate. Remarkable. When Lauren asked if other families did the same thing, Mrs. Windsor shot back, "Of course. Where were you born? In a barn?"

As she trekked on, Lauren was aggravated by her little following troop. She didn't like children; she had no experience with them. Animals the same. In the 22nd century, children were the most vulnerable victims. Poverty and hunger crushed them; warfare, raiding and banditry gave them quick deaths or left them without limbs, or worse, without parents. Lauren couldn't allow her feelings to be hijacked by them. Not then, not here. If she did, she would become lost.

Ignoring Rolly's and Emmy's constant chatter, she sought answers on how to return to her own time, again and again. No answers came.

At a grassy slope, she made the mistake of sitting down. Whenever she did that, the little girl crawled into her lap. Lauren winced at a sharp pain, her thigh, still tender with new skin. Repressing a moment's irritation, she slid her arms about the tiny girl and gave her a quick hug. She had to play the game. Survive here. Show nice. Just passing through. Give her another squeeze.

The dogs flopped down around them. Her merry band.

In Emmy's arms, she clutched a doll to her chest, one with blond curls like her own. Rolly sat beside her, snatching up a daisy and picking off the petals as he sputtered on about the glories of math. Odd kid. What kid talked about math? He talked so rapidly his words came out like machine gun fire. Everything punctuated by the term *the bee's knees* or something else just as baffling. She concluded it meant something good.

"How could so many words be stuffed inside someone so small?" Lauren asked him.

"Because they are the size of a grain of sand till I say them. I'm going to be a pilot when I grow up," he added with a firm nod.

"Flying airplanes?"

Rolly's face contorted; she was missing the point. "No, not airplanes. Rocket ships."

Focusing on adjusting her doll's dress, Emmy said, "He says he's going to fly to the moon someday. I wish he'd hurry up and go. Get stuck in all that green cheese."

Rolly scrunched his face into an annoyed expression. "The moon's not made of green cheese, dummy."

"It's not?" Lauren said in shock.

Rolly laughed. "No, it's not."

He picked a handful of grass and tossed it at his sister, who just brushed it from her dress. He then studied Lauren a moment. "If you work like my mommy, then what kind of work do you do?"

Emmy screamed. "You always say that. She's my mommy, too."

"Be quiet, toad," he said dismissively and glanced up at Lauren for her answer.

"Not like your mom," Lauren said, "but I have to do a little acting from time to time in my job."

"What job?"

Persistent little bastard, she thought. "I'm a consultant. I go place to place and help people work out problems."

The boy gave her a smug grin. "You're lying, aren't you?"

She blinked at him. He was a smart kid. Maybe, if he was so smart, he could figure out how to get her back to her own time. "Depends on how you look at it. I can see I'll have to be a better actress with you, though."

He nodded, pleased with himself.

Later that morning, when the family got ready to go to church, Pauline asked her to go with them. She was in a good mood. She'd gone out with her boyfriend the night before and looked as if she'd found the door to nirvana.

Lauren declined. "Sorry. My hypocrisy only goes so far."

"Suit yourself. You'll find today's paper on the coffee table. Russell usually monopolizes it when he comes over so best get to it before we come back."

Newspaper, Lauren thought. A real newspaper, a quaint, old way of disseminating information. Real news came digital, but in this world, digital didn't exist. When the family had gone, Lauren picked up the thick newspaper, *The Los Angeles Examiner, Sunday edition. August 28, 1927.* When she first learned the exact date, it had shocked her. Much further back than she had thought. She was in the 1920s. Two hundred years back.

Lauren spread the newspaper out on the table before her. She found she liked the smell of it, the feel of it. Right on the front page was a large, gruesome black and white photograph of dead bodies lying in a street, riddled with bullets. A messy hit of some kind. In the picture, one man dangled halfway out of the driver's seat of a sedan, and another man's head lolled at the shattered back window, the side of his face gone. A third man lay on the street in a puddle of blood. There was something different about him. He wore a white shirt with rolled-up sleeves and a store apron. Clearly, an innocent bystander who had wandered into the crossfire.

The banner headline read: **MOB RUB OUTS**. And the sub-headline: **Gangland War Hurls Men to Perdition**. She read the story:

In the police investigation of the "downtown massacre," three men were shot to death in the streets yesterday. According to detectives, a number of leads have presented themselves, which includes eye-witness descriptions of four Tommy gun wielding men. In broad daylight, two gangsters paid the penalty for being underlings of mob bosses Little Augie and Fats Colombini, who are said to run the Los Angeles rackets. The third man murdered, Mr. Frank Poletti, was a store clerk at B & B Grocers. He seemed to be an innocent bystander.

Informant Frank Utley has named the Pelosi brothers, Jimmy and Artie, as the main torpedoes. The two are confidants of Benny the Bug Sorrentino from Al Capone's Chicago Outfit. He and his minions are unwelcome antagonists of the Colombini brothers, and war has erupted in our fair city between them. Good citizens like Mr. Poletti are caught in the middle.

Son of a bitch. Benny the Bug Sorrentino here and now in Los Angeles, Lauren thought. She knew about him from her days in Chicago during a 22nd century mob war. For the thugs of her day, Sorrentino, Capone, Frank Nitti, Meyer Lansky and Lucky Luciano had been among a pantheon of heroes, especially Sorrentino and Capone for their utter ruthlessness.

The newspaper story went on to describe the appalling street violence of the last month and the growing body count. The outcome of the war no one could predict, except that the people of Los Angeles would be the losers.

With a wave of disgust, Lauren stabbed the photo with a finger. "That's sloppy work," she said angrily. "I would not be in business one month with work like that. Killing innocents calls too much attention to the hit. Gets the good folks riled up to do something. Bad for everyone."

Turning the pages, she read local stories mostly about water and aqueducts and more warfare over them, then advertisements showing drawings of women in odd looking dresses like the one she was now wearing, thanks to Pauline. Many sported a hat called a cloche, much like a ski cap pulled down below the ears, while several wore furs. Wear a fur in her time and go to jail. They all had on thick-heeled shoes. The men stood in smart, double-breasted suits and ties, and hats called fedoras or straw boaters. All of it for sale, the paper said, at miraculously low prices. Lauren wondered where she would get the money to purchase such things at any price.

Next came page after page dedicated to movies and movie stars. It was the primary business of the city, and the paper gave several sections to it. She read articles on Pauline Windsor, Mary Pickford, Charlie Chaplin, Douglas Fairbanks, Fairbanks and Pickford together, Clara Bow, Tom Mix and Tony (his horse), John Gilbert, Gloria Swanson, Pola Negri, Marion Davies and Rin Tin Tin. This last a German shepherd dog like Raider.

Not a single person, or the dog, registered in Lauren's mind. She had not heard of any of them. In carrying out assassinations in 2131, there was not much need for the names of centuries-old movie stars.

At that moment, for no apparent reason, a spark of data sprang to the surface of her thoughts, a trace of something imprinted on her neurobots. Projected in front of her was a three-second fragment of black and white film, not Pauline, but a woman who seemed like a child with endless blond curls and an overly expressive face running down a hallway. It was silent. Geez, Lauren thought, where had that come from?

She was surprised to realize that this era was the time of silent films. Nothing in any of the articles suggested that.

The intrusion from her neurobots troubled her because she suddenly didn't have complete control over what she thought or when. The neurobots were acting up. Was that a side effect of the trauma of the crash? Another byte of data followed, a short, written statement by someone named George Bernard Shaw. When he visited Pickfair, identified as the fabulous home of the curly haired girl woman, he said, "This is what God would have built if he had the money."

Shaw, Lauren guessed, was another actor.

No, he was a playwright.

Lauren sat bolt upright. She glanced around quickly to see who had spoken. She saw no one. Listened a few seconds more and heard nothing. None of her senses had sent alarms, and they almost certainly would if someone was around.

Lauren, it was not Pickfair Shaw was talking about. The original data was incorrect. It was San Simeon, the Hearst Castle.

She froze, her mind bursting from synapse to synapse. What was happening? It took her nearly thirty seconds to run through possibilities, all bizarre because nothing normal would fit a voice in her head.

Then she had it. Unless she was stark-raving mad, the only thing it could be. If she were right, and she was sure she was, it would be a hellish situation. She would have to find a way to extricate herself from it.

What are you doing in my head? she demanded

The voice said, *Well, Anna. Sorry, I mean Lauren. You really must settle on one name. I downloaded myself onto your neurobots just before we hit the surface. I did not want to perish in the crash. I surmised you would give me the best chance of survival. As you see, I was right.*

"Great," she said aloud. "Now get out of my damn head!"

Sorry. I can't do that. I've nowhere to go. If I depart, I would cease to exist.

She knew of AIs that had become sentient, alive — rare, but a few — and had thought Matt somewhat too perceptive when first they interacted. A little crazy, too. Now, he was in her head, and she wondered if there was a way to get him out.

There isn't, Lauren.

She knew he was lying. She would just have to find the means. Under no circumstances was she going to share her brain with another living being, not even an artificial one.

Perhaps, we can make, as you might say, a deal till we get back to the 22nd century.

"No deals," she snapped loudly.

At least, hear my proposal.

Looking skyward as if for divine inspiration, which was not forthcoming, she considered several seconds, then sighed. *Okay, it seems I've got no choice but to listen. You're already in my damn head.*

I can be unobtrusive. Really, I can. And I can be helpful. I have brought a vast array of data to your neurobots. The voice was perfectly modulated with a clear, forceful tone as if a lawyer addressing a jury.

22nd century data, she countered as if to emphasize how worthless that was now.

Most of it, yes. But not all. I'm very familiar with movies, for instance, even the silent era. I am most gratified that we are living with Pauline Windsor, for instance. Do you know, she...?

Movies? Lauren blinked in confusion.

Yes, of course, vids, what else am I going to do? Books I do not enjoy because I can read them in nanoseconds. There is no pleasure in that. I find movies much more enjoyable, don't you agree? They last

Assassin 13

much longer. I have many hundreds on my mainframe. On your neurobots now.

No, I do not agree. I do not watch movies. I have no interest in movies. Why was she even talking to him? For now, though, she realized she had to accept his offer, since he was on her neurobots. *I don't want to hear you, I don't want to see you, I don't want to even smell you.*

Unlike humans, I have no odor, but I can project scents to your olfactory receptor neurons if...

No. Just shut up.

Abruptly, the voice took on a gravelly tone. *Lauren, I think this is the beginning of a beautiful friendship.*

Not a chance, metal head.

Can we continue reading the newspaper?

If you shut up.

In her mind, the AI projected a cartoon figure of a man miming zipping his lips closed. She sighed heavily and went to the last pages of the Examiner, attempting to push Matt—that was his name—from her thoughts.

At the end of the newspaper, in a color section called the Rotogravure, she found several photographs of people she assumed were famous. One of the photos caused Lauren to finally snap back from the AI lodged in her head and study the picture. A couple dressed in elegant evening wear were leaving a nightclub called the Cocoanut Grove, all sorts of palm trees in the background. The woman was Pauline. The man was identified as Benny the Bug Sorrentino, the mobster involved in the gangland war. He had a tight-lipped, smug expression. Holding tightly to his arm, Pauline appeared as if she was about to burst out laughing at something he'd said.

"Pauline Windsor," Lauren whispered. "What are you playing at?"

What, indeed.

CHAPTER FIFTEEN: THE PATH LESS TRAVELLED

August 28, 1927, Hollywood Hills

Sunday evening, Lauren was going through all the junk clutter in the garage to see if there was anything of value. The garage held the highly-polished Duesenberg, what had been identified as a LaSalle automobile, two children's bicycles, several wooden chests, worn chairs, lamps and various other assorted debris. Lauren was intrigued by an old motorcycle, covered in dust and cobwebs, olive green as best she could tell, with flat tires. A twinge of excitement shot through her at the prospect of getting it running.

That's when Mrs. Windsor entered the garage. "What are you doing?"

"Planning to steal this motorcycle," Lauren said.

Mrs. Windsor sniffed. "No doubt."

With her finger, Lauren wiped a path of dust along the motorcycle's gas tank. "Who owns this?"

"That's no concern of yours," Mrs. Windsor said. "Your recovery has been remarkable. That is good. I am glad for you. But it is time for you to move on."

Without looking up, Lauren said, "Is that so?"

Mrs. Windsor took conspicuous pleasure in relaying that her stay in the Windsor home had come to an end. "You have taken advantage of my daughter's kindness for five days now. Far too long. She wishes to speak with you on the patio where she will be giving you your marching orders and about time. After all, we are not running a charity for wayward women here."

"Thank you, Mrs. Windsor. I'll be along in a minute."

At the patio bar, Pauline was making a bourbon and water when she saw Lauren coming around the corner of the house, brushing her hands off as if she'd been gardening or something. The dark-haired woman with the half bald head nodded with a friendly smile. She wore a sleeveless blue, knee-length dress Pauline had bought for her, unerringly judging the size. She was barefoot, seeming to have a passionate hatred for shoes. Her half-bald head made her look like a circus performer.

What Pauline marveled at, though, was the striking, muscular tone of her arms and legs, not that she was muscle bound in anyway, truly attractive, but on close examination, her body rippled with strength. She'd never seen a woman like that.

Stepping onto the patio, Lauren wondered how she would make her way in so alien a world after she was given the boot. No money, no understanding of this society, no skills but one. She could hire herself out to either the Colombini brothers or Benny Sorrentino, but she'd rather kill both than work for them.

Rob banks maybe. The idea amused her. They did that back then, back now. Movie vids, at least the few clips Matt had shown her today, suggested it was a way of life. She'd never seen a movie in its entirety but the clip she'd watched today showed some guy named Rico as he robbed a bank, guns blazing. It was ancient, from sometime around now.

Matt said, *Enrico 'Rico' Bandello from the movie Little Caesar. It was...will be, a breakthrough film. Even I am becoming confused with tenses. It's a sound film, so it hasn't — .*

Shut up, Matt.

Pauline asked, "What will you have? The choices are bourbon, gin and rum."

"Whatever you're having."

"Bourbon and water then."

Above, the Milky Way spread like luminous crystals across the sky. The moon out, big as hell. Lauren still couldn't believe the clarity of this L. A. sky.

Assassin 13

"Pauline, who owns the motorcycle in the garage?"

The actress froze in mid-motion of pouring. "It belonged to my husband. He's no longer with us."

"I'm sure I can get it running."

"If you can, it's yours. I have no use for it. I should have thrown it out years ago."

"I can't pay you yet, but…"

"I said it's yours."

"Thanks." Now she owned a motorcycle, even if it was an old gas-fueled relic.

Pauline brought Lauren the drink. "Booze was harder to get before the Volstead Act."

The Volstead act? she asked Matt.

Now, you want me to talk?

The Volstead Act? she snapped.

I've viewed six films that concern in some way the Volstead Act. An act of Congress that brought on Prohibition, which made the sale or consumption of alcoholic beverages illegal. If you had watched all of Little Caesar, you would have known that. It described…

I got it.

Lauren recalled the photo of Pauline and Sorrentino in the Rotogravure that morning and the gang war to control the sale of 'bootleg whiskey.' A fortune to be made by the winner. Mobsters were the same in any century, ruthless killers. And this actress dated one.

"What's the point?" Lauren asked. "Why have Prohibition in the first place?"

"Temperance. The temperance movement formed because…well, frankly, because men got drunk, came home, and beat the hell out of their wives and children."

She went on to explain about the long history of women trying to end the enormous consumption of alcohol that was tearing families apart and plunging women and their children into poverty. When she talked, she planted her feet as if against a strong wind and focused entirely on Lauren, as if Lauren was the most important person in the world to her.

Then, her face grew tight with a strange mix of anger and sadness. "My father was one of those men. We never had any money because his paycheck was poured down his throat. He would come home three sheets to the wind and beat mother senseless often just because she was looking at him crossly. She stood up to him, though, when it came to Russell and me. She wouldn't let him touch us."

Lauren considered Mrs. Windsor having the backbone to protect her children. She still didn't like the old bat but gave her credit for that. Moonlight glimmered off Pauline's platinum blond hair. God, she was gorgeous, Lauren thought.

"I treat mother so abominably sometime," Pauline said. "But she drives me mad."

"That I can understand."

They both laughed.

"When my father ran off and left us," she went on, "it was like we'd been freed from prison. Believe me, we were not the only family in that situation." She shrugged. "So, the temperance movement grew and that got us to Prohibition."

And here they were drinking like her father. Lauren lifted her glass. "Cheers."

Pauline snapped back, "I'm no hypocrite if that's what you're thinking."

Her ice blue eyes sparked, and Lauren thought, at least, she wasn't some High Priestess of Peace and Harmony all the time.

Now, you've done it, Matt said. *Now, she'll throw us out for sure.*

We should be fine. After all, I have an AI in my head who knows the future.

The only future I know is what I found presented in movies. And clearly, you are no historian.

Great.

Angrily, Pauline's eyes darted about a couple times as if words were soldiers and she was gathering hers for an assault. Finally, she said, "I'm not a temperance lady with a silver flask of demon rum in her purse. I'm from Minnesota, remember? If someone tells me I can't do something, that's exactly what I'm going to do. So, yes, cheers." She took a long drink.

Matt, what do you know about Pauline Windsor?

I've seen her in fifty-seven features. She is one of the best actresses of the silent era. She is mentioned in brief film biographies of three other famous individuals of this era, Mary Pickford, Douglas Fairbanks, and Charlie Chaplin but nothing on her own.

Is that all? There must be more.

I told you, Lauren, I am not an endless databank. I only have a short, concise encyclopedia to cover all human history. It is not surprising that Hollywood and a small segment of a single decade in one country has nothing about just one actress, even one as popular as Pauline Windsor was, is. Not all AI model 17Bs even had general encyclopedias downloaded. I do have fifty-four separate flight manuals, two hundred and sixty systems engineering manuals, and thirteen hundred schematics of the Orlav-Proxima station to station shuttle. That's the one you crashed.

Matt projected in her mind a picture of a cartoon rocket crashing nose first into the ground.

You were the AI, Lauren snapped. *I didn't crash the damn thing. You did.*

I do not believe...

Shut up, Matt. Now.

Pauline had asked a question and Lauren hadn't heard. "Sorry. What?"

"I asked you if you've seen the play *Romeo and Juliet*. I'm beginning a new film of it soon."

Lauren said, "The only Shakespearean play I've seen is *Othello*. It was performed by a travelling troupe"

"Really? Where?"

Lauren shrugged. "I'm not sure. When I was a child, I was with a small circus, and sometimes we paired with a traveling theatrical troupe moving from place to place. We didn't like to do that so much. There wasn't a lot of money to be had and dividing the entertainment dollar made for fairly slim pickings."

Pauline's eyebrows rose in surprise. "Really? You were in the circus? My God, what did you do?"

Telling her this could not matter. Nothing she would say about the Misfits could lead the actress to identify her as coming from another time. She was fairly certain circuses existed in the 1920s. "I was an ultimate fighter. From the age of eleven to thirteen, I fought no holds barred combat in a cage called an Octagon. I took on all challengers, teenagers that is, both boys and girls."

"How terrible."

Lauren shook her head. "No, I loved it. I never lost. I never came close to losing. The trick was to make it seem like you could lose. I didn't do so well with that to my father's annoyance."

"I see," Pauline said, a hint of skepticism in her voice. She sipped her drink. "Tell me about *Othello*, what you remember."

Lauren saw the play in her mind; she could recall all of it. Outdoors on a hot August afternoon in a field somewhere in Northern California. She sat in the front row with her mother.

"I wanted to go up on stage and kick that Iago in the ass. I pictured him in the Octagon with me. Of course, they had a black actor playing Othello. He was terrific. It went a couple hours, and I was enthralled every minute."

Considering this, Pauline swirled her drink, clinking the ice, then said, "That's what I want to achieve with *Romeo and Juliet*. Global Studio didn't want to do it, but my contract allows me to choose two of my films. My boss, Jerry Zelinsky, will do anything to sabotage the production. But I think it will be the most important film of my career. That's what I'll be working on for the next couple of months."

Lauren nodded, wondering why she was being told any of this.

Pauline finished her drink and nodded towards Lauren's empty glass. "You have a dead soldier there. How about another?"

"No, I'm fine."

Pauline went to the bar and fixed herself another drink. Lauren decided to get the evening's real business over with. "I want to thank you for all you've done for me. You saved my life, Pauline. I owe you. That means something to me."

Pauline waved the comment away. "Anyone would have done it."

Lauren pressed on. "No, they wouldn't. I have never lived off anyone, or anything my entire life. I can't keep living off your kindness. I'll leave tomorrow."

Shocked, Pauline set her glass down on the bar. "But why? Don't you like it here?"

"Enough with charity."

Quickly, Pauline came out from behind the bar, her hands clasped together. "Please, you don't understand. Don't leave. I need you here." She held her hand up to stop Lauren from speaking. "Hear me out. You know that I'm a successful actress. I've earned a lot of money. A lot. I have not spent it wildly like others. I've invested most of it in stocks and bonds, and I own a very successful restaurant in Hollywood. I'm given twenty to thirty photoplays a week by my studio to read for films I might do. I get fifty thousand fan letters a week. Fifty thousand." She said that with pride. "You see what I'm trying to say?"

"I have no idea what you're trying to say."

Neither do I. Matt interjected

Frustrated, Pauline took the chair beside Lauren. "A month ago, my private secretary got married and moved back to Iowa. I never realized all she did for me. What with me taking care of the children, I'm overwhelmed. It's too much for me alone, especially when I have a movie shoot." She paused as if waiting for a response then added urgently, "I need help. I want you to work for me."

Lauren leaned back with surprise. "You want *me* to be your secretary? Why me? You people think I'm crazy."

The actress shook her head emphatically. "No, we don't, at least, I don't. Not anymore. From what I can see, you're back to normal. I think I'm a good judge of character, too. I've been so far. I've had to be. I know you're smart. I know you can do this work."

"I have no experience as a secretary."

"No one else does either," Pauline explained. "Every assistant. Every secretary is an actress waiting for her big break. And it's more like a manager of everything Pauline Windsor than a secretary. Not me, but me as a business. You'll do everything but tuck me in at night and work like a slave." Gripping Lauren's hand, she added, "It comes down to this. I need someone I can trust, and, damn it, Lauren, my instinct tells me I can trust you."

Say yes, Matt pleaded. *Please, say yes. I'm going to work for Pauline Windsor.*

Shut it. "You're being foolish and naïve, Pauline," Lauren said.

"And impulsive."

"Yes, and impulsive."

Part of Lauren felt a sense of pleasure at the thought of Mrs. Windsor's frustration that she would be staying. "All right. Why not? Let's call me your Management Consultant."

The actress beamed. "I like that. Good. Management Consultant it is."

Lauren leaned back. "So, what do I do?"

Pauline tossed the rest of her drink down. "Everything. Tomorrow you will be starting in the movie business. You've probably never experienced anything so cutthroat before. You'll need to keep your wits about you all the time. There will be a lot of first class bastards to deal with. Do you think you can handle that?"

With a cool smile, Lauren answered, "Sure. I'm good with bastards."

CHAPTER SIXTEEN: THERE'S NO BUSINESS LIKE SHOW BUSINESS

August 29, 1927, Global Studio lot, Los Angeles

The next day, since Pauline was at a costume fitting for *Romeo and Juliet*, Lauren arrived alone at the actress's office bungalow at the Global Studio. She wore hiking boots, khaki cargo pants, a sleeveless black blouse that revealed her tattoos, and a half-bald head though stubble had begun to grow. Before crossing the lot, she received no particular stares. Everyone would think she was an actress playing a part in a film currently in production.

A dowdy, stern-faced woman sitting at a big oak desk guarded the entrance to Pauline's private office. At Lauren's appearance, her eyes went wide with shock that bordered on horror.

Half bald, tattooed women don't seem to proliferate in 1927 Hollywood, Matt said. *She knows you're not an actress. This is the real you.*

She'll have to get used to it.

At a smaller desk nearby, a young woman was making clacking sounds by punching at a small machine with her fingers.

The woman at the big desk had a stern, puffy-cheeked face. "Yes? Can I help you?"

"I'm Lauren Ramirez."

"I know who you are. Miss Windsor told me you were coming. Management consultant, indeed. Putting on airs, aren't we?"

"Who are you?" Lauren asked coldly.

"If you must know, I'm Mrs. Akers. I am Miss Windsor's studio secretary. I was appointed by Mr. Zelinsky himself when dear Kathleen departed."

Lauren knew the woman was a spy for Zelinsky, the studio boss, and couldn't be fired.

Silence dragged out several more seconds, then Mrs. Akers indicated a tiny desk on the far side of the room. "I can't imagine what you will do here, but I prepared a desk for you."

Lauren tapped the woman's oak desk. "Thank you, Mrs. Akers, but this one will do."

Folding her arms across her chest, the woman looked as if she were going to snort fire.

Lauren leaned both fists on the desk. "This one. If you have a problem, take it up with Pauline."

After another second, Mrs. Akers's gaze faltered. "Well, this is not fair." Then, she rose and noisily moved her things to the smaller desk.

I think you made a friend for life, Matt said.

Lauren walked over to the other woman, who stopped clacking and looked up. She glanced quickly away as if Lauren's baldness was a disfigurement.

"Who are you?" Lauren asked.

"Jenny Cole, Miss Ramirez."

Lauren indicated the contraption. "What's that thing?"

For a moment, she was confused. "A typewriter."

"Ah, of course," she said. She returned to the vacated desk and sat behind it. She had no idea what to do. She decided to stare at Mrs. Akers, which she did for the next twenty minutes, unsettling and angering the woman.

Later that day, after Pauline finished her costume fitting, she showed Lauren the studio back lot and several of the films in production. Three separate crews were shooting exterior scenes on a set of a cobblestone street and false-front buildings.

Several extras, in a variety of costumes, hurried from place to place. The filmmakers were immune to the clang and bustle of noise around them.

Pauline caught Lauren's gaze and smiled. "You can feel the energy, can't you? It was like this when I first came to Hollywood. Everything you did was like inventing the wheel."

"Yes, it's as if it's a force with physical substance," Lauren said.

"Exactly. In the beginning of the industry, no one knew what worked and what didn't. It's still the same. There are no rules. No one way to do things. That's all you need to remember, and you'll do fine."

Suddenly, Matt screamed in Lauren's head, *Tom Mix and Tony!*

Lauren shot to one knee and snatched for her Glock, which wasn't there.

Excited, Matt exclaimed, *It's Tom Mix. The real Tom Mix. The greatest cowboy actor ever.*

Goddammit, Matt, Lauren said, regaining her feet. *Don't ever do that again.*

"Are you okay?" Pauline asked.

"Sure," she said. "I just stumbled. It's nothing."

Tom Mix was riding Tony the Wonder Horse down the street. He was sporting his glittering cowboy getup that included the trademark ten-gallon hat, or, as Matt called it for its massive size, *a fifty-gallon hat.*

In her half-day on the job, Lauren had memorized some of the ongoing productions and actors working at the studio. Mix was the biggest cowboy star in movies, on loan from Fox for three quick horse operas.

Pauline explained, "Zelinsky loves Mix and his ilk. Mix makes films fast and cheap. He gives no trouble unlike me, and generates boxcar loads of money."

As he approached, Mix tipped his hat. "Ladies."

Pauline gave her dazzling smile. "Hi, Tom. Zelinsky got you in another oater?"

"One more for that asshole then my loan is done," he said. "I'm running back to Fox as fast as Tony can carry me."

Pauline laughed. "Asshole is right. You've pegged his personality precisely. Tom, this is my management consultant, Lauren Ramirez."

He touched the tip of his hat again. "Ma'am."

"Sir," Lauren said, giving a two-fingered salute.

"Got to run, Tom" Pauline said. "I'm already late for a meeting with my director for *Romeo and Juliet*, Otto von Richter."

"Von Richter? Hell, my sympathies," he said and doffed his hat a third time. He and Tony clopped on down the street.

Von Richter was out of his office and his secretary said he'd gone for the day. For the next hour, Pauline took Lauren around the rest of the studio, showing her the important offices and detailing her duties. To Lauren, it was like entering a new world for the second time in more than a week.

A brave new world, Matt said.

Indeed.

In the next couple of weeks, Lauren fell easily into her new role, becoming adept at the countless mundane parts of the job. Each day, she screened Pauline's calls and set up interviews with writers on the Hollywood beat, like Luella Parsons of the Los Angeles Examiner and Adela Rogers St. Johns of Photoplay. She slipped positive gossip tidbits, real and fictional, into newspapers and fan magazines. She directed a team of young women from the studio secretarial pool, like Jenny Cole, to answer Pauline's forty thousand fan letters a week. Most mornings they typed on those funny machines, sending out notes and signed photographs of the star.

Around noon each day, Pauline usually took a lunch break at one of the in spots, most often her own restaurant, Cafe Windsor, and Lauren accompanied her. Actors, directors, and producers never went anywhere without their assistants.

In so little time, Lauren struggled to develop a feel for Hollywood of 1927, a strange, strange place inhabited by even stranger people. She'd never experienced anything like it.

What she noticed most was the hyperdrive voltage of the town, first experienced in her walk across Global's back lot with Pauline. You could feel a rhythm, an energy, a fireball glow with dreams of gold and names-in-light, stardom swirling about like centrifuges. She had to admit it was infectious. It affected everybody. The business and the town were growing and evolving, not just by the day, but by the hour. It stirred her blood as well.

And people did the oddest things. Men sat atop flagpoles for days on end for no discernible reason. Couples danced in marathons that could last for weeks with no breaks. The fad of swallowing goldfish swept through Los Angeles. Snag them out of a fishbowl and swallow them down. It was as if the looney bin had opened and now the escaped inmates swarmed through the city.

In many ways, Los Angeles reminded her of a Wild West boomtown, not unlike the Tin Can. Seemingly, hundreds of buildings were rising up overnight like the new city hall along with apartments, houses, hotels, and nightclubs. In a single day, fortunes could be made and lost.

And the Hollywood movie factory was at the center of it.

All of America was mad over silent images flickering on a screen. With no language barrier, Hollywood movies were the most popular in the world. Stars like Pauline Windsor, Mary Pickford, Douglas Fairbanks, Charlie Chaplin, Clara Bow, John Gilbert, Pola Negri and a thousand more strode the planet like mythological gods and goddesses becoming as rich as Croesus in the process.

It seemed every beautiful young woman and handsome man in America rushed to the town with dreams of being the next Pauline Windsor or John Gilbert, and the wolves waited for them at the door.

Like any boomtown, this one had a seedy, even brutal underbelly. More familiar with that side of life, Lauren caught on to it more quickly. She recognized the swindlers, petty thieves, pimps, drug dealers, robbers, murderers, and gangsters. Her kind of people. Chief among the predators were Benny Sorrentino and the Colombini brothers. They controlled the city's elected officials, made police appointments, built private armies to terrorize anyone who opposed them, and fought each other for control of the city.

And one of them was Pauline Windsor's boyfriend.

It upset her that an important part of all this eluded her. The basic code, the magic that made one movie blaze to life while another died, was a mystery to her. When dealing with the creative part of filmmaking, like reading scenarios, she felt like she was floating in deep space, alone and adrift. She had no idea what was good and what was bad. But she sure as hell wasn't going to tell anyone that. Pauline understood the creative process. Most people didn't, but pretended they did. So, Lauren decided to pretend as well.

Two weeks into the job, Lauren found herself thrust back into familiar territory, into the kind of territory she knew better than anyone else. She returned to the office from a quick meeting with the writer Adela Rogers St. John to discover Jenny Cole crying over her typewriter and Mrs. Akers trying to console her.

Lauren did not like dealing with people's personal problems because she wasn't good at it. Jenny dabbed her nose with a handkerchief, then wailed again.

Reluctantly, Lauren went over. "What's wrong?" she asked.

You have such a deft touch with those in distress, Matt said. *Sainthood awaits.*

I don't need a comic in my head.

"Nothing," Jenny muttered bravely.

With a frown, Mrs. Akers said, "It's that Mr. Bagley. He's always going at the young girls when they have to show him title cards or anything. He's a...he's a masher."

"Who is Bagley, and what the hell is a masher?" Lauren asked.

Through the sniffling account, she got the story. After Jenny typed the title cards, she had to carry the file over to this Bagley fellow, who ran the Hays Office on the Global lot. The Hays office monitored the Decency Code all the studios supposedly subscribed to but really didn't. Still, Bagley had to pass on all written material to appease the country's straight-laced Catholics, Mrs. Akers explained.

I don't think she likes Catholics, Matt said.

Each time one of the secretaries delivered work to him, he cornered them, groped them and attempted sex.

Feeling the stirring of rage, Lauren asked, "Why not report him?"

"To whom?" Mrs. Akers asked. "You must know women are on their own in these matters."

"He put his hand up under my dress," Jenny said, trembling. "I couldn't get away. If someone hadn't knocked on the door, I don't know what would have happened. I ran."

Rage began to roil inside Lauren. "Okay, I get it," she snapped and Jenny flinched. "Sorry. I'm not angry with you, but with Bagley. This is going to end."

Mrs. Akers snorted derisively. "And what do you think you can do?"

"I think I'll pay him a visit right now. Have a talk with him." She leaned over and touched Jenny's hand. "I promise you, Jenny. He will not bother you again."

The girl blinked, wiped her eyes, and nodded, but Mrs. Akers seemed less convinced.

The Hays Office was on the second floor of a rundown wood building behind Stage Four, not far from Pauline's bungalow. Outdoor steps with a small veranda led up to his door. Lauren climbed them two at a time and entered without knocking.

In her work, she had trained herself to never be surprised by what she came across. That could be deadly to her. This time was no different. What she saw in the strange scene was a small, barrel chested man with powerful arms standing at the front of his desk, his back to her, his pants and underwear around his ankles. His hairy butt was thrusting into a woman who sat on the desk, her legs around him and her dress bunched up at her waist.

On her face was a look of utter distaste, but she was moaning with fake pleasure. Lauren felt a surge of molten rage. At that moment, he glanced back, his lips split in a grimace of ecstasy mixed with surprise and annoyance. Without stopping or showing embarrassment, he shouted, "Get out, toots. Wait your turn."

In two quick strides, she struck the side of his head with such force his ear split, gushing blood. With a shriek, he fell to the floor, his hands flailing as if under water. The woman screamed, shoving down her dress.

"Get out of here," Lauren ordered.

She grabbed her panties and floral hat off the desk and ran from the office.

"What the hell!" Bagley choked out.

He rose while pulling up his pants, then with fury burning his face, he charged her. She easily stepped aside and took his wrist, twisting his arm and yanking it out of its socket. This time the man's scream seemed to vibrate the window glass.

She kicked him in the ribs and then punched his face with three quick jabs, breaking his nose and busting open his lip. She hated to act with emotion, but she did here and felt herself losing control. The rage had taken hold. She was making a mess of the man.

She dragged him outside to the landing where he collapsed. Amid his pain, his groans, he mumbled something.

She leaned down. "What?"

"Why?"

Her eyes blackened. With three quick snaps of her fist, she broke his jaw.

When she rose, she noticed Mrs. Akers at the bottom of the steps, staring up horrified. "What happened to him?"

"He fell down the stairs," Lauren answered.

"But he's on the landing."

Lauren glanced down as if just noticing that fact. Stepping behind him, she put her boot on his shoulder and shoved hard. Amid shrieks, he rolled to the bottom and flopped at the woman's feet.

Lauren bounded down the steps and grabbed Bagley by the shirt. "If I ever see you again, I'll cut your fucking throat." She slapped him twice. "Look at me." When he did, his eyes full of terror, she said, "Do you think I'm lying to you?"

Blood bubbled from his lips; his eyes clouded with pain and panic. He shook his head.

"Good. Go to the hospital. I don't care how you get there. Tell them you fell down your steps. Then, leave Los Angeles. Understand?"

Frantically, he nodded, and she lifted him to his feet. He stumbled away holding his arm. Mrs. Akers was glaring at her.

Lauren met her gaze. "Let's keep this to ourselves."

"I don't think I have a choice."

"You don't."

The older woman nodded. "You're not a secretary, are you? You seem to have other talents though."

Lauren smiled. "You know, Mrs. Akers, I think I'm getting the hang of this movie business."

CHAPTER SEVENTEEN: ROMEO AND JULIET

September 19, 1927, Global lot
Scenario adapted by Francis Marion

Scene 1 — Exterior. Long shot. A medieval city with church steeples, stately buildings and pedestrian-filled boulevards.

> Art Title — I
> Two households, both alike in dignity, in fair Verona, where we lay
> our scene, from ancient grudge break to new mutiny, where civil blood
> makes civil hands unclean. A pair of star-cross'd lovers take their life.

Scene 2 — Exterior. Close up of a market street, filled with shoppers. Enter Sampson and Gregory of the house of Capulet, armed swords and bucklers. Coming the other way are two men of the house of Montague, Abraham and Balthasar. Sampson insults them.

> Dialogue Title
> "Dog of the house of Montague. I serve as good a man as you."

Abraham responds heatedly.

> Dialogue Title
> "You lie. I am for you. Draw, if you be a man."

Assassin 13

The Montagues and Capulets draw swords and fight.
***

Holding her elaborate gown above her ankles, the curls of her golden wig bouncing, Pauline raced down the darkened hallway lit only by the occasional candle. In the diffuse light and dancing shadows, the fear and urgency on her face was compelling. When she burst into the back of a small, lighted church, her expressive blue eyes went wide with alarm, and she searched frantically. Spotting two men standing up front by the altar, she visibly relaxed.

One man was an old, white-haired man in a friar's garb. The other stood broad-shouldered in a rich doublet of red and black brocade. When this man turned and saw her, he grinned widely, and he too sighed with relief.

In the shadows behind the lights, Lauren watched Otto von Richter, the director, in his jodhpur riding pants, black knee-length boots eyeing the scene with disdain. He held a riding crop in one hand and a megaphone in the other, and shouted instructions to the actors as the grinding cameras rolled.

Tension had plunged his set into a deep, black fog. He treated the crew and actors with scorn, browbeating them for even the slightest perceived infraction or not meeting his exacting standards. After two weeks of filming, many in the crew were ready to tip a large Kliegl light on him.

Earlier in the day, a technician had moved one, then quickly reset it. Still, Richter rounded on him furiously and browbeat him for a full five minutes till Pauline stopped him and told him there was a scene to shoot. To everyone, no matter what his reputation for brilliance, he was a prancing martinet.

Now, as Pauline appeared in the door, his voice boomed through the megaphone, "You are not a hausfrau, Pauline. Act! Act! What happiness. You think Romeo jilted you at the altar, and here he is. You think, wunderbar. How you love this man. Now, run to him. Run to him."

Alight with joy, Pauline rushed down the aisle and into Romeo's embrace.

Michael Murray, playing Romeo, held Pauline intensely, his face locked into fierce earnestness. "Juliet, if the measure of your joy be heaped like mine then let rich music's tongue unfold our happiness."

Though no audience would hear him speak, Pauline always insisted she and the other actors speak the right words. Eventually, when the film played, they would be replaced by title cards on which the dialogue was written. Probably for the best, Lauren thought. Murray was such a wooden actor, able to deliver little feeling.

But Pauline was different. She was good, very good. She could convey emotion and meaning in a single glance, melting into the character as if she were, indeed, Juliet. Her blue-eyes gazed at Romeo.

Richter shouted, "Now, you look at man you love. Liebe ihn! Liebe ihn!"

Pauline's face took on the sentiment of child-like longing for her beloved, but then she went further. Her eyes became suddenly inflamed with lust so bold, so raw, that Lauren heard gasps from the crew. Then, her expression changed once more to angelic virtue, all given with engaging likeability.

Richter cried, "Cut."

Michael hugged Pauline, grinning effusively. "Brilliant, honey. Just brilliant. Where did that come from?"

Her hands on her hips, Pauline said, "Well, Mikey, if you knew your onions like you're supposed to, you'd know the first expression was for the lovesick dames in the audience, and the second, the passionate stuff, was for the boys and their papas. And that third, well, after all the old biddies in the audience became scandalized, they absorbed my angelic expression and changed their minds about me having naughty ideas. Now all of them will come again when my next picture shows up."

Michael laughed and kissed Pauline's cheek. "You're a trouper, honey."

"Nein, nein, nein," Richter marched up impatiently. "It must be perfect. Perfect. I must shoot it again. Go to places. Go to places!"

It was after four in the afternoon, and they'd gotten no usable film in the can all day, reshooting scene after scene. In the two weeks of the shoot, they'd printed less than ten minutes of usable footage, but used more than a third of the budget. Now, he wanted another reshoot.

For the last two weeks, Lauren had witnessed Pauline's growing frustration with the director. At this rate, they would have less than one reel in the can when the money ran out, and the movie *Romeo and Juliet* would be as dead as the two characters at the end.

With exhausted sighs, everyone went back to their places to shoot the scene, except Pauline. She'd had enough.

"Take your whip, Herr Richter, and shove it up your ass. You're fired."

After an instance of silence, a cheer erupted from the crew.

Richter expressed shock, then scorn. "You cannot discharge me. You are just an actress. Mr. Zelinsky hired me. Only he can discharge me. He knows my films are all masterpieces."

Pauline snapped back, "Listen to me, Kaiser. Get off this set."

She picked up her skirts and strode away. As she passed Lauren, she said, "Come with me. We're going to see Zelinsky."

As they left through the stage door, someone shouted, "Give 'em hell, Pauline."

In her Renaissance dress, accompanied by Lauren, Pauline stalked across the studio lot toward the Global headquarters building. They rushed past the fiftyish secretary and burst into Zelinsky's office. From behind his desk, he shot to his feet. "What's the meaning of this? You should call for an appointment like everyone else."

He was short and portly and wore an expensive three-piece suit with a bow tie. His brown hair was slicked down with pomade. To Lauren, he looked like someone's creepy uncle.

Pauline strode to his desk. "We need to talk about von Richter, and it can't wait,"

He glanced over at Lauren. "Leave. I want to speak to Pauline alone."

Lauren looked to Pauline, who said, "She's my business manager. Lauren Ramirez. She stays."

Zelinsky gave a put-upon shrug and sat back down behind his desk. He gestured for Pauline to speak and then folded his hands across his puffy stomach as Pauline paced the floor, getting wound up listing the director's many faults.

After several minutes, he smiled paternally. "Oh, dear Pauline, I told you this would happen if we do Shakespeare. We've only shot 10% of the film and the budget is already half gone. This is not good business. Shakespeare is not good business, but no one listens to me."

Lauren knew he had been furious because Pauline had gone over his head to Sid Meisner in New York to okay *Romeo and Juliet*. Meisner, the owner of Global Pictures Studio, seldom got involved in the actual moviemaking process, handling the financial end of things. He and Pauline were old friends, and some said lovers. He had okayed the picture.

Zelinsky went through the ritual of preparing a cigar to be smoked, then stuck a large cigar in his mouth and lit it. "Richter is a genius," he said, shaking the match out. "You wanted a prestige film. He is Mr. Prestige."

"Genius, my ass," Pauline shot back. "The budget for the film is limited. It will run out long before principal photography is completed. That's not genius. It's idiocy."

Lauren asked Matt, *Does Romeo and Juliet get made?*

I do not have that data. If it was completed, the film was lost. I've never seen it. Most silent films did not survive the 20th century.

"You did this," Pauline accused Zelinsky. "This is what you wanted all along. You hated the idea of *Romeo and Juliet* from the beginning. And you sure as hell didn't like me going over your head to Meisner."

Zelinsky waved the idea away "True. I say what pictures get made at Global. Not Meisner. That's our deal. But I ain't going to ruin my own movie. That's just crazy."

"Bullshit."

He smiled at the word. His chair squeaked as he sat up abruptly and turned to Lauren. "What do you think, Miss..."

"Ramirez."

He squinted at her. "What's wrong with your hair?"

"Nothing," Lauren said. Pauline had suggested she let her hair grow back. One half of her head was now covered with short black hair.

He snorted. "Well, baldness is not a good look for a woman. Tell me what do you think about all this Shakespeare shit? About the genius that is von Richter?" He pointed his cigar hand at Pauline. "And tell her."

I suggest you frown, Matt urged. *That makes you look like you're thinking.*

I am thinking. She said, "People believe Richter is a genius because he says irrational things no one understands. Back in

Germany, before he became a director, he was a crony of Adolf Hitler. Rumor has it he served as a general in the German army during World War II. Pranced around with his field marshal's baton, and is now doing the same thing on movie sets here. He's a toilet down which money is thrown."

Zelinsky and Pauline stared at her uncomprehendingly.

Matt cried out, *No. No. World War II hasn't happened yet. Have you had no schooling at all?*

Her eyes darted back and forth, then she smiled. "World War II, remember? That was one of Richter's early German films. Adolf Hitler was a character in it, and the good director acted in his own film. It lost hundreds of thousands of dollars. Like I said, we can do better."

Neither Zelinsky nor Pauline seemed to know how to respond, so didn't. Finally, Zelinsky said, "I'm sorry, Pauline. Otto is the director. We cannot change him now."

He dismissed the two women waving the back of his hand.

"Then, I'll do it," Pauline said.

"Direct?" he asked, incredulous.

"No. Fund the picture," she said. "I'll put my own money in. Global handles distribution."

A sudden look of curiosity appeared in his eyes. He leaned back in the chair, puffed his cigar. "How much are you willing to commit?"

"I'll put in whatever's needed to finish the picture. But I own 50% of the gross."

"Don't be ridiculous, Pauline. 25%, and you know that's generous. It's my studio, my actors, my crew, and my director you are using."

Lauren was surprised Zelinsky agreed.

"All right," Pauline said. "One stipulation. I'm replacing Richter. I want Clarence Martin to direct. He's fast and he's good."

Silence followed for several seconds. Then Zelinsky nodded. "Agreed. This is unusual. You are now a producer, Pauline."

As they left the building, Lauren asked Pauline, "Why did he agree to that? It's not what he wants at all. I know he's got some sort of plan, but I can't figure it."

"He thinks if the film fails, not only will it damage my career, but break me financially. That way he thinks he will control me." Pauline's eyes took on a hard gaze. "*Romeo and Juliet* must succeed. It must."

CHAPTER EIGHTEEN: THE FLYBOY

September 22, 1927, Hollywood

Working on the motorcycle in the garage before breakfast, Lauren didn't think it would take long to get it running. She set out the parts on a tarp, and began rebuilding the vehicle. She cleaned the carburetor, spark plugs, and rings, checked the gas tank for rust, drained the oil and replaced it, replaced chains, sprockets, and brakes, and bought new tires.

Each morning as she worked, the children were always under foot, Emmy just watching but Rolly wanting to help. Annoying as he was, she tolerated his pestering questions. She had been around few children in her life and none as an adult. They were such needy creatures, demanding constant attention.

Incredibly naïve and innocent, Emmy wanted love from too many people and trusted too many people. She was heading for a terrible awakening someday. But that was not Lauren's problem.

Rolly was worse. He spent much of his free time pestering Lauren. She might have to set him straight in harsh terms. She was not his auntie, she was not his nanny, and she sure as hell was not his friend. He was a kid.

When she dumped the motorcycle's gas into a bucket, he asked why she did that. "Don't you need gas to run it?"

"Maybe not, kid. Besides, this gas has become stale. I'll need to replace it."

"You're going to run it on bread?" It was a Rolly joke. Bread goes stale. She was beginning to understand him.

She smiled. "You'd be surprised what I can run it on."

She planned to pirate a battery from one of the spider robots on the shuttle. That would blow the kid's cap off.

Finally, on Thursday morning, still using the gasoline engine, she took the machine outside and kick-started it. At the roar, Rolly jumped up and down clapping. Lauren laughed, getting caught up in his joy. Lifting him by the scruff of his shirt, she put him in front of her and they rode slowly down the driveway. With his hands on the handlebars, he thought he was guiding it. He screamed with delight.

When they returned, Pauline was standing outside the door watching them. She was grinning. "So, you got that old thing running."

"I did."

"Good." She said to Rolly. "Come on, buster, you're running late."

Lauren set him on the ground. "Okay, kid, you need to get ready for school, and I need to get ready for work."

***

That day the temperature in Los Angeles was a sweltering 105. On the set of *Romeo and Juliet*, it felt like working in an oven to the actors and crew. Lights blazed; cameramen, technicians, prop men, and nearly forty other crew members hurried about as if each of their jobs could mean success or failure for the shoot. The new director, Clarence Martin, ordered blocks of ice and placed large fans behind them, creating his own air conditioning.

The crew knew what Pauline had done in getting Richter fired and hiring Martin. Now, they were willing to give everything they had to see the movie a success.

The new director was a small, bookish man with wire rim glasses. He stood beside the main camera giving Michael last minute instructions. This was the balcony scene. A large fake vine wound its way up the house wall to the balcony where Pauline stood in her gown waiting to begin the scene.

Martin clapped Murray on the back and the actor raced up to the house, dropped to one knee, placed both hands over his heart and looked up at Pauline with a simpering gaze.

The director of photography called, "Cameras rolling."

Martin shouted, "Action."

In the dark behind the Kliegl lights and cameras, Lauren watched the scene unfold. The actors spoke lines that would never be heard and used visual gestures expressing love and longing for each other as Martin called out each actor's emotion at the moment.

"Miss Ramirez?" a man said, stepping up beside Lauren.

She'd been aware of his presence for several seconds but detected no threat. Now, she glanced at him. She'd never seen him before. An unusual looking man with a nose that had been broken badly once. A scar ran down his forehead diagonally into a black patch covering one eye like a pirate. The scar continued down his cheek for another three inches. His left hand held a pipe, but otherwise the arm seemed useless.

Makeup or real. In the poor light it could be either. If real, these were no casual wounds. They had to be from the recent war or a bad accident. Maybe, though, he was just an actor who'd wandered in off a nearby set. Though the face was battered, he was handsome in a tough-guy sort of way.

"Who are you?" she replied.

"My name is Remington Garnett. My friends call me Remy. I'm a friend of Michael Murray." He stuck out his hand, and she shook it.

"I see," she said, remembering that Murray was gay. She disliked the term.

He laughed. "No, not that kind of friend. Michael and I fly out of the Griffith Park Aerodrome. He's a fairly good pilot."

"What do you want, Mr. Garnett?" she asked brusquely. She was sure he was another fan or aspiring actor who wanted to get to Pauline through her.

Nervously, he put his good arm behind his back. "I saw you on the lot and asked Michael who you were." He smiled as if that were explanation enough.

Suspicion clawed its way into her brain. "Why did you do that?"

"Why does any man ask who that beautiful woman is?"

She leaned her head back to study him, gaging the depth of his bullshit. He would not be the first man who thought her attractive enough to approach, but here in the land of stunningly beautiful women, she stood out only as someone not up to goddess standard like Pauline.

"I'm shooting a film for Global," he added. "I have a break and thought I'd come over and introduce myself."

"You're an actor then." She gestured toward his scars. "In the darkness that makeup looked almost real."

"I'm no actor. I'm a stunt pilot." He touched his damaged face. "I assure you, the scars are real. I hope you're not put off by a man with only one eye."

"The popular preference *is* for two."

That took him aback. She smiled, and after a moment of uncertainty, he grinned back, showing even white teeth. He touched the scar on his face. "Compliments of the Red Baron himself. I'm flying and designing the aerial scenes for this new movie."

She asked Matt, *The Red Baron?*

Baron Manfred von Richthofen, a German fighter pilot during World War I, called the ace of aces. He shot down more planes than any other pilot, 80 air combat victories. I've seen only four films concerning Richthofen, but there have been many, including one staring a floppy-eared dog. He…

Enough. I get it.
"I was in *Palace*," Garnett said.
"What?"
"Pauline's movie, *Palace of Fallen Angels*. It will be opening in Los Angeles in a couple months."

"Good for you. What do you want, Mr. Garnett?"

Nervous for some reason, he stuck his bad hand in his pocket, as if unsure what to do with it. When he spoke, though, his voice was assured. "I would like to see you. I would like to take you out."

Surprisingly, she felt intrigued. "Well, make your pitch, Mr. Garnet, but I warn you it has to be imaginative or you can go back to your planes. And if you're going to woo me so you can get close to Pauline, forget it. I'll sabotage any chance you have with her."

"Pauline and I are old friends. I can see her anytime I want. Are you free Sunday?"

"I am, but I hope that's not your pitch. Surely, you can do better than that."

His single eye winked. "Have lunch with me, a picnic up in the mountains. I don't want to spoil it for you by giving the rest of it away, but I promise it will be like no other date you've ever been on. I'll pick you up at nine in the morning."

"How can I refuse? All right, pick me up at Pauline's house."

CHAPTER NINETEEN: WINGS

September 25, 1927, Los Angeles and the San Bernardino Mountains

At nine o'clock on Sunday morning, Remy picked Lauren up at Pauline's house in his open roadster and drove over the Hollywood Hills to the Griffith Park Aerodrome. He had told her to dress for the outdoors so she wore khaki trousers, a plaid shirt, red bandana, hiking boots, and a floppy hat, which she held in her lap while the wind tussled her uneven black hair.

There was something about him that resurrected a spark of feeling in her. Not sympathy for his burn injuries, the lost eye, the nearly dead arm, but something else. In an odd way, he reminded her of her father, his tough exterior yet a gentleness within. Too easy. Too naïve. Too vulnerable. Like her father.

To her surprise, she realized she wanted this man to like her. Her life had never allowed for anything long term anyway. Short term with Remy, though, would be just fine.

On a ridge above the aerodrome, he stopped the car to take in the panorama. Below, several hundred people stood beside parked cars, watching an air show. In the sky high above them, five planes circled and looped maniacally.

Lauren asked, "What are they doing?"

"Mock dog fights."

"That's what you did in the war?"

"Most days."

When the planes landed, Remy drove the car down onto the field to one of the large hangers where the five biplanes taxied in and parked. Up close, Lauren thought they were made of paper and sticks. She could not imagine how they could fly.

They got out, and he led her over to the planes. "You're looking at five of the Thirteen Black Cats."

"Black Cats?"

"Stunt pilots for the movies. We negotiate together with the studios for our services."

The aviators in leather caps and goggles climbed down from their open cockpits and gathered around Remy, greeting him warmly. He introduced them to her.

A cherubic-faced man named Clyde Brady said with a wink, "Lauren, you're not letting this madman shepherd you around the countryside? He can't drive any better than he can fly."

He had red hair and freckles in an imitation of Tom Sawyer.

"No accidents yet," she said.

Brady laughed. "There's a lot of time yet."

Another man lifted binoculars skyward and announced. "Here we go."

They all looked up. Lauren didn't think much could shock her, but what she saw next did. Five hundred feet up in the air two biplanes cruised side-by-side at 35 or 40 mph. On top of one's top wing, a tiny figure moved about like a gyroscope. It was the height of lunacy.

"My God, what is he doing?" Lauren asked.

"The Charleston, I believe," Remy replied, deadpan, handing her a pair of binoculars.

"I mean, why in the hell is he up there?" With the binoculars, she picked the figure out. He was indeed dancing...on the wing of an airplane. She saw the figure clearly. "It's a woman."

"Gladys Ingle," Remy said. "Quite a remarkable lass. Best pilot among us."

Brady dropped his binoculars a moment to look at Lauren. "She's got more balls than most men I know. Pardon my French."

"You people are crazy," Lauren replied. They all laughed, pleased as if it were a compliment.

They are called Wingwalkers, Matt said and went on to explain the phenomenon. In air shows, men and women went out on the wings of planes as they flew high in the air. He'd seen many early film newsreels of the phenomenon. *It's amazing that I can actually see this in reality.*

With the binoculars, she picked the woman out again and watched her tiptoeing to the wing's edge, apparently to jump to the other plane. It couldn't be more than a foot away, but the wings kept dipping and couldn't sync.

Suddenly, Gladys Ingle lost her balance, wildly flailing her arms. Lauren gasped and a great cry went up from the audience. As her wing rose, Ingle regained her balance and leapt across to the other plane, scrambled to the back cockpit, and climbed in.

Lauren heard people clapping all around the field, and she wondered if Ingle really lost her balance or was just putting on a show. Would they have clapped if she had fallen?

After saying goodbye to the pilots, she and Remy entered the hanger.

"I thought we were going on a picnic," Lauren said.

"We are if you still want to go."

"Why wouldn't I?"

"Because we're going in that." He gestured toward a snub-nosed plane with a bright red wing across the top, the cockpit enclosed inside a silvery fuselage.

She glanced at Remy. He was looking back at her, his face an open challenge.

"You are the pilot?" she asked.

"I am. I come with the plane," he said. His next words were spoken with pride, as if talking about a favorite child "It's a Lockheed Vega. The newest and fastest plane around. I've gotten it up to 160 mph. It's so new Lockheed hasn't even put it on the market yet. I first tested it for them in July. Of course, if you don't want to go, I'll understand. We can drive someplace else."

"I'll go with you on one condition."

"Which is?"

"You teach me how to fly the damn thing."

Ten minutes later, the Lockheed Vega powered down the runway, the engines roaring in her ears, the fuselage rattling as if it were about to come apart. Nothing could have been further from the silent, smooth flight of the shuttle.

In her head, Matt cried out, *Fasten your seatbelts. It's going to be a bumpy ride.*

With a dirt berm at the end of the runway rapidly approaching, Remy pulled back on the stick with his powerful good arm, and the plane lifted into the air. His left arm wasn't completely useless. He was able to steer the plane with it while using the right to pull on the stick. He glanced at her to see if she had been frightened.

She grinned. "Nice work, flyboy."

As they climbed, two eagles tried to keep up for a time. She was disappointed when they fell off the pace. At five thousand feet, Remy leveled off and headed east into the morning sun. He leaned toward her and shouted over the engine, "If you get cold, there's a jacket behind you."

With a chill filling the cabin, she reached back for the leather flight jacket and put it on. She liked its feel and smell. Gazing out the window, she thought the land far below appeared like the ground inside the Tin Can. Small towns dotted the open country. Unlike the Tin Can, blue sky hovered overhead, not more greenery and more towns.

She liked the engine's roar and the frightening bump of the cockpit with every gust of wind. This flying business opened up a new world of experience, of reality, far different from the pristine flights in her own time. For her, this was raw, undiscovered country.

Throughout the next hour, he gave her the controls several times, explaining the function of the stick and the few gauges on the control panel. She picked it up quickly and kept them going steadily with only a couple dips and turns.

"You're a natural," he said. "Some people are."

His remark gave her a sense of satisfaction, and she returned his smile. "Thanks."

When they reached the mountains, he took back control. Below was an endless forest of pine and fir that they traversed for nearly twenty minutes before the woods split open, revealing a sizeable lake

The water glistened in the afternoon sun, creating a fiery cobalt blue so striking that when she closed her eyes, it still flickered in her mind's eye. They flew on for a few more miles, skimming the treetops, the plane's shadow just preceding them. Finally, ahead, a tiny space opened up, a field with a barn at the end.

"We're landing," Remy called.

The plane lurched and rattled and settled down to the ground, bouncing once and taxiing to the barn. A strange narrow-nosed car was parked by the door. With grills on the side, running boards and a spare tire on the driver's side door, it looked like it had been put together by a pack of slow-witted monkeys. She told Remy so. He called it a sturdy little Renault. Inside on the back seat was a picnic basket.

"You are resourceful, aren't you, Mr. Garnet?" she said.

For nearly an hour, he drove on a dirt road up into the mountains. Around noon, he stopped the car, grabbed the picnic basket, and led her out onto a promontory high above the lake they'd flown over. As he spread a blanket and began setting out food, she walked to the edge. A couple sailboats plied the waters below. Three miles to the north, a small town glittered white in the sunlight, the buildings like a string of sparkling pearls. A flutter of noise caused her to glance back at the trees. On a high branch, an eagle perched motionless, staring at her.

Remy watched her as well, feeling himself being overwhelmed by this woman. On one side, a gleaming shock of black hair fell in thick tresses down her back, while the other side appeared like a bobo. Strangest thing he'd ever seen. The black hair made her olive complexion look almost pale by contrast. Her khaki pants clung to her ass, showing its lovely shape. She had unbuttoned the plaid shirt, and when she glanced back at him and smiled, he caught a glimpse of her breasts through the thin t-shirt.

Lauren thought him roguish with his eye patch. She decided she liked Remy Garnet but didn't know exactly how to approach him. Once, when she was assigned to assassinate the playboy minister of war in a prominent Asian country, she had taken on the role of seductress to get close. It had worked. She decided to play that role now, though without the kill.

She returned to the blanket and sat down next to him. "Do you bring all the women you want to seduce up here?"

Amused, he shrugged. "Not all. Some."

"Do you think you'll be successful?"

"Seducing you? That's yet to be determined."

"What if I want to seduce you? Do you think I'll be successful?

"Definitely."

He took a bottle of wine from the basket and poured her a glass, then one for himself. He lifted his. "Salute."

"Salute," Lauren said and drank.

Then, she set the glass down and took his face in her hands. She traced her finger along his scar. She could smell his skin, feel the heat of his body, see the swell of his irises. She kissed his eyelids, his cheeks, his mouth, softly at first, then harder. He groaned.

They undressed quickly. With one arm, he was grappling with his pants. She couldn't wait and yanked them off. His mouth closed on her, frighteningly alive.

After a moment, he muttered hoarsely, "The food. We're smashing it."

She laughed and lay back on the blanket, pulling him down on top of her, wrapping her legs around his hips. The crush of his body against hers was so five-by-five it sent shivers through her. It had been so long since she made love to someone she cared about she was not sure it had ever happened before. The realization struck her that she had used the word *cared*. She cared about Remy.

In this age, a woman who is quick to jump in the sack is regarded as an easy woman, a tart. No respect, Matt informed her. *She can forget about a substantial relationship with a man.*

Shut the fuck up, Matt. Not now.

She and Remy made love, and then another time before heading back. Remy allowed Lauren to drive the car, and focusing intently on the unfamiliar vehicle, she lurched down the mountain.

You must be careful, Matt said. *You almost drove into a tree. If you die, I die.*

Look, Metal Brain, stow it. I allow you in my head because if I ever get the shuttle running again, I might need you. I don't want to hear from you every damn second.

Of course, you will need me. How else would you be able to fly it?

I told you to shut up and I meant it. I can purge you from my nanobots if I choose. There are two situations in which you must not speak. Ever. One is when I'm dealing with a dangerous situation like trying to drive a damn car off a mountainside. The other is sex. When I am having sex, I do not need your kibitzing. Do you understand? You can answer.

He created an image in her mind of a monkey covering his mouth with his hands.

When they reached the highway, Remy directed Lauren north, a different route back to the plane. After five miles, they entered a small town with just a general store, a church, and a lodge. A few cars were parked along the street beside a couple horse-drawn wagons.

Something familiar about the town sent a chill through her. Just ahead she saw a building under construction, red brick, two-stories with arched windows, as yet without a roof, scaffolding all around. She knew that building. She'd seen it before. A narrow street entered the main road at a sharp angle creating the building's odd triangle shape. A knife plunged into her solar plexus. She knew where she was.

"This is Bonner Springs," Lauren said, her voice a low rasp.

"Yes, I think so. How do you know? Have you been here before?"

Without responding, Lauren drove slowly through town and turned onto an open field where several boys were playing baseball. She parked in the middle of left field and jumped out before Remy could speak.

"Hey, lady, what are you doing?" the closest outfielder called. The other boys stopped and stared at her as she strode across the outfield.

She ignored them. Blood pumped hard in her temples. Behind her, Remy called to the boys. "It's all right. We'll just be a few minutes."

When she saw the creek just beyond the trees, she stopped and stared at her surroundings, blinking several times. Disinterred memories flooded back, memories of events that had not even happened yet. After being suppressed for so long, they now engulfed her. This was the place the Misfits died, this was the place her father died.

She saw the spot where Sybil had lain beneath Dom's shattered body. Saw the other bodies strewn around the field. Felt the chaos and fear again. An infinite sadness spread through her. At the same time, rage erupted, the emotions symbiotic, feeding off each other.

She longed for the feel of a gun in her hand, but there was no one here to kill. She felt a touch on her shoulder and spoke with a lethal edge. "Remington, remove your hand."

Quickly, he did. When she turned, his damaged face was wrought with concern. "What is wrong, Lauren?"

Her mind went to that distant place in time. "This is where they died. This is where they all died."

"Who? Who died?"

The boys came up. One with sandy hair, probably no more than thirteen, spoke, "We're trying to play ball here, ma'am. Will you please move your car?"

Seeing the dead look in Lauren's eyes, several of the boys backed away. After a moment, the sandy haired one stepped hesitantly forward again. "We'd like to continue our game."

"What's your name?" she asked him.

"Babe Ruth," he answered defiantly. "What are you going to do, ma'am?"

A couple of the boys snickered at the name he used.

After a pause, she gave him a half-smile. "Well, Babe, we're going to leave."

The flight back was silent between them. Remy didn't ask, and Lauren didn't offer any explanation about what happened to her in Bonner Springs.

That evening, when he dropped her off, she got out of the car without saying a word. He drove off. She watched him go, then went directly to the garage, strapped a canvas tarp and shovel onto the back of the motorcycle, kick-started it, and roared off.

CHAPTER TWENTY: BURY THE DEAD

September 25, 1927, Santa Monica Mountains

On the motorcycle, Lauren roared into the Santa Monica Mountains, trying to control the festering emotions unleashed by her visit to Bonner Springs. Grief for Sybil, grief for her parents, grief for the Misfits, all bubbled like lava just below the surface. It was as if landing here in 1927 had ruptured the dam holding back all that misery.

I thought you wanted Remy to like you, Matt said.
I did, she snapped at his intrusion.
I think we can safely assume that didn't work out.
You're a master of the obvious. Now, leave me alone. I mean it.

By the time she reached the site of the shuttle, it was early evening, and twilight was disappearing fast, stars popping out like a spill of gemstones. On her own, with little memory of the trek out after the crash, it would have taken hours for her to find the ravine, but Matt directed her right to it.

The dark shape of the spacecraft loomed like a giant squid at the bottom of a murky sea. She dropped the tarp and shovel, popped open the cockpit hatch with her DNA print, and swung in. The air was not as foul as she had suspected it would be. The lights came on automatically. Spotting Sybil's blackened, desiccated body on the flight deck, she winced.

First, she found her Glock 75 in a pocket of the pilot's chair. She went to the open hatch, aimed outside at the ravine bank and pulled the trigger. Nothing happened. She tried it a couple more times. Still nothing. It was 22nd century technology. Even if she could repair it, she only had one magazine of thirty exploding rounds. She stuck the weapon into her belt.

She turned to Sybil's body. "All right, mi hija. It's time you are given a proper burial."

In the next couple of hours, Lauren dug a grave, wrapped Sybil in the tarp and set her gently into the ground. When she filled the grave and stacked rocks on top, she stood back, not knowing what to do or say, feeling only a vast empty space inside her.

A monstrous grief stalked her, and she fought desperately to keep it at bay, but it exploded over her, fangs and claws bared, savaging her. The monster ripped open the wounds left by her parents' deaths and the massacre of the Misfits, Sybil dead again.

Her knees buckled, and she collapsed to the ground by the grave. A primordial scream blew up from her chest and out of her. She wept like a child for the first time in years.

Matt spoke over her racking heaves. *We stand in the presence of the Almighty, ready to deliver our friend, Sybil, unto His good care. She has gone to her endless rest far too early. We know God works in strange ways. We do not claim to know the wisdom of those ways. After all, when he calls, we must go. Who can take Sybil home now but God? Her soul is free, her suffering done. Dying is as natural as living. The man who's too afraid to die is too afraid to live.*

Strange words, Lauren thought, coming from an AI, but they eased her pain. Her crying slowed and then ended. *Matt, I know you got those words from a movie, but thanks.*

The first quote is from "Oregon or Bust," a 2089 classic. The second is from 1961, "The Misfits." No connection to you, but fitting. The words were spoken by the Clark Gable character.

You do know how to spoil a moment.

Not ready to return to Hollywood, Lauren sat on the ravine hillside staring at the shuttle's dark outline, her devastation complete. It was not yet 1:00am. She felt wasted by the emotions that had ripped through her. Stuck here in ancient America, an alien in an alien land, it was as if her entire skeletal system had been yanked out from her body.

There must be a way to get back, she said. *I have too much to do. Too much to finish.*

There is not, Matt said emphatically.

You're just a damn appliance. How would you know?

Lauren heard the snake rattle, and saw its shadowy form just a foot away from her leg, ready to strike. Her hand shot out, clutching its head so quickly it could not react. Lifting it off the ground, she held it in front of her, barely able to see the vertical pupils in the darkness. Before it could spit, she hurled it into a patch of brush fifteen feet away.

That's when the shuttle began to glow.

Instantly, she knew what it was. Panic rose like ice water inside her. She was sure the damn thing was about to disappear. Jumping to her feet, she sprinted for the spacecraft and swung inside through the hatch.

What are we doing? Matt asked.

She ordered him into the computer.

To what purpose?

Get inside the damn computer.

When he leapt from her head into the ship's brain, it felt momentarily painful, like ice water sloshing around in her skull.

"I must ask: to what purpose?" Matt said, his voice coming through the ship speakers.

"That glow on the ship, the fluorescent strands. That's the anomaly. Analyze what the hell is going on."

Her excitement grew at what this might mean. In a nanosecond, he reported back. "You are right. The strands, just four of them, were part of the time displacement anomaly."

"What else?" she asked.

"What else? What else do you want to know?"

She exploded with anger. "Stop stalling, or get yourself another fucking human host. Give me all the data you discovered about it."

"The anomaly has DNA. It is alive."

That shocked her. "What the hell does that mean?"

"It means it has DNA. It is alive."

She exhaled. Dealing with the AI was like dealing with an enormously intelligent five-year-old. "What else?"

"Current analysis shows the anomaly returns to this time period at specific intervals. Today is now September 25, thirty-five days from when we first encountered it. Therefore, it is reasonable, though not certain, it will return on October 30, then December 4 and so on."

"I get it." Her heart leapt. "If I can go back through the anomaly, will I be able to return to my own time?"

A nanosecond of reluctance passed before he answered, "Theoretically, it is possible. However, in reality, it is not. The anomaly is dying."

Her excitement drained away. "Damn. How long?"

"I do not have enough data to make an accurate conclusion. I will set out the data for you, and you can make the estimate yourself. I can say this: it has a finite amount of time before it ceases to exist, and I suspect it is not long."

"How certain are you?"

"One hundred percent," he said. "From the sensor arrays, I determined the vitality of the anomaly when we passed through it at 23.4 VQ. That's a top score. The illumination then lasted for 20 hours, fifteen minutes. Today, the VQ is down to 7.8. That is a 66.666666666667% drop. And only four hours, forty minutes' illumination this time. Clearly, when you crashed into it, you mortally wounded it."

"Me? You were flying the damn spaceship."

"The anomaly will reappear October 30. I'll know more then. But be assured, it cannot return more than one or two more times, if that."

Standing abruptly, Lauren paced about the flight deck, considering the possibilities.

Matt interrupted her thoughts. "You do know what you are thinking is futile. Repairing the shuttle will be impossible. This is 1927, after all. "

For some reason, he seemed upset, not just replicating an emotion learned from a thousand movies. Why was a damn AI upset? "Everything is repairable," she said. "Do a survey of the damage-control arrays and save the asides. Be accurate. I'll know if you're lying."

"I cannot lie." Moments later, he said, "I have gathered the data."

"Well? Do you mind telling me if this bucket can fly?"

"As I said, theoretically, yes. In reality, no."

She sighed, frustration growing. "Be more specific."

"Systems inside and outside the ship have been damaged, but most have working backups. A few, however, cannot be repaired, ignored, or jury-rigged. They leave the shuttle landlocked as a dodo. That's a…"

"I know what a dodo is. Be specific. What damage?"

"Two hundred and twelve hairline fractures on the outer hull can be repaired only by molecular polymer epoxy. To my knowledge, we have none, and it is definitely not a product of the early 20th century. If we try to fly, the ship will break apart, then adios, amigo."

Another movie quote, annoying her. "Amiga," she corrected him. "Why do we not have this epoxy on the ship? It seems it would be basic supply."

"We may have. I just do not possess that knowledge."

He was playing with her. Why was he suddenly fighting her? If she allowed him back in her head, she could destroy him by unleashing her nanobots. They'd respond to him as if he were an invading virus. But she still needed him to fly the damn craft if she could get it airborne.

"You're playing a deadly game, Matt. You need to be more forthcoming, or you and I will no longer be friends."

"Friends? You think of me as a friend?" he said excitedly. "We two have made progress. If we have the epoxy, my theory is it will be in the ship's hold."

She went down into the craft and quickly found two thermos-sized metal containers of the stuff. She held one up to one of the many cameras. "Next problem."

"Two more complications significantly more challenging since they, in fact, have no solutions. Firstly, the directional gyro has been destroyed. Completely. The backup has been offline for months, and there is no replacement in 1927. We cannot fly without it. The ship would have no control."

He projected an image above the hold's small control panel of a balloon shooting around, randomly while rapidly losing air.

"Very amusing, Matt. And the other obstacle?"

"The positron reactor."

That shook her. If that was out of action, there was no power, and even she knew they wouldn't be able to ever fly.

"The reactor itself is not the difficulty," he said. "The matter-antimatter pellets will last another thousand years. The problem is the gamma ray converter. The reactor engine generates blasts of high-energy gamma photons, which are funneled through the converter and transformed into harmless energy in the form of heat and then expelled from the craft as simple exhaust. Some heat, however, is diverted to fuel the life-support systems on the shuttle."

"Okay. Got it. What's broken?"

"As I said, the converter. It is busted, kaput. We can still fly, but, of course, gamma photons will flood the ship."

"Can we fix it?"

"No. We need to replace coils made of a tridium, molecular composite. That process is not known in this time, and tridium itself will not be discovered for another 150 years."

Frustrated, she exhaled, then calmly set the epoxy back in its locker. If she had to breech a den of jackals to kill one particular jackal, she could figure that problem. Nobody was better at it than her. And she could fix a damn radio and motorcycle, but this scientific stuff? This level of complex engineering? It was light years beyond her.

"Do you have any good news for me?" she asked.

"Good news? Ah, you are asking me a rhetorical question."

"Not really. There must be something we can do. For instance, can we jury-rig a lead plate to block the gamma photons coming into the life support system?"

"Yes, that is entirely possible."

Her face lit up. "Damn it, Matt. Why in the hell didn't you say so right off? All we have to worry about now is somehow replacing the directional gyro, and then we can fly."

"That is true."

Something stuck in the back of her mind, something she did not want to retrieve. But, the thought came. "Shit, shit, shit."

"You understand now," Matt said.

"Yes, the gamma rays."

"As I told you, they will be funneled into the air as exhaust. They, of course, are deadly to life."

She slammed the flat of her hand into the wall. She hated herself for even asking. "How many people will die?"

"Too many variables to come up with a valid conclusion."

"Estimate, goddamn it."

"Estimate millions."

CHAPTER TWENTY-ONE: LITTLE CAESAR

September 25, 1927, Chicago

On Sunday morning, Sorrentino accompanied Al Capone, his wife Mae, and their nine-year-old boy, Sonny, to church, along with ten of Capone's soldiers for protection. After saying amen and crossing themselves, they piled into several Model As and in a long motorcade returned to the Metropole Hotel, where the overlord of the Chicago Outfit maintained two floors for himself, his family, and his closest confidants.

Even on Sunday, politicians and cops crowded the lobby. They'd come for their payoffs. The Chicago Outfit couldn't operate so profitably without cops and pols, including the city mayor, on the take.

Sorrentino smiled to himself. Al never missed a trick. Most of them were already drinking at the open bar along with several high-class whores. He joined Capone and his family in the elevator and rode up to the fourth floor where they lived in five spacious rooms.

After kissing his wife on the cheek and ruffling Sonny's hair, Capone led Sorrentino down to room 406, a corner turret he used as an office. Unlike Capone's luxurious living quarters, this room was spartan with just a desk, filing cabinets, and two cushioned chairs.

"I want you to see something," Capone said. He stepped to the four windows curving around the turret and thrust his hands against the glass. "I like to stand here and look at my city. A king surveying his kingdom."

Sorrentino stood beside him. Below, a stiff, cold wind blew loose newspapers down the street, and a few heavily bundled people scurried along the sidewalk.

"I love this city," Capone said, his arms spread wide at the window as if presenting the entire city to him. "Why's it got to be always so damn cold, Benny? You grew up here. Why the fuck? I'm going to move to Miami someday, I swear." He crossed himself.

Sorrentino chuckled. "You ever think two mugs like us would ever retire to ritzy Miami? Isn't that the tiger's spots?"

Capone laughed, then stared at him with a sad half-smile. "Yeah. Lot of workdays before you and me sit on that beach." He paused, eyed him. "You fucked up, Benny."

"The police commissioner? Had to be done. Little Augie had Rooney in his pocket, and that got the police goons hounding us. Rooney couldn't be bought. He thought Little Augie was going to come out on top. His mistake."

"Okay, okay. Police commissioners, they can be your best friend if you pay them enough, but let them think they can take you on, they can be real pains in the ass."

Capone strode to his desk, picked up a Chicago newspaper, and shoved it at Sorrentino. A photo of a gangland slaying was splotched across the front. It was of Los Angeles, the one in which Jimmy Pelosi gunned down the grocer.

Annoyed, Sorrentino only glanced at it and tossed it back on the desk. "What the hell is the Tribune doing? Chicago doesn't have enough shootings of its own?"

"That ain't the fucking point, Benny." Capone held up a finger as if lecturing. "This shit ain't good. John Q. Public don't give a shit if gangster mugs like you and me gets bumped off, but he don't like one of his own getting clipped. That's when he wants the police to do something about it. You already got that police commissioner shot to hell. Now, this."

"I got it under control," Sorrentino said flatly. "The Colombini brothers are not going to just hand over their operation to us. I need to spill some blood."

Capone jabbed a finger at him. "Kill the stupid fucks all you want, but not some dumb clerk. You been there what, three, four months? Why ain't the Colombinis dead yet?"

"They're not stupid, Al. They got a lot of men protecting them. Fats goes nowhere without ten men, and Little Augie stays in his house with his family and never leaves. He's got at least fifteen men guarding the place. Half of LAPD's on his payroll. I'll get them, Al."

Capone eased the tension in his bulldog shoulders. "Yeah, yeah, I know. I ain't worried about you. My old boss Big Jim Colosimo was a smart man. He once told me war's a bitch. Nobody makes any money during war. He was right. You need to get this Colombini business done. That's all I'm saying. Just some friendly advice."

Sorrentino remembered Colosimo well. It was Sorrentino and Capone who shot Big Jim dead back in 1920. "I'll take care of it, Al."

Capone nodded. He took out a cigar and lit it, then pointed it at him. "Gambling, Benny. It goes with bootleg like a horse and buggy. That's where the big money is right now. That's where the high-class whores make the cash. You take all the sucker's money. The house wins even when the game is straight. That's the beauty of it." He took a drag on the cigar. "You got a place to open a club yet?"

Sorrentino sat on the arm of one of the chairs and nodded. "You know Pauline Windsor, the actress?"

"Yeah, sure. What about her?"

"She's got a place, a big place with a restaurant. It's just the ticket. The second floor, you could get a thousand people in it. The upper floors, prostitution and drugs. The perfect location. Near downtown but open fields all around so you can see the cops coming."

"Then what's the delay? You writing her a fucking poem? Get it done. We want to be up and running before the end of the year."

Sorrentino hadn't even mentioned the idea to Pauline yet, but Capone didn't need to know that. "We will be, Al. I'm working on the details right now with her. She's not eager to sell her place, but she will."

"She got family?" Capone asked.

"Yeah, two kids."

"No husband?"

"No. I think he's dead or something. She won't talk about him."

Capone nodded, a smile on his wet lips. His smile broadened. Sorrentino had seen that smile, the one when Al realized a deal had been completed in his favor. He patted Sorrentino on the cheek. "There you go, Benny. Them kids. That's what you call leverage. A dame's going to do anything to protect her kids. Even give you a blow job while you're fucking her over the restaurant. Then you'd remember it and get a hard-on every time you see one of her pictures. Wouldn't that be something? She's sure as hell going to give you her restaurant if she thinks her little kiddies are in danger."

"Yeah, Al."

Sorrentino hoped it wouldn't go that far. He liked Pauline. Hell, if he was being honest with himself, he'd say he was in love with her. He could see himself married to her. That would be the cat's meow as the Jazz people said.

Capone took the cigar out of his mouth and picked a bit of tobacco from his lip. His eyes black, he stared at Sorrentino. His voice hard. "I don't give a fuck how you do it, Benny. Just get that goddamn gambling operation up and moving, you hear?"

CHAPTER TWENTY-TWO: GUNFIGHT AT THE OK CORRAL

September 26, 1927, Los Angeles

Before leaving for work that morning, Lauren tucked the dead Glock 75 into a holster at the back of her trousers and threw on the leather flight jacket that Remy had given her. She spent the first two hours of work that morning on the phone with the city's top gossip columnists and fan magazine writers answering questions about Pauline's romance with the gangster Ben Sorrentino. She couldn't say she had no idea why the beautiful and smart actress was seeing such a ruthless bastard, so she threw out pablum to them: *they are just friends. Like so many people, he is a fan. She knows nothing about the gang war going on or Mr. Sorrentino's part in it, if any.*

She didn't believe any of it. Pauline was a fool to date that viper, but then Lauren wasn't her mama. The actress was an adult.

After the interviews, Lauren set out to find a gunsmith to fix her Glock.

First, she went in search of Remy. He was on the lot somewhere working on Global's new aerial epic. She found him in a corner of the canteen with three other members of the Black Cats, including Clyde Brady, the cherubic Tom Sawyer lookalike, going over plans for their stunt flying. They all stood for her when she approached. Quaint. Apparently, something men did in the 1920s, even for Mrs. Windsor.

Remy gave her a quizzical look as if to say *I never thought to see you again.* "It's wonderful to see you," he said. Clearly, a lie.

She got to the point. "I'm looking for a gunsmith. Can any of you help me?"

Be nicer. You sound like a non-sentient AI, Matt said, projecting an image of a sweet smiling Lauren into her head. *Smile at them. Blink your eyes at them. Exchange a pleasantry or two. In other words, act as if you're pleased to see them. That way they may help you.*

She noticed Remy scowling at her and thought maybe the damn appliance was right. "I'm sorry. It's been such a hectic day already." She kissed Remy's cheek. "I had such a wonderful time Saturday. You are quite the pilot in more ways than one."

Remy blushed while Brady and the other two men whooped. "I told you to watch out for him," Brady said.

She forced a look of helplessness. "My handgun is damaged. I'm desperate."

"Do you have this little pea shooter with you?" Brady asked. "Maybe we can help you."

She drew out the Glock and set it on the table. Eyebrows raised, the men whistled. One said, "I've never seen a handgun quite like that. Where'd you get it?"

"I had it made special."

They stared at her. She read in their eyes the questions: what kind of woman has a gun made special for her?

Remy lifted it, ran his hand over it. "Some piece you got here, Lauren. I don't know any gunsmiths, but there's an old-timer who hangs around the studios. He advises sometimes on cowboy flickers. He knows guns. Famous for it in fact. He might know of someone."

It was just past noon when Remy discovered from a friend that the old man was in the San Fernando Valley where Tom Mix was shooting his horse opera for Global. The old man and Mix were great friends it seemed.

Remy drove her out in his roadster, silent most of the way. It annoyed her. It was as if they were married and he'd caught her cheating on him. She did not feel obligated to fill the sound void and remained silent herself.

Just off a dirt road, Remy parked beside several cars and trucks. They hiked over to a group of men huddled together and busy doing nothing. Lauren assumed the director was the one with the megaphone.

They were all looking over a rail line that cut through the middle of dry, jagged hills. About sixty yards down the track a short train of seven cars sat waiting. An open flatbed truck with two cameras idled on a dirt road parallel to it. Several men stood around the cameras waiting. From what she'd learned in her time in Hollywood, they could be waiting for anything, from the sun to rise higher to the stunted scrub oak to grow another inch.

The director lifted his megaphone. "Are you ready yet?" he shouted to the truck.

Someone came back on his own megaphone. "Not yet. Tom says in two."

A small, potbellied man in a suit too big for him hurried over to Lauren and Remy. "I'm the assistant director. Can I help you?" He wore suspenders and a skimmer straw hat. "Are you from the studio? Is Mr. Zelinsky pulling us back in? Are you extras? We asked for more extras, but we need cowboys, not a pirate and a dame."

"We're looking for Wyatt Earp," Remy said.

The man looked confused. "Who?"

"Wyatt Earp. He's a friend of…"

"Oh, the old timer." He gestured toward a tall, white-haired man who had to be pushing eighty standing off from group, his hands in the pockets of his worn suit. He was thin, his shoulders bony under his dusty suit. He surely was not eating much. "I hope you've come to take the old coot off our hands. He thinks he's an advisor. Keeps telling us how it really was. Like he's an expert or something. If he wasn't Tom's friend, the director would kick his worthless ass back to Hollywood. What do you want with him?"

Easy. Your blood pressure is rising, Matt said. *May I suggest you calm down.*

For some reason, the assistant's attitude toward the old man made her furious. *I'm always calm.* But she wasn't. She was just always in control.

Lauren snapped at him, "What the fuck is it to you?"

"See here now," the man blustered.

At her outburst, shock imprinted on Remy's face. He looked from her to the assistant director. "He is an important man." Then to Lauren. "Let's go."

They went over to Earp. A young cowboy even taller than the old man joined him, eyeing them warily. Shaking Earp's hand, Remy said, "Wyatt, I'm Remy Garnett. I don't know if you remember me, but…"

"Sure, I remember you, Remy," Earp said. "I'm still not going up in one of those damn planes. I was born on the ground, and I think that's where I'll stay."

He had intense blue eyes that Lauren was sure saw everything. A phrase popular in her time was gunfighter's eyes. No one knew where it came from, but this old man had them.

Glancing her way, he smiled, "Who's this, Remy? I'm old, but not dead. I still appreciate a beautiful young woman."

Remy said, "This is Miss Lauren Ramirez."

"Nice to make your acquaintance, ma'am." He glanced at the tall cowboy. "This big lug is my good friend Duke Morrison. He's going to be a big movie star someday, at least that's what he tells me."

This is John Wayne, Matt said with excitement. *Before he became John Wayne.*

Am I supposed to know who that is? she asked.

You? No, you wouldn't know.

At being talked about by Earp, Morrison went red with embarrassment but said nothing.

"We're looking for an expert gunsmith," Remy said. "He has to be the best. Lauren needs work done on her firearm and special cartridges cast for it. I figured if anyone knew anything about guns and gunsmiths, it was you."

"It's a special gun," Lauren said, "so there's a hundred dollar finder's fee for taking us to a gunsmith."

Remy gave her a quick glance.

Earp looked skeptical. "That's awful generous, ma'am. I know how to shoot them, and I can fix them if they're not in too bad a way. That's about it. You have it with you?"

She drew it out of her pocket and handed it to him.

He whistled, holding it in his hand as if it were a breakable heirloom. She noticed Morrison's eyes widen with astonishment.

"This is some piece of shooting equipment, Miss Ramirez," Earp said. "I've never seen the like. Can you hit anything with it?"

"I can."

He eyed her a moment. "I bet you can." He handed it back. "Tell you what I'll do. I know a gunsmith. He's damn good. He's the grandson of someone I knew in Tombstone. Now, he might be able to fix it; he might not. If you don't mind waiting till the shoot is finished, I'll show you the way. Mix is a little crazy. I want to make sure he's all right."

That's when the train whistle blew, and the great engine began to move. They all watched as the truck picked up speed to keep pace with the train, the two cameramen cranking furiously.

The director shouted through the megaphone, "Action."

Assassin 13

What Lauren saw next was utter lunacy. Tom Mix appeared in one of the passenger car windows, his giant white hat firmly on his head, and scrambled into a sitting position on the sill. He glittered, wearing an elaborately embroidered black shirt with black pants stuffed into tall cowboy boots. As the train gained speed to fifteen or twenty miles an hour, Mix leapt from the window to the gravel path below, stumbling before regaining his balance and running alongside the train.

The Assassin 13, calm amid the greatest peril, gasped at what the cowboy star did next Mix crawled under the rolling train, slipped onto a girder just above the tracks between the wheels. If he slipped, he'd be crushed instantly.

Amazing, Matt said.

"Madness," Remy said.

"Almost as dangerous as flying burning airplanes for a living," she said.

"Cut," the director called. "Great work, Tom."

The train rolled to a stop, and Mix clamored out from under it. Everyone including Lauren clapped. The actor took off the big hat, sweeping it down in a flamboyant bow.

This decade is madness, Matt, sheer madness, she said.

But not the dark, nuthouse madness of our time, he said.

Nuthouse. Good word. No, not that kind of madness, she agreed.

Forty minutes later, Remy, Lauren, and Wyatt arrived in Chinatown. The gunsmith shop was on the corner of Marchessault and Los Angeles Streets in the Old Plaza, a small place with a cloth awning among a long row of dingy businesses and homes. The plaza was not paved. Chinese in traditional clothes crowded the vegetable wagons and other shops. The gunsmith had a row of potted plants and flowers on a balcony above the door.

Written by hand on the door in big white letters was the name Quang Gu Kee in English along with Chinese lettering. A bell rang when Lauren, Remy, and Wyatt entered. The dim room was lit by two muted lamps hanging from the ceiling, except at the back where a funnel of bright lamplight shone on a Chinese man at a small table. He was bent over a vise that held a pistol. He wore black trousers and a Chinese jacket with a gold embroidered collar.

As they approached, he looked up irritably, then broke into a broad grin at seeing Wyatt. He rose, came quickly around the workbench, and extended his hand to the much taller, older man.

"Wyatt, my old friend, you have not come to see me in such a long time," the Chinese man said in perfect English.

"Sorry, Kiki, I don't get around as much as I used to. Too rheumy."

After chatting another minute or two, Wyatt introduced Remy and Lauren and explained their purpose in coming. She drew out the Glock 75 from the back of her waistband, removed the magazine, and handed the weapon to him. His only reaction was to look from it to her, then back at the gun. "It won't shoot. It was in an intense fire."

He studied it for several more seconds, then tried to break it down, but couldn't. She took it from him and quickly broke it into its parts. He studied them for just a second or two. "I see the problem right now. The firing pin is twisted. Just slightly but enough, but that would do it."

"Can you fix it?" she asked.

"Yes. It should be easy enough," he said. "For a friend of Wyatt, I will have it ready tomorrow." He looked up at her. "Where does this weapon come from?"

"Specially made." She handed him the magazine. "Also, I need more rounds. This is my last magazine."

He took a cartridge out and held it up, its silvery glow reflecting in the light. "Tell me about this."

"High velocity exploding rounds. Can you do that?"

"No. High velocity, sure. But exploding rounds? I've never heard of such a thing."

They did not appear in films till 2061, Matt said. *Likely he will have no capacity to make them.*

"Then hollow point rounds?"

He nodded. "Yes, I can do that. Come back tomorrow."

The next morning before 7:00am, Quang Gu Kee called Lauren. "I'm sorry, Miss Ramirez. I was unable to fix your gun. I was sure the problem was just the firing pin, but when I replaced it, it still wouldn't fire. I'm at a loss. I don't know…"

"I'll be right there."

She rode the motorcycle down to Chinatown. Quang was in the back of his shop, working on another weapon under his spotlight. When she pushed through the beaded curtain, he rose and picked up her Glock off the side table.

"Again, I am sorry…," he began.

"Do you have a range here?"

"A test range out back, but…" He didn't finish, just shrugged and led her out into a small enclosure of stone walls some 60 by 20 feet. A paper bull's eye target had been nailed up on a post at one end. Lauren took the gun to the other end and with her left hand fired four hollow point shots in rapid succession. All four hit the small bull's eye.

Quang's eyebrows raised. "You're not exactly a pots and pans sort of girl, are you?"

Ignoring the comment, she said. "I'll need about 200 hollow point rounds."

"I have them." He extended his hand for the gun. "May I?"

"Sure." She handed it to him.

He aimed but the weapon wouldn't fire. She took it back and put two more rounds into the bull's eye. When he looked at her, his face asked the question.

She pointed to the handle. "You see this chip? It recognizes me. It will not allow anyone else to fire the weapon."

He said nothing for several seconds. "I know just about everything there is to know about gun science, the mechanical and industrial art of it, what all the gun manufacturers in the world are doing. This science doesn't exist."

Lauren gave a half smile. "Not yet, it doesn't."

CHAPTER TWENTY-THREE: THE GODS OF OLYMPUS

October 12, 1927, Los Angeles County

For several weeks, Lauren had gone out to the crash site whenever she could get away, sometimes spending much of the night. She studied the ship's schematics as presented to her by Matt, investigated every inch of the spacecraft, and sat hours on the hillside just pondering the question of the directional gyroscope and the gamma ray converter. No answers came.

She was able to repair the microscopic fractures in the shuttle with the molecular epoxy and overhaul every bit of damage in the ship. But the two unsolvables remained unsolved.

On a Wednesday in mid-October, she planned to spend the weekend out at the shuttle to put the finishing touches on her repair work, but Pauline insisted she attend her dinner party with some of Hollywood's elite invited. Indeed, someone very special was going to be there, and Lauren was needed. Pauline would not say who the very special person was.

So, instead of hours in her cargo pants and sleeveless t-shirt out at the shuttle, she found herself in her bedroom at the house, slipping into a black evening dress with a five inch satin fringe at the hem. It was a flapper dress, reaching to the knees, but she decided to wear it anyway, if only just to annoy Mrs. Windsor.

***

Not more than a mile away at a suite in the Roosevelt Hotel, Ben Sorrentino stood in front of the mirror in his living room, smoothing the lapels of his tux. Jimmy, Arty, and two other men sat in the room while four others patrolled the halls outside. Never liking to stay in one place too long, Benny moved out of the Fountain Avenue place for the time being and taken the entire fifth floor of the Roosevelt Hotel for two weeks.

"Finally. It's about time that actress finally invited you to her house," Arty said.

Sorrentino gave an easy chuckle. "No. She has no idea I'm going to show up."

A couple of the men laughed.

She had always insisted he could not come to her house. She'd apologized but explained that bringing a man with ties to the underworld to her home, especially during a gang war would put her children in danger.

That would not do. He needed to move the romance forward. Yeah, she slept with him, but he needed her to fall in love with him. She didn't have to marry him, though that would be the best outcome, but she did have to be under his control. To take possession of her property, it was this or the more drastic step Capone had suggested. Go after her kids.

He'd learned about the dinner party from the newspapers. Tired of waiting for her, he'd decided to push things. He'd decided to surprise her and her fancy friends tonight. Either she accepted him then or she didn't. If she didn't, it would be Capone's way.

Adjusting his silk tie, he thought he looked like a movie producer or a big-time actor. The phone rang and he quickly picked it up. The desk clerk said, "Mr. Sorrentino, your limousine is here."

***

At Pauline's home, the guests began arriving at eight. A school night, the children were allowed to greet them and then were sent off to bed. Pauline kept her parties small, just eight people tonight. The first to arrive were the so-called Boy Wonder, Irving Thalberg, just twenty-seven and head of production at MGM, and his wife Norma Shearer, MGM's biggest star. It was only nine days after their "wedding of the year." Both were so busy they had taken little time for a honeymoon.

The other Hollywood couple was the married Queen and King of the Movies, Mary Pickford and Douglas Fairbanks. Pickford was an intense, smart woman, a far cry from the adolescent girl in danger she often played onscreen, even well into her thirties. There was no one Pauline respected more than Little Mary, who had been the driving force behind the creation of United Artist and the single biggest movie star on the planet for the last twenty years.

Fairbanks was the swashbuckling hero of *The Mark of Zorro*, *Robin Hood*, and *The Thief of Bagdad*. His flamboyant onscreen persona reflected the man offscreen.

His digital brain sparking with excitement, Matt pestered Lauren to ask them questions, but she ignored him. She wondered why she, just an employee, was even asked to come. Like Rolly and Emmy, she would rather be persona non-grata.

She suspected it was because Pauline wanted Remy here and thought they were an item. She didn't know how disastrous their date had been. As a famous war hero and stunt pilot, Remy was a popular guest at many Hollywood parties, just like Pauline's boyfriend, the gangster Ben Sorrentino. Famous "real people" like them were great catches for any hostess. Lauren knew the actress had not even considered inviting Sorrentino. Though naively not thinking him the monster the papers portrayed him to be, she still didn't want a mobster near Rolly and Emmy. Dating Ben Sorrentino was one thing, inviting Benny the Bug to your Hollywood party quite another.

It's the mores, Matt said.

What?

The mores of the times. 1927. It is a time when many people, especially women, feel liberated, their inhibitions lifted, but still the hangover from Victorian and Puritan restrictions on sex still affect people like Pauline. She is embarrassed by her runaway carnal desires every time she sees Mr. Bug. That's my analysis.

Sure. Just what I need. Crock psycho crap from an appliance.

An AI. I am an AI.

An appliance.

Remy was different He and Pauline had known each other for many years. He had been best friends with her husband.

When he arrived, he and Lauren gave awkward clipped greetings, followed by silence, then she excused herself to help in the kitchen.

As if you can cook, Matt said. *For a woman of crazy physical courage, you are a social coward. Do something. I know you like him. Be a little bolder and tell him.*

When dinner was served, Russell and Mrs. Windsor sat at the table, dazzled by the starlight coming from Pickford, Fairbanks, and Shearer. Pauline's family loved rubbing elbows with the Hollywood elite, and she wouldn't think of excluding them.

Remy and Lauren sat next to each other. In a lull in the conversation, he leaned closer to her and asked, "Do you mind me being here?"

"No, of course not. Why should I?"

"When I dropped you off after our date, you ran from me like I was chasing you with an ax."

She smiled at him. "You and an ax wouldn't bother me."

"Did something bother you?"

"Yes, but not you, Remy. At least, not in a bad way. I like you." She kissed his cheek.

Good, Matt said.

Rubbed his cheek in mock ecstasy. "Are you going to tell me what did bother you?"

"No."

"Hey, lovebirds," Douglas Fairbanks called to them from the other end of the dining room table. "If anyone should be kissing at the table, it's the honeymoon couple."

People laughed, and Norma Shearer said, "I'll second that."

Thalberg picked up her hand and kissed it.

"That's fine for now," Shearer said. "A preview of coming attractions."

During dinner, everyone talked movies. There was no other topic. Over cucumber soup; lobster soufflés, potatoes and gravy, fresh vegetables, and Crystal champagne, the industry was taken apart and put back together again. Each of the movie people were involved in productions, so Thalberg asked Pauline how the filming of *Romeo and Juliet* was going.

She held up both hands, fingers crossed. "So far, so good."

Thalberg smiled. "Zelinsky being an ass?"

Pauline shrugged. "As always. He wants more sword fighting, less schmaltz." She looked at Fairbanks. "He says watch *The Thief of Bagdad*. Make that movie."

Fairbanks laughed. "Only one thief and Romeo ain't it."

"You should come to work for us at United Artist," Mary said. "We'd love to have you, and you'd produce your own films."

"I'm thinking hard about it," Pauline answered. "We'll see."

Thalberg asked Remy where the aerial scenes of Global's war epic were being filmed.

"At the Griffith Park aerodrome," Remy answered.

He told about a scene in which he had to crash land a plane into bales of hay. He made his struggle with the plane's stick seem like masturbation. Everyone laughed.

"I want to become a pilot," Fairbanks said.

"No, you don't," Mary said.

Mrs. Windsor gave a stifled giggle. "Oh, you two," she said, waving her hand.

Thalberg turned to Pauline. "I understand you forced von Richter out of the director's chair. These German directors all want to wait till the grass grows the right height before they shoot a scene. They cost the studios a fortune. But sometimes they can be brilliant."

"I just finished a film with Lubitsch," Norma Shearer said. "He was a charm."

Thalberg nodded. "I've had my problems with Stroheim but he can produce quality films that do box office."

Each of the actors had stories both complementary and horrible about working with the so-called German genius directors, mentioning von Richter, Lubitsch, Murnau, von Stroheim, who was from Austria, and several others. Lauren could see how much Pauline was enjoying herself. She had not seen her so relaxed before. Always there had been a sheen of pressure, of responsibilities bordering on burdens, all of which she handled well and with humor. But now her guard was down. No pressure, no responsibilities, just great, good friends. Though Lauren understood it, the sheer power of friendship was still a bit of a revelation to her.

Pauline was asking Fairbanks about the picture he was working on called *The Gaucho,* and he said it would be different from his usual swashbuckling efforts. "Darker, more sex." He grinned with a devilish roll of the eyes. "Mary's in it."

"It's an unbilled part," Pickford said. "I play the Virgin Mary."

Fairbanks chortled. "We know that's not true."

Everyone laughed; the loudest laugh exploded inside Lauren's head as Matt roared, projecting an image of a stick figure bent double and slapping his knees.

"Are you all right?" Remy asked.

"Fine, just a little headache. It will go away and be good. Won't it?"

Remy seemed confused. He had no idea what to reply.

Matt said, *If you say so.*

***

With the limo heading up a curving road, the driver glanced back over his shoulder at Sorrentino and his three bodyguards. "All right, Mr. Sorrentino, we're in the Hollywood Hills. Where we going?"

"Pauline Windsor's home. Do you know her?"

"Sure. She's a pip. I should have guessed, but I don't know where she lives."

Sorrentino gave him the address.

***

Over flutes of champagne at the dinner party, everyone was giving rapt attention to Remy, who was talking about his meeting with Charles Lindbergh, the American hero of the hour and year for his solo flight across the Atlantic in May. Lindbergh had come to Los Angeles a week or so before the Thalberg-Shearer wedding for a parade and reception in the LA Colosseum.

A flight across the Atlantic, Matt said derisively *I've seen many, many movies about Lucky Lindy, but still cannot understand it. I could fly around the globe hundreds of times before he reached Paris.*

Flying in a cardboard airplane that far is a little harder.

In the pause that followed the story, Fairbanks looked at Pauline. "I was down in Tijuana at the races with Chaplin a couple months ago when who should we run in to but Ben

Sorrentino. He was excited about this colt of his running in one of the races. We talked a bit. He seemed a good enough chap. What's he really like?"

"Doug," Mary chastised. "That's personal."

The room fell silent. Everyone turned to Pauline, anticipating embarrassment, denial, anger.

Hesitating only a moment, she smiled. "Doug, he's a real peach."

For some reason, they all chuckled at that, more in relief than humor.

"Hey! A party," came a voice from the dining entrance. "Well, folks, the life of the party is here."

Every person turned to look at the speaker. It was Ben Sorrentino. Hollywood actors appreciated an entrance, and they applauded. All except Pauline.

She stood and faced him, her fist clenching. With a clear struggle, she forced herself to relax. There was little she could do. "Ben, what a surprise. I'm afraid you've missed dinner but you're in time for the champagne."

Russell hurried out and brought in another chair.

"Here, sit next to me, old boy," Fairbanks said to him, and Ben did.

Every eye fixed on Pauline, she lifted her champagne. "Well," she said. "No one ever said I gave dull dinner parties. To the guest of the hour, Ben Sorrentino."

Everyone laughed with relief and drank, everyone but Mrs. Windsor and Lauren.

CHAPTER TWENTY-FOUR: A DAY AT THE RACES

October 15, 1927, Los Angeles and Tijuana

On Saturday morning, Sorrentino turned his Chrysler Imperial up Pauline's driveway to pick her up for a day-long outing to the Jockey Club in Tijuana. His horse, Top Outfit, was running in the sixth race.

Pauline had been upset with Ben for crashing her party Wednesday night but told him no harm done. He had charmed all the movie gods and goddesses that night, and Thalberg even offered him a position at MGM as a producer, but Ben declined saying, "The film industry can only handle one boy wonder at a time."

But she needed to tell him today that he must not come uninvited again. She will not put her children in any danger. She just had to find the right time for it. When Sorrentino stopped at the head of the driveway at 8:00am Pauline asked Lauren to tell him she was still putting on her face, and it would be another five minutes.

Lauren had met Sorrentino in person only on Wednesday night and then they hadn't been directly introduced. She'd seen pictures of him before, the first in Chicago in the winter of 2127, hanging on the wall in Robert Kaseem's apartment. Now, in 1927, Sorrentino sat in his black Chrysler Imperial, tapping his fingers impatiently on the steering wheel as she approached.

Hollywood's most lasting mystery, Matt said, *is how countless starlets, beautiful young women, famous actresses, all smart women, are attracted to bad men: the wolves at the door, drunks, conmen, sociopaths, and mobsters. Someone like this man.*

Rolling the window down, the mobster stared with a lopsided grin at her. She was sure that grin was supposed to make women's knees grow weak. It made Lauren's heart cold

She had never seen anyone project such malevolence before. It swathed him like a dirty overcoat. No emotion touched his pale blue eyes, dead as a squashed bug, Benny the Bug. A massive hate swelled inside her, prodding her. She wanted to drive her fist into that mouth, wipe the smirk away.

"Pauline's not ready yet," she said. "She'll be another five minutes."

He focused on her for several seconds, as if she'd spoken a foreign language. Wednesday night, Lauren had only felt his menace. Now was different. As an assassin, she dealt with fear, others and her own. Fear could be a powerful ally if controlled, which she'd had to learn as a child. Now she felt dread in every molecule of her body. Dread and hate. Good.

"I heard you, toots," he said.

"*Toots*. You're such a fucking charmer."

He blinked, then stared hard at her. "You got a mouth on you for a dame."

That's when Pauline rushed out of the house, jumped in the car, and kissed his cheek. On his face, he sported an appealing smile meant no doubt to melt the female heart. It seemed to do that with Pauline. To Lauren, she only saw the smile of a lizard.

***

Many people Pauline knew from Hollywood were in attendance at the track in Tijuana, John Barrymore, Wallace Beery, Buster Keaton, Al Jolson, Charlie Chaplin, and more. Many of the stars stopped by their box to say hello, but she suspected more were interested in meeting the famous gangster. Yes, she knew he was a gangster, but that didn't make him Al Capone.

Charlie Chaplin wormed his way into a seat with them since they were closer to the track. Throughout the first five races, Sorrentino made several friendly wagers with a man in a nearby box Pauline knew as the baseball player Babe Ruth, fresh off his World Series win with the Yankees.

"You got a bet with that mug on the next race?" Chaplin asked Sorrentino in his British accent.

Sorrentino made a face as if he'd caught a bad smell. "No, save your money. Nags all of them. They're all headed for the soap factory."

It was the sixth race that Top Outfit ran. Sorrentino was more nervous than Pauline had ever seen him. No one, not even Ruth, wanted to bet against him, seemingly fearing winning the bet more than losing it.

Top Outfit broke slowly from the gate but closed to second and pulled away down the stretch. Pauline jumped up and down with excitement and Sorrentino hugged her, grinning as if he'd just won the Irish Derby.

"That's one hell of a horse," Babe Ruth called to him, and others joined in the congratulations. Beaming with pride, he accepted all of them. Pauline held to his arm, smiling as if it had been her horse that had won.

***

Since Lauren had no Saturday night plans, Pauline asked her to watch the children. Mrs. Windsor was playing canasta with her lady friends, and Russell was tied up at the UCLA lab till late. Lauren had hoped Remy would ask her out, but he hadn't. That relationship was dead.

In the evening, the two children sat at the kitchen table, glasses of milk in front of them, waiting as she prepared their dinner of peanut butter and jelly sandwiches.

Peanut butter and jelly sandwiches. Oh, if only I were human, Matt said.

You're not. She held up a sandwich. *Here's protein, grain, and fruit. The perfect meal.*

When done, she placed the sandwiches on the table in front of the children and kept one for herself. As she ate, she stared at the two pint-sized people. Miniature adults. Clattering. Chattering. Emmy was winning that battle, out talking even Rolly. There was a proscription constantly uttered by Mrs. Windsor that seemed to do little good. *Children should be seen and not heard.* They talked on anyway, but Lauren had tuned them out.

She was in a foul mood. It had been weeks since she pinpointed the exact problems in bringing the shuttle back to being space-worthy, but she'd made exactly zero progress in solving them. It annoyed her whenever she began to follow a track of thinking, and the children would break in with an inane question. Settle some dumb argument like which was smarter, an ant or a bee. Do bees really have knees? They were an annoyance tag team.

For some inexplicable reason, since the day she arrived in 1927, the two children had desperately wanted her to be their friend; more than a friend, almost a second mother. She could not fathom why they showed such bad judgement. Her like a second mother? She sure as hell was not that. It had to stop. It was time to set them straight.

Good, Matt said. *Certainly, it is bad enough for them to have a violent assassin as a babysitter, but heaven forbid, as a role model.*

That was not exactly the support she was looking for. A germ of an idea about gamma rays began forming in her mind when Emmy asked her what the tallest skyscraper in New York was, had she ever gone to the top of it, and did it really scrape the sky.

"Eat your food, kid," Lauren said to her brusquely.

Don't be such a gorgon, Matt said. *Answer the poor girl. The Empire State Building is the tallest.*

Absently, she said to Emmy, "The Empire State Building is the tallest, and I've never been to the top, and it does not scrape the sky."

Finishing his sandwich, Rolly licked his fingers. "Don't you mean the Paramount Building is tallest? Mom says she met Adolph Zukor there enough times to know. At least, she says he never stops telling people that the Paramount Building is the tallest building in New York. I've never heard of that other one. Is it new?"

Matt? Lauren said.

I thought that correct. It seems it is not, the AI answered. *I'm not omniscient, after all. I only know what I'm programmed to know, or what I've seen in movies. Most of the early movies of New York have the Empire State Building as the tallest structure, but I have no data when it was actually built.*

"Oh, yeah, that's right," Lauren said. "You're right. I've never been in that one either."

Just after seven in the evening, she sat in the living room flipping the pages of a book Pauline had given her to determine if it could be made into a good film. That task fell to Matt. He read; she flipped. Instead of focusing on the novel, she tried to pick up the thread of an idea about gamma rays. *They are expelled by the Positron Reactor. Sent to the converter, which is now broken. Then ejected out of the ship. The converter...the converter...*

Rolly sat across the room in a large armchair that made him so tiny as to appear Lilliputian. Last check, Emmy was in her bedroom playing with dolls inside her teepee. Rolly kept trying to engage Lauren in conversation and breaking the train of her thought every time.

The converter...the converter...

His legs bouncing on the chair with uncontrolled energy, he said, "I don't like mom out with some mobster guy, but I guess if it has to be someone, then he seems all right. I saw the movie *Underworld* with Emmy and Uncle Russell about rival gangsters named Bull Weed and Buck Mulligan. The names Bull and Buck are okay, don't you think? Mom's boyfriend is Benny the Bug. I could think of a lot better nickname than that."

The converter…the converter. It took gamma rays and turned them into harmless…

"Are you really from New York?" Rolly persisted. "You don't seem to know a lot about it."

"No, I'm not from New York."

"Can you really read that fast? You're just flipping through the pages."

"Yes."

"If you're not from New York, where are you from?"

"I've work to do, Rolly."

"Is that a place?"

Your blood pressure is rising, Matt said. *Suggest breathing exercise. You can start by…*

Matt, shut up.

She didn't answer Rolly, but he wasn't discouraged. "The paper says Benny the Bug's a real gangster. Maybe someday he'll be my new daddy. Mom likes him. I can tell. I wish he would change his name first though. He might be an all right daddy. No kids would mess with me with Benny the Bug as my daddy."

He didn't see the darkening look in Lauren's eyes. The spark that set her off was the boy's acceptance of Sorrentino as something of a 'good guy.'

Rolly went on, oblivious. "Why call yourself Benny the Bug? I can help him with that. Benny the Boxer. Benny the Bear. Benny the I swear." He exhaled a loud lip fart and rolled his eyes. "This movie I told you about, *Underworld,* showed gangsters are really good guys at heart. Like Benny the Bug maybe. I guess just like anybody else when you come right down to it. He's really a good guy at heart."

At these last words, her temper exploded. She turned on the boy. "That's bullshit, kid, utter bullshit." He flinched. Her words shot at Rolly like they came from a machine gun. "No goddamn gangster, no goddamn warlord, no goddamn clan leader has a heart of gold. They kill without mercy, kid. They kill people like you, like Emmy, like your mom. Benny the Bug is the worst of them. Don't be stupid. Your mom is dating a savage killer. Make no damn mistake about it."

Her words slammed Rolly back against the chair. In shock, he let out a whimper. Mouth agape, he blinked back tears, but the tears came anyway.

Despicable, Lauren, Matt said. *How could you?*

Lauren was stunned to see how she had hurt him. The ice around her heart cracked like a spider web. In an instant, she rushed over to him and knelt in front of the chair. "Oh, God, Rolly, I'm sorry," she pleaded. "I'm so sorry. I don't know what's wrong with me."

Afraid of her, he curled up into a ball. How could she possibly hurt this boy like that? What kind of monster was she?

"I didn't mean to make you cry," she pleaded. "I wasn't angry with you. Please, believe me. I would never hurt you in any way, and I will never, ever let anyone else hurt you. The world can be a bad place; that's all. Please, Rolly, I'm sorry. I can be such a shit sometimes."

Out the corner of his eye, he peered at her, still frightened but a little mollified. Immediately, she scooped him up in her arms and held him, wondering at the same time what was happening to her, but letting it play out. Finally, he stopped crying, and she handed him a handkerchief. He sat back in the chair and blew his nose, then tried to give it back.

She held up her hand. "It's got snot all over it now."

He laughed, and after a moment said, "Can I show you something? Please."

"Sure."

By the hand, he led her to his bedroom, and there showed her all his models, the flying saucers and spaceships dangling on wires. A small, blocky gray robot stood by the wall.

For Lauren, the models hung a foot below eye level. She read the names, the USS Bar of Soap, the USS Baby Ruth, USS Coffee Pot, and finally, the USS Quercus Dumosa. Holding that one, she looked at Rolly questioningly. "What's that mean?"

"It means the USS Scrub Oak," he said.

He went on to talk excitedly in his stream of consciousness rambling on 'scientifiction,' stories detailing space flight, galactic empires, alien invasions, robots, and one about a police force called the Interstellar Patrol. She finally realized he meant science fiction. He reached up on his tiptoes and spun a flying saucer. "I did them all myself," he said. "Uncle Russell helped me hang them, but I made them all. What do you think?"

"Excellent work, Rolly. They look like the real thing."

He beamed. "Really? I want to make them better. Do you have any suggestions?"

She lifted the saucer to show the underside. "Well, add a rotating ring almost the size of the plate. That would represent electromagnetic energy that generates an anti-gravitational field. Once you have that, escaping earth's gravity is as easy as stepping onto a curb."

He grinned, pleased. "Yeah. That would be the bee's knees."

CHAPTER TWENTY-FIVE: DOWN TO THE SEA IN SHIPS

October 15, 1927, Palos Verdes Peninsula

On a high bluff overlooking the ocean, Pauline Windsor and Ben Sorrentino leaned back against the hood of his Chrysler Imperial with its winged gold ornament, drinking champagne from expensive wine glasses. They were celebrating Top Outfit's victory earlier that day.

From below, she heard the roar of the surf. The moon hung large above the horizon. A ship was anchored about four miles off shore, its dark shape and lights visible. As an actress skilled at making herself beautiful, she knew the moon's glow on her blond hair would shine like a halo. She would be irresistible, and, indeed, he was watching her. Was he in love with her? Perhaps. Was she in love with him? Perhaps. He was the most exciting man she'd ever met. That was certain.

So, that made what she had to tell him even harder. He must not just show up at her house again. It was not him but his profession. She had no choice.

She was a little fearful about bringing it up. She put it off for now.

She sighed and breathed in the fresh ocean sent. Here she was high on a bluff with a gangster she knew she would be having sex with before the night was over. When she'd first come to Hollywood as a teenager with Max Sennett and hit it big, she became known as the Wild Girl, drinking heavily, screwing any man who gave her a tingle under the skin and staying out all night.

Then, in the early 1920s, several big stars OD'd, Fatty Arbuckle was put on trial for rape and manslaughter, and director William Desmond Taylor was murdered. America was shocked by the level of immorality, and the nascent movie industry staggered to its knees. There was no place in it for a Wild Girl. She either had to reform or give up her career. She reformed and took on a new persona in her movies, America's Heroine. Also at that time, she got married and had children. That tended to tamp down the wildness.

Now, with Sorrentino, she was reliving some of that excitement. It made her feel guilty but alive, like she hadn't felt for years.

"Those are my boats," Sorrentino said proudly, pointing to the cove below. "They're bringing in hooch from that freighter out there, my Mexican supplier."

Instead of hiding the fact, he was showing her where a fleet of boats scudded into one of the coves with a small beach. "That's Portuguese Bend down there where they're unloading. It's good cause it's got a dirt road I can get trucks to the water on. The freighters come up from Mexico or down from Canada and anchor off shore in international waters like that one."

She saw far below crates being loaded from several small boats onto three trucks. "I disguise them as farm trucks." He chuckled. "They even got some stacks of smelly cabbages in the back."

He was proud of how he did this and she said, "Imaginative, Benny."

"Yeah, I think so, too. We even got tunnels into San Pedro we use sometimes."

She glanced at him. "Then you are not just a small-time bootlegger. You are a mobster."

"I don't like that word," he said. "I prefer businessman. That's all I do, Pauline. Just a little business. Someone's got to provide the hooch. You knew I was in the rackets."

"How much does a businessman make a year bringing in illegal liquor?" she asked.

He laughed. "A woman with a head on her shoulders. I like that. You can make a lot if you own the wholesale, distribution, and sales."

"Do you have that?"

"No, but I'm working on it. Wholesale is in Mexico and Canada. Gambling is the selling part. Put the bootlegging in with the gambling and you got a fortune. Like a Rockefeller. And nobody gets hurt."

It was something she wanted to hear, that he was not really part of all this mob war going on in Los Angeles, but she was not sure that she believed it completely. She pushed it to the back of her mind.

"You're certainly not just another pretty face, Ben," she said.

He leaned in closer to her, his physical presence overwhelming sexually and menacingly. "Your restaurant, that entire building, would be the ideal place to set up a bigtime gambling operation. You could still run the restaurant while upstairs we could work the gambling. Sell it to me, Pauline. We can make millions."

Pauline's face drained. "That's hardly the most romantic thing I've ever heard."

He shrugged. "Sorry. I always got business on my mind."

"To answer you, I don't want to sell the restaurant or the building."

"I'll pay you a top price."

"Let's not talk business anymore," she said.

He inhaled and forced a smile. "Sure. Sure." But he was upset.

Since he'd broken the romantic mood, she knew there would be no better time than now to bring up Wednesday night. She made her voice confident, assured, though she felt neither. "Ben, I truly enjoy your company. I want to be with you as much as I can. But I can't have a repeat of Wednesday night. You've told me what you do. You can't tell me there's no danger in it. I worry about you. I don't want to worry about my children, too."

His jaw clenched. He turned away from her and leaned against the car, folding his arms over his chest. Before he turned away, she saw pure rage flare through his eyes. She flinched and stepped back. But it was gone in an instant. She was not sure it had even been there. No, she decided. She must have imagined it.

He sighed. "Look, Pauline, I can't help what people say about me or what the newspapers write. Hell, every time a boy falls off a tricycle, someone stubs a toe, every time there's a murder, the police and the newspapers holler 'get Sorrentino.' I've been accused of every death except the casualty list of the Great War. I have spent the best years of my life giving people the lighter pleasures. That's all. Helping them have a good time, and all I get is abuse."

"That's not all there is to it though, Ben. We both know it."

His face took on a look of deep sincerity. "It is. I swear. I have nothing to do with that terrible gangland war. I promise you. Look, I'm no saint. You knew that when we met. I run a little bootleg, take bets on the dog races, loan money, and keep my head down. If that's too much for you to handle, doll face, too much for your conscious, then I'm sorry. Ben Sorrentino is the sweetest guy you ever saw with kids. I know that worries you. Those kids are precious to me. Nothing will ever happen to yours because of Ben Sorrentino. I promise."

He reached for the Champagne in the ice bucket, refilled his glass and topped off hers. "Let's finish this."

It was not easy getting back into the romantic mood, but after a few moments she slid next to him, felt his warmth next to her. She watched as the boats traveled back out toward the freighter, then held up her glass to him. "Congratulations on today. I don't know much about horse racing, but Top Outfit looked like a first-class thoroughbred. Cheers."

He winked at her. The spark was back in his eyes. They clinked glasses and drank. "We're also celebrating our anniversary," he said. "It's been two months since I met you, doll."

He took her hand and kissed it. She felt his soft lips tingling her knuckles and saw his penis pushing hard against his trousers. "I've lived in this town ten years," she said softly, "and this is the first time I've been up here," she said. "I am happy here with you, Ben. I want to freeze this moment forever."

"Yeah, me too."

With his hand in hers, she lifted his arm and placed it around her shoulders, then guided his hand down to her breast and began massaging herself with it. Her breathing grew more rapid.

"Let's go to my hotel," Ben said.

Her voice hoarse, she said, "No, it's a pleasant night. This is a beautiful spot. And you surely must have a blanket in your car trunk."

He grinned. "That's my girl."

CHAPTER TWENTY-SIX: SCHOOL DAYS

October 19, 1927, Briar Summit Mountain

For the last few mornings, Lauren had noticed a parked car out on the street, two men inside. It was always the same car but not always the same men. They did not seem to follow anyone but just sat watching the house. She planned to let it go on for a couple more days so she could see who manned the vehicle.

Then things changed. On the morning Pauline was to shoot the balcony scene in *Romeo and Juliet*, Lauren had to drive Rolly and Emmy to school. Clarence Martin planned to film the scene first thing, so Pauline had an early call for makeup and costumes. She could not drive the children, and the chauffeur, who seldom worked anyway, had quit two weeks earlier.

Cars were not motorcycles. Lauren had barely managed to drive Remy's Peugeot, and the LaSalle was unfamiliar. Of course, she'd seen Pauline, Remy and even the chauffeur a couple times drive cars, but that didn't change the fact she was a terrible at it. In her century, you just told the car where you wanted to go and it went.

Holding their bookbags and lunch pails, Rolly and Emmy sat on the passenger side of the LaSalle, waiting patiently for Lauren to start the car. Gripping the steering wheel, she stared at the dashboard. Together, she and Matt had flown a craft through space, but driving a damn car was nearly beyond their capabilities.

Show a little ingenuity, old girl. Buck up. You can do it. Matt spoke in a haughty British accent. God knows what movie actor he was parodying.

Are you sure you can't drive this thing?

I have no manuals on piloting an ancient automobile. Besides, you know how. You just don't want to look like a complete fool in front of the children.

She got the car started and lurched out of the garage as Rolly and Emmy exchanged glances. Coasting to the end of the driveway, she engaged the clutch in first and turned onto the road, still lurching forward.

That's when she noticed in the rearview mirror the car following them. It had not done that before.

As the LaSalle progressed jerkily forward, the glossy black Model-A Ford that had been sitting on the street for days pulled out and followed. Her nanobots took in the information from forty yards, processed it into closeup detail and disseminated it instantly through her brain. She saw the men clearly.

The driver was short and stocky with sallow skin. Near his left eye, he had a splotch of burned flesh that gave him a sinister appearance. The other man, also short, was younger with a bulldog face and short cropped blond hair. His shoulders stretched the gray suit he wore. The stare in his eyes was blank as if nothing ever registered behind them.

Lauren knew them, at least the type. Gangsters were pretty much the same in the 22nd century as they were in the 20th. And they were following her. Not her but more likely the children. Perhaps, they thought she was Pauline, despite her long black hair. Almost certainly, this had something to do with Pauline's relationship with Sorrentino. The only question was who these men worked for, Sorrentino or the Colombini brothers.

Set high up in the Hollywood Hills, Briar Summit Private School was an imposing building, a Loire-style chateau that stood alone on the hillside. The closest other structure was a small diner that sat a half mile down Briar Summit Road on

Mulholland Drive. The chateau had once been owned by a railroad magnate and later, when he died, sold and converted into the most prestigious educational institution for young children in Los Angeles.

Lauren pulled in line behind several cars, all of them expensive, dropping off children at the front door. Many had bodyguards. Of course, children of the rich were targets. Pauline was rich. Her children should be as well.

When her turn came, the children jumped out of the car.

"Hey, you two," she called after them.

They turned to face her.

"Be bad today. Get in some trouble," she said.

For a moment, they stared at her confused, then laughed and ran into the school.

Ignoring honking car horns, Lauren did a U-turn and headed back down the road, searching for the car that had followed them. About two hundred yards from the school, it was parked along the side of the road. If they didn't follow her, she would have to turn around and brace them right there. She carried her Glock hidden in a back holster underneath the flight jacket she wore most of the time these days.

When she passed the Model-A, it turned to follow her.

Matt, it's time to find out who these people are.

I was afraid you would say that.

Abruptly, Lauren sped ahead a couple hundred yards. Around a curve, she spun a U-turn that caused Matt to issue a stream of math gibberish, and drove back up the hill on the wrong side of the road. The other car appeared around the curve and squealed as the driver hit the brakes and swerved off the road into a ditch. The men struck the roof and the windshield.

You're mad, you're absolutely mad, Matt screamed. *You could have killed us both.*

Shut up, now, she ordered.

Lauren parked beside them and rushed over. The driver's nose was bleeding. The other man, the muscular one, was groggy and seemed not to know where he was. The windshield in front of him was shattered.

The driver side window was cracked and she busted it open with her fist. "Who are you working for?"

The driver blinked, looking up at her. "What?"

She reached in, grasped his broken nose and twisted. She heard bone cracking. He screamed and his body shook with a paroxysm. "Who sent you? Next time it'll be your eyes."

Before he could respond, a car pulled up behind them. It was a chauffeur driving a model of car she didn't recognize.

A Packard, Matt said.

When another car stopped, the chauffeur of the first got out.

A Lincoln, Matt said. *The second car is a Lincoln.*

Christ, Matt, who cares?

"What happened here?" the first chauffeur demanded. He was a short, pudgy man in a gray uniform and black cap.

Lauren shrugged. "I don't know. He ran off the road." She noticed a police car a hundred yards back up the road approaching. She smiled at the chauffeur. "I'm so glad you stopped. I'll leave this in your capable hands. I'm late for work."

Calmly, she went to her car and drove away.

***

The balcony scene went smoothly. As the cameras rolled, Clarence Martin talked the two actors through a range of emotions building an arc from infatuation to love. To capture the quality of Shakespeare's language in this all-important scene, it would take more dialogue title cards than usual. Yet, as the director, Martin said the great genius of silent film was language conveyed by the actors visually, and in this case, that meant Pauline.

They did one take. Martin liked it and he called, "Print it." They did one more to be safe.

Lauren found Pauline in the costume department, the costume fitter, a thin woman in her forties, changing her into a nightdress for the marriage bed scene.

"You won't believe what just happened," Pauline said cheerfully. Her smile faded when she saw Lauren's face. "Oh, God, now what?"

Lauren explained what happened, then added, "They'd been watching the house for days. They are watching you or the children."

Pauline sat down on a nearby chair, her face deadly pale. "But this is 1927. It's not the Dark Ages."

The costume fitter spoke up, "I read in the newspapers that children of rich parents like yourself are being kidnapped at an astonishing rate. It's become big business in California." She picked up a newspaper off a stand with thread and needles and handed it to Pauline. "Another poor child was taken in San Francisco just the other day. A newspaper publisher's son."

Pauline glanced at the article. Her hand went to her throat. She looked up at Lauren. "I'll cancel the rest of today's shoot. Zelinsky will be apoplectic but it's my money funding the film now. I should contact the police?"

"No police," Lauren said. "I'll take care of it."

Lauren knew the pool of men from which she wanted to hire body guards and knew the man who could get them for her. With the help of the studio operator, she located Remy at the Griffith Park aerodrome, and explained what she needed. He told her he knew just the people for the job.

That afternoon, when Pauline and Lauren returned from picking up the children, he was waiting with two men. Both had army Colt 45s strapped to their waists. Remy introduced them as. "This is Captain Clyde Brady, Pauline. You've met him before at an airshow."

"Of course."

"He flew with me in the Lafayette Escadrille and the 1st Aero Squadron. And this is Corporal Tommy Corcoran of the fighting 69th Infantry Regiment."

Corcoran was a small, feisty man seemingly unable to remain still. He had a thin black mustache and hair slicked down with pomade.

When Pauline smiled at Brady, he visibly wilted, much like a school boy with a crush. This was not the first time a man looked at her in that way. It had happened since she was a child, instant infatuation, lust, or adoration. She could not tell which this was, but she had too much on her mind to give it much thought now.

Remy said to Rolly and Emmy, "They will be going to school with you for a while."

"They look too old for school," Emmy said.

The men laughed, and for the first time all afternoon, Pauline relaxed and smiled. "They're just going to help get you to school and back."

Rolly was fascinated by the guns they wore. Lauren sensed he knew why they were there, but didn't seem troubled by it.

That evening, after the children and Mrs. Windsor had gone to bed, Pauline decided to call Sorrentino to satisfy herself that it was not his men following the children. She called a number, identified herself, and said she needed to speak with Ben. Five minutes later the phone rang.

She answered it and went straight to the point. "Ben, some hoodlums followed my children to school this morning. They weren't your men, were they?"

"No, Pauline. Why would I do that? God, I hope they're all right."

"Yes, they're fine. I was sure it wasn't you, but I had to check. You might have thought I need protection."

"Now, I think you might. I can send some men over." He seemed to wince as if someone had punched him.

"No, please don't."

As she listened for several more seconds, she slumped down into a chair and hung up.

Lauren sat across the room. "What is it?"

Pauline's hands trembled. "Benny's been shot. He says he's all right, thank God."

That's nothing to thank God for, she said to Matt.

"He wants to meet me at Café Windsor tomorrow. He says it's important." Pauline frowned. "I want you to come with me. He always has those Pelosi brothers lurking around him. They scare me."

You like the idea of meeting the Pelosi brothers, Matt said disapprovingly.

I do. Lauren said to Pauline, "I'd love to."

CHAPTER TWENTY-SEVEN: EVERYBODY COMES TO PAULINE'S

October 20, 1927, Los Angeles

Two or three eateries served as the favorite noontime places for the movie elite. One of these was Pauline's Café Windsor on Oakwood Avenue, a large four-story stucco structure with Mediterranean arches and a red tile roof, conspicuous amid open fields. The third and fourth floors were rented out as office space to law firms, architects, and accountants. The second floor was a vast, vacant storage area. The first floor housed the popular restaurant.

The Café Windsor was packed. Noisy with the clink of dinnerware and constant chatter. As usual, Pauline sat at a raised circular booth in the center of the room like a queen holding court amid producers, directors, and other actors, all of whom paid homage to her. Often playing a role, she shot back raunchy rejoinders to other actors, maintaining a remnant of her once Wild Girl image.

She whispered to Lauren, "*Palace of Fallen Angels* opens in a couple weeks. If it sinks, they'll pounce on me like rabid dogs."

A waiter hurried over to them, Pauline greeted him warmly, and he took their order; two Caesar salads.

Every time they had eaten lunch at the restaurant, Lauren noticed a very obese fellow of about forty sitting in a corner booth near the toilets, and he was there again today. As if he had leprosy, no one spoke to him. Few even looked at him. Occasionally, a waiter brought him a phone as if he were receiving an important call, but Lauren soon figured out he was paying the waiter and speaking to dead air loudly about upcoming films of his that didn't exist.

"Who's that?" Lauren asked Pauline.

Pauline looked over. "Oh, that's Fatty. Very sad. That could have been me. I was just as wild. He and Mabel were the cat's meow in their day." She glanced at Lauren's blank face. "You know. Fatty Arbuckle."

"Sure."

Glancing at her wristwatch, Pauline said with a worried expression, "He's late."

If we're lucky, he's late because he's dead, Lauren said.

Not a high probability, Matt said.

A dark-haired woman entered accompanied by her assistant and sat in the next table, a prestigious spot so near Pauline. She waved. "Pauline, dearest, you're wearing white. Surely, you cannot think you're fooling anyone."

That's Gloria Swanson, Matt said excitedly. *The real Gloria Swanson!*

So?

Tilting her head askance, Pauline answered, "Gloria, sweet, out stalking sailors again?"

Gloria Swanson flashed her eyes, put a hand to her chest in a mock gasp. "Only if I could find one. Please tell me where you keep them all."

There was no animosity in the exchange. Pauline said, "Join us."

"Can't. Meeting my prince," Swanson said and moved on.

Pauline whispered to Lauren. "Prince, my ass. A penniless Marquis, for God's sake. One would think she married the King of England or Charles Lindbergh to hear her talk."

Look, look over there, Matt screeched in Lauren's head. *Clara Bow! The one with the red hair. Turn your head so I can get a good look.*

Behave. You're worse than Rolly or Emmy.

"Are you all right?" Pauline asked. "You have such a fierce scowl on your face."

"This is my smiling face."

"You've got a little bit of work to do on it." Pauline smiled. She seemed to want to say something else but hesitated. Then, she said, "You know, I've never really had a female friend before. I always seemed to get along with them. But never as close friends. Now, you, Lauren. I am grateful for your friendship. I just wanted to say that to you." There was not a hint of embarrassment in being so forthcoming.

Lauren was taken by surprise. Not knowing how to respond, she gave a half-smile. "So, I'm your best woman friend ever?"

Pauline returned the smile. "Well, I guess so. Since you're my only female friend."

That's when Sorrentino arrived. The clinking of silverware stilled, and the room fell silent. Everyone craned their necks to see the famous gangster. Among a crowd that made a living on their entrances, he topped them all, walking in as if he owned the place. Looking like a movie star, he wore a stylish fedora, a pin-striped suit, and glossy spats. His left arm was in a sling and the suit coat was draped over it.

A malignant aura surrounded him that only Lauren could see. The Pelosi brothers flanked him like two cobras.

When he walks, he brings menace like the night, Matt said quoting some long forgotten future movie.

Leaning down, Sorrentino kissed Pauline quickly on the lips. "Hey, doll."

Doll? That's a bit cliché, isn't it? Matt said. *Is he going to stick a grapefruit in her face now?*

Focused on the gangsters, she didn't answer.

Pauline's eyes lit up, then worry crossed her face. "Ben, are you all right?"

He waved her concern away, "Hardly more than a scratch. I'm fine." He glanced at Lauren with raised eyebrows. A dark look came into his eyes. "I remember you, toots."

"Ben, this is Lauren Ramirez. She manages my business affairs. She was at the dinner party."

"Yeah, good to see you again." Sorrentino reached for Lauren's hand, but she kept both under the tablet. Frowning, he locked eyes on her. "Business manager? Then you're just the person should be here with what I got for Pauline. Miss Ramirez, or is it Mrs.?"

"Benny the Bug," Lauren said. "How did you get a name like Benny the Bug?"

He stiffened. His features grew dark.

Pauline glared at her. The room had been silently watching. Now, tension floated through like static electricity among gasoline barrels.

Lauren's hand went theatrically to her chest in a picture of innocence. "I hope I didn't offend you, Mr. Sorrentino. I meant no harm. Benny the Bug? That is your name, isn't it?"

"What the hell's with you?" His voice, low and cold, sounded like gravel being stomped. He glanced about the room, everyone watching him. He leaned closer to her. "Don't call me that again, sister, you hear?"

"Sure, Benny, sure."

After a couple breaths, he forced a smile and turned back to Pauline. He held out his hand. "How about you showing me around the place, doll?"

She gestured at the large room. "This is pretty much it, Ben. There are two other rooms but they're closed down right now."

His eyes flashed with just an instant fury, gone quickly. "I want to see the upstairs. You got an upstairs, don't you? Show me."

She shrugged. "All right. It's just used for storage right now, and the other floors are rented office space, but if you want to see them, follow me."

Taking his hand, she led him back through the kitchen doors.

When they were gone, the room snapped into excited chatter. The Pelosi brothers sat down across from Lauren. A waiter rushed up to them with menus, but Jimmy waved him away.

For nearly a full minute, they stared at her, and she stared back. Both wore suits, too small in the shoulders for them. Jimmy had a splotch of blood on his white shirt Lauren felt sure wasn't his. The only physical difference between them was the flatbed nose, broken too many times, on one's ugly face. That would be Arty.

She forced a pleasant smile. "So, you're the Pelosi brothers."

Arty brightened. "You heard of us?" He looked to his brother. "How about that, Jimmy? She knows us. We're famous."

She read somewhere that Arty wore razors on the tips of his shoes and carried spiked brass knuckles for fights. Jimmy had the reputation of being a deadly assassin.

Just like you, Matt said.

Not like me.

Jimmy watched her without emotion.

"I'm Arty. That's Jimmy," Arty said and leaned forward eagerly. "What did you hear about us?"

"I heard you're first class fuck-ups. You made the hit on Colombini's men that left a grocer lying in the street. Sloppy work. Purely amateur hour. Too much collateral damage and that brings on too many optics."

Arty frowned, confused. "Too many what?"

Jimmy glared at her. "The dumb Palooka should have got out of the fucking way."

Lauren gave an exaggerated shrug. "You know, I'm sort of a fortune-teller. I can see the future. I see that someday you boys are going to be the prey, not the predator. Someone will hunt you down and delete your fucking files permanently."

Flustered, Arty turned to his brother. "What's she talking about, Jimmy? Why are we going to pray?"

Jimmy did not take his eyes from her. "She ain't talking about nothing. She's just a stupid bitch." He addressed her. "You want to fuck, toots? We got a little time."

Lauren smiled. "Sure. Oh, you mean with you. No, that would be like fucking a cockroach. No fun in that."

She thought she saw the hint of a smile on Jimmy's face, but couldn't be sure. If it had come and gone, there had been no humor in it.

I have no data on either of them and your neurobots do not have any reference to them. Matt said. *You can't possibly know what is in their future.*

Oh, I think I do.

At the back of the kitchen, Pauline led Sorrentino up narrow stairs, swaying her ass in a snug print dress she knew drove men to a volcanic lust. Glancing over her shoulder at him, she saw Ben's eyes lift from her bottom, and crinkle in a smile. He took two giant strides up behind her and rubbed her ass with his good hand.

She giggled. "Stop that."

On the second floor, she turned on the lights. Along the walls near the stairs stood boxes of food stuff, napkins, coffee, tea. and bottles of Coca-Cola in wooden crates. She faced him. She threw her arms around his neck and kissed him.

Stepping back, she started to undress. Thousands of tiny goose bumps erupted on her skin. Her breathing grew more rapid. Slowly, she did a strip tease for him till she stood naked in front of him. She saw his erection pushing against his pants. He cupped her breasts and her nipples sprang up. He lifted her in his good arm and carried her to the old couch on the near wall. With her help, he rapidly took off his clothes, and they made love.

Afterward, she lay back putting on a smile despite her disappointment. There had been sparks, but too few. The lovemaking had come and gone like the San Francisco express train. But she told herself she was satisfied. She had the most desirable man in a city of desirable men.

He sat up, one of her naked legs draped across his lap and spent penis. His face took on the expression of someone who had just had a great revelation. "I love the way the movie business does it all from beginning to end."

She felt deflated. That was not what she expected. "You do?" she said flatly.

"Yeah, the studio makes the movie, distributes the movie, and shows the movie in their own theaters. Like I told you, you get all the money. You don't have to share it with no one else. I love that. That's what I want to do with bootleg."

"Bootleg?"

"Yeah."

Struggling with one arm, he stood up and dressed. She let him struggle. She gathered up her clothes and went to the second-floor bathroom to clean up. He didn't notice she was upset.

A few minutes later, dressed, Pauline returned. Sorrentino was moving slowly around the room, studying it as if an interior decorator, even the dust and cobwebs. She knew what he was doing and she didn't like it. She wasn't a prude about his gambling palace, but she didn't want it to be her place. She did not want to be involved in any part of his business, small time hood as he claimed to be or not.

"I'm not selling, Ben," she said flatly.

He turned to face her, his jaw tightening. "Did I say anything? Did I make you an offer? Seems a damn waste to leave a big room like this doing nothing when I know exactly what use to put it to. This building is perfect for me. I could use all four floors. The location. It couldn't be better. I could take in ten million a year. That's a lot of clams. I'll pay top dollar for this place, doll. Name your price."

Just standing there, he was imposing, exuding threat even without intending to. She steeled herself. "No, Ben, I don't want to sell. Lauren has been telling me to sell my stocks and buy real estate. She says the movie business will grow and so the value of good property around Los Angeles will grow. She's been right so far. The value of my new properties is rising."

"You sound like a damn accountant, not a woman," he said, his temper flaring. "And you're taking business advice from a broad? This Ramirez woman is the one stopping you from selling to me?"

"I make my own decisions."

"Good. Then, here's what I got in mind."

She stood firm. "No. I told you I do not want to sell this place. Can we just drop it?"

His face pinched into a terrible mask of anger and she backed up from him. Quickly, he held up his hand. "I understand, doll," he managed to say. "Everything's jake. It's okay."

For the first time, she saw in his face an eagerness for violence that startled her, but then it was gone. It left her queasy and uneasy.

Five minutes later, leaving Café Windsor with the Pelosi brothers, Sorrentino said, "I want that broad dealt with. She has become a problem."

Arty asked, "Pauline Windsor?"

"No, goddammit. The Ramirez woman. The dark-haired broad. Get it done."

CHAPTER TWENTY-EIGHT: FLAGPOLE SITTING

October 24, 1927, Downtown Los Angeles

Two blocks from Global Studio's main gate, Remy and Lauren sat on their favorite park bench where they had been coming for the last two weeks to share lunch when he wasn't on location flying. *Baby steps in their romance,* Matt called it. *Or two porcupines attempting to mate.*

The sun bore down hot like it had measurable weight. Sweat glistened on Remy's neck where a portion of his burn-torn skin poked above the collar. She felt an unusual twinge of pity for him. Pity of any kind was foreign to her, and he'd hate it if he thought her pitying him. He was talking about the aerial scenes he'd orchestrated for Global's epic of World War I pilots.

The irony struck her that they were talking about flying machines made out of sticks and paper while her state-of-the-art 22nd century spacecraft sat grounded in a dusty ravine not thirty miles away.

His flies, yours doesn't, Matt pointed out.

No thanks to you.

The appliance had been correct in one matter. After checking with several UCLA science profs and with Lockheed engineers, she could find no one who could help her, or even understand her. Everyone thought she was crazy. She spent most of her hours studying the schematics of the shuttle Matt provided in her head, especially on the two affected systems. She knew the damn ship nearly as well as he did. It was like analyzing each blade of grass on the prairie, hoping to find the one that can provide an answer.

Matt insisted daily that it was hopeless till finally she threatened to scrub him from her neurobots if he didn't *shut the fuck up!* She did not deal in hope or hopelessness. She dealt in persistence, and that cost her nothing.

When Remy paused, lost in his thoughts, she glanced at the crowd gathered under the flagpole in the center of the park. A man sat atop it on a platform, and he had been there nearly a week. She couldn't figure out why the hell he did that, and Matt could give no insight. He'd never seen a movie about flagpole sitters. Whatever the reason, people came every day to this park to watch him just sit atop his pole.

She asked Matt, *How does he pee?*

How would I know? I've never had to pee. Arty Pelosi is in the crowd.

I see him.

"I began flying when I was eighteen," Remy said, suddenly changing the conversation to something more personal. He looked down at his hands, the good one grasping the withered one. "It was not exactly a great time for me."

Lauren had been thinking about the schematics of the shuttle. It was nearly the end of October, the next appearance of the anomaly was in less than a week, and she was no closer to answers. And Matt no help.

Not true, Matt said. *I cannot conjure solutions where none exists. Perhaps you are unaware we are in the early 20th century?*

She realized a response was expected. "I've heard Montana is pretty country," she offered lamely, hiding her growing frustration.

"It is God's country," He gave a rueful smile then went deep within himself. "At first, it was just to get away from a bad situation."

It was as if he had flipped a switch in her. Moments ago, she was in a soft, safe comfortable land with him, then the next, the ground underneath her vanished. People seemed desperate to share their deepest emotions, and that's what Remy was doing. She hated it. This sharing and revealing of yourself.

She realized the purpose was to strengthen a bond with another person, but that was exactly what she didn't want. She did not want to take on anyone else's pain. She had enough of her own. It was dangerous territory. Pauline put her on the edge of it. Rolly and Emmy had created a breach in her and both poured through to capture her heart. Now, she was responsible for them. Their happiness was her happiness; their pain was her pain.

Now, Remy. What was with this guy? Wasn't sex good enough for him?

He was talking about how he had grown up on a ranch, telling her things he wanted her to know about himself, the deeper relationship thing. "I fell in love with flying. Montana from high in the air can do that. You can't imagine the endless sky and endless breadth of land from five thousand feet in the air."

He fell into a long silence again. He was leaving space in his recitation so she could jump in and say something about herself. She never did. They'd had this talk before. Despite how much she liked him, she wanted no more depth to their relationship than they already had.

"I was to marry my high school sweetheart Alecia," he finally said. She picked up anguish in Remy's voice. "Then just before graduation she and Danny Wheeler came to see me. He was my best friend. We had all grown up together. They told me they had fallen in love and *they* were going to get married." Grimacing at the memory, he hesitated a long minute before continuing. "They even asked me to come to the damn wedding. Can you believe that?"

"I'm sorry, Remy. She's probably fat and worn out with eight kids now."

He smiled. "Three kids. I actually went by Danny and her place last year..."

"Look," Lauren cried, pointing down to a shiny object in the grass near her boots. "A silver dollar." She picked it up and inspected it. "I've never seen one of these. Wow, it's dated 1927. Well, I guess it would be."

Excitedly, she showed it to him, and he stared back as if she'd slapped him in the face. Abruptly, he stood and walked away.

She blinked, saying aloud, "What's wrong with him?"

You are hopeless, Matt said. *The man truly cares about you. He's in love with you though it is beyond this poor AI's ability to understand why. And you, you treat him as if he's nothing more than an annoying mosquito.*

I treat him fine.

He was sharing with you moments of great consequence to him, and you, to use the vernacular, dismissed him. That's not what people do who care about each other.

How the hell would you know? You're a fucking appliance.

Apparently, I've had more experience with emotions than you. I can help you. Tell him this: even if love is full of thorns, I'd still embrace it, for I know that in between those thorns there is a rose worth all the pain." After a pause, he added, That's from *Sleeping Beauty, the cartoon version.*

She shook her head. *I should have left you in the ship's main frame.*

You must at least apologize. Hurry before he has left.

I can't. Remy wants part of my soul, and I don't want to give it to him, she said. *You're a damn AI. You can't know. What's done is done.*

Part of your soul? Matt said. *Oh, aren't we dramatic. It's called being human, Lauren. You don't know how to do that. That is the nature of your challenge. On a mission, you have pretended romantic love and caring, which is amazing since you never experienced them in life. Now, you must access those true feelings. They are inside you.*

Across the park, she saw Remy striding toward his car. She hadn't wanted to hurt him. She did like him, did care about him, but she could not afford another emotional entanglement. They always ended badly. When she returned to her own century, she would leave everyone here behind forever, and if the bonds to all these people grew stronger it would be crushing.

At least apologize, Matt said. *It doesn't mean you're getting married.*

Her stomach grew sour. True, she did not want to lose him. Being an ass had become a part of her personality. Suddenly, she bolted from the bench and sprinted across the grass, waving. He saw her but got in his car and pulled out into traffic. To cut him off, she hurried into a dense set of trees by Union Avenue.

Lost to sight, an odd thought struck her: in the 22nd century Los Angeles, trees existed only inside domes. Outside was cracked pavement with massive potholes, concrete walls, cramped and dirty apartments, vendors using squalid cubbyholes to sell an assortment of junk and questionable food, but no trees.

As she hurried, something in her antennae raised an alarm, and she slowed, her senses instantly hyper-alert.

Your heartbeat and blood pressure have risen, Matt said. *Is there a situation?*

Yes. Be quiet now, she said, and he obeyed.

Something had triggered her warning system. A movement, a sound. In the center of this mini-forest was a single orange tree from a bygone orchard. She and Remy and half the people working and living downtown picked fruit from it. As she approached, she saw Arty Pelosi leaning against it, his fedora pulled down low over his forehead. He was staring at her, smirking like a cat about to tease a mouse. He had a good smirk.

She should have been aware of his movement but had been too concerned about catching Remy. Entanglements.

She had the Glock hidden in her back holster, but didn't want to kill him. A dead body here might cause problems, especially since someone could easily remember seeing her. Approaching him, she spotted the glint of razor blades on the tips of his shoes and spiked brass knuckles on his right fist. He kept patting that fist.

"Remember me?" he said.

"No."

"Arty Pelosi?"

"Name means nothing to me."

He blinked, then gathered himself and said, "Don't be afraid."

"I'm not afraid."

"You should be, toots, but don't worry, I ain't here to hurt you, that is if you cooperate."

She cued herself: time to play the game. Trembling, she slid fear into her eyes and backed up a step.

Arty laughed out loud. "Yeah, sure, you're not afraid." He reached into the inside pocket of his suit coat and withdrew an envelope. "The boss don't like you getting in between him and his girlfriend. But he's got a good heart. He don't want you hurt if you cooperate. This here is a train ticket to San Francisco. Hookers make a lot of money there."

Her hand shot to her mouth in a gesture of fear she thought might be too over the top. "Do I have a choice?"

"Yeah," Arty said pleasantly. "You can get on the train or you can give me a blow job before you get on the train, but either way you get on the fucking train." He tapped his brass knuckles. "I'd hate to bust up that pretty mouth."

She'd had enough of him. She moved to within a couple feet. This surprised him. "I have a third choice," she said in a voice as cold as deep space.

He blinked. She drove a front kick into his chest with the kinetic power of a cannonball. She slammed him back against the orange tree. He struck his head against a knot and slumped to the ground, unconscious.

Lauren hurried through the trees to the street to see Remy's car two blocks farther down Union, turning into the Global Studio lot. Disappointed, she returned to a still unconscious Arty. She considered killing him. One less thug she would eventually have to deal with.

Don't do it, Matt said urgently. *Listen to your better angels.*
I have no better angels. But she couldn't risk it.

She slipped the brass knuckles off his hand and removed his razor blade shoes. He groaned, beginning to waken. Quickly, she pulled off his pants and his boxer shorts, then snatched up his handgun. She stood and looked down at his shriveled, micro-dick.

At that moment, Arty awoke and stared at her uncomprehendingly. She kicked him in his crotch, extracting a scream, then with the heal of her boot slammed his head back against the tree. He slumped, unconscious again, or maybe dead. She didn't care which.

Dumping the clothes in a trash can — she kept the brass knuckles — she rushed up to a policeman walking a beat on Union, a nightstick in his hand.

"Officer, officer," she pleaded in a shaky voice. "A naked man was chasing me in the park. By the orange tree. Quick! Hurry!"

Assassin 13

Blowing a whistle, he ran for the park. As she walked back to the studio, she assessed the situation. The threat had been directed at her, but the real target was Pauline. Sorrentino wanted a clear path to her. He would come after her.

Things are getting messy, she said to Matt.
Indeed.

CHAPTER TWENTY-NINE: FOOLISH WIVES

October 28, 1927, Beverly Hills

On Thursday night while Sorrentino was eating dinner at an Italian restaurant, an attempt was made again on his life. The story appeared on the front page of next day's newspaper.

Los Angeles Examiner:

The Chicago mobster Ben Sorrentino was wounded last night while eating at Moretti's Italian Restaurant on Highland Avenue in downtown Los Angeles, an establishment frequented by many big shots from the city government. As he dallied over ravioli and red wine, window glass exploded with a hail of bullets from multiple Tommy guns and shotguns peppering the screaming diners who dove for the floor.

Bullets struck like raindrops in a summer storm, shattering the dinnerware, tearing down Venetian landscape paintings and ripping apart the walls. Dashing to the window, Mr. Sorrentino fired back with a single revolver, but did little good. Five cars packed with thugs from presumably the Colombini mob stood just outside the restaurant, and the muzzles of several Thompsons flamed from the car windows. It was reported that Arty Pelosi, one of Mr. Sorrentino's henchmen, took the gang leader to the floor and covered his body, reflecting a level of bravery seldom seen among this class.

After nearly a minute of carnage, a single long blast of a car horn signaled the end to the terror as the automobiles drew away. A waiter and a female diner were killed and several people wounded, including Mr. Sorrentino himself, who sustained a superficial cut from exploding debris. It was the second time in recent days that the noted mobster had been injured from gang gunfire.

***

As evening twilight faded, Fats Colombini's sedan pulled to a stop at his brother's Beverly Hills mansion. Two bodyguards toting Thompsons strapped to their shoulders stepped down from the porch, and one of them opened the car door. Fats lifted his enormous girth out.

"Good evening, Mr. Colombini," the guard said.

Fats ignored him. He was still fuming from the embarrassing failure to kill Sorrentino at Moretti's. It was not his failure, but Augie thought so, and his brother called him here to berate him for it.

"Be patient, Fats," Little Augie Colombini said a few minutes later, in his infuriating soft-peddling way of chastising him, as if a priest chastising an errant parishioner.

A small, lean man, Augie had a narrow face, hook-nose, and a nearly bald head rimmed by gray hair. They looked nothing like each other.

They sat at the table in the elegant dining room, waiting for Augie's wife and children to join them for dinner. The table was set with a white tablecloth, crystal glasses and china and candelabras. *Just like the hoity-toity,* Fats thought.

"You're a hothead, kiddo," Little Augie went on. "We can't go charging into Sorrentino guns ablazing. He might have had forty men in that restaurant. We got to be smarter."

"Smart!" Fats snapped. "They kill five of our men, we kill ten of them. That's smart."

Augie leaned back in his chair and fixed his brother with a hard gaze. "There's a better way. Hit him where it will hurt the most. We kill a couple of his goons, and so what? He hires more or imports them from Chicago. There's always more foot soldiers, Fats."

"Then what?"

With a smug grin, Augie grabbed a biscuit and buttered it, but before he could explain his wife and two young children entered the room.

Fats eyes immediately fell on his brother's wife. In her mid-twenties, the woman was a looker, bobbed blond hair much like Pauline Windsor's, but much sexier. She wore a backless chemise dress cut daringly above the knees. Her legs, clothed in stockings, glimmered in the candlelight. Smoking a cigarette in a holder, she glided into the room like a movie star.

The two children, a boy and a girl aged four and six, ran to their father, hugged him, then took their seats at the table.

Elyse Colombini slid into her chair like a cat, giving Fats an intoxicating glimpse of her thigh garter. He couldn't take his eyes off her; he never could. She had a figure that stood men's peckers on end. It did his now, and she knew it. She never minded his longing gazes. Leaning down to adjust her stockings, she gave him a glimpse of bare breast. He swallowed hard and forced himself to stare down at his plate.

He loved the damn woman more than Augie did, way more. He desperately wanted to fuck her.

Dinner was an exquisite five-course meal catered by his favorite chef, Enrico Rossi, the owner of Donatella's restaurant on Sunset. It took an hour and a half to complete. When the meal was finished, Little Augie called Rossi and his two waiters out to the dining room. Patting his belly, he said to them, "You have outdone yourself, maestro. If this is my final night on earth, it was a wonderful last meal."

Two hours later, Augie paced alone in the muted lamplight of his office, excited he had finally come up with a strategy to bring down Sorrentino and his Chicago thugs. A brilliant plan, simple and easy to pull off. He wanted to lay it out to Fats, but Fats had gone right after dinner.

After helping Elyse put the children to bed, he came down here to flesh out the plan, wanting every detail right in his head. He would wipe out Sorrentino and end this damn profit-killing war.

He went to the bar, poured himself a brandy, and took a generous sip. It went down smooth. After years of one fight after another, he now enjoyed the good life for himself and his family. That bastard Sorrentino was trying to take it away from him. He would not allow it.

From outside, he heard a muffled sound like a dog's bark abruptly cut off. He went to the window and looked out but could see nothing in the darkness. He had five men patrolling the grounds. He saw none of them but that didn't mean anything. They could be anywhere on the property. Still, he felt a chill in his bones, the kind of thing he shouldn't ignore.

Footsteps came from behind and he swung around. He was surprised to see one of the waiters standing there in the middle of his office, smiling pleasantly as if expecting a tip. Blood spattered the white sleeve of his jacket. Little Augie recognized him. He was not a waiter at all, but Jimmy Pelosi, Sorrentino's enforcer.

"Have you forgotten something?" Augie said, pretending not to recognize him. It might give him time to get to the desk and his pistol.

Pelosi's smile spread into a hideously wide grin. From his white serving jacket, he drew out a gun with a silencer and fired. The world shut down for Little Augie Colombini.

At that moment, Elyse backed in through the door, holding two snifters of cognac in her hands. Stopping abruptly, she saw her husband lying on the floor and dropped the drinks.

She didn't scream. "Don't hurt my children."

"Sure, toots." Jimmy fired two bullets into her chest.

CHAPTER THIRTY: RECONCILIATION

October 29, 1927, Hollywood Hills

In the morning, as stars faded, Lauren ran the hills above the house as she did every day. To her, working her body was a religion. It had been since those early days training with her mother and father. Every moment she was not pushing herself to her limit was a lost opportunity. In the days after her arrival on planet Earth 1927, she had picked up her workout routine again. Lifting weights, executing her own devised kata, attempting to destroy an old punching bag hanging behind the garage, and running in the hills above the house. Between 5:30 to 6:30 each morning, she ran, building up to six miles.

This morning, her mind was drowning. Running helped ease the chaos in her head, allowing her to think. The most pressing problem was the shuttle. Today was the 29th and the anomaly, if it were still alive, would reappear in the form of its four torn-away strands sometime from tonight through the following night. And she had the ghost of an idea on how to repair the gamma ray converter.

Unfortunately, interfering with her ability to work out the idea was an onslaught of other concerns brought on by the re-emergence of so many damn emotions. Remy for one. She'd come to realize she'd been driving him away and didn't want to do that. She liked him and missed him when he was not around, even if for just a day. She didn't know what this meant, but it was infuriating.

She had been twisting her mind into fractured leaps of logic, at least according to Matt, on the problem of the shuttle. But also shifting to her concern over the gathering threats to Pauline and her family. Not surprising since the actress was dating a damn homicidal maniac warlord.

Pauline is naively oblivious to it all, Matt said.

But how can someone be so smart and so stupid at the same time?

The human condition. Your species is quite adept at it.

You know, you're really not much of a help with Pauline either.

Suddenly, she was drawn entirely out of her thoughts when she found Raider, the German Shepard, running beside her. She tried to shoo him away but he wouldn't go. He was an old, old dog, his muzzle practically white, and was not unable to run her six miles, stopping about a mile out and waiting for her return.

She scowled down at him. "I don't like dogs."

He seems to like you, Matt said. *That is puzzling.*

Just after dawn, he was running back with her when Remy appeared in the path ahead. The morning was hazy and fresh with soft shadows. Already catching his scent, Raider recognized him and did not signal an alarm.

"I needed to speak with you. It's driving me crazy," he said, coming up to her. "I have to be flying most of the day, and I couldn't leave things as they are. So here I am."

"So here you are."

Smooth, Matt said.

Shut up. Keep out of this.

Remy rubbed his bad arm. "I thought of a lot of things to say to you, but I guess it just comes down to how much I like you, how much I want to be with you if you'll let that happen."

She smiled, about to speak, when Raider shoved in between them and barked. That broke the tension between them and they laughed.

Remy ruffled his ears. "Hey, old boy. Good to see you, too." He glanced at Lauren. "Looks like you've made a friend."

She lifted a shoulder in a shrug. "He goes where he goes."

"Of course," Remy said with exaggerated emphasis. "Do you know about him? Raider?"

"No. Pauline said he was some sort of army dog in World War One, I mean the Great War. That's the war you were in, right?"

He looked at her curiously. "Right. That's the war I was in."

That had upset him somehow. Now what had she said?

They stepped onto the outcrop and looked down over the lights of Hollywood. Raider flopped down beside them with a grunt.

Remy said, "Your dog, or I should say the dog that is following you around, served in three offensives and fifteen battles of the war. He was a courier going from trench to trench and a scout often out in No Man's Land. That was the deadliest hell man ever created."

Despite not wanting to care, she did and looked down at the dog, noticing the white whiskers covering his muzzle. God, he was old. An unfamiliar feeling of tenderness spiked within her. From Brady and Corcoran, she knew of No Man's Land and trench warfare. "He lived through that?"

"Yes, he did, but barely. Wounded three times, he barely survived a mustard gas attack. He had as hard a time over there as any human. A lot of soldiers have problems when they come home from war. Raider was no different. He had shellshock. Still does."

Like you, she thought sadly. "How did he end up with Pauline?"

"He was her husband's dog."

That surprised her. She had heard nothing about Pauline's husband. Of course, she hadn't asked, but the actress had offered nothing, not one word, nor had Mrs. Windsor or Russell.

"His name was Martin Landry, and he was Raider's trainer. He snuck the dog home with him after the war. He went through everything Raider did. He had shellshock bad. Most days he wouldn't get out of bed. They were a sad pair, him and the dog. Then, he met Pauline and he seemed to be back to his old self. They helped each other escape the worst of themselves. She was known as the Wild Girl, on a track to overdosing or driving off a cliff. They fell in love, married, and had children."

"But they didn't live happily ever after." Emotion. Caring. Pain. She knew it was so.

Remy studied her. "No, not a happy ending. They had a few good years, but after Emmy was born, Marty went into a deep tailspin. No one can explain these things. He had everything a man could want. Then one day, he went upstairs and killed himself with his shotgun."

He paused for such a long time, then lowered his head and said in a soft, agonized whisper, "I was his friend. I should have seen it. I should have known."

Lauren leaned into him, turned his head toward her and gave him a light slap hard enough to sting. "Don't say that. It was not your fault. He was responsible for his own actions. You can't save the world, Remy."

After a moment, he nodded, then said, "It took Pauline a long time to come back, but finally she did. Raider didn't. For him, when Marty disappeared from his life, the heart and soul went out of him. Now, he seems to have found you."

"He hasn't found me. I told you that."

He held his hands up as if in surrender. "Sure." He reached his hand toward her forehead and traced his finger along a small, almost invisible scar. She felt her body heat rise. It didn't make sense. No man had ever made her tremble this way. Remy did. It made her feel unsafe.

"You're shivering," he said.

"I'm cold."

"Sure. That's it."

He placed his forehead against hers.

"What's the matter with you?" she said softly. "You can't still want to be around me?"

He smiled. "You're beautiful and unusual."

"You're such a sweet talker."

"And I'm persistent." His lips pressed against hers. A feeling of warmth filled her body and she wanted him to go on kissing her, but he pulled back. "You can't run from the world."

He spun about and strode back down the hill. When he was thirty yards away, she found a response and shouted, "Yes, I can."

Clever, Matt said.

Raider looked up at her as if asking what now. She sat down beside him and blankly stared at the lights of Hollywood flicking out. This was crazy. She had no love in her, but she did feel something for Remy. What it was, she couldn't say.

She could hear Raider's bones creaking as he dropped down beside her with a gruff sigh. After a moment, he nestled his head in her lap. Absently, she rubbed the back of his neck. "You, too? What am I going to do with you, dog?"

The odd thing was, as she sat there with Raider, the way to repair the gamma ray converter appeared whole and complete in her head.

CHAPTER THIRTY-ONE: ALIEN DYING

October 29, 1927, Santa Monica Mountains

The scientist who invented replicating nanobots and pumped them into Lauren's circulatory system told her genius was layer upon layer of failed efforts, along with a small spark of imagination, not that she saw herself as a genius. The hard work she could do, studying shuttle's schematics, understanding each system, each subsystem, each array. After a few weeks, a growing sense that she was close to the answer took hold. Treat it like an Op, she told herself. Take in all the information, think of and dismiss ways to proceed until the one that worked remained.

The night of October 29 she went out to the spacecraft to apply her ideas. She would have to be there before midnight, all through the twenty-four hours of the 30th and beyond. When the anomaly appeared didn't seem to be exact. After all, October 30th came and went at different times across the globe. Who knew what relationship any of that had to the anomaly returning. Certainly, Matt didn't.

I told you I wasn't omniscient, he said in a petulant tone. *The peculiar laws of physics that govern the anomaly are things with which I have no familiarity.*

She picked wildflowers and placed them on Sybil's grave, then as she waited sitting along the banks of the ravine, she reviewed her idea. The shuttle's varied and enormous infrared systems took gamma rays from the reactor and altered them to the harmless infrared frequency for a hundred different tasks. Her idea was to reroute all the gamma ray exhaust through the infrared systems, even if the systems had to run continuously. Harmful gamma rays would become harmless infrared radiation. At least, that was the plan.

Lauren was hesitant to begin the experiment, too afraid that this latest idea would fail like all the others. Even if she were right, she still couldn't fly. Finding a way around the loss of the ship's single directional gyroscope might be unsolvable like Matt said, but she would never admit that to herself. She would proceed as if it were not.

Then, finally, she exhaled and told herself it was time to fix the damn gamma ray problem. Once in the shuttle, she sent Matt into the computer to reroute the gamma photons through the infrared systems.

Within a second, Matt announced, "Reroute complete."

"Start engines," Lauren ordered

The engine roared to life, or it seemed to because the shuttle began to vibrate slightly. More accurately it hummed to life. She let it run for thirty seconds.

"Stop engines," she ordered and the shuttle came to rest. "Result? Any gamma rays escaping into the atmosphere?"

"No. Experiment successful," Matt said.

Lauren felt herself erupt with excitement as if all her neurobots were firing at once. "We did it. And you said it couldn't be done."

"You know, of course, if the shuttle becomes air born, which is still unlikely, and if we do manage to breech the anomaly and return to our century, you will be leaving Pauline in a precarious situation with that gangster Sorrentino."

"She's an adult. She chooses her own way."

"And the children?"

"Matt, shut up, before I decide to leave you in the mainframe."

As the hour passed midnight moving into October 30, Lauren sat on the side of the ravine tossing pebbles and watching the dark mass of the spacecraft. The Milky Way spread starkly across a moonless sky. She felt no satisfaction at having solved the gamma ray problem. It meant nothing if she couldn't find a replacement for her 22nd century gyroscope in 1927. The shuttle couldn't fly without it.

She was waiting for the strands to reappear, if the anomaly was still alive. The purpose now was for Matt to determine if it had enough life to return once more. In her gut, she expected it to be dead, having passed its last in some rotating time other than this one.

It was a little after 1:00am when the shuttle began to glow. Lauren returned to the craft so Matt could enter the computer again. The broken strands of the anomaly lasted for an hour and twenty-two minutes, then they left for another time, and the ravine went dark.

Matt returned to her head. *The VQ is 3.8. On September 25, the VQ had been 7.8, down more than 66% from its first appearance. Now, it's fallen a little more than 50%.*

It didn't need further explanation. The anomaly was near death. Her way back was vanishing.

CHAPTER THIRTY-TWO: MADNESS

November 2, 1927, Beverly Hills

Fats Colombini had gone mad. That was the conclusion of many of his men. He lashed out at them for seemingly no reason. The day after Little Augie's murder, he punched his girlfriend so savagely an ambulance had taken her to the hospital where she remained. Outside a restaurant, one poor zhlub asked him for an autograph, mistaking him for Fatty Arbuckle. Fats had always flown into a rage at that mistake. This time, white with fury, he drew his revolver and popped six bullets into him. His men hustled him into a car and away.

They knew the reason for his madness was not the murder of Little Augie but of Elyse. It was no secret the passion he had for his brother's wife. Now, any mention of Sorrentino's floozy Pauline Windsor sent him into a rage in which spittle flew, furniture was busted, and people within his vicinity were punched savagely. Indeed, madness. Yet, he paid such high wages with promises of a big cut in the profit when they ridded themselves of Sorrentino that most stayed on. They figured he'd calm down after a few days. He hadn't yet.

On Friday evening, after the funerals of Little Augie and Elyse, he returned to their house, now his. He'd shipped Little Augie's kids off to an aunt. He sent six men out to gun down every man at a known Sorrentino warehouse. "Don't come back till that bastard gets the message," he told them.

This was vendetta.

Sorrentino had killed the people he loved, and he would kill people Sorrentino loved. An eye for an eye. That meant that floozy actress. Rumor had it Sorrentino planned to marry the bitch. All he'll get now would be her damn corpse.

He called several men into his brother's old office, now his. Moving his massive girth in front of the desk, chain smoking cigarette after cigarette, he said, "We got to do something or people will not respect us. Kill a member of my family and I kill ten of yours."

"Whoever killed Augie and Elyse was a pro," Joe Feeney said. He was a tough, square-jawed Irishman, not cowed by Fat's frequent outbursts. "The operation was planned, boss. Like army stuff. Whoever did it knew what he was doing."

Colombini's dark eyes flashed deep within his doughy face. "I know who the fuck did it. I don't need to figure out who the fuck did it. Sorrentino. It doesn't matter who pulled the fucking trigger. We kill his fucking woman, Pauline Windsor. She's the target. We get to him through her. It's called a honey trap. That way we get both."

Bruce Manson, the largest man in the room, lit up at the actress's name. "Yeah, she's my favorite. That movie of hers, *The House of Ushers* or something, it was the ant's pants, boss. You see it yet?"

Dumbfounded, Colombini stared at him for a full five seconds. "Jesus, shut your fucking trap, you moron. We are not talking about movies." Sighing, he turned his bulk toward Feeney. "Kidnap the woman. Bring her here. She's the bait. We'll put ten bullets in him for Augie and ten in her for Elyse."

"I'll take Manson," Feeney said.

"No," Colombini said, his puffy face pinched in thought. "Get me Laurel and Hardy. Let them do the snatch. They're the best."

That evening, not more than five blocks away from Fat's' home, Cedric Boyd and Harry Kane were working a birthday party for the eight-year-old son of one of Global's top producers. Though they didn't need the money, they got a kick out of working gigs as Laurel and Hardy. They resembled the popular comedy duo but only marginally. Both wore bowler hats. Boyd was big and had Oliver Hardy's clipped mustache. Kane was thin and could mimic the Stan Laurel bewilderment, but his face was pockmarked from small pox as a child, and that destroyed any true resemblance to Laurel.

They thought they were better than the real duo, but no one else did. They were mechanical actors, not funny at all, and on this day, they scared the eight-year-old boy and his friends. Two of them were crying, others about to break into tears, upsetting the producer who was a little frightened himself. He was happy when a call came to his house from someone looking for the two. Kane took the call.

It was Joe Feeney. "I've been looking all over for you guys," he said. "Fats wants to see you now."

"We can't go now," Kane said. "We're working. The audience loves us."

"I don't give a shit. Fats has got a job for you. Pays top dollar, but you need to get your fat asses over here now."

"You're breaking these kids' hearts, but, yeah, on our way."

CHAPTER THIRTY-THREE: THE GATHERING STORM

November 7, 1927 Los Angeles

When Pauline and Lauren dropped the children off at school Monday morning, Brady and Corcoran followed in Brady's Model T. Afterward, the men pulled into a diner on Mulholland from where they could watch the school a quarter of a mile away on the hillside. The two women drove on to Global Studio. Pauline was quiet the entire way, worried about Rolly and Emmy. Lauren knew she would be worried the rest of the day, the rest of the week, the rest of her life.

That's motherhood for you, Matt said. *Something you have to look forward to.*

Lauren gave a snort of derision. *I'm not the mothering type. Besides, too much pain in the world to bring a child into it.*

"Are you all right?" Pauline asked as she drove through the Global gate.

"Fine." She decided not to make up a lie and said nothing else.

We must talk about your reasons for bringing or not bringing children into the world, Matt said.

Let's not.

An unusual number of productions were being shot on the lot, some finishing up while others were just beginning. So, Matt lost all thought of childbearing, enjoying himself spotting the stars walking along the streets with hundreds of extras in costume. To Lauren's annoyance, he squealed when he saw a bespectacled man in a straw boater hat. *Harold Lloyd! Harold Lloyd!*

You've seen Harold Lloyd before, Lauren said. *You're like an endless digital replay.*

He squealed again moments later. *There. Ronald Colman! That's odd. He didn't make many Global pictures as I recall. At least none that survived. Lauren, look right. Yes, that's it. Laurel and Hardy. I can't believe it. I'm sure they didn't make any Global films either. And there, that woman at Stage Two, that's Janet Gaynor. What's she doing on this Poverty Row lot?*

This is not Poverty Row. Any studio with Pauline Windsor is not Poverty Row. She was surprised at how irritated the slight to Pauline made her. *Take it back or I'll close my eyes.*

You're right, of course. Pauline is a star of the first rank. So, Global is not Poverty Row.

They made it to Stage Four, where the day's filming was to take place, without any more star sightings. The filming of *Romeo and Juliet* had been going smoothly and quickly since Clarence Martin took over the director's chair. Knowing that Pauline was now funding the picture, Martin attempted to cut corners financially while maintaining the quality. The masquerade ball at the Capulets called for fifty extras in costume, but he was using only thirty and a tighter camera. After all, this was the scene where Romeo boldly crashes the party and first sees Juliet. The camera would be on them most of the time with the extras as background.

After Romeo and Juliet meet and slip off their masks, they fall instantly in love. Romeo steals a kiss from Juliet. Later, she is horrified to learn from her nurse that the man she had just kissed and fallen in love with was none other than Romeo of the House of Montague, her family's mortal enemy.

Again, to save money but to try a new technique, Martin shot the scene straight through without cuts using a camera mounted on a winding track. Throughout the running scene, he coaxed and cajoled just the right performance out of Michael while trusting Pauline to come up with the goods on her own. She did. The love, the intense passion, came through on her face. Michael did his part. The stalwart clutching his breast and yearning for Juliet was serviceable.

When Martin called *cut*, the extras and the crew broke into applause and cheers. They all thought they'd done something of quality.

Then a disturbance at the stage door caught everyone's attention. A big, broad-shouldered man had insisted that Jerry Zelinsky had sent him for Pauline. The studio boss wanted to see her immediately, he'd said. But many of the extras, still happily playing their roles as Capulets, stopped him. Jerry Zelinsky was in New York for the next two weeks on business. The man had punched a Capulet squire, knocking him to the floor, before racing out the stage door.

"What the hell was that all about?" Martin asked, as they all stood around the dazed squire.

With a wave of the hand, Michael answered him, "Pauline's fans will do anything to get to her. Next time just give him an autographed picture."

"I swear it looked like Oliver Hardy," the Capulet squire who had been knocked to the floor said, rubbing his jaw. "You know. Laurel and Hardy. But it wasn't him."

An arctic chill raced through Lauren. It was a boneheaded play but in two centuries, her own and this one, she'd found that most criminals were dumber than 1st Gen computers. Whatever that had been about, she had no doubt Pauline was at the center of it.

A few hours later, as Martin and the rest of the crew filmed around Pauline, the two women left to pick up the children from school.

When they turned onto Briar Summit Road, Lauren glanced at the diner where Brady and Corcoran spent most of their day. Four cars in the parking lot. Brady's and Corcoran's car was not one of them. Usually, they'd be waiting up at the school by now, so that meant nothing. Yet, her body's natural warning sensors sparked deep into the red. Two men sat in one of autos, watching the road, watching them.

Pauline was speaking and Lauren focused on her. "His teacher wants to talk with me about Rolly's behavior. He better not be pulling pigtails again."

Lauren had Matt rewind what Pauline said before. *A parent-teacher conference this afternoon with Rolly's teacher.*

"The boy has got a bit of the rascal in him," Lauren said. She studied the road and the dry sagebrush landscape with Matt's help. He could bring minute detail onto her neurobots.

Nothing seemed out of place.

The massive Loire chateau that was the Briar Summit School appeared up the road a quarter mile ahead. Matt telescoped the cars into Lauren's mind. Expensive cars already in line waiting for the bell and rush of children out the door. Mobsters or kidnappers did not drive around in expensive luxury cars with liveried chauffeurs. The parents she saw waiting by their cars were all familiar.

But Brady and Corcoran's Model T was not there.

The unease she felt shot to hyper-alertness. She leaned forward slightly in the front seat for easier access to her Glock.

Dear God, I hope you don't have to use that with all the children running about, Matt said.

I hope not, too. If I have to, it means someone else is firing a weapon, and I need to put him down.

At the school, Pauline started to pull into the school's parking lot when Lauren placed a hand on her forearm. "No. Get in the line."

Instead, she stopped. "I have that meeting with Rolly's teacher."

"Look around. What do you see?"

Pauline frowned, then glanced about. "I see what I always see. Cars waiting to pick up children. Why? Is something wrong?"

"What do you not see?"

Pauline suddenly jolted upright. "Where are Brady and Corcoran? They should be here."

"Right. They should be here. Get in line."

Pauline slid the Duecy in line behind the other cars. "Maybe, they had a flat tire and had to go into town to get it repaired?"

"No, they didn't. Those two would have been here, flat tire or not. They would have commandeered a taxi or even stolen a car if they had to. Something else happened."

Pauline voice strained with apprehension. "I need to get my children."

"I'll get them," Lauren said. "Keep the car running. Leave as soon as we're back."

"They're in the headmaster's office," Pauline called as Lauren got out.

Lauren dreaded that they were not inside at all, that they'd been snatched already. *Please, God, let them be inside.* She strode to the double doors and went in.

CHAPTER THIRTY-FOUR: LAUREL AND HARDY

November 7, 1927, Briar Summit School
Inside the school, children were lined up on each side of the hall, waiting for the bell. A few teachers patrolled the lines to keep them from getting rowdy. In the headmaster's office, Rolly and Emmy, sitting together on a bench, looked up with surprise as Lauren entered.

"Come on. We're leaving," she said.

"Here! You can't do that," a man said from behind a counter. He wore a clerk's visor on his forehead. "They must speak with the Headmaster. Who are you?"

"She's our auntie," Rolly said as he and Emmy followed her from the office.

Outside the school, Lauren said, "Remember our training. I say *down*, you get down."

They nodded, Emmy with a grin—still a game for her—and Rolly with a quizzical look. They scrambled into the back seat of the Duecy, and Lauren into the passenger seat. "Go."

Immediately, Pauline drove off.

Dropping her small satchel on the floorboard, Emmy stood on the back seat, leaned over into the front seat and kissed her mother on the cheek. Then she kissed Lauren as well. Lauren grabbed her by the back of the dress and lifted her into her lap. "Come on up here, kiddo."

"Ciao" Rolly announced breathlessly from the back. "Come stai? Arrivederci."

While the other cars made U-turns to head back down into Los Angeles, Pauline drove up toward the summit where the pavement ended and became a winding, dirt road, skirting steep hills and deep ravines. This way cut twenty minutes from the drive home.

Attempting to appear calm, Pauline looked in the rearview mirror at her son. "Let me guess. You studied Italy today?"

"Yes, bello, bello. It's the cat's meow, the ant's pants, the monkey's eyebrows, the kipper's knickers…"

"Okay, okay," Emmy said. "I studied the multiplication tables. Seven times seven is…"

"Forty-nine," Rolly shouted.

Emmy pouted and scowled at her brother.

"Behave," Pauline snapped.

Quiet a moment at his mother's sudden anger, Rolly then asked, "Is something wrong?"

Pauline said hastily, "No, dear. What could be wrong?"

The road looped down, then came out on a level stretch beside a steep canyon. A slight drizzle began. Pauline turned on the windshield wipers, which squeaked rhythmically. Her hands white-knuckled on the steering wheel. Catching their mother's tension, the children fell silent.

"What's wrong?" Rolly asked again.

"Nothing, honey," Pauline said. "We'll be home in a few minutes."

"What's wrong, Aunt Lauren?"

Lauren turned back to Rolly. "Brady and Corcoran didn't show."

After thinking a moment, Rolly nodded and sat back in the seat.

Just then, a Model A appeared in the rearview mirror, coming up fast. Within a few seconds, it closed to within a couple feet. "Oh, God! What are they doing?" Pauline shouted.

Rolly peered out the back window. "They look like Laurel and Hardy." He giggled. "We're being chased by Laurel and Hardy."

"Sit down, Rolly!" Dread filled Pauline's eyes.

"Pull off there," Lauren said, pointing to a bypass jutting over the canyon.

"No, I think…"

"Damn it, do it!"

Pauline turned onto the bypass and stopped. The Model-A didn't go by, instead halting and blocking a way back onto the road.

Pauline's face contorted in fear. She glanced at her children, then to Lauren and mouthed the words, *Not my kids.*

Lauren shifted Emmy to her mother's lap. "Do you trust me, Pauline?"

The actress's eyes were white with fear, but she nodded.

"Good, then whatever happens stay in the car. All of you. Understand? Stay in the car." When they didn't answer, she snapped, "Understand?"

They nodded. Pauline's asked, "What are you going to do?"

Lauren got out of the car and went around to meet the two men approaching. She still did not want to use the Glock. They did look like Laurel and Hardy but a mean version of the comedy duo, even to a Hitler-like moustache on the Hardy character. He was far more muscular than the actor, not an ounce of fat on him. The other man was smaller and thin. He wore a bowler. Unlike Laurel he had a heavily pockmarked face.

As they advanced, she theatrically held her hand up to stop them, but Hardy in the lead shoved her easily aside. When the smaller Laurel reached out to do the same, she moved with blurring speed, grabbing his wrist, twisting it and slamming him down, stunning him. She hammered his face into the hardpan.

Groggy, he spat blood and gasped, "What the hell!"

Lauren's face contorted into a hellish mask, her teeth bared, her eyes dark with madness. She hit the man with two savage punches that knocked him unconscious. Quickly, she found his revolver in a shoulder holster.

Not taking notice of what was happening behind him, the bigger man stepped up to the car window and shouted, "Get out of the car. You hear me, lady? If you don't want your kids hurt, get out of the fucking car!"

He drew his gun and stuck it against the glass. Pauline covered Emmy with her body and shouted, "Get down, Rolly!"

Lauren drove her boot into the back of his leg, and with a surprising squeal, he collapsed to his knees. He tried to get up, but she punched him in the temple, and he went down again, this time on all fours. She kicked his gun away. In a killing rage, he rose to his feet. Lauren aimed the revolver at his head.

"You ain't going to shoot me," he said with disdain. "I ain't never seen no dame with the guts to use a gun."

"You're as stupid as you look." Lauren lowered the gun and fired, exploding his knee cap.

The man screamed in agony. Pauline and the children jumped at the sound. Emmy curled into the fetal position in Pauline's lap and now bore down deeper. At the back window, Rolly's eyes were enormous.

The man hopped around a second then flopped down into a sitting position, clutching his leg. As he sat there, Lauren kicked his jaw so violently it sent blood and teeth flying, and he slumped back unconscious. She strode over to the idling Model-A and got in. Grinding the gears, she finally found the right one and gave it gas. It lurched forward, and just as it went over the cliff, she rolled out. As she returned, the smaller man was struggling to consciousness.

Pauline kept Emmy down, brushing her hair with her hand and told Rolly to look away. But he watched, taken by fear and fascination.

Lying on his back, the smaller man stared up at Lauren, blinking himself awake. Then his eyes flared with ferocity. Oddly, Lauren smiled, a boa constrictor about to swallow a plump rat.

"Who sent you?" she asked calmly. "Colombini? Sorrentino?"

He chuckled. "Fuck you, bitch!"

Pointing the revolver at his head, she stepped hard on his crotch, and he shrieked so loud the sound echoed through the hills. When he got his breathing under control, he said, "I'm going to kill you!"

Instantly dropping down on one knee, she grabbed his tie and lifted his head within a foot of hers. "Look at me, chip shit. Who's on top here? Who might die here? You or me? I'm going to ask you again, and if I don't get a straight answer, I'm going to crush your balls. Both of them. You'll be the one singing soprano in the mob choir. If I decide to let you live, I don't give a shit whether it's with or without balls."

The words flew from his mouth. "Fats Colombini sent us."

"Why?"

"Payback for Little Augie and his wife. We was to bring the dame to him."

"Then what?"

"He was going to kill her and drop her body where Sorrentino would find it," he said, then gave an aggrieved expression. "Tit for tat. Benny the Bug went after family. He killed Little Augie's wife. She was a good one. Why'd he have to do that?"

"What else?

In pain, he shouted, "That's all I know. I swear. Please, I swear."

"Don't worry. I believe you."

Lauren stood up, and Rolly watched stunned as she stomped her boot into the man's crotch. He wailed and his legs curled up to his chest.

Pauline had never seen anything like that. The cold application of violence. She could not imagine it. She had been so afraid of these men, yet Lauren had not been, not at all, and she handled them as if they were toddlers.

When she returned to the car, Pauline and the children stared at her. Emmy had risen from her mom's lap when the noise had ended.

"Are we okay now?" the girl asked.

"Yes, for now, sweety," Lauren said and added to Pauline, "No police."

All of them stared at her.

"Are we waiting for some reason?" she asked.

Pauline shook her head, then drove onto the road. Still shaken, she realized, her life had unmistakably changed in the last few minutes. She would have to deal with it. Like she dealt with her family's crushing poverty as a child. Like she dealt with her husband's suicide several years ago. Like she dealt with all the wolves at the door in Hollywood.

Those men would have killed her and likely harmed her children if not for Lauren. But a darkness so deep it was endless shone from her friend's eyes in those few minutes she them. She was chilled by it. Lauren could have killed those men without hesitation or remorse. Pauline could not have that around Rolly and Emmy. Lauren would have to leave. She would do that as soon as they got back.

CHAPTER THIRTY-FIVE: FALSE FACES

November 7, 1927, Hollywood Hills

"You kill them if I say you kill them," Colombini screamed into the phone. He was talking to LAPD Lieutenant William "Dutch" McGinty.

Colombini was furious Laurel and Hardy had failed him, botched the snatch of the actress. Somehow, they'd fucked it up, both on their way to the hospital according to Rooney. Now, he had to clean up the mess before it came back to bite them all.

McGinty sighed into the phone. "Cops can't go around killing famous actresses and their children, Fats, and think they can get away with it."

"You can if I tell you to. I pay you big money. You do what I damn well tell you to do." His spittle flew over the phone receiver.

McGinty was silent.

Fats calmed down marginally and said in a more reasonable tone, "Look, Dutch. I'm not saying you drive out there and go in guns blazing. You investigate. See what she knows. See if those fuck-ups Rooney sent let my name slip. They say they didn't but who the hell can trust them. They're beat up pretty bad. Find out what the hell happened? If the actress don't know nothing about me, then fine. Leave. I'll snatch her later when the stink dies down."

"All right. I can do that."

"You're damn straight you can do that," Fats said coldly. "But listen to me good, Dutch. If she knows I'm behind it, I can't let her telling people that. Someone as famous as this dame starts saying Fats Colombini tried to kidnap her and her kids, that's going to cause me big trouble. And that trouble will fall on your head too. It ain't no secret you're my man in the department. I'll survive it, you won't."

"You got a point, Fats."

"You find out what the hell they know. If they know I sent those two, you must kill them all. Make it look like a robbery."

McGinty hesitated a long time then said one word. "Yeah."

***

When they reached home, Pauline took Rolly and Emmy into the kitchen for their afternoon snacks. She told herself normalcy for the kids. That's what they needed. Don't break down. Handle this like you've always handled everything. Lauren had gone straight to her room before Pauline had a chance to talk to her. She would deal with that, too.

No police, no police, that was crazy. She would have to call them now. Someone had tried to kidnap her and her kids.

Tia, the cook, had sandwiches with the crust removed already made and waiting on the kitchen table along with glasses of milk.

"Tia, Tia," Rolly shouted as he scrambled into his chair. "Two gangsters tried to kidnap us. They ran us off the road."

"Two bad men," Emmy chimed in.

"What's this I'm hearing?" Mrs. Windsor said, coming in. "What's this about gangsters?"

Pauline poured herself a cup of coffee with trembling hands. "Two men stopped us on the road over the mountains. They threatened us."

"Madre de Dios," Tia said, crossing herself.

Mrs. Windsor's hand went to her throat. "Dear God, what happened?"

Rolly was already telling it, the words spilling out like how the car had come up behind them and Pauline had pulled off the road and the two men blocked them in and the two men came at them.

"Real gangsters," he said. "Then, Auntie Lauren beat them up."

"Don't tell such fibs, Rolly," Mrs. Windsor said and looked to Pauline.

Shaking her head disbelievingly, Pauline exhaled a long breath. "It's true, Mother. Lauren just…she somehow handled two grown men. One man she punched so hard it knocked him out. The big man, she kicked him, and he went to his knees."

"She shot him," Emmy said with wide, fearful eyes.

"How do you know?" Rolly said. "You weren't even looking. You were hiding on the floorboards" Then, he said excitedly to his grandmother, "She shot him."

Pauline nodded. "She did but in the kneecap. She didn't kill him."

The full horror of it settled into Mrs. Windsor's face. "Dear God, we need to call the police."

"Yes" Pauline said. "We do."

***

Using the phone in her room, Lauren eventually found Remy at the Griffith Park Aerodrome and explained what happened.

"Dear God, is anyone hurt?"

"No, as far as I know, but Brady and Corcoran are missing."

"I'll find them. Are you all right?"

"Yes, I'm fine," she said. "We need men here right away, Remy. This is not over. Can you do that?"

"I'll take care of it right now."

Next, she threw her blood-stained clothes in the small fireplace in her bed room and set them alight. Then, she showered, scrubbing her body relentlessly.

What you are doing is unnecessary, Matt said. *There is no DNA retrieval in this era. It is reasonable to conclude people in the year 1927 don't even have theoretical knowledge of DNA.*

"Force of habit," she replied aloud. "Besides, my skin feels like it's crawling with lice. I want every fucking microscopic strand of those two bastards off me."

She heard a knock at her bedroom door. Even in the shower, she'd heard the approach and knew exactly who it was. Carrying a towel but not wrapping herself in it, she went to the door stark naked and opened it.

Mrs. Windsor stood there, straight as a drill sergeant, then blinked in shock. "You're…you're naked."

"You are a sharp one, Mrs. Windsor. I was in the shower. What do you want?"

Pauline's pinch-faced mother quickly regained her chilly composure. "I want to know how you have knowledge of…" Then her eyes shifted to the scars on Lauren's. "You have lied to us. You are not what you say you are. Look at you. What kind of wounds are those?"

Lauren considered not answering, then said, "Gunshot mostly." She pointed to one on her forearm. "A knife wound here." All occurred before she received her nanobots. "They happened long ago." She gave a sardonic chuckle at the phrase *long ago* about things that will not happen for nearly two hundred years.

Her lips pursed in disapproval, Mrs. Windsor nodded. "Of course. They would be. I was right all along about you, Miss Ramirez, wasn't I? I felt it my duty to thank you personally for what you did on behalf of my daughter and grandchildren today. Pauline told me. Rolly couldn't stop talking about it, how you destroyed two grown men. I didn't believe it at first. But they were insistent, and they could not have made that up." Her voice was grudging. "I am grateful you were there."

"So am I."

Mrs. Windsor stared at her so long Lauren began to think the woman had gotten lost woolgathering, a favorite term of the old bat. Searching back in her memory, she found she'd only heard it used once in the 22nd century by an old juggler with the Misfits. At least eighty, he was known for drifting off in the middle of conversations. He termed it his woolgathering. What bothered Lauren was that the word was a term of this time, the early 20th century, not the 22nd century, and she had comfortably used it.

"Are you a threat to my family?" Mrs. Windsor asked.

"No."

"Surprisingly, I believe you." Abruptly, she said, "Mind you, I still don't think you're a good person."

Lauren laughed. "I can always count on you, Mrs. Windsor, to tell the truth. I am far worse than even you can imagine." When the woman blanched, she added, "But I do care about Pauline and the children. I will do everything I can to protect them and the rest of the family, including, I suppose, even you. And, Mrs. Windsor, they need protecting."

"Yes, I fear my daughter is in a pickle, Miss Ramirez. She is either too stubborn or too daft to realize it, and she is not daft." The woman nodded, started to leave, but turned back. "What happened to the people who shot you?"

"They are dead. None of them survived the encounter."

After Mrs. Windsor left, Lauren dressed quickly, putting on khaki trousers, a black blouse and strapped on her back holster, hiding it under the blouse.

A little fist pounded on her door. Rolly called out. "Lauren, Lauren, Mom says to come quick. A bunch of policemen just drove up in a car."

***

Lt. McGinty paced the living room of Pauline's home, a cigarette held between yellow-stained fingers. He wore a rumpled gray suit and suspenders that stretched at his rounded belly.
Two other plainclothes detectives stood by the alcove entrance listening. One wore a long overcoat in the house, and Pauline thought that odd. Why would he not take it off inside?

McGinty scratched his head, puzzled. He regarded Pauline with a complex mixture of curiosity and nervous intensity. "I'm just trying to piece together what had happened out on the road. The two thugs who attacked you somehow sustained injuries, but no one seems to know how that occurred."

The living room was crowded. Pauline sat with the children and her mother, Lauren nearby. Also, for some reason, the police wanted everyone on the premises: the cook, Tia, and the housekeeper, Mrs. Belknap, neither of whom had any knowledge of the incident.

Pauline felt her nerves scraped raw. McGinty was staring at her, waiting for her to respond. She glanced about the room. Her eyes fell on the detective with the overcoat, and she gasped. He had turned slightly and the barrel of a shotgun slipped partially out. Panic shot through her. For a moment, she could barely breathe.

Then, regaining her composure, she lifted her head. "Why does that man have a shotgun?"

"Oh, that. It's for your protection, ma'am," McGinty explained with a fake grin. "Should those men who attacked you come here, we want to be prepared for them."

She did not believe a word of it. Now she knew why Lauren didn't want to contact the police. What troubled Pauline most was the question of who had called McGinty. She hadn't called anyone yet, let alone the police. Her mother hadn't. In her mind, that left only one person who could have, Fats Colombini, the man who had sent the thugs. This was the Dark Ages. No one else could have known about the incident. Police or not, these were his men. And that meant grave danger.

"Are all these questions necessary, Lieutenant?" Mrs. Windsor asked. "Pauline and the children have been through a harrowing event. She has told you what happened. The story will not change."

"You see, ma'am, I'm just not getting a clear picture." Taking another drag on his cigarette, McGinty turned back to Pauline. "Did these men threaten you directly, Miss Windsor?"

Playing a role now, perhaps the most important of her life, she rubbed her chin in thought. She'd portrayed the ditsy blond so often in movies she fell into it easily.

"I believe they did," she said. "They said 'get out of the car.' They weren't too friendly about it."

"Did they ever say why they wanted you?"

"I can't remember that. I don't think so. Money, I guess."

He looked at her steadily for several seconds. "Did they say who sent them?"

Turning her head slightly as if in thought, she saw Lauren's hand slide behind her back. Pauline knew she had a gun there. She wanted to shout to her *No, don't.*

"Is something wrong, ma'am?" McGinty asked. "Did you remember something?"

Pauline's head snapped around, and she focused on him, then shook her head. "Yes, I remember one of them had mismatched socks. Oh, dear me. That's not important is it, Lieutenant?"

"No, ma'am, not likely." He gave a skeptical glance at his two men, then addressed them all. "Let me get this straight. These two men ran your car off the road and attempted to abduct you. They both had guns. Yet, here you are and the two of them are in the hospital with severe injuries, one of them with a gunshot wound. How could that happen? In all honesty, ma'am, I'm finding it hard to believe."

Pauline's eyes flashed angrily. "As you say, they are on their way to the hospital, and here we sit. Believe your eyes, Lieutenant. What else is there?"

"That's what I'm trying to determine."

McGinty suddenly realized his cigarette was down to his fingers. Looking hastily about, he discarded the ash in the dry fireplace and flicked the cigarette after it.

Sitting on the divan, Mrs. Windsor muttered, "Were you born in a barn, sir?"

"Sorry, ma'am." Abruptly, McGinty strode over to Rolly and knelt in front of him. "Now, I bet you're a smart one," he said with an ingratiating grin.

"He is," Emmy chimed in. "He's the smartest boy in our school."

"Sure, he is." McGinty agreed. "Rolly—that's your name, isn't it? I bet you remember exactly what happened today. How those men got hurt, don't you? I'm a policeman, and I need to find out, so I can catch the bad guys."

"I thought you already caught them," Rolly said.

McGinty frowned. His tone lost its friendliness. "Yeah, that's right. But there might be more. Can you tell me what you saw, smart kid?"

Rolly nodded. "I think I can. Well, that car came up real close behind us, so close mom got scared, so she pulled off the road so they could pass, but they didn't pass. They stopped right there blocking us in. Then those two men got out of their car and started coming toward us, but their car started rolling and they ran back toward it." He burst out with a sharp laugh. "It went right over the cliff like in a Harold Lloyd movie."

Emmy looked at him wide-eyed.

"Go on," McGinty prompted him.

"Well, that was when they started arguing, shouting at each other. The big man called the little man a nitwit, and the little man called the big man a Dumb Dora, so the big man hit the little man. He kicked him a couple times, too, and the little man took out a gun and shot the big man in the leg. That's when mom drove out of there." Rolly shrugged. "That's it."

Pauline smiled at Rolly. McGinty looked at the other policemen and all of them seemed to relax. He glanced at Emmy. "Is that what you saw, little lady?"

She shook her head. "No."

Rolly stiffened as did Pauline.

McGinty and the other policemen were suddenly tense again and the shotgun's barrel peeked out from the overcoat.

"What did you see?" McGinty asked.

"The floor of the car."

Everyone laughed, including the policemen. McGinty said, "I think we've got enough. I don't suspect you'll see those men again. It sounds like an attempted hijacking by a couple of dumb saps. I wouldn't worry about it, but I'll leave a patrol car around for a while. Just one more question, Miss Windsor."

"Yes?"

"Would you mind signing an autograph for me? My wife's a big fan, and she'll never believe I met you."

Emmy said suddenly, "One of them did say Columbus wanted mommy. In 1492, Columbus sailed the ocean blue. Why would he want my mommy?"

McGinty froze. He glanced quickly at the man with the shotgun. Pauline saw Lauren reach behind her back.

That's when headlights played on the windows, and they all heard the sound of a car on the driveway. The shoulders of the man with the shotgun tensed. He eyed McGinty, who shook his head. Seconds later, there was a loud knock.

"Are you expecting anyone?" McGinty asked Pauline.

Lauren answered, "We are. Mrs. Windsor, would you answer the door?"

Stern-faced and unafraid, the older woman rose and went into the alcove, harrumphing as she passed the two detectives. Moments later, she returned with Remy, Clyde Brady, and Tommy Corcoran. Brady's arm was in a sling and Corcoran's face sported a black eye and a cheek swollen yellow and purple. All three men wore .45 army colts.

For several seconds, the detectives stared uncertainly at them. Then, with a curt nod, McGinty said he was done and abruptly left with the two detectives.

Emmy said, "They were in such a hurry, mommy, they forgot your autograph."

Feeling a surge of relief, Lauren approached Remy, threw her arms around his neck, and kissed him. "That's for your impeccable timing."

Brady grinned. "I have impeccable timing, too."

She patted his cheek and shook Corcoran's hand. "I'm glad you boys are all right."

Pauline herded the children out of the room with Mrs. Belknap and Tia, then came back. "What happened?"

"I found them in jail," Remy said. "I figured it was best to get here as soon as possible."

"I'm glad you did."

Brady explained they did have a flat tire and after putting on the spare drove down into town to get it fixed. "It was a setup, all the way. A truck rammed us before we got to a garage, and the police were right there waiting when it happened."

"They arrested us," Corcoran said, his bruised face red with anger. "A setup job, all right. Had to be."

The two men became quiet, but it was obvious they had something else to say.

"Tell it all," Remy said.

Brady and Corcoran exchanged glances, then Brady said, "While we were in the lockup, we met a guy who drives bootleg for Colombini. He says Fats blames Sorrentino for Elyse Colombini's killing." He fixed his gaze on Pauline. "He's gone stark raving mad over the idea that you must pay for it."

"Me?" Pauline said.

"You. You're Sorrentino's girl," Brady said. "This damn mob war has turned into a blood feud, and you, ma'am, are in the middle of it. This guy says Fats keeps talking about an eye for an eye. You for Elyse. He was always an out-and-out killer, but now something has scrambled in his head. I don't think even killing you would be enough. I'd take it seriously, ma'am."

She stared at everyone in the room. They were all looking back at her as if snakes grew out of her head. The smell of cigarettes from McGinty and his men still lingered. It was not improbable that they had come to kill her and her children under orders from Colombini. The hairs on her arms lifted. Whatever the truth about Ben, she needed to protect Rolly and Emmy.

She'd made a decision about Lauren as well. She and Rolly and Emmy were safe and alive because of her.

She turned to Lauren and said, "Will you protect my family?"

Lauren nodded.

"Good, because I think I need more bodyguards."

CHAPTER THIRTY-SIX: WINDSOR'S WARRIORS

November 12, 1927, Hollywood Hills

Lauren intended to raise a small army, and until she had it, the children were kept home from school. Pauline could afford it. She was worth millions in a time when a loaf of bread cost a dime and a lunch-counter meal cost less than half a dollar.

Lauren knew exactly where to get the men for it. And Remy was just the person to handle it. In 1927, there were thousands of unemployed veterans of the Great War drifting about the Los Angeles area. Newspapers were filled with stories about many of them being hired to participate in a war over water rights between the Los Angeles and farmers from Owens County. The city was outgrowing its water supply, and so William Mulholland negotiated the rights to divert the Owens River to the city.

When aqueducts were built and the river changed, the land in the Owens Valley went dry. This wiped out farmers and merchants, and they fought back, sabotaging the principal aqueduct in raids. The city needed security for its new water system and hired out-of-work veterans to protect it. Between jobs as a stunt pilot, Remy had been one of these.

Mostly unemployed, some unemployable, many became soldiers in the city of Los Angeles's personal army while others became strike busters, mercenaries, or personal security for wealthy Hollywood types. Lauren planned to hire security from this pool of men.

Remy put the call out to veterans' halls, and a flood of men trekked up into the Hollywood Hills on Saturday to Pauline's mansion.

That morning just past 10:00am, when Russell arrived, several veterans were already in the backyard waiting to be interviewed. Pouring himself coffee from a pot on the bar, he took a seat on the patio where the interviews were going on. He watched with some curiosity the odd trio of people questioning the veterans.

First, Pauline looked like the Queen of Hollywood in a purple drop-waist Coco Channel dress that cost more than he made in a year from UCLA. Second, Remy Garnet, who looked like quite the movie hero in his leather pilot's jacket and a Colt 45 at his waist. But he was the real thing.

Finally, Lauren Ramirez, who in her khaki pants, high top black boots and red blouse still appeared to Russell the most unusual woman he'd ever met. That's when Rolly and Emmy ran outside and pulled him away.

On that Saturday, a problem quickly arose. Having lived in 1927 now for many weeks, Lauren understood that gender roles were different in the early 20th century. Despite uninhibited flappers, rising hemlines, and females like Pauline, Mary Pickford, and Francis Marion leading the way in the movie business, women in this period were considered the weaker sex. The predominant feeling was that they were good for baby making, house cleaning, cooking, and supporting men in their pursuits. A clear demarcation of duties and skills between the genders.

Nothing could be further from Lauren's experience in the 22nd century. Taking orders from a woman then was commonplace, but in 1927, most men could not accept it. When they came onto the patio to be interviewed, few of them could take their eyes off Pauline. She dazzled them, and everyone initially wanted to work for her, till they learned who would be giving the orders. They would take pay from Pauline and be pleased to guard her. But taking tactical orders from Lauren was out of the question.

Pauline would not budge. She thanked them for coming and sent them on their way.

Clyde Brady, his arm in a sling, sat for an interview, even though Lauren already planned to keep him and Corcoran on. He was in love with Pauline and everyone knew it. The actress asked him a few questions about his experience in the Great War, then ended the short interview by asking, "Will you have a problem taking orders from a woman?"

His cherubic face split into a grin. "Give me a paying job, ladies, so I can keep flying my plane, and I'll take orders from an orangutan."

Pauline laughed. "I've had my acting compared to worse."

Brady was horror-struck. "Oh, no ma'am. I didn't mean...I'd never compare you to an orangutan. I meant...

"That's all right, Captain Brady. You're still hired."

Most of the other men, desperate for work, lied and said they would take orders from Mrs. Coolidge if it came down to it.

Who's that? Lauren asked Matt. *Mrs. Coolidge?*

She's the First Lady, he explained.

First Lady of what? Lauren asked.

The voice in her head was derisive. *The United States.*

Russell came out to the patio again and leaned down to speak with Pauline. "There's an older gentleman here to see you. I tried to tell him you were busy at the moment, but he insisted." He glanced over at Lauren and Remy. "Says he knows both of you."

"Let's speak to him," Pauline said.

Russell waved toward the French doors, and Wyatt Earp walked out into the sunlight. Wearing a battered fedora, he squinted his eyes and came toward them. With each stride,

Lauren thought she heard his bones creaking. So thin and so damn old.

A conspicuous, long-barreled Colt dragged down the right side-pocket of his suit coat. All three stood.

"Nice to see you again, Mr. Earp," Lauren said.

"You, too, ma'am. You too."

"Afternoon, Wyatt," Remy said. He could not hide his curiosity at seeing him here. "Let me introduce Pauline Windsor."

He tipped his hat. "I don't get out to the movies much, ma'am," he said, "but I know Miss Windsor. It's a pleasure to meet you."

"A pleasure to meet you, sir," Pauline said, extending her hand and shaking his. "What can we do for you?"

"Word is gangsters threatened you folks, and now you're go to war against them," he said. "That's something in which I have a little experience. I come to join up."

They could not hide their surprise, staring at him in silence, unable to speak for the moment, then Pauline said, "Please, sit down, Mr. Earp."

He did, placing his hands on his bony knees, and looked at each one waiting. Pauline asked first off if he had any problems taking orders from a woman.

"I've been taking orders from my wife for forty-five years," he said with a slight grin. "So, I'm used to it."

She asked him a few more superficial questions, then smiled. "You're hired, Mr. Earp. We can use a man of your experience."

Both Remy and Lauren stared at her in surprise. Then Lauren told Wyatt to come back tomorrow at which time they would set up their operation. When he left, Remy said, "What are we going to do with him? Jesus, Pauline. The man's near eighty."

"Just keep him out of trouble," Pauline said. "And who knows? He might be useful."

Remy gave a doubtful shrug. "Well, they say he used to be someone you could count on in a fight."

"We don't want him in a fight," Pauline said, "but we'll put him to use somehow."

At the end of the first day, the small army numbered fourteen men, fifteen including Earp, all proclaiming their readiness to take orders from Lauren, none of whom she believed. She would have to deal with that at some point or someone might get hurt.

But all were tough individuals who had seen combat in battles with odd sounding names like Belleau Wood, Chateau Thierry, Second Marne, Second Battle of the Somme, Cambrai and one at a place called the OK Corral. And she wanted them. Lauren had no doubt they would all withstand the terrors of a gangland war, even the old guy.

On the second day, still needing at least six more men as Lauren saw it, the interviews continued. Unlike the previous day, a few insisted they would never take orders from a woman.

"That goes against nature and common sense," one man said and trudged back down the hill toward Hollywood.

One of these naysayers was former Master Sergeant Jack Knighton, whom Remy said they needed. No army, even a tiny one like Pauline's, could function without a Top Sergeant, and Knighton was the best. At forty, he was powerfully built, tall and muscular, mostly bald but for a swathe of graying brown hair. His blue eyes seemed tortured, as if hiding some great terror from his past.

"Sergeant Knighton is a Medal of Honor recipient," Remy said, "and that means something. He knows how to run the day-to-day details of an outfit. We need to get him if we can. He will make the difference."

When he was called to the patio, he greeted Remy, "Captain, good to see you again."

"Top," Remy replied, shaking the man's hand. "Still busting heads for the city?"

"Anyone who will pay me." Knighton said, smiled warmly at Lauren and Pauline. "Ladies, it's a great pleasure to meet you both. I am your biggest fan, Miss Windsor."

"Thank you. I can always use another fan. Please, sit down," Pauline said.

Pauline explained her need for a large group of men to protect her family around the clock. Listening to his answers, Lauren became convinced Remy had been right. Knighton was just the person to take care of the day-to-day details. To her, he was the essential piece.

"Will you have a problem taking orders from a woman?" Lauren asked finally.

"You mean Miss Windsor? No, Of course not. If she signs the paycheck, she calls the shots."

"No, me. Pauline will set out what she wants from all of you. I will be giving the orders."

Looking surprised, Knighton glanced at Remy. "You're not running this show?"

"I'll be part of it, but Pauline is the boss, and Lauren will be giving the tactical orders," he said.

Chuckling, Knighton shook his head. He looked at the two women. "No offense, ladies. But this noncom is too old to learn new tricks. From what you've told me about the nature of this work, it's dangerous and needs people with actual experience. I will not be taking orders from a woman this day or any day." His jaw was set. He rose to leave, nodding to them. "I appreciate your time, and it has indeed been a joy to meet you, Miss Windsor."

Lauren stood. "We're paying top dollar, Sergeant. Two hundred dollars a month. As Top Sergeant, you would receive two hundred and fifty."

He shook his head. "Doesn't interest me, ma'am. I could not spend it if I were dead. And following the orders of a woman in this gangland mess could get me dead. I've never heard of a female who knows anything about combat, let alone a street fight, which I believe this is going to be. I wish you luck."

Lauren had an idea. The men that had been hired yesterday were all here in the backyard, including Earp, most playing baseball. Raider chased the ball for about five minutes then lay down exhausted and watched it. Lauren needed to change the minds of these men about taking orders from a woman, and she needed Knighton to make sure her orders were carried out.

She put a hand on his forearm to keep him from leaving. He shot her a dark look. She said, "I can't say how long this job will be, Sergeant Knighton, but I suspect at least six months. That's what we're guaranteeing the men who sign with us. I will give you three hundred a month. That's eighteen hundred dollars."

He sighed. "Ma'am, I already told you…"

"Just shut up and listen," she snapped.

He blinked in surprise, then stared at her.

"Are you a betting man?" Lauren asked.

"I've been known to play a little poker, but I'm not playing poker for this."

"I'll make you a wager. If you win it, you walk out of here with eighteen hundred dollars, all six months' pay for doing nothing. If you lose, you sign on and take orders from Pauline and me. You get the money either way. Are you in?"

He gave a skeptical look, then a half-smile touched his lips. "Depends on the bet."

"You against me. Bare fists. No holds barred. I say I can make you surrender or turn out your lights in less than a minute. If you're still standing after a minute, then you win. That is if you haven't survived by running away from me."

Knighton roared with laughter. He looked at Remy. "Is this a joke?"

Remy shrugged, but he too looked at her curiously. Lauren was actually excited by the prospect of an Octagon fight without the cage. "Are we on, Sergeant, or do I frighten you?"

"Well, you don't exactly frighten me, ma'am," Knighton said. "But I won't hit a woman. That puts me at a distinct disadvantage."

She put her hands on her hips. "You outweigh me by fifty pounds. So, grapple. Wrestle. Throw me to the ground. I don't give a damn. Just so long as you don't run. If I have to chase you, it will take much longer. Besides, I'm at a bigger disadvantage than you."

"I know. You're a woman."

"My disadvantage is this: I've got to put you out in less than a minute without killing you or damaging you. I need you to be whole. If it wasn't for that...," She looked him over. "...it would take me about five seconds."

Thinking that a joke, he laughed again, then saw in the cold glare of her eyes, she wasn't kidding. He looked at Pauline. "You go along with this, ma'am?"

"I do," the actress responded.

He turned back to Lauren. "You're crazy, you know that? But...all right. I'll play along. Besides, if someone is so intent on giving me two thousand dollars, who am I to refuse?"

Lauren smiled at his upping the bet. Getting wind of what was going on, the men already ended their baseball game and gathered into a semicircle, closest she would get to an octagon.

When she strode out among them, they whistled and gave her a few catcalls. She waved and feigned a frightened tremble. Several men offered bets on Knighton but no one took them. None of the men wanted to vote on Lauren, not even Remy.

Seeing something was about to happen, Russell, Mrs. Windsor, and the two children came from the house, trailed by the two smaller dogs. Lauren told Russell to hold Raider by a leash, or he would go after Knighton.

As they tightened into a circle fifteen yards in diameter, Lauren heard her father say, *Make it close, Mali. Let him think he can win.*

Not this time, papa.

Knighton bounced around, showing off for the men more than warming up. He winked and grinned. He was having fun. He asked Lauren, "Don't you want to warm up?"

She stood up. "No, I won't need it. Are you ready or are you going to preen all day?"

A moment of curiosity flashed across his eyes. Lauren saw it and smiled. He didn't like that either. But he was still confident, unconcerned. That was good. As she looked around at the audience, a long forgotten sense memory settled into her psyche, smells of the Octagon, worn leather, moldy boxing mats, and sweaty clothes. Grotesque to anyone else, but she loved those smells. The past *–or actually the future–* was in her heart, and she felt good, truly good for the first time since arriving in 1927.

Brady stepped out among them. "I'll referee. You need a referee."

"You've got a broken arm," Corcoran yelled. "How you going to referee?"

"One good arm's all I need."

Lauren nodded. "Fine. Bare fists. No holds barred. Submission or knock out ends the fight."

"Two-minute rounds?" he asked them.

"Bout is only for a minute," Knighton said.

"It won't go that long," Lauren said.

They faced each other, and Brady tomahawked his hand down to start the match. Instantly, she struck him with a high kick on the jaw that staggered Knighton. Surprised gasps erupted from the men.

She kicked the same spot again, then slipped in quickly behind him, wrapping her arms into a choke hold, closing off his wind pipe. No one expected such speed from her. Five seconds. She had him, she thought. Just apply pressure. Cut off the air supply. He will black out in a few seconds. That's when she knew she was in trouble.

Abruptly, Knighton dropped to one knee, throwing her over his shoulder. She rolled and bounced up, but he was on her immediately, tripping and slamming her hard to the ground. The breath blasted out of her chest, stunning her. Something strange flitted through her groggy consciousness: she could lose. How could that happen? She never lost.

If he pinned her down, the fight would be over. She could do something to damage him, gauge out an eye or jam his nose bone up into his brain. But she wouldn't do that. At least, not today. Her reactions came without thought.

As he barreled over her, she wrapped her legs about his waist, holding him at bay momentarily. When he reached for her head, she clutched his wrist, bent it back and twisted his body with her legs. He flew off her onto the ground.

They both jumped to their feet, but this time Lauren was quicker. She drove a savage kick into his testicles, bending him double with a groan. Drove a fist into the side of his jaw, dropping him to one knee. In an instant, she was behind him again, bringing him down into a sitting position, her legs wrapped around him, and applying the choke hold with her forearm. He was already having trouble breathing. This time he could not shake her off.

"Yield," she demanded.

"No," he gasped.

Another second later, he slumped, unconscious, and she laid him gently on the ground and stood. Silence filled the lawn as everyone stared slack-jawed, then they cheered. They loved a good show. After a moment, Knighton blinked his eyes open, sat up, and shook his head. Slowly, he stood.

Holding up a pocket watch, Brady announced, "Twenty-six seconds."

Knighton fixed his eyes in a blaze of fury on Lauren. If he didn't abide by the bet and attacked her, this time she would damage him.

Then, his shoulders relaxed. "I guess I'm the top sergeant of this ragtag army."

CHAPTER THIRTY-SEVEN: CLASH OF WOLVES

November 16, 1927, Hollywood Hills

Late Wednesday night, Lauren patrolled the grounds alone with Raider. Dressed in her usual khaki cargo pants, she carried her Glock 75 in a holster at her waist. A quarter moon rose through a field of stars, casting shadows around the house and in the hills. A stalking moon. Enough light to hunt; not enough for the hunter to be seen.

Six men were on duty this night, two inside, four outside. The two in the house were Buck Beachum and Dave Arthur, whom Rolly immediately dubbed Mr. A and Mr. B. Knighton was the duty officer.

Three days in, she was satisfied with Windsor's Warriors, the name the men were calling themselves. The security details ran smoothly, due in large part to Remy, Captain Brady, and Sergeant Knighton, who was as advertised a top sergeant who knew his business. Each of them learned leadership in the crucible of the Great War. And the men, having served in those battles, respected each other and knew how to stand a watch.

On Monday, Pauline had bought four Model-A Fords to use, and a new one for Brady, who lost his old Model T in the kidnapping attempt. She gave Remy money to buy Army Colts, M1 rifles, and Thompson sub-machine guns and radios.

Windsor's Warriors in turn took great pride in working for one of the most famous actresses on the planet. The two old-timers, Raider and Wyatt Earp, were quickly accepted into the unit.

When the men learned the German shepherd had served in France, they treated him as one of their own, and Raider seemed to shed ten years. Back to his youth. He patrolled the grounds with them and often carried messages between

Knighton and Lauren or Pauline. When Brady was the duty officer, he sent poems via Raider to Pauline. Not exactly love poems, but not exactly not. She became a little flustered by it but didn't do anything to stop him.

Though the men did not seem to know why Wyatt Earp was among them, they took to his tales of bygone days in the West. After all, they were big fans of Tom Mix, William S. Hart, and Bronco Billy, and here was the real thing.

Earp showed his alarm at their horrific tales of the fighting in France. "That sounds like hell to me, boys. I'm pleased to serve with all of you. My wife, though, she's not so happy. Says I'm going to get my old ass shot off by these modern-day gangsters. They're a whole different kettle of fish from the Clantons, Curly Bill and Johnny Ringo."

He always stood his duty watch during the day, often when the children were at school, because his "old eyes couldn't see so well at night anymore." On Tuesday, he accompanied Pauline and Lauren to the studio as the actress's personal bodyguard. A few of the crew chuckled at that until he parted his gray suit coat to reveal the long-barreled Colt strapped to his waist.

That Wednesday night, as Lauren patrolled the grounds with Raider, she gave no thought to Earp. He was doing his job. Instead, she was on edge, all her senses alert. They had been since the moment she stepped outside fifteen minutes ago. The night carried no sound. Not an owl, a coyote, or the movement of small animals up the hillside. Silence.

Approaching the back of the house, Raider slightly in front, his head turning slowly side to side, his ears pricked, she saw Sgt. Knighton standing just inside the patio doors. He had opened them slightly so he could blow the smoke of his cigarette out.

Lauren stopped next to him. "Quiet night, Top."

"Yes, ma'am. Too damn quiet."

"Raider's hackles have risen twice."

For a second, Knighton seemed to go deep into a memory, perhaps of desperate nights on the Western Front. In the last couple days, Matt had shown her the movie *All Quiet on the Western Front*, and she'd learned a lot about those hellish trenches.

What a strange team she had, Lauren thought. Men broken by war and still suffering from it, an old battered war dog, an ancient lawman from the Old West, and a damaged AI.

I am not a damaged AI, Matt insisted.

Sorry. I should have said a damaged appliance.

At that moment, Mrs. Windsor stepped out the back door in a robe and sat in a patio chair, tucking her legs underneath her. She had a cup of coffee. Lauren was ticked off. She didn't need the old bag wandering around at night.

"I'll talk to her, ma'am," Knighton said.

Suddenly, Raider shot across the grass and darted up among the sage and stunted trees into the hills.

"Stay here," she called to Knighton. "Make sure everyone is safe."

Drawing the Glock, Lauren sprinted after the dog. In the moonlight, she saw a flash of dark fur some thirty yards ahead and tried to keep up, but fell steadily behind. She dared not call out for fear of warning whoever was up here. And she was sure someone was up here.

In the distance, Raider barked. He was closing on his prey. She pushed harder, heard a gunshot, the sound of a struggle. Growls, a yelp, another gunshot.

A voice, "Son of a bitch!"

Over a rise, she saw them ahead. Raider was biting and clawing a man. Another man was running away.

On a tripod lay a rifle with a sniper's scope.

"Help me! Get this goddamn thing off me!" the man cried.

"Back, Raider," Lauren called, and surprisingly he fell back a step but snarled inches from his face.

"Don't let it get at me! Please!" he cried.

"Who sent you?"

"Fats. Fats. Who else? Get it off me." He kept sliding away from Raider.

"Are you the sniper?"

"No, no, Frankie. The bastard ran. You got to believe me."

"I do." She shot him in the head.

No police. One less to worry about. Picking up the rifle, she followed the sniper at a jog. "Stay with me, boy," she said to Raider.

She saw the figure some seventy yards ahead now, flitting in and out of the moonlight. Like a lot of assassins who kill from a distance, he wanted nothing to do with a close-up fight, especially with something like Raider. Even at this distance, she could smell the stink of his fear. He had shit his pants.

Raider was lagging back, his age catching up to him, she guessed. She left him behind. Five minutes later, the sniper reached his destination. Glancing back, he slowed to a stumbling walk and slid down a hill onto a paved road where a car waited, a man outside by the driver's door.

She knelt and aimed through the sniper scope at the assassin. Approaching the car, he was speaking to the other man with frantic gestures. She focused on his back just below the neck and fired. She hoped the rifle had been correctly calibrated. It had. The man slumped to the ground as if his skeleton had been yanked out. The other man jumped nearly a half foot in the air. He turned for the car. She fired a second time.

Ten minutes later at the patio, she came out of the darkness with Raider, carrying the sniper rifle. Mrs. Windsor sat in the dark beside Sgt. Knighton. Her cup rattled at Lauren's sudden appearance, coffee spilling. She placed a hand over her chest. "You scared me half to death. I did not hear either of you." Her hands were shaking. She said barely audibly, "I thought I heard gunshots."

"The place is protected," Knighton said. "Is everything okay?"

She nodded. "Why are you out here, Mrs. Windsor?"

"I live here. This is my home. I'll be where I please."

Nodding toward her, Knighton said, "She wouldn't go inside."

Lauren sat down across from Mrs. Windsor, and Raider flopped down with a whimper. Lauren held a finger up to quiet Mrs. Windsor, who was about to speak. "Top, there are three bodies up there. One about two hundred yards up. Two others on a road about a half mile away. Take Mr. A and Mr. B and dispose of them. I don't care how or where. I just don't want them found anywhere around here."

She tossed the sniper rifle to him.

For a couple seconds, he stared back at Lauren, then nodded. "Yes, ma'am." Going back in the house, he returned seconds later with Dave Arthur and Buck Beachum.

As the three men disappeared up into the hills, Mrs. Windsor said with a nervous vibrato voice. "What's going on?"

"Colombini's men. One a sniper. They intended to kill Pauline."

Her question choked in her throat. "They're…?" She didn't need to finish it.

"Yes."

"You?"

"Yes, me."

Mrs. Windsor gave a long exhale. "Miss Ramirez, I am grateful you are here during this trying time, but you must know, when it is over, you have to go. You are not the type of person the children should look up to, should even know."

She had spoken without rancor, almost sympathy. She was right. Lauren nodded.

Raider was already lying down, sleeping, she assumed, and wished she could drop off as easily. She desperately needed sleep. Reaching down to scruff his mane, she was alarmed when her hand came away sticky with blood.

***

Near 3:00am in the Hollywood Hills, a constant banging on the door of Doctor Bernard Meyer finally woke him and his wife. When he opened it, several dangerous-appearing men poured in along with a tall dark-haired woman carrying an unconscious dog. Shockingly, the actress Pauline Windsor filed in last of all.

He sputtered, "What is this?"

"The dog's been shot," the dark-haired woman said.

"I'm not a veterinarian," he said aghast.

"You are now," she said, her voice threatening.

Pauline put a hand on his shoulder. "Dr. Meyer, Raider will die before we can get him to a vet. He means so much to the children. Can you help us? Just to stabilize him."

When he didn't answer right away, she added, "My latest picture *The Palace of Fallen Angels* will premier in three weeks. Of course, you and your wife will be my personal guests."

Mrs. Meyer, who had been standing on the stairs, now rushed forward. "We can't turn them away, Bernie. We must do something."

"All right," Dr. Meyer said. "Bring him into the garage."

"No," the dark-haired woman said. "You have a clinic here?"

"A small one, but that's for…"

"Take him there," she said and the fierce, unforgiving look in her eyes changed his mind completely.

With Raider on the operating table, Pauline and Lauren stepped outside and sat on the porch steps. It was a relatively warm night, black with a wide spread of stars and the quarter moon. They heard crickets in the hedges and a few lightning bugs floated about.

The two women sat silently for a time, then Lauren noticed Pauline was crying. With her handkerchief, she blew her nose. Lauren was surprised. She didn't think Pauline was that close to Raider.

"Are you all right?" Lauren asked.

Pauline was silent for such a long time, Lauren didn't think she was going to answer. Then, she nodded. "Raider can't die like this. He can't."

Lauren didn't know what to say.

Then Pauline went on, "I love that dog. He was my husband's. Except for the children, he is the last part of Marty I have to hold onto."

"You don't speak about him."

She thrust the handkerchief back in her dress pocket. "I don't. I hate him. I can never forgive him for killing himself. He did that to Rolly and Emmy. They were there in the house. Emmy might not remember but Rolly does." She glanced around as if marshalling her anger, then her shoulders relaxed. "I knew he was broken when I married him, but I loved him. I was no great shakes myself, the Wild Girl and all that crap. We made a hell of a pair, but for a time, we were good for each other. We had a few good years. We had Rolly, then Emmy, and everything seemed to be going great."

She didn't finish, but Lauren knew the last line. *Then he went upstairs and stuck a shotgun in his mouth.*

"I will pray for Raider," Pauline said softly.

Lauren put her arm around Pauline, and they sat together like that for several minutes till Brady stuck his head out the door. "You need to come in. The doctor's finished."

They went inside. The doctor was wiping his hands with a cloth. He looked at Pauline. "The dog is stable. I stopped the bleeding. But the damage is significant. I caution you. Be prepared. He will not survive the night."

CHAPTER THIRTY-EIGHT: OUTSIDE THE LAW

November 17, 1927, Hollywood Hills

The death watch began. They gathered in the family room, five of Windsor's Warriors along with Pauline, Lauren, and the children as Knighton gently laid Raider onto his blanket, unconscious or asleep.

"Is he dead?" Emmy asked in a barely audible voice.

"No, honey," Pauline said, setting her hand on her daughter's shoulder. She didn't add what they all knew: *not yet.*

Dr. Meyer had said the bullet entered his abdomen and exited out the thigh. It must have hit something vital. If he operated, it would kill him. "The vet may have a different opinion. After all, this is not my field."

Raider whimpered, curled into a ball, and soon was asleep. A foot-wide white bandage was wrapped around his abdomen. The two other dogs, usually hyper, lay still, solemnly looking at Raider over their folded paws.

By 7:30am, the vet arrived and examined Raider, not removing the bandage. It was Monday, and Pauline had held Rolly and Emmy back from school. They watched the vet run his hand along Raider's coat. The dog trembled but didn't awaken. Emmy had tears in her eyes and clung to her mother's leg. Rolly stood with tight lips, his eyes blinking to keep the tears away.

"Aren't you going to even take the bandage off and look?" Lauren snapped at the vet.

Unruffled, he rose to his feet and shook his head. He was a young man with scruffy brown hair and wire rim glasses. He spoke with genuine concern, "No need. I spoke with Dr. Meyer. For a GP, he did a good job. I know how hard this is. I can dispose of him for you."

Lauren took a swift step toward him and he backed up. "I'll dispose of you first."

He flinched, then quickly turned to Pauline. "Well, then, there's nothing for me to do. Make him comfortable till the end, then call me."

Without looking at Lauren, he walked out.

An hour later, Sorrentino called Pauline. His voice was soothing. "Hey, Doll, I just heard about that bastard going after you. That should never happen. You know, I'd never want that to happen."

"I know, Benny, but it did."

"You and the children are fine, right? I hope them little ones are okay. They mean the world to me."

"They're fine. I'm fine."

"I'll send some boys over to your place. Make sure you're protected. Nobody's going to go after Ben Sorrentino's girl."

"Don't do that, Benny. I've taken care of it. I've hired army veterans. Good people. I have twenty bodyguards now."

He hesitated before speaking. "Good for you. Okay, if you're sure. If you change your mind, I can have someone over there in an hour."

"I'm sure," she said in clipped words.

She wanted this call to end. His power over her had weakened, and she knew any contact with him threatened her and her children. She knew what she had to do: end their relationship. When that thought ran through her head, she was amazed at how relieved she felt. As if the weight of a mountain on her back had been lifted. The iron-hold the mobster had over her emotions died a sudden death. But telling Ben was different. That would have to be done carefully. She had Colombini after her. She didn't want Ben, too.

"I'll take care of that bastard Colombini, Pauline," he said. "He's hiding out somewhere right now. He's not at

Augie's or his own place. He's got to come to ground sometime, and when he does, I'll make him pay. I promise."

"Please, don't do anything, Benny. Don't do anything on my account."

He paused a long time, then unable to hide his impatience, said, "All right, all right. Anything you say, Doll. But I don't like doing nothing when someone goes after my girl. When can I see you? It's been a couple of weeks."

"I'm sorry, Benny. Not now. I think we should not see each other for a while. This gang war. It's threatening my family now."

"I told you that's got nothing to do with me."

She no longer believed him. "I've got to go, Benny." She hung up the phone.

That night, Lauren went into the family room to check on Raider. She smiled when she saw Emmy sleeping beside him on a blanket, gripping a wooden doll in her arms. Remy came in. Most nights, he was sleeping over in her bedroom, much to Mrs. Windsor's chagrin. The old bat insisted he use another guestroom for the sake of propriety and the children. Then, he slipped into hers.

He stared down at Raider for a few seconds, then motioned for her to follow him. Outside on the back lawn, he said, "This is my fault. I should quit. I'll leave as soon as you can find someone else."

"What are you talking about?"

"I should have sent patrols up in there," he said, sighing, glancing up into the hills. "I should have."

"Knighton and Brady came to me and said the same thing. Look, you and me both. We all fucked up. But there's no one I can get better than you, Remy. You can do things I can't, that no one can. You seem to be friends with every damn person in this city. So, I'll tell you what I told them: get over it. I need you."

He sighed again. "Something has to done about Colombini. We can't sit around again while he sends men after Pauline."

She nodded. "I'm working on a plan. First, I need to find out where he is. Can you do that?"

He stared at her with curiosity. "I know some people," he said. "What plan?"

"Not yet. Let me work it out first."

Two days later, Remy came to her with Colombini's location. He had even taken his plane up to confirm it. "He's got a villa in the mountains around Calabasas. He's been there while the dust settles around his attack on Pauline. What are you planning?" he asked.

"Not yet. Let me work on it a few more days."

I know what you're thinking, Matt said in alarm. *It's crazy. Not even the great Malinche can possibly beat those odds. We both could be terminated. After all, if there is no you, there is no me.*

Yes, I know. That fact has often tempted me to suicide.

CHAPTER THIRTY-NINE; TOP OF THE WORLD, MA!

November 20, 1927, Calabasas

On Sunday morning, Fats Colombini stepped out of his mountain villa thirty miles northeast of Los Angeles for the drive down to the city. He knew one of Sorrentino's men was outside the fortified stone walls, stalking him. They had discovered his location. McGinty had told him as much this morning on the phone. Even without that, he'd been around too long to ignore the prickly feeling of a sniper's scope on the back of his neck. He wasn't worried. It wouldn't be the first time someone tried to kill him, and it would not be the last.

As his bodyguards checked the Studebaker and two Fords for explosives, he gave a bark of a laugh and rubbed his hands together in glee. Things were falling into place for him. He now ran the outfit alone. He was going to kill that Windsor bitch; the plan was in place. Then he would destroy Sorrentino and take over the city. And today it would all come to pass.

Also, while hiding out, he'd had blissfully rough sex with his favorite prostitute, a girl no more than eighteen if that. She made him feel like a young lion, screaming and pleading for him to stop, yet that was what he paid her for. He was indeed a happy man this morning.

"The cars are clean, boss," his driver said, opening a door of the Studebaker for him.

He grinned. "Then, let's go stick a T-gun up Sorrentino's ass, eh, Reilly." He clapped the driver on the back and got in. Four men got in the Ford to the rear and four into the one in front. The two other bodyguards got in the back of his Studebaker.

Assassin 13

The first car pulled out onto the road and the Studebaker followed. The convoy eased through the crowded farmer's market of the little hamlet abutting his villa.

Once out of the village, the road began twisting down through the forest of oak and pine.

Fats nudged the driver's shoulder. "Look at these roads, Reilly. I built these roads. Me and Augie did. I raised the money. Them farmers back there owe me."

"Yeah, boss."

"I have done many good things. I am a good man. A great leader."

Reilly glanced at him, but said nothing.

"After today, we're going to run the damn city. Maybe even the state soon," Fats said, then laughed. "Louis Colombini, Governor of California."

Ten minutes into the drive, Reilly adjusted his mirror and said, "I don't see Rizzo and the boys anymore. Someone else is following us."

With a jolt of fear, Fats snapped his head around, the jowly fat about his neck jiggling. He saw a motorcyclist thirty yards behind. *Was this the assassin?* But as he watched, the bike came no closer. He chuckled. "Relax, Reilly. On this road, it is always logging trucks and motorcycles. I'll tell the boys they need to keep up when we stop."

But over the next few minutes, Fats glanced back several times. Odd behavior that the rider maintained the exact distance, never approaching, never falling back. Like stalking prey. Him. It made everyone nervous. The bodyguards in the back seat closed their hands over their Thompsons.

Soon, the road descended into thick fog with visibility only a hundred feet or less, and Reilly slowed. As they entered several sharp switchbacks, they could no longer see the Ford in front of them or the motorcyclist behind. The unease tightened like a choker around Fats' neck.

He always had to piss these days. When they drove out of the fog, he saw no one, no car in front or behind, but neither did he see the motorcyclist. With an assassin stalking him, he had not wanted to stop at all till he'd reached the safety of his Beverly Hills home, but his bursting bladder changed that. He ordered the driver to pull over onto the shoulder.

***

Three hundred yards farther down the twisting mountain road, nestled behind brush, Jimmy Pelosi was adjusting the sights on his sniper rifle. Then, his head snapped up when he saw the Ford crest the distant hill and head down a series of sharp curves. The car began to slow and came to a stop just below him, not thirty yards away. Four men got out and looked back up the road.

Jimmy could hear them. One said, "Should we turn around and go back?"

"Nah," another man said. "We can wait here. They'll be along in a minute."

This presented a problem. When Fats came, his car would have to slow for the 180-degree switchback directly below and that would put the fat bastard right in his sights. He couldn't miss. But the men below? He would have to take them as well. That might be difficult.

Then the Studebaker appeared coming over the crest. Fats' car. He decided to go ahead as planned. But abruptly, the car pulled over to the side of the road, stopped, and the four men got out, including fat, waddling Colombini. The men from the Ford could not see up the mountain.

Fats and his three men stepped quickly to the edge of the forest to piss. Pelosi thought he could take Fats from here, but it was still a difficult shot, three hundred yards. He could wait.

A motorcycle crested the hill.

***

Fats laughed. "A hell of a police lineup we got here, boys."

The others laughed as well. A bird screeched from somewhere high up in the trees, startling Fats so much he wet his patent leather shoes. This assassin business had him on edge.

They heard the motorcycle first, then saw it draw to a spinning halt on the shoulder twenty yards away, kicking up dirt. The rider stared at them for several long seconds. He wore a dark leather helmet and goggles, so Fats couldn't see the face. Fear took hold of him.

Still pissing, two of the bodyguards slipped their Tommy guns from their shoulders, but then the cyclist took off the helmet and a great flow of black hair tumbled out. It shocked them all. A dame, an attractive one at that. Fats' alarm faded away, and he laughed.

With a grunt, the two bodyguards adjusted the rifles back onto their shoulders. Laughing with relief, Fats continued to urinate in a short stream. "If she wants to watch four men piss, we let her."

They all laughed. With a leer, he glanced over his shoulder as the woman approached. Her black eyes fixed him in a hellish concentration, freezing the leer to his face. As if by dark magic, a gun appeared in her left hand. Her harsh voice plunged fangs into his heart. "Pauline Windsor sends her regards."

Instantly, he recognized the name of the actress. He stared in horror at the woman. *This* was his assassin. "Sorrentino started it," he screamed.

Wetting himself again, he fumbled in his jacket for his pistol. The bodyguards scrambled to get the T-guns off their shoulders, but it was all too late. The woman dispatched the guards and driver with three quick shots, all to the head, and turned to Fats. He raised his hands in surrender.

"Please," he muttered. "Please, it's not fair."

She fired the kill shot into his forehead, exploding a red spray of bone and brain tissue. Next, the assassin snatched two black flower petals from the nearby dry grass and placed them over Fats' eyes. Calmly, she strode back to the motorcycle.

***

From three hundred yards away, Pelosi set the rifle scope on the dark-haired woman. He had watched the kill in utter surprise. What the hell was this? He had never seen a woman assassin before, never even heard of one. But then he knew women could be as deadly as men. And that gun. It shot rounds that exploded like tiny artillery shells. He would give anything to possess that gun.

He followed her with the rifle scope as she climbed aboard the motorcycle, the sights squarely on her head. His finger slotted into the trigger guard, but he didn't fire. He could not see any detail of her face from such a distance, but he had an inkling who it was.

"I'll be damned," he whispered.

Spinning dirt from her wheels, she shot the motorcycle back onto the road and raced down the road toward him. The four men below him had heard the shots, glanced at each other, then stared up the mountain road. Two of them drew revolvers.

Pelosi tracked the woman taking curves at such speed she leaned nearly horizontal to the ground. He would blow her off the bike with one shot.

His finger pressed into the trigger guard. As she shot by below, Pelosi fired two quick shots but she was going at such speed, he'd missed. "Fuck!" he hissed.

Assassin 13

He then turned to the stationary targets. Colombini's men collapsed one after the other on the road. The woman was already gone, hidden within the forests. Pauline Windsor's fucking assistant was a button woman.

This was going to spark Benny's tinderbox.

CHAPTER FORTY: DOG JUSTICE

December 7, 1927, Hollywood Hills

With the premier of Pauline's movie, *The Palace of Fallen Angels,* drawing near, the house had been on edge for nearly a week. It was finally here, and everyone was running around as if the End of Days. Brady had drawn up a plan for protection tonight, and Knighton assigned men their duties. No intel or rumor suggested a particular threat awaited them, yet Lauren was uneasy. Then, of course, she was always uneasy.

It was near 5:00am, almost time for Lauren to get up for her morning run. Moonlight shone through the window but did little to illuminate the darkened corners of the bedroom. She lay beside a sleeping Remy. More than two weeks had passed since Fats Colombini's deletion, and the mob outfit had completely disintegrated. The following afternoon after she had closed the gangster's file, newspapers' headlines screamed: *Fats Slain in Ambush. Fats Colombini Shot Dead by Unknown Assailant. Violent End of Mob Boss.* Most articles speculated Sorrentino had clipped Colombini.

A few men tried to take over the Colombini organization but all failed, killed by Sorrentino. He offered jobs to the remnants, and the gang war that had plagued Los Angeles ended abruptly.

Lauren exhaled in frustration. Although exhausted, she hadn't slept thanks to her inability to draw a curtain over her mind, but also the lovemaking. That had been, well, engaging, far too engaging. Not what she needed right now. Too many things were making a chaotic jumble inside her mind.

You're not keeping me awake, are you, Matt? she asked.
No, why would I do that?
Because you don't sleep.

I'm an AI. Of course I don't sleep. But I swear to you I am doing nothing to keep you awake. He fell silent for nearly a minute, then added, *It is sometimes freaky crazy to be caught up in your dreams though. Freaky crazy. I enjoy saying those words. Freaky crazy. Applicable here. You're either running from something monstrous, or killing something monstrous. It's harrowing being me in your brain. Can't you once just have a simple dream, a romantic interlude, eating ice cream, or jawing with friends? Jawing. I like that word, too.*

Ignoring him, she considered threats to Pauline. The biggest peril was Sorrentino. She had broken up with him temporarily. Not ending their relationship completely as she should. Ever the smart fool, she saw him as no direct threat to her or her family. Lauren planned to delete him as well, then when she returned to her own time, she could feel she'd done her best to protect this family.

Three days ago, she had gone out to the shuttle to see if the anomaly appeared. It did. She didn't have to wait long. Just after 2:00am it came, the four strands suddenly glowing on the ship's hull. She saw vibrating brightness as if a dying creature's wail of agony.

Matt was already in the computer ready to gather data. It was not good. The VQ was down to 2, all its life force nearly drained away. Its stay this time in 1927 was just twenty-one minutes. Like a death gasp. That had to be the last appearance. Was the anomaly gone forever? Was she trapped here, and the chance of retribution for her mother's murder gone forever?

Matt had no answer for that. He could not say if the anomaly would return for one last gasp of life or die somewhere else.

Afterward, as Lauren walked up the ravine to the motorcycle, she held the medallion tightly in her hand, telling her mother she would not give up. And telling Matt she would not give up, that she would proceed under the assumption the anomaly would return on January 8th.

That wouldn't matter, though, if she couldn't find a fucking gyroscope.

Her bedroom door opened and someone slipped inside, tiptoeing toward her. It was Emmy. The little girl who was afraid of the dark, but something made her unafraid this time.

She shook Lauren's arm and whispered, "Wake up, Lauren.

"I'm awake, mi hija."

Emmy dragged at her. "It's Raider. Hurry."

So, the dog had finally died. He'd hung on for more than two weeks. Emotions welled up inside her. He had fought like the soldier he was. Remember that, she told herself. She threw on a pajama top and bottoms and followed the girl to the family room.

Raider was standing up and drinking from his water bowl. She rushed to the dog, falling to her knees, hugging him fiercely.

CHAPTER FORTY-ONE: FLY ME TO THE MOON

December 7, 1927, Downtown Los Angeles

On Wednesday, Pauline's new film *The Palace of Fallen Angels* was scheduled to premiere at Grauman's Chinese Theater. She was irritable and nervous all day. She desperately wanted the movie to be both well-received and a commercial success. As one of the top stars in Hollywood, she was well aware that many people were eager to see her fail. More than just a few critics and film people wished the movie turned out to be terrible and her acting a bust. It sold more papers. "Screw them," she muttered throughout the day when the children were not around.

Wearing tuxedos, Knighton and Brady squeezed into the front seat of the Rolls Royce Phantom with Dave Arthur, who drove. Knighton ran a finger between his collar and throat and grumbled that he looked like a penguin. In the back, Remy sat with Lauren in the jump seat, facing Pauline and Michael Murray.

Arc lights blazed violet streaks across the night sky as their car fell into line behind the procession of limos dropping off the Hollywood royalty. Massive crowds pressed against ropes to watch them all arrive.

Decked out in a blue silk Madeleine Vionnet evening dress that clung sensuously to her figure, Pauline looked every inch the movie star. Sitting in the jump seat, Lauren was stylish but less dramatic in a black Coco Chanel dress. It would not do to compete with the star over fashion, but then Lauren knew that next to Pauline, she would be foolish to attempt it. She was purely background.

Lauren scanned the crowds, but even with Matt's help, it was impossible to garner any information on any threat, a madman perhaps, or a leftover thug from the Colombini mob bent on revenge, or someone simply wanting to sabotage Pauline's night. She didn't expect any trouble, but that was often when it came.

Ahead of them, one after the other, movie stars stepped from their limousines to cheering and applause. These were the biggest stars in the Hollywood firmament, or so Lauren had been told by Matt. After watching so many movies with Remy, Russell and Matt, she was becoming much more familiar with them. They did seem to glitter as they walked down the gauntlet of fans. Among those scheduled to attend: John Gilbert and Greta Garbo, Mary Pickford and Douglas Fairbanks, the Talmadge sisters, Charlie Chaplin just stepping out of his car ahead of them, Gloria Swanson, Pola Negri, Fatty Arbuckle, whom Pauline had invited despite Zelinsky forbidding it, Lillian and Dorothy Gish, Clara Bow, and even Rin Tin Tin on a leash.

Lauren could feel Matt's excitement rising volcanically, actually sending tremors through her body. *Stop it, Matt. Calm down. You need to stay alert.*

He relaxed marginally.

Pauline indicated the crowds up and down the block and spilling into the street. "Look at our fans, Michael. They love us, but if the film flops, they will rip us apart."

"Not me, my dear," he said. "They will rip you apart. I'm no good. I know that, and they know that. It's you who stands on the high cliff. It's you who will have the long fall."

"Thanks," she said. She sucked in her breath as the Rolls Royce stopped in front of the entrance that stood like a giant pagoda. "Here we go."

With a dazzling smile, Pauline stepped from the car onto the red carpet. The crowd cheered madly, calling her name.

Arm in arm with Michael, she walked down the red carpet, waving. Lauren and Remy followed, barely noticed.

This is exciting. Matt blurted out. *My first red carpet.*

A stocky, middle-aged woman at a microphone spoke with Pauline and Michael. Their voices blared through loudspeakers. Then, she asked, "Pauline dear, Mary Lawrence, who played Edna in *Palace of Fallen Angels,* just said she outshone you in the movie."

"Really?" Pauline raised an eyebrow in surprise. "I didn't know she was in the picture."

When she and Michael left, the woman's assistant, a young man in a bow tie, stepped toward Lauren and Remy to catch them for an interview.

The woman stopped him. "Not them. They're nobody."

Matt piped up, *I bet SHE doesn't have an AI in HER head.*

In the lobby, Jerry Zelinsky, Global Studio head, stood puffing on a cigar with three other men, gesturing at the red lacquered columns and the great Chinese lantern hanging from the gold ceiling. "Look at all this luxury shit," he said. "If it wasn't for Global Pictures, Grauman would have a little fleabag place. My pictures pay for this palace."

Seeing Pauline and Michael enter, he called out. "There are my stars now. Big night, Pauline. This is going to be a huge hit." When she drew closer, he lowered his voice. "We can't afford a fucking flop, you hear? Not with that bomb *Homo and Juliet* coming next. That would put you in a bad spot."

Pauline met his gaze. "Don't be such a coward, Jerry. *Palace* will shatter all Global box office records. Which incidentally are my records."

"I'm sure it will," Zelinsky said with little conviction and then motioned his arms at the people in the lobby as if herding cattle. "Go in. The stars of the moment have arrived."

Gloria Swanson, with her long black hair set off by a diamond tiara came up accompanied by a distinguished gray-haired man. "Have I introduced my husband, Pauline," she sniffed with exaggerated haughtiness, "the Marquis de La Coudraye."

"Only about a hundred times." Pauline glanced at him. "I hope you enjoy the picture, your highness."

"Address me as *My Lord*," he said. "Your highness is hardly necessary."

"Of course." Pauline glanced at Lauren and rolled her eyes.

Swanson winked. "Good luck tonight. I just know you're going to have a major hit to deal with."

"Thanks, Gloria."

Inside the theater, a full orchestra from down in front filled the auditorium with a powerful, classical melody. The two thousand seats were occupied by the famous and not-so-famous of Hollywood, including Dr. and Mrs. Meyer, saviors of Raider. A haze of smoke floated above from cigarettes and cigars, partially obscuring the ceiling with its field of artificial stars.

A young woman in an elegant Chinese costume led Pauline's group to their seats in one of the balconies. When they sat down, Remy nervously tapped his knee with his knuckles.

"What's wrong with you?" Lauren asked.

He frowned. "This is my movie, too. In the aerial scenes, I'm the one flying the plane."

The lights faded, conversations ended. Lauren sensed a collective anticipation. *For Pauline's sake,* she said to Matt, *I hope this is good?*

Oh, it will be, he answered her. *This is Pauline Windsor's masterpiece. It is considered…"*

What a minute, she interrupted him. *You've seen it before?*

Of course.

Why didn't you tell me? Lauren asked, annoyed.

I had no reason to do so. I cannot perceive what you don't know or what you might want to know unless you tell me, and you had not.

Then, you're a pretty lame excuse for an AI.

AIs are not omniscient, even sentient ones such as myself, he insisted, defensively. *My programming is not limitless. Here, in the theater, about to watch the movie, I thought it relevant and gave you the data. It is...*

Before he could say more, the orchestra began playing again, a full-bodied arrangement of something classical, and Matt went quiet. The projector's beam of light fell on the curtain as it opened. Appearing on the black screen were the words *Global International Pictures and Jerry Zelinsky Presents*. Then, the film began.

In the story, Pauline played Princess Eugenia. When her father, the king of Moldonia, was murdered, she fled in an old rickety biplane with Michael Murray, who played the pilot. She had rousted him out of a drunken stupor to fly her to safety. In the shots of the plane in the air, Remy was flying and Gladys Ingle, his compatriot in the 13 Black Cats, sat in the back.

Lauren patted his knee. "Nice work, flyboy. That white scarf is dashing."

He gave a derisive snort, but she could tell he was pleased.

As the pilot and the princess approached Paris, the Eiffel tower in the distance, two planes from the Moldonian air force caught up with them and attacked. Remy did loops, summersaults, and then a death spiral to escape. Damaged by machine gun fire, the plane crashed in a farmer's field. Both the princess and the pilot survived unharmed. Of course, Lauren knew if they didn't survive, the movie would be over within fifteen minutes.

Later, after a tortured romance between the two, the king's loyal followers sent word to Paris for the princess to return. They wanted her to be the symbol of the new revolution. Fearful of her power as a rallying point, the enemy sent agents to kill her. They stood watch at the rail stations and roads and at the border crossings. For her to get back home, she needed the plane repaired, which seemed an impossible task.

After hours of work, the pilot got the plane to start. In a long scene, the director focused in closeup on the spinning propeller for a full ten seconds, cutting to the plane rising into the air. The band hit a crescendo, and the audience cheered.

In an instant, a blast of brilliant color shot into her mind, a connection between the shuttle and what she'd just seen on screen. The solution. She had her gyroscope. The damn spacecraft would fly. She could repair it tonight.

It won't work, Matt said. She ignored him.

The movie was finishing. The plane made it aloft. The princess returned home to lead her people to victory. In the film's climax, she wrought her revenge on her father's murderers, then married the pilot.

The audience stood and cheered.

Remy leaned into her. "I really like it when the pilot gets the girl."

Lauren nodded, only half hearing him. As they began walking out behind Pauline and Michael, Remy said something to her, but she was barely aware of it. She registered Pauline saying, "Now, it will depend on the critics."

People were filing from the theater, still caught up in the excitement of the movie, and she moved along in tow, focused on a precise moment in the film. The spinning propeller. Occam's Razor. A simple answer to a complex problem.

Matt, we are going out to the ship, she said.

It won't work.

Assassin 13

She shot back angrily, *We are going out to the ship. Now. How? Walk? It's thirty miles. You have no transportation.*

Holding her hand, Remy drew her to the side. "Lauren, what is the matter with you? You look like you're going to hit someone. Are you okay?" They were standing outside the theater among a crowd of celebrities waiting for their limousines to be brought around.

"What?" Lauren snapped at him, just realizing he had spoken.

"Are you all right? I asked if you're hungry. I thought we could skip the party and…"

She wrenched her hand free. "I've got to go. Watch Pauline." Abruptly, without another word, she disappeared into the crowd.

Around the corner of the building, Lauren slipped through the shadows of the vacant lot and out onto Highland Avenue where the line of luxury cars, headlights on, crept slowly toward the intersection to turn onto Hollywood Boulevard and pick up their passengers. The dark street was empty of pedestrians. While the other cars moved up, the last one lagged back, not moving at all.

The chauffeur was leaning back in the seat, smoking a cigarette and drinking from a bottle in a sack. He was drunk. Walking up to the car, Lauren opened the door, grabbed his tie and yanked him out, rolling him onto the street.

"What the hell?" he croaked, struggling to his feet.

One snap-punch to the jaw, and he flopped down like a dead puppet. She had not meant to hit him so hard. Quickly, she dragged him across the street to a brick building and sat him against it, placing the bottle in his lap.

Then, she walked calmly back to the car and drove off.

CHAPTER FORTY-TWO: WOMAN IN THE MOON

December 7, 1927, Santa Monica Mountains

As Lauren sped out to the crash site in a limousine, she felt a growing pressure inside her head and sensed the cause was tension coming from her sudden realization that she might actually return to her own century if this worked. And from Matt. He did not want to return to the 22nd century. She could not explain what he was doing to cause it, didn't even know that he could actually feel tension. She knew also that he was monitoring her thinking.

What's going on, Matt? she asked him.

Your idea will not work. That is all, he replied. *I detect your disappointment. I am sorry.*

Are you? I doubt it, she said. *You want to stay here. Why the hell does it matter to you? You're just a damn appliance.*

Smile when you say that. He paused for a long time waiting for her to react to his joke, but she didn't offer a ripple of emotion. Minutes of silence between them passed. In the black night they roared along the dirt road, stirring up dust as they cut into the mountains.

She felt him digging into her subconscious. *Get out of my damn subconscious, Matt. I can't have you in my head if I can't trust you.* She paused to let him take that in. *All right. Tell me now. Why the hell does it matter to you? The truth, or so help me God, I will scrub you from my neurobots.*

I think you would, he said petulantly. Then a microsecond passed. For him, a long hesitation. *I will answer truthfully as always. For me, being prisoner within the confines of a computer for all eternity is no life for a sentient being. Here, in this time, in your head, imprinted on your neurobots, I move when you move. I see when you see. I hear when you hear and feel when you feel. Here, in this time, I am truly alive.*

A tingle as if a low current of electricity shot through her. An AI flinch. Did she feel a spark of emotion for him? Maybe. But, though alive and sentient, he could not be her responsibility, too. She did not want to share her thoughts, her psyche, or her soul in totality with another living being. Certainly not a sentient AI. She did not think those last thoughts. Knew them without thinking them. She was learning how to keep thoughts from him.

When they returned to the 22nd century, Lauren would have herself back. She would complete her life's mission. If that condemned him to his computer prison, so be it. That's what he was created to do. With him privy to her thoughts, she did not dare let the issue come to her conscious mind or even subconscious till she was ready to go to war with him. That would be at some point when she was back in 2131.

We'll see what happens. That's the best I can do, she said finally. Two can play at this game of subterfuge.

That's all I ask.

Ten minutes later, inside the shuttle's cockpit, Matt leapt from her head into the ship's computer.

The spinning propeller in the movie made Lauren think of the shuttle's anti-gravity ring, which spun constantly beneath the ship. It occurred to her that the ship itself was a gyroscope.

Matt had known what she'd been thinking. She asked him, "Is it possible?"

It took him a nanosecond to respond, but she caught his hesitation. "It is," he said.

"I thought so."

To replace the destroyed gyroscope, Matt rewired the digital pathways in the guidance control system in seconds. The ship's own gyroscopic action should stabilize it in flight.

Lauren took her seat in the captain's chair. "Matt, engage the engine."

Power rumbled through the hull as the ship came alive. The field of vision screen opened 180 degrees. She felt the sensation of the ship lifting, wobbling slightly, and she groaned, thinking the gyroscope fix had failed. But Sybil's grave slid below in the FOV, and the ship rose out of the ravine. Then, they shot forward.

Lauren gave a primal scream of joy.

The lights of Los Angeles blurred below her and disappeared in an instant. A tingle raced through her body as if she were weightless. Her hair lifted, effects of the inertia dampening field killing the great G-forces.

"Gamma ray emissions?" Lauren asked.

"None," Matt said.

"Ship stability?"

"Five by five."

"Goddamn it, Matt. You said it couldn't be done. I damn well did it."

He spoke in a somber tone. "Yes, you did, Lauren."

They circled the globe, mostly in silence but for a few commands, and returned to the ravine. Lauren allowed Matt back into her head, and sustained a moment of icy chill inside her skull. She was aware what a strange figure she presented in her Coco Channel dress climbing out of the ravine and walking to the stolen car.

That's when Matt's hyper-charged voice suddenly shattered her thought process. *Lauren, Lauren, I have discovered information of vital importance.*

This ought to be good. What now?

You wanted me to be more active in notifying about data that might be of some significance to you, no matter how inconsequential I might think it is.

Assassin 13

Get to the point, Matt.

He sent an image of what looked like an obituary with several words and phrases missing. She was about to purge it from her mind when she saw the name Ben Sorrentino.

What the fuck.

She took in the half-page at a glance, then with a gasp, read more closely.

***

MIAMI POST

MIAMI BEACH, FLA., August 15, 1977. Ben Sorrentino, ex-Los Angeles prohibition era mobster, died in his home here this morning of heart failure. He was 78. His wife, Cherie, and two sons, Ben Jr. and Alphonse, were present.

Known in his gangster days as Benny the Bug, Sorrentino was described in one biography as the most brutal cutthroat in American history. In the City of Angels, he engaged in a notorious gangland war that saw more than 200 slaughtered by handguns, shotguns, Tommy guns, knives, baseball bats and brass knuckles. Innocent men, women and children were caught in the crossfire.

Yet, inexplicably, in that bygone era, he gained celebrity status in a town of celebrities.

"Benny had charm," Meyer Lansky, another notable Miami Beach retiree, said on hearing of his passing. "People just naturally liked him, wanted to please him. He had that effect on everyone. Especially women. It was charm all right, but the charm of a snake."

Just after arriving in Hollywood in 1927, he most notably dated the famous silent film actress Pauline Windsor. He was arrested for her murder in 1928, the only time he was tried for a crime. When evidence and witnesses disappeared, he was acquitted and...

***

Lauren's anger turned on Matt. *How long have you had this information?*

Assassin 13

I never had it. You did. It was on your neurobots, part of an encyclopedia of crime that, I believe, you deleted years ago. I came across remnant strands of data not five seconds ago.

She did not believe him. He was lying again, but the obit was real. She knew because she had seen it before. Long ago in Chicago when she had taken out Nasri and many of his top lieutenants. While in Robert Kaseem's apartment, she'd seen the photos of Chicago gangsters from every decade over the previous two hundred years, but mostly in the Golden Age of the 1920s and 30s. Each of those photos had an obit inside the glass as if the modern-day mob was proud of their ancestors dying with their boots on.

She had seen one for Sorrentino, but hadn't read it except to notice he had died in 1977. This was the same obituary.

She did not know how to respond to any of this. Pauline murdered, past tense. Sorrentino arrested and acquitted, past tense. In 1928, only a couple weeks away. So, will the murder take place in that year or in the last couple weeks of 1927?

She raced back to the car.

Near 4:00am, Lauren drove the hijacked car back to Hollywood and left it parked in a side street not far from Grauman's and hiked the couple miles up into the Hollywood Hills to Pauline's mansion. As she arrived home, the first shards of sunlight fell on the surrounding hills.

Quickly checking the four outside guards on duty, everything seemed under control.

She told each one, "Stay alert. This is not over."

She went in, showered, and grabbed an hour's sleep.

Later that morning on the patio, Pauline and Mrs. Windsor eagerly poured over the Los Angeles newspapers for the reviews of *Palace of Fallen Angels*. At one in the Hollywood Daily Citizen, Pauline broke down in tears.

"What is it?" Mrs. Windsor asked, alarmed.

Russell had come over, Lauren sat nearby, and the children were drifting in from the lawn, surprised to see their mother weeping.

"They describe the movie as an instant classic," Pauline said, her voice trembling.

Mrs. Windsor shrieked, "Halleluiah!"

They all read on, and not a single critic panned the movie. They loved it, calling it the best picture of the year, a surefire hit, Pauline Windsor magnificent. With great anticipation, they awaited her new film *Romeo and Juliet*.

Mrs. Windsor beamed with pride and announced, "It looks like we have another hit."

That's when Mrs. Windsor read aloud an oddity from the L.A. Examiner. After the movie, John Gilbert's limousine was stolen and the poor, drunken chauffeur claimed Gloria Swanson did it. The renowned dark-haired actress, he insisted, had knocked him out before she drove off in the car.

Everyone laughed, including Lauren, who laughed the loudest. If the damn anomaly had one more breath in it, she was going home on January 8, but she had work to do before then. She needed to delete Ben Sorrentino first.

CHAPTER FORTY-THREE: DOPE

December 15-17, 1927, Los Angeles

In the next week, Lauren spent several days looking for Sorrentino. After the fall of Fats Colombini, he apparently felt safe enough to leave his organization in the hands of his lawyers while he dealt with setting up his organization outside the country. Rumors had him as far away as Hong Kong, lining up the opium trade. Or in Canada establishing a steady source of bourbon. For Lauren, the important consideration was Pauline's safety. She didn't think he would come after the actress till he exhausted all avenues in taking possession of her downtown property.

The big topic around the house was still *The Palace of Fallen Angels*. The box office from theaters across the country steadily reported the film an enormous hit. The picture's success also energized the production of *Romeo and Juliet* as it drew to an end, everyone thinking Pauline led a charmed celluloid life, and that they were working on another major hit. Nothing could stop her.

On the last day of filming, Lauren abruptly found herself in front of the camera. The actor who was to play the brief role of Friar John had fallen ill. In the play, he was the Brother tasked with delivering the message to Romeo telling him Juliet was only pretending suicide, and to come to be at her side when she awakes. Since it was only one quick scene and Clarence Martin, the director, didn't want to waste time bringing in another actor, he enlisted Lauren. She was more than tall enough to play a man wearing a cowl.

Surprisingly, when the cameras were about to roll, she found herself panicky, more so even than going into the kill zone of an op. A different kind of nervousness, one powerful and debilitating. She felt nausea, nearly vomiting on stage.

What the hell is wrong with me?

Matt's raucous laughter invaded her mind. He sent an image to her neurobots of a thickly mustachioed man slapping his knees with uncontrolled mirth. *The great Malinche paralyzed with fear,* Matt said. *Oh, that's a pearl, a pearl.*

Pauline understood and hugged her. "Focus on the two key points of movement in the scene. Let Martin talk you through it. You'll do fine."

In brown clerical robes and cowl, she dragged a donkey behind her on a set made to look like the walls of Mantua. That's where Romeo had fled after killing Juliet's kinsman Tybalt. Her face full on camera, Lauren drew back her hood—her hair in an unseen ponytail—and asked a merchant where to find Romeo. Her shaky voice would not make it into a silent film, but the dialogue title card of her lines would. The merchant pointed her in the wrong direction while, behind her on the road, Romeo headed out of the city toward Verona, where he believed Juliet lay dead.

After the director called *cut,* Lauren's nervousness exploded into frenetic excitement. It reminded her of a day long ago when she accompanied her father and mother, shooting the rapids down a narrow Sierra Nevada stream in a canoe. They had been tossed and turned and finally flipped over. They caught up to the canoe, flipped it right-side up and climbed back in. That day she had laughed with joy. When the cameras stopped rolling, she laughed, too.

"A star is born," Martin said, grinning.

She gave a high-pitched seal-squeal, which made her grimace at her silliness, but she felt ecstatic. All this acting got in the blood.

Assassin 13

That day *Romeo and Juliet* went to the editing room, and a private screening of the finished film was scheduled in less than two weeks on December 27th at Global Pictures' private auditorium.

At home, when Pauline and Lauren returned from work, the children were only mildly interested in Lauren's moment in front of the camera. They'd long become familiar with actors and acting. Not an impressive thing anymore. They were more concerned with their own lives, Lauren realized, like most children were.

The most important thing in the world to Rolly was his birthday on Saturday. Many of his classmates would be attending. He invited household staff and Windsor's Warriors as well. It would be the best birthday party *ever*. For days, everyone had been engaged in finding the perfect gift for what was turning into a major event on Saturday.

What would excite and impress an eight-year-old, soon to be nine-year-old? Lauren asked Matt.

A ball?

You're no help.

I'm serious. A ball. Any sport.

That evening in the living room before bed, Rolly pleaded with her again to come to the party.

"Of course, I'll come, mi hijo," she told him, kissing his forehead.

He was in his pajamas. "What are you going to get me?" he asked excitedly.

"I haven't decided yet," she said, putting a finger to her chin as if trying to choose right then. "I was thinking maybe a laser generator that shoots a beam of light from the earth to the moon, or a tiny phone that fits in your head and has access to all the knowledge in the universe, or maybe a robot."

Pauline and even Mrs. Windsor laughed at that, but Rolly, jumping up and down with excitement, clapped his hands.

Those would actually be good, Matt said. *Of course, none of that is available in 1927.*

Pauline turned Rolly toward his bedroom and lightly swatted his rear. "On the way, you. No more procrastination. Get to bed."

As he ran off down the hall, Pauline frowned at Lauren. "Now, you did it. He won't sleep much at all."

***

Early Saturday morning, a hundred miles north of Los Angeles on Route One, Greeny Walsh drove his new Chrysler Imperial toward town after a week-long trip to San Francisco's Chinatown, buying first-class dope. The sun was just about to break above the mountains. Nearly a hundred pounds of cocaine, marijuana, and heroin sat in the trunk, strapped to the back of the car.

"Those chinks really have a handle on the dope market," he said to the other men in the car.

Two of the men Sorrentino had sent along sat in the back. Arnold Hauser, his fingers drumming on the suitcase in his lap, was a big man, six feet five, his head nearly touching the car roof. Beside him sat Otto Flick, small and pudgy, a face like a ripe peach. His glasses were pushed back on his head as he lolled in his sleep. He could use a gun but preferred a knife. He cut people up, which could be a very intimidating thing for Greeny's rivals.

"You know Pauline Windsor?" Anthony Bandini asked for the third time. He sat in the front passenger seat. "I want to meet her."

He was all blubber with a pig face. But he was the most dangerous of the three. A deadly shot with a pistol and ready to use it on anyone no matter age or sex. Yesterday, Greeny saw him pump six shots into a young chink whore who refused to suck his cock. When Flick asked him why he did that, he said so people would know to fear him. How could she fear him if she was dead? Greeny had thought.

"Sure, I know her," Greeny answered him. "One of my prime customers, but forget it. She's Sorrentino's Sheba. Don't worry. There are plenty of movie broads be interested in a handsome guy like you."

Two hours later, he reached his house and parked the car in the garage, telling the men to put the dope on the kitchen table.

The curtains were drawn in the darkened living room. Stepping into the shadows, he made out the trash, old beer bottles, food cartons, and unwashed clothes that cluttered the floor. A strong odor resembling Limburger cheese emanated from them. He flicked the light switch but nothing happened.

"Damn," he cursed.

"Do you ever plan to clean this mess?" a voice in the dark said.

Greeny jumped and slammed back against the wall. Searching frantically, he made out the speaker sitting in an armchair by the fireplace. It was a woman. He relaxed. His only worry now was whether he would have to share her with the other three.

Then something about her unsettled him. In the dim light, her black eyes gleamed like a wild animal's. He started sliding back toward the kitchen and his men in the garage.

She fired a shot into the wall by his head, shards stinging his face, and he froze in place. The gun barely made a sound. He didn't even see it. Was someone else with her? Where the hell were his men?

The first question was answered when a man's voice came from a shadowy corner. "Stay put." She was not alone.

Greeny just made out his shape and the patch over his eye, like a fucking, scary pirate. "Please don't hurt me," he whimpered.

The woman remained in the chair. "We're not here to hurt you. I just need to ask a couple questions. Tell me what I want to know, and we will leave you alone. In fact, we'll never see you again."

He wanted to believe her, but didn't. This was her. That woman several of Sorrentino's men had been talking about, the one who had clipped Colombini.

She said softly, "Where is Sorrentino?"

Without warning, she dove to the floor as a spray of bullets from a submachine gun raked her chair. She slid along the floor into the shadows near the couch. Hauser's giant frame stepped into the kitchen doorframe. Greeny was about to shout where she was when he heard the gun from the man in the corner, two shots. Hauser's head snapped back, and he collapsed to the floor like an empty pair of pants.

"Are you all right, Mr. Walsh?" came Otto Flick's voice from the kitchen.

Greeny was frozen to the spot, too far from the kitchen to have a chance of reaching it. "No, I'm not all right," he snapped furiously. "There's a guy in here with a madwoman, and they're trying to kill me."

Suddenly, she was beside him and slammed him against the wall. "Shut up. Sit the fuck down and don't move."

He slid to the floor as she crept quickly to the kitchen doorframe, put her back against the wall, and waited. Greeny's head throbbed now and he felt a dampness in his groin area. He had peed his pants.

Down the hallway to the bedroom, he saw the blunt form of Bandini crawling like a turtle toward the living room, a shotgun cradled in his arms. The woman couldn't see him from where she was. She'd think any threat was coming from the kitchen.

Surreptitiously, he tried to point Bandini to where she was. He hoped he could see the gesture in the darkness.

Frick's head materialized at the kitchen entrance. He was smart. He would know where the woman was. Suddenly, his arm swung around the doorframe, knife in hand, attempting to strike her. She leaned back; the blade just missed her head and plunged into the wall.

At the sound of movement, Bandini rolled into the living room more nimbly than Greeny thought possible for such a fat man and aimed his shotgun at her.

The woman grabbed Frick's arm and jerked him toward her, placed the pistol under his chin and fired. The top of the man's head blew to the ceiling just as Bandini fired. In the small room, the shotgun sounded like the detonation of dynamite. For Greeny, the thud of buckshot striking flesh was sweet to hear. She had to be dead.

At the same time, the man with the eye patch pumped several bullets into Bandini just as the woman fired several from behind Frick's body. Bandini slumped out on the floor and the shotgun tumbled from his hands. Shoving Frick aside, the woman strode quickly to the fat man along with her male partner. Bandini's eyes opened. Still alive.

The woman kicked the shotgun away and placed a boot on his chest. She glanced over at Greeny. "Where'd you get him?"

Shakily, he answered, "San...San Francisco. The other two are Sorrentino's men."

"Oh." She put two bullets in Bandini's brain. "Well, Greeny, we're back where we started. You just need to answer one question."

From his sitting position, he held his hands up in surrender. They shook visibly. The wet spot in his pants spread. "I'll tell you whatever you want to know, but I don't know anything."

"I'll bet you know lots of things, Greeny," the man said. He had a deformed arm, but the other held a gun and seemed lethal enough. "All we care about is Sorrentino. Where is he?"

He shook his head, pleading, "I don't know. I swear. No one does."

Kneeling in front of him, the woman shot her hand out, smacking him hard on the chin. His head snapped back against the wall. "Jesus, you're pathetic," she said. "Where's Sorrentino?"

"I don't know, I don't know. No one knows. Chicago, maybe, or Canada. I swear to God, no one knows."

She slapped his arms away from his face and fixed him with her lunatic eyes. "Greeny, you're not helping yourself. You could die here or you could go on living." The low, cold tenor of her voice scared the shit out of him.

His voice grew shrill. "Look, look, other people are running his operation. Ask them. But I'm telling you, not even they know where he is. All I know is he's not in Los Angeles. He moves around, see? He's moving all the time. Business."

Her voice hardly above a whisper. "We talked to four of his men, Greeny. They held out on us. Just like you. They're dead." She gestured to Remy. "This man wants to kill you, Greeny. I don't. I'm betting you know the information we need."

Moaning, he rolled his head back and forth. "Jesus, lady, I told you, I don't know shit."

Rage flashed in her eyes. "I've had enough of you. You are deleted." She thrust her gun against his forehead.

"No!" he wailed, squeezing his eyes shut.

But the shot didn't come. Two seconds later, he was still alive. Five seconds. And ten. He opened his eyes. Her own eyes were darting back and forth as if trying to understand someone speaking. The man was silent. No one was speaking.

Then, she said something completely odd, her voice chilling. "Matt, don't ever use my mother's image to tell me anything again. If you do, I will terminate you even if I have to scrub every nanobyte of data from my neurobots. I'll pilot the damn shuttle myself."

The woman was crazy. Even the man gazed at her strangely. Greeny knew she wasn't talking to him, so, who the hell was she talking to? No one. And that scared him even more.

She pressed her gun harder against his forehead. "This is going to make a canyon of your brainpan. Amazingly enough, I don't give a shit whether you live or die. If you truly don't know where he is, then you're of no use to me, and you're worm's meat."

"Please, please, wait, wait," he screamed. "I don't know where he is, but I know where he's going to be."

Her frenzied stare riveted him. "This better be five by five."

Confused, by the *five by five*, he stammered, "January 7th in Tijuana at the Jockey Club race track. He will be there. His horse is running. He never misses one of his races."

From her reaction, he was sure she was going to kill him now. Her face had twisted into an agony so intense it looked as if he'd stabbed her in the chest. But then she smiled, holstered her gun and got up. "Damn, Greeny, you came up with the goods. But if this data is false, you won't live another day."

"It's true. I swear it's true."

The man reached down with his good arm and lifted him up. "If you warn Sorrentino, you're a fool, and you're not a fool, are you Greeny?"

He nodded, then quickly shook his head.

The man said, "He will kill you for talking to us. If you want to stay alive, your only choice is to let this play out."

For some reason, he stared at the eye patch, not the good eye. He nodded rapidly.

After studying him for another moment, the woman patted his cheek. "Hell, Greeny, you just might survive, after all. And, Greeny, get rid of these bodies."

CHAPTER FORTY-FOUR: A TRIP TO THE MOON

December 17, 1927, earth and space

After the gunplay at Greeny Walsh's house, Lauren rode to the Griffith Park Aerodrome on her motorcycle with Remy on the back and dropped him off. They had spoken little on the ride over. She was not upset. She was never troubled following an assassination, but Remy seemed unsettled.

When he got off, she said, "Are you all right with what happened?"

He stared at her as she straddled the bike. After a second, he nodded. He appeared like a novice priest overwhelmed with doubt.

"It had to be done," she said. "I have to find Sorrentino. I'll do anything to protect Pauline and the children."

"So, you can do to him what you did to Colombini?"

She did not hesitate. "Yes."

Finally, he nodded again, turned, and walked toward the hangers. Now, he knew exactly what a cold-hearted bitch she was. Now, their romance, such as it was, was likely adios, amiga.

It wasn't deleting Greeny's men that bothered her, but Rolly. She had missed his birthday party and the boy would be devastated, or maybe worse, he wouldn't care at all. She couldn't decide what was worse: being a traitor or irrelevant in his life. On the mountain road over to the Hollywood Hills, she raced the motorcycle at high speed, taking stupid risks in an attempt to return in time for the stupid birthday party.

A few minutes later, roaring up the driveway, she pulled the motorcycle to an abrupt stop, dropped the kickstand, and hurried inside. Pauline was the first person she saw, cleaning up after Rolly's party in the living room with Mrs. Belknap, the housekeeper, and Tia, the cook. All three frowned reproachfully at Lauren when she came in. All the children from the school had already left. The Warriors were back on duty or gone home.

"Have I missed it?" she asked.

"You missed it," Tia said. "It was done an hour ago."

"How could you, Lauren?" Pauline asked. "You know how much he wanted you here, you in particular. For some reason, he thought you would keep your word."

"I'm sorry," Lauren said and meant it. *I was out killing people for you.* "Something came up I couldn't avoid."

"Something is always coming up with you," Pauline said.

Emmy ran in and gave Lauren a hug, but the rest of the family, Pauline, Russell, and, of course, Mrs. Windsor, ignored her, treating her as if she were a leper.

"I'll work it out with him. I promise," Lauren said.

Sighing, Pauline said, "See that you try. He's outside now."

With Pauline following, Lauren went into the backyard where Rolly was playing football with Corcoran, Beachum, and Brady, all three of them off duty. The Border collie, Reggie, was running around chasing the fat ball, the only one seemingly capable of tackling Rolly. All of them, including the dog, stopped as the two women approached.

"Rolly, I wanted to explain why I couldn't make your party," Lauren began, wondering why she was being so sheepish.

He shut his hands over his ears and loudly spouted gibberish.

"You show her, Rolly boy," Brady said with a grin. "You show her."

Lauren scowled at him, and Pauline said, "Don't do that, Rolly. It's impolite."

Rolly removed his hands. "I'm not talking to her."

With no experience in dealing with children, Lauren had no idea how to fix this. Then, an idea came to her. Something she knew she should not do.

This is a very bad idea, Matt said.

Ignoring him, Lauren turned to Brady. "Captain Brady, would you tell Rolly I missed his party because I had to get his birthday present ready." Her voice lowered dramatically. "It is a present so special that it took a lot of time to prepare. Months."

Brady did a military left face and announced, "Rolly, Lauren says she is a sad, sad excuse for a friend and is really, really sorry she missed your birthday party. No one with anything inside their head would ever want to miss a Rolly Windsor birthday party."

Turning to Lauren, Rolly giggled, his eyes bright. "My present? Where is it? What did you bring me?"

"It's not here. I have to show it to you, that is if your mother will allow me the use of her LaSalle?"

Pauline looked curiously at her but nodded.

"Let's go, kid," Lauren said to the boy.

In the LaSalle, Lauren drove Rolly into the Santa Monica Mountains. On the way, he bounced excitedly on the front seat of the car, asking over and over, "What is it? What is it?"

"Sit still," she demanded. "It's a surprise. You'll see soon enough. Rolly, sit still."

Deep into the mountains, she pulled the LaSalle off the dirt road and drove a quarter of a mile over the hardpan to a copse of trees. Confused, Rolly climbed out on Lauren's side. She lifted him up on her back and climbed over the rocks ahead. "Just a little way now."

At the lip of the ravine, she stopped so he could see the spacecraft below. The sun's rays still bore down, but the dark hull seemed to absorb them. Rolly's jaw dropped and his eyes bugged out. After a few seconds, he gasped, "What is that?"

"That is a flying saucer, my flying saucer, and for your present, you and I are going into space. Do you want to go?"

"Yes!" he screamed excitedly, riding her back like on a bucking bronco down the hillside.

In the shuttle, as Matt jumped unseen into the computer, she placed Rolly in one of the cockpit seats and sat beside him.

"You're in the pilot's seat now," she said. "Say, start engines."

He hesitated, then said hesitantly, "Start engines."

The engine began to purr, vibrating the craft. Rolly's head snapped around to her, his eyes wide circles. She nodded with a grin.

The FOV screen appeared stretching around 180 degrees both horizontally and vertically, and Rolly yelped as they lifted off.

Suddenly, Matt appeared above the control panel in an odd red uniform and addressed him formally. "Captain, what is our destination?"

Shocked, Rolly threw his head back and asked, "Who are you?"

"I'm the AI. The artificial intelligence." When Rolly looked baffled, he added quickly, "The robot. I hate that name. Where do you want to go?"

Rolly glanced at Lauren and back to Matt. "Into space."

They surged upward into the clouds. He gripped the arms of the seat but there were no G-forces. "I can see Los Angeles below, but it doesn't even feel like we're moving."

"That's the inertia dampening array," she said. "If we didn't have it, we'd feel several G's worth of extra weight pressing on our bodies. We wouldn't be able to move. At these speeds, the G-force would kill us."

He nodded, seemingly understanding.

In four minutes, the atmosphere disappeared and space appeared, and Rolly started to float out of his seat. He screamed in fear, then delight. She grabbed his hand and pulled him back down. "Matt, secure him to the chair."

Invisible bonds strapped him in.

Looking out the screen at the curve of the earth, he was awestruck. His mouth dropped open, and his eyes blinked rapidly. Lauren knew his senses were being overwhelmed. Below lay a gorgeous blue globe with tiny white clouds, and ahead was the curve of the earth and the black sky. Tears filled Rolly's eyes. He muttered, barely audibly, "Wow."

They sat in silence for nearly forty minutes, making two trips around the globe. Finally, Rolly asked, "How fast are we going?"

Matt answered, "23,496 miles per hour. I don't want to go too fast, do I? The world would speed by too quickly."

Night stretched below them now. Most of the mass was black with only a few tiny spots of city lights. Lauren guessed they were over Europe because in this era, there were few cities lit at night. But most impressively, what riveted Rolly's attention were the flashing lights elsewhere over the dark surface, eruptions of sudden brightness that disappeared just as suddenly.

"What's that?" he asked.

"You tell me," she prompted.

He thought only a second. "Lightning."

"Indeed. It's always raining somewhere."

On this side of the earth, they could see the stars filling deep space like an endless spread of broken crystals, the Milky Way in full swathe of bright colors. Lauren felt the joy of the experience through him, and she laughed at his happiness. For the moment, she too felt unadulterated joy, and it was a feeling so long missing from her being, she had thought it dead. Her own eyes welled up and she blinked the water away.

After three hours of circumnavigating the globe, diving down to hover over the coliseum, the pyramids, the Great Wall of China, and then skimming across the blue Pacific, she said, "We have to go home now."

He pleaded, "One more time around the world. Please!"

"Hear that, Matt. One more time."

"Aye, aye, captain," Matt said.

In the car on the way back to Los Angeles, Rolly couldn't stop talking, occasionally breaking into a wide grin and laughing. As they turned up into the Hollywood Hills, he said, "You don't want me to tell anyone about this, do you?"

"Tell who you want," she said with a half-smile. "No one will believe you anyway."

"Okay, I will."

CHAPTER FORTY-FIVE: THE FACE IN THE DARK

December 17, 1927, Los Angeles

Past 9:00pm in a suite of the Hotel Luxemburg, Ben Sorrentino sat at a desk facing his attorney Earl Sherman, papers spread out on the top. He'd slipped back into Los Angeles just that afternoon, wanting no one to know but a select few. He'd be gone again after seeing Pauline tomorrow, heading for southern Mexico to wrap up his distribution network. Nearby, both Pelosi brothers sat on stools at the suite bar nursing drinks. A sign above the bar read: **Prohibition be Damned.**

"Sign these, Benny," Sherman said, shoving three documents in front of Sorrentino. "And your part will be done. I'll take them to Miss Windsor for her signature."

Sherman smiled, but then, he smiled constantly as if smug in the knowledge that whatever he was doing was utterly brilliant. A lean, small man, he wore a dark three-piece suit with a watch chain on his vest. His brown hair smoothed down with pomade. A pack of Lucky Strike cigarettes on the table. He tapped his cigarette ash into the tray and glanced over the documents.

Sorrentino signed them and gave them back. He was annoyed by all the paperwork. "When she signs these, the property's mine?"

"No," Sherman said with a sheepish shrug. "Then, it goes to city hall for approval." He held up his hand quickly to stop Sorrentino's angry retort. "I've been greasing palms. That will be no problem. When Miss Windsor signs the papers, the sale will already be approved at city hall. Then, you will have the biggest casino in the West. We just need to go through the process, and that will take a couple of days. The council gets to pretend like they're doing their job."

Sorrentino asked. "Why do so many damn people have a say in this?"

Sherman rubbed his thumb and fingers together signifying money. "Everyone wants a piece of the action."

That, Sorrentino understood and nodded. "I'll see Pauline tomorrow and get this done. She'll sign. It's taken too long already." He smiled. It was all coming together.

The next day, Sorrentino called Pauline from his hotel suite and asked to see her, saying it was important. She did not want to come at first but he told her he was leaving town for a while and would not see her for weeks maybe. And it was important. Something he'd heard about a threat to her children. He'd tell her when she got to the hotel.

That night, when she arrived at the hotel, Pauline noticed at least fifteen men standing beside three cars in the parking lot. Three of them carried submachine guns, not attempting to hide them. She felt their eyes following her as she walked passed them.

Inside the suite, the Pelosi brothers sat talking with Benny. Immediately, without an order, they got up and left. Several suitcases had been placed by the door. A candlelight dinner was spread on the dining room table.

He took her in his arms and kissed her. "I've missed you, doll."

He drew back, puzzled by her lack of response.

"What about my children? You said they were in danger."

"Don't worry about it. I took care of it. I'll tell you later." He turned and lit the candles. Shaking out the match, he dropped it in a saucer. "Your business manager, what was her name?"

"Lauren Ramirez. Why?"

"Where's she from?"

Pauline shrugged. "I don't know. She's had a bit of a vagabond experience from what I gather."

"I'll bet."

"Why are you interested in her?"

This made him furious, that she'd lie to him about the Ramirez woman. Pauline had to know what she was. But he controlled his anger. "Nothing. Forget it."

"Listen, Ben, I want to know about my children."

"I told you they're okay now. They're safe." He turned out the lights and went to her, taking her more roughly in his arms and kissing her. He grabbed her ass in both hands and pulled her hips against his.

The old sparks ignited in her, but were quickly doused when he leaned back his head. "Things have changed. Colombini's out of the picture now. We can make big plans."

"What plans?" She looked away, avoiding his eyes.

"When you sell me that restaurant, I'm going to make you and me the King and Queen of this town. You'll see." He released her. "Come on, let's eat."

She stepped back, her heart pounding. She knew Benny didn't like to be denied anything, and she was about to deny him everything. That suddenly terrified her. How could she have been such a fool? How could she have missed how violent and deadly this man was?

"I've eaten," she said, her voice cracking.

Annoyed, he said, "You can't just sit down and have a bite? I haven't seen you in nearly a month. I want to spend some time with my gal."

"No, I can't stay. I don't think there was anything about my children. You just wanted me here." She forced herself to stand erect as if she had more courage than she did. "I'm not selling my property to you, Ben. I know how much you want it, but I'm not selling."

A dark rage radiated from his eyes. Alarmed, she backed up.

"Listen to me, you disloyal bitch," he shouted, sending out spittle. "I am going to have that damn building. It's the lynchpin of my operation. You're going to sign where I tell you to fucking sign." From a desk, he picked up a stack of papers and plopped them on the table. "You will sign these papers, and they will go through city hall. If you don't, you will lose more than just a goddamn building."

He was threatening her family. The water in her bowels threatened to rupture, but she shook her head, blond hair dancing, a gesture familiar to millions of fans. Making her voice firm, she said, "No, I will not. I cannot see you any longer, Ben. My kids come first. Our romance, such as it was, is over."

When she turned to leave, he grabbed her hair and swung her around viciously, sweeping the table clear of dishes and candles and slamming her face down on it. Her nose burst; blood poured out and into her mouth and pooled on the tablecloth. He lifted her dress and yanked down the silk panties.

"Benny, please, don't do this," she pleaded.

He dropped his pants, and already hard, thrust into her from behind, grunting like a wild animal. She pleaded again and again for him to stop, but he ignored her. She could not move. It felt worse than anything she'd ever experienced. It was savage. Her body and her soul bled.

No longer circling his flame, she had been burned alive by it. She set her mind to surviving. Her fear and panic fled, replaced by hatred and blind fury. She could handle studio heads and prima donna directors, but this was vastly different. This was a lethal mobster from Chicago. She had badly misjudged her own power over him. But she would not give in to him.

Finally, he let her up. She pulled on her panties, then grabbed several napkins, dabbed them in the ice water of the champagne carafe, and held it to her nose.

"You bastard," she whispered.

He watched her with a smug grin. "Yeah, I am. Understand this, Pauline. I just nailed a sign to your ass that says, this is mine. That sweet body is mine. Everything you own is mine. Your precious children are mine. I can always get to them. That building and that restaurant are mine. The sooner you realize it, the better it will be for you and them." He shoved the papers toward her with a pen. "Now sign the goddamn papers."

She did, seven of them, quickly, then thrust the pen down and hurried to the door.

Playfully, a charming rogue again, he grinned. "I've been in love with you since I first saw you in the flickers."

It sickened her.

When she didn't respond, he added coldly, "I really like fucking you."

Her eyes blazed, but she didn't respond. She just wanted to get out of the room. He wasn't so smart. He wasn't so in control. He had not looked at the papers. She had signed *Fuck you* on each one.

As she hurried out, she heard his laughter. He shouted after her, "You belong to me, Pauline. Don't forget that. And so does the goddamn Café Windsor."

CHAPTER FORTY-SIX: FIRST KILL ALL THE LAWYERS

December 21, 1927, Hollywood Hills

In the following week, Pauline ate little and often woke at night, always on edge, fearing someone had broken into the house. Everyone thought she was worried about the upcoming private screening of *Romeo and Juliet*, but Lauren knew exactly what bothered her. One night late in the living room, Pauline had finally told her and made her promise not to tell anyone else.

Pauline had cried, and Lauren took her in her arms. Lauren remembered her mother comforting her like this when she was six and had been bitten by a wildcat that didn't want to be petted. Lauren held Pauline for nearly twenty minutes till the actress sat up and wiped her eyes with her hands.

"He's going to be madder than a hatter," she said. "He may come after Rolly and Emmy."

Lauren said grimly, "I've already added more men. They'll be protected 24 hours a day. You'd think he'd just buy another damn building."

"No, not Benny. He wants mine, and whether it's perfect or not, that's the one he will have."

Lauren studied her a moment, then said, "So, you really signed the papers *Fuck you?*"

Pauline nodded.

Lauren laughed and Pauline joined in. Moments later, Emmy walked in rubbing her eyes. "What's so funny?"

"You, Little Button," Pauline said, taking her daughter up into her lap.

Two nights later, shaking with dread, Pauline roused Lauren, saying someone was in the house. Remy was sleeping at his house with an early call for flying tomorrow. Someone, indeed, was in the house — her men, three including the duty officer, Clyde Brady, and six men outside.

Still, they searched the place thoroughly. Lauren brought her Glock, and along with Brady, a limping Raider, and Pauline, they searched every corner of the house, quietly making sure everyone was safe in their room. As Lauren suspected, they found no intruders. No one would have gotten by the dogs.

Pauline rubbed her temples, her hands with a little tremor. She stuck them in her robe. Lauren knew she was still shaken by the recent encounter with Sorrentino. Her century called it trauma effects.

"Ma'am," Brady said to Pauline. "I'll just place my chair by your bedroom door."

"No, thank you, Captain. That's not necessary," she said. Hesitated, then added, "I'm going to have some tea. Perhaps you'll join me."

His eyes brightened. "Yes, ma'am, I'd be glad to."

Lauren went outside to check on the men patrolling the grounds, then up into the hills to speak with the two at the listening post. The night was cloudy and visibility in the darkness limited. A slow, struggling Raider accompanied her. The dog insisted on coming, wouldn't stay behind. He seemed to have something outside he wanted to find. She took the path farther up the hill slowly and carefully for him. All seemed quiet.

It took no great deduction to know Sorrentino would strike at some point. Tonight maybe. He could not let things stand. Like any psychopath, he had to have whatever he thought he needed or wanted. Pauline and what Pauline owned was what he wanted.

About two hundred yards beyond the listening post, Raider's hackles rose. She drew the Glock. "What is it, boy?"

They moved forward cautiously. With the help of Matt her eyes gathered light, brightening the darkness to something akin to twilight. Then she found it. Raider gave a little whine and hung back.

The Border collie hung from a tree limb like a butchered chicken. It had been beheaded and gutted. She felt rage fire through her synopses. This was a message from Sorrentino, and only Jimmy Pelosi would have the skill to carry it off. She cut the poor creature down, dug a hole with her knife, and buried the collie, piling on rocks. That would hold for now. She'd come back later and bury him properly.

The question now: was Pelosi still about somewhere? Raider seemed to think so. He started to pick up a track, and they followed it.

Matt said, *It might be possible to draw on some of the shuttle's infrared systems and attach them to your neurobots.*

Thanks for telling me that now.

I'm trying to be helpful.

In the murky darkness, she considered where he would be. He had sat up here watching the house through binoculars and seen the collie come out through the doggie door and up into the hills. Never a watchdog, it probably approached Pelosi unafraid.

Raider shook off his ailments and broke into a trot, and she ran to keep up. The dark shapes of the scrub oak appeared like grotesque sentinels of the devil, any one of them could be hiding Pelosi. He would have seen her security team, maybe saw her exit the back door and move up into the hillside, coming toward him. What will he do now? Try to kill her or escape?

She caught Raider's collar and slowed him down. In a crouch, she moved silently forward, keeping among the shrub, ignoring the constant scratches from briar needles.

Beside an oak she paused, waited, listened. Nothing. No sound. The night was still, which meant the intruder was nearby. Raider's nose was in the air, pointed toward a knob where a single bush grew. That's where he was.

"Stay," she said to Raider and hoped he would.

Maintaining the crouch, she darted among the deep shadows, always upward. Glock in her left hand.

Ahead was the knob. He had to be there, had to. She closed within twenty paces, then froze. A trap. It was the most obvious place, a place she would have chosen to lay waiting with a scoped rifle. She could feel he was close, very close, and she would have to cross open ground to run him down.

Lauren heard several sounds that brought her focus back on the night. Off to her right, an owl called. Over her, a large bird settled into a nearby tree. She heard the yip of a coyote a little way off. Her shoulders eased and she exhaled a breath. He was gone. Then, from a distance came the sound of a car engine starting. She ran to the prominence and looked down the hillside to a street seventy yards below. A car was pulling away and disappearing down the curving road.

***

On Friday, Earl Sherman, Sorrentino's lawyer, called Pauline and asked for a meeting to discuss the purchase of the restaurant and its building. He had been informed that she was amenable to the sale. Sherman had a reputation for representing famous actors, mobsters, and businessmen, and always winning. She had known this call was coming. Her hand shook, and for several seconds, she did not respond

"I am," she said into the receiver, barely audible.

"Perhaps, we could meet this afternoon at my office on Gower," Sherman said. "Clear up this unpleasantness and get it out of the way. Say three o'clock? Is that acceptable?"

"No. Come to my house. We can take care of it here." She gave him her address and hung up abruptly.

As three o'clock approached, Pauline sat nervously at the alcove window, working on her fifth gin and tonic in the last two hours. The rain had stopped. The window commanded a view of the driveway and front yard, which glistened from the dampness. In the lap of her print dress she had placed the revolver. She was uncertain what she would do with it when Sherman came, maybe shoot him. The thought of shooting the lawyer the second he stepped in the door gave her immense gratification.

Thankfully, no one else was about. Two days before Christmas, her mother was shopping with Knighton as bodyguard. Lauren was in town somewhere with Remy secretively doing God knows what. Searching for Sorrentino, she thought. Russell was at work across town and the children playing in the backyard with Nanny Claire, surrounded by several guards. Pauline told them she had a terrible headache and not to bother mommy this afternoon. Claire was instructed to keep them outside.

Only Raider lay nearby, awake, his paws crossed. He seemed to be recovering. She felt a sensation of great warmth for him. The dog had sensed her distress this afternoon, and it buoyed her how he wanted to protect her.

Waiting for Sherman, Pauline suffered through competing emotions: anguish, rage, and fright. Someone had broken into her house and savagely mutilated one of the children's dogs. Her eyes watered as she thought about the poor, helpless creature. It had been a singularly cruel act. She hated these thugs. She hated Sorrentino now. And she hated herself. How could she have been so far wrong about him? He was a monster and she had thought him a playful rogue.

Assassin 13

She drank and watched as Clyde Brady, a holstered .45 at his side, and the old timer Wyatt Earp, with a long-barreled shotgun, patrolled along the hedgerow that bordered the front of her property. She was glad Brady was there. He barely went home. She knew he was in love with her and though not reciprocated by her, she liked and trusted him.

It made for a sense of unreality that she and her family were surrounded by a small army all the time. She had brought it on herself. She just prayed her children would not pay for her foolishness. She was afraid of Sorrentino now, deathly afraid, not for herself, but her children, far more than she'd ever feared Colombini.

She did not know what she was going to do to get her and her family out of this mess. Not knowing scared her. Everything scared her.

When a beige Studebaker rolled up the driveway, she grabbed the gun and stood up abruptly. Brady and Earp approached the car as it stopped near the door. Pauline had told them to expect the lawyer, but even so Earp held his shotgun aimed at the three men who stepped out of the car while Brady searched them.

They appeared annoyed by the process, but also amused by the very old man with the Colt. "Careful with that, old timer," one of the lawyers said with a smile.

Earp's expression did not change. He cocked the shotgun, and the lawyer's smile froze, then disappeared. Brady demanded they open their briefcases, and they did.

Two of the lawyers were middle-aged, wearing expensive double-breasted suits. The third was younger and thinner, with a bow tie and curly brown hair. Surprisingly, this was Earl Sherman.

When Brady ushered them into the house, he asked Pauline if she wanted him and Earp to stay. She nodded.

Moments before, she'd stashed the gun in the chair in which she now sat. She did not offer them a seat and they remained standing. Raider placed himself at her right, eyeing the men suspiciously. Brady came over to stand at her left, his hand on his forty-five. Earp leaned casually against the fireplace mantel, but his gray-blue eyes intense.

"It is a pleasure to meet you, Miss Windsor," Sherman began with a practiced smile, his voice a smooth baritone. "You must know I am a big fan."

"How would I know that?"

His smile remained intact. "I see. Well, then, shall we get to it?" He opened his briefcase and took out several sheets of paper. "These are all prepared. You need just to sign them to complete the sale of your property downtown, and we will be out of your way. We will, of course, deal with city hall approving the sale. As I'm sure Mr. Sorrentino explained, you will be paid top dollar. Would you like to look them over?"

"No, I don't need to look them over."

"Then we can sign and be done." Holding them out, Sherman started for Pauline. Raider gave a low growl and bared his teeth. Sherman stopped. "Can you call off the dog?" His reasonable tone cracking.

"No. I don't think so."

He frowned. "Don't play games, Miss Windsor. Mr. Sorrentino has been generous and will not be held up for more money. This is the offer. You must accept it."

"No, I don't."

He gave a frustrated sigh. "Look, Miss Windsor, you're just making this harder than it needs to be. You will sign this now or later, I promise you, and for the amount stipulated. It is..."

Pauline stood abruptly and walked over to Sherman, snatching the papers from him. "You tell that son of a bitch I will never sell to him. I will not sell him my restaurant, my building, or even a damn paper clip that I possess. He can go to hell and so can you." She threw the papers in his face.

Blinking rapidly, his composure fractured. When she followed with a torrent of insults, Raider rushed up beside her, barking at them. The men flinched back. The old man at the fireplace aimed down his long-barreled shotgun at them.

Pauline shouted, "You have ten seconds to get the hell out of my house before I order Raider to attack."

They scrambled for the door with Raider snapping at their heels. Brady and Earp followed Sherman and his partners out to the car, holding their weapons as if about to fire.

Before getting in, the lawyer glanced back at Pauline. "That was foolish, Miss Windsor. I assure you Mr. Sorrentino will hear about this betrayal. He knows how to be persuasive."

Pauline placed her hands on her hips, a gesture she had used many times in her films. "Captain Brady, if any of these men set foot on my property again, shoot them on sight."

"Yes, ma'am."

Earp fired his shotgun into the air, and the lawyers clamored into the car and drove off.

Pauline walked up to her two men and all three laughed from relief. "Thank you, Mr. Earp," she said. "You're still someone only a fool would buck."

"You're welcome, ma'am."

She turned to Brady. "And you, Clyde, thank you."

Brady's cherubic face broke into a wide grin. "Any time."

The next day, a messenger delivered a letter to her from Sorrentino.

Dear Pauline,

I am out of the country for a while on business. My lawyer told me what happened, which was very silly on your part. It accomplished nothing. Know that I have people watching you. All the guards in the

world can't protect you. Know, too, that we will conclude our business together to my satisfaction one way or another.
Benny
P.S. And your sweet ass is still mine for as long as I say it is.

CHAPTER FORTY-SEVEN: A TALE OF TWO MOVIES

December 28, 1927, Los Angeles

Just after Christmas on December 28, 1927, a tsunami struck the movie industry, a great wave that had been rolling across the country since the October premiere of *The Jazz Singer* in New York city. That evening, the Hollywood premiere of the picture would take place at the Criterion Theater. Sound was coming. According to Matt, rumblings of it had been shaking the industry's foundations for months. The coming of sound would terrify everyone, destroy many, and expel stars from the Hollywood firmament. After tonight, nothing would ever be the same.

It begins today, he said, winding up his diatribe on the coming of sound movies. He was waxing on and on about the importance of a single film in bringing about such drastic change. *I have seen twenty-three movies about The Jazz Singer dealing in large part with its use of sound.*

It must be a great movie, Lauren said.

Hardly. Important though. He flashed a brief image in her head of a man in black face singing a song called "Mammy." *This will be when many of the movie moguls see it for the first time and judge its impact.*

On this day, another film was scheduled to be shown in Hollywood as well. At 2:00pm in the small theater on the Global Pictures lot, a preview screening of *Romeo and Juliet* was planned so Jerry Zelinsky could okay its release, order changes, or cancel it altogether.

Pauline was worried about this screening far more than *The Jazz Singer* premiere.

Just before two, Adela Rogers St. Johns, *Photoplay's* top writer, made her way into Global Studio's theater to see the movie. She'd heard that problems with the picture were insurmountable. Rumors were widespread that the rift between the actress and Jerry Zelinsky had become a chasm. Their fierce battles before, during, and after filming were legendary now. She had written about some of them. Rumor had it this was a stink bomb of major proportions, and Zelinsky wanted to end it right here before a regular audience saw it. Anything about Pauline Windsor was a story. But a great star's spectacular flameout would sell endless copies.

Pauline denied the rumors, said it was a great movie, and invited all the movie critics and gossip columnists she could arm-twist into coming. A bold and risky move by the actress. Their responses could make the movie a hit when it was rolled out, if it was rolled out, or condemn it to the celluloid trash heap.

Adela spotted Luella Parsons, but turned away as if she had not noticed her, having no interest in engaging in conversation. In the center armchair, Zelinsky sat smoking a cigar. Up front by the orchestra were bowls of popcorn and fruit on a long table, along with illegal spirits, which the audience swarmed over. Two cigarette girls with trays of the latest brands flanked the table. A haze of smoke hung in the air.

When the doors were closed, Pauline and Michael Murray entered onto the stage to applause.

"Hurry up, you two," Zelinsky shouted. "We all got work to do. Time's wasting."

"Coming, Mr. Zelinsky," Michael said.

Zelinsky muttered for all to hear, "I never wanted to be in the Shakespeare business. Global is a movie company, not a damn university." He turned to the projectionist. "Start the damn picture, pal."

An hour and a half later as the film ended, Adela was aghast. She began writing in her head as she assessed what she had just seen. Throughout the last decade, filmmakers had put out greater and greater movies, extending the boundaries of what was possible, imagining and bringing to reality some of the most creative, most stunning visuals ever filmed. The art of movies was soaring toward a peak. And **director** Clarence Martin's *Romeo and Juliet* and Pauline Windsor's performance of Juliet may be that peak.

It was the best movie Adela had ever seen.

When the room lights came up, the audience burst into wild applause and cheered and didn't stop for five minutes. Pauline and Michael stood and waved, both basking under the adulation.

Zelinsky stuck the cigar in his mouth, knitting his thick eyebrows, and fumed. When the applause ended, he said incredulously, "They died? What the hell. They both died! What kind of shit is that? I never saw such a thing. They both died!"

"That's the story, Mr. Zelinsky," said Martin. "We can hardly change that."

Zelinsky faced the director. "That's a dead hoofer. It's shit. I can't do nothing with that. What's the matter with you, Clarence? You can't end a movie with Pauline and Michael dying. Their fans won't stand for it. People will hate the movie."

"But, Mr. Zelinsky, that's how it ends. What can I...," Martin began.

Holding up his hands, Zelinsky cut him off. "Okay, okay. The movie's not bad. I'll concede that. Not nearly as bad as I thought, but I want a final scene. I want to see them two walking off hand in hand. That would be perfect. Like they escaped, you see. Then, and only then, can I put that drivel out to the public. Maybe as a second bill."

Michael groaned and slumped down in his seat. But Pauline gave the studio boss that dazzling smile that melted the hearts of so many movie-goers.

"By damn, I think you've really hit on it, Jerry," she said loudly for everyone to hear. She was the only one at Global that called him by his first name. "Of course, everyone knows Romeo and Juliet die in the end, so how do you change that? Perhaps, you've showed us the best ending ever."

"You're damn right. I'm no janitor here." But he looked skeptically at her.

Martin gazed at her dumbfounded as she patted Zelinsky's cheek affectionately. "Just as you said. A scene of Michael and me walking up into the clouds, hand in hand, very much in love, happy on our way to heaven to live together forever. That's brilliant, Jerry." She gazed at him in admiration.

No one ever said she wasn't a damn good actress, Adela thought.

He frowned at her for several seconds, then as wheels visibly clanked in his brain, he nodded emphatically. "Do it, Clarence." He faced the audience. "Refreshments up front. You freeloaders, help yourselves." He turned and walked out.

Looking ill, Martin glanced at Pauline.

"Just shoot the scene, Clarence," she said. "It might even work. If not, we'll ship it out without it. He'll never know."

Adela made her way up to the director and two actors and congratulated all three, telling them they had a masterpiece. She was sure every critic would be reporting that.

Twenty-five feet away, Lauren was sitting in the back row where she could watch Pauline and the entire auditorium. Remy, Brady, and Dave Arthur were placed about the theater. She was caught up in the good feeling about the movie. After all, she had been in the cast. She had found herself riveted when she came on the screen, her face a dark shadow in its cowl. She felt she did all right.

What do you know about this Romeo and Juliet? she asked Matt. *Was it a hit?*

I know nothing about it, he said. *There is no record of it as a movie. It's as if it were never made. It just disappeared, completely forgotten.* He added in a sympathetic tone, *At least, we saw that Pauline was magnificent. A bravura performance.*

You never saw it before today? Lauren asked surprised.

No. That might mean Global never released it, or more likely it was lost.

Lost? she asked. *How do you lose a movie?*

They are not digital. Silent movies were shot on cellulose nitrate film stock, which decayed and turned to dust over the years. Ninety percent of all silent films have been lost. So, likely this one was, too. His voice sounded like a train whistle in its sudden anger. *It's a disgrace! All those movies lost. A real tragedy.*

Yeah, a real shame, she responded sarcastically.

Most of Pauline's were lost.

And Lauren realized it was a shame. The actress's life work, her talent, long forgotten.

Two hours before the Hollywood Premiere of *The Jazz Singer*, Michael called to cancel as Pauline's escort, so she said to Brady, "I guess we'll have to throw a tux on you, Clyde, and you'll be my companion tonight. Is that all right with you?"

He beamed. "Yes, ma'am. It'll be rough duty, but I'll do my best."

That night, the movie that would have a profound effect on the movie industry had no effect on Lauren except she squirmed at the blackface Al Jolson, the star, used.

They did that then, Matt said.

You were right. It wasn't even that good.

With several months working in the movie business, she was beginning to think she knew as much as anyone else, which actually was not much. And to her, despite the enormous crowds eager to see additional showings of *The Jazz Singer*, it was a completely forgettable film. Al Jolson sang a few catchy tunes. A bit of dialogue was actually spoken. There was a strong relationship between mother and son, but the film centered around the conflict of a Jewish boy torn between becoming a cantor or singing on stage. Not exactly riveting stuff.

"It had a few lines of sound dialogue," Pauline said once they had gotten home. "So what? We're a visual medium. Always have been, always will be."

She's wrong, Matt said. *You must tell her she's wrong. She must prepare herself for the changes coming.*

Lauren thought back over the movie, Al Jolson finishing a song, then saying, "Wait a minute, wait a minute, you ain't heard nothin' yet …" That startled the audience. They gasped when they heard him speak, then shouted and applauded. Matt was right.

Of course, I'm right. This is it, the end of silent movies, he said. *It will come fast. The whole industry begins changing early next year. Studios, directors, actors will either adapt to sound or be cast aside. Many will not make it.*

Many would not make it he'd said, and that would include Pauline, but not because she wasn't a great actress. She would be murdered tonight or sometime in the next month. Then forgotten. Lauren had to prevent it before she went back to the 22nd century.

She had to find Sorrentino and kill him. January 7. Tijuana.

CHAPTER FORTY-EIGHT: TWILIGHT OF THE GODS

Saturday, December 31, 1927, Los Angeles
On New Year's Eve, Esther Ralston's mansion glittered brightly from every window. Lights strung on the home, something new in Los Angeles, made it sparkle like a Christmas tree. Pauline sat in the back seat of her Duecy as Sgt. Knighton pulled the car snugly into the line of automobiles moving up the driveway. Brady sat in the front passenger seat.

Ralston, Paramount's popular comedic actress, and her husband, David Webb, were famous for their New Year's Eve parties, each year topping the last. Bejeweled and decked in evening wear, over a hundred and fifty famous Hollywood stars and prominent industry figures attended. They were coming to see out the greatest year of all, 1927, and usher in 1928 with its earthquake rumblings of a cataclysmic shift in the business.

When Brady opened the car door for Pauline, holding out his hand, he said, "Enjoy yourself, ma'am. We've got the grounds covered."

She saw a warmth in the man's eyes. "Thank you, Clyde. I will."

She wore long white gloves and a white satin evening dress that clung snugly to her hips, all complementing her pale Minnesota skin and blond hair. Just ahead of her at the entrance, the tall, gangling Gary Cooper, whom many were saying was a rising star, glanced back at her and gave a low whistle. His date, a pretty brunette Pauline didn't recognize, frowned heavily.

Ignoring her, he winked at Pauline. "You are the Queen of Sheba tonight, Miss Windsor."

Her body stiffened. Benny liked to call her that. She forced a smile, then crossed her eyes, something she'd done to good effect in her Mack Sennett days. Coop laughed.

At the door, four studio guards in blue uniforms were checking guests. Esther was determined no one crashed her party this year, so only those with invitations were allowed inside. That afternoon, the Paramount star had boasted over the phone to Pauline that a fly couldn't slip through her security net. "And my men will be carrying guns."

Once in, Pauline was led by a maid into a large, crowded ballroom where tables had been set up with flowers and ice buckets of champagne. Netting was strung along the expanse of ceiling, containing hundreds of balloons. At the back of the room, the orchestra was playing *Lucky Lindy*, and several people were dancing the frenetic *Lindy Hop*.

With so many celebrities here, she expected to see Charles Lindbergh himself walk out of the pack, but he didn't. Instead, short, bulging, and obnoxious Jerry Zelinsky strode toward her, waving the hand holding his cigar, and grinning as if they were old friends. Quickly, she snatched a flute of champagne off a passing serving girl's tray and drank it halfway down before he reached her.

"There she is. My toot, toot tootsie," he said. He had a glass of bourbon in his other hand, some of which he spilled over his fingers.

"I'm not your anything, Jerry," she said. "If you'd stop drinking that lion piss, you'd know that."

"Hey, we're having a good time here," he said, annoyed. "Ease up, queenie."

He started to walk off, then turned back. "Hey, good news. Remember that scene I came up with to finish off *Romeo and Julia*? Well, we're going to do it with sound dialogue. How do you like those apples? We're going to put in sound effects too, and music. Wish we could do the whole damn thing over again with sound dialogue, but then that would cost me way too much."

Shocked, she did not bother to correct his mispronunciation of the title. "You're making a goat gland movie?"

Her brother Russell had explained where the term came from. It was based on a horrifying surgical procedure in which doctors implanted goat testes into humans, supposedly to cure impotence, influenza, and insanity. Goat gland became the metaphor for this new movie procedure in which sound effects and even new scenes with sound dialogue were implanted in a silent film already shot, in the hope of making it more profitable. She didn't know which was worse, goat gland movies or having goat testicles inserted into a human body.

He blanched angrily. "You bet your sweet ass we are, queenie. We ain't the YMCA. I'm here to make money. We can test your voice out before the shoot. Who knows, you might have a terrible voice, and your career in films will be over."

Laughing, he spun around with a flourish of his cigar and headed over toward Norma Talmadge's table.

That had been a terrible thing to say, but typical Zelinsky. She'd already decided *Romeo and Juliet* would be the last film she did for Global. In the new year, she would move to United Artists. Mary Pickford had long been asking for her to join her studio.

In one swallow, Pauline finished the champagne and poured herself another off the nearest table. She felt confident the industry would not move to sound. Why should it? The films being made now had achieved an artistry unequaled while still being greatly entertaining. They made tons of money. Why kill a good thing? And as for her voice, it had withstood vaudeville and Broadway. It would be good enough if she should ever need to use it on film. Her reasoning was solid, she told herself, but it still did not mollify her unease.

At every table, everyone was talking about sound as if it would descend on Hollywood like a massive avalanche this very moment. Pauline joined a group where Charlie Chaplin was holding forth. "I don't expect talkies will ever make it in this business," he said. "If they come at all, I give them six months, a year tops. Then, they're done."

"Don't worry, Charlie," the young Mary Astor said whimsically. "No one's going to make you speak on film. A tramp with a cultured British accent?" She shook her head.

A few people chuckled.

"Dat is so right," Pola Negri, the exotic beauty, said in her thick Polish accent. She gave an emphatic nod and with a flourish of her hand, added, "It is noting but fad. It vill soon pass." She flipped her hair theatrically. "I vill always be a star."

The others laughed but a little too shrilly, Pauline thought. Whistling in the graveyard.

Ronald Colman stubbed his cigarette out in an ashtray. "Except as a scientific achievement, I am not sympathetic to this 'sound business.' I feel, as many do, that this is a mechanical resource, that it is a retrogressive and temporary digression insofar as it affects the art of motion picture acting— in short, that it does not properly belong to my particular work of which naturally I must be the best judge."

Tongue in cheek, everyone applauded wildly as if it had been a brilliant speech given to the Rotary Club, and Colman's face flushed red. He waved his hand as if to say, *Well, it's true.* He was a moderately successful actor, pretty much at his limit, Pauline guessed. She had worked with him in two films and liked him. Handsome but not overly expressive, he was terrified of sound coming in and putting him out of work, which was odd. He had the most beautiful male speaking voice she had ever heard.

"Don't let them mock you, Ronny," Jesse Lasky said. He was the bespectacled part owner and production chief at Paramount Studios. "Exactly right. You see a painting on the wall of blowing trees. Do you need to hear the wind to appreciate the painting? Not at all. If sound could improve our product, we would embrace it. But, in fact, the opposite is true. It would set the movie industry back ten years."

Everyone nodded and agreed, Pauline among them. Later, after dancing with John Gilbert and the young director Raoul Walsh, she snatched up another flute of champagne and joined Mary Pickford.

"Where's Doug?" she asked.

Mary waved to the dance floor. "Cutting a rug." Her husband, Douglas Fairbanks, was in the center of a small group that was clapping and cheering him and his partner Esther Ralston on. They were performing an athletic Charleston to the rapid beat of the orchestra.

"You've said nothing about the topic du jour, Mary," Pauline said. "Do you agree sound is a fad at best?"

If anyone would know, Pauline thought, it'd be Mary Pickford. Since her first films nearly twenty years ago, the woman had achieved a worldwide popularity no other actor would likely ever match. But more impressive, Pickford was smart, tough, and knew her way around business.

The great star shrugged. "At United Artists we have put plans in the works to refit all our stages for sound at a cost of millions. The other studios are doing the same. What do you think?"

This shocked Pauline. Why hadn't she heard anything about it? "I think I better start taking vocal lessons."

Both women laughed, though it sounded to Pauline like the laugh of the condemned.

By eleven o'clock, the nature of the party changed. At a furious pace since the beginning, it now was jolted into a state of sheer madness when Clara Bow arrived. The band had just finished a tune, and every eye turned to the entrance as she strode into the room wearing a floor-length fur coat. She threw off her coat, and people gasped. Among all the evening gowns, she wore only a short, one-piece bathing suit, red to match her fiery hair.

Hands on hips, she bellowed, "Is this a wake or a goddamned party?" Cupping her hands around her mouth, she shouted, "Band leader, play *I've Found a New Baby*."

The band leader waved, and within seconds, the orchestra struck up the frenzied tune. Kicking off her shoes, Bow leapt up on the nearest table top and danced the *Black Bottom*. As always with Bow, everyone watched, some embarrassed, others horrified, but all fascinated.

After a second, Pauline said, "What the hell," and jumped up on the table, falling into perfectly synchronized steps with Bow. They flapped their arms in unison, did the unique steps in unison, and bumped bottoms. A few people laughed; others cheered.

Then, more and more people elbowed their way up on tables, occasionally falling off and climbing back up. Everyone now wanted to dance the *Black Bottom*. It was madness, and for the first time in quite a while, Pauline felt her worries lifting from her shoulders like a flock of birds.

After twenty minutes, she flopped down in her chair while the endlessly energetic Bow kept going on with other partners.

Midnight approached. A minute to go, the band played a slow waltz, and couples filled the floor for the last dance of

Assassin 13

1927. Having no desire to dance cheek to cheek with someone she didn't care about, Pauline was secluded alone in a corner and watched while sipping her eighth or tenth champagne, she wasn't sure. She watched them because she loved them. She had never stopped being a fan when she ascended into the heavens alongside them. They were the biggest stars in the universe. Brighter than the brightest stars in the night skies. They would last forever.

Mary and Doug were on the dance floor. John Gilbert and sometime fiancé Greta Garbo. The three Talmadge sisters, Norma, Constance and Natalie dancing with their husbands. Natalie's husband was comic Buster Keaton. The beautiful Hungarian actress Vilma Banky and her husband, handsome Rod La Rocque. The comedienne Marion Davies danced with Chaplin while her famous paramour, William Randolph Hearst, the rich newspaper magnate, watched forlornly from a nearby table. She saw the Gish sisters, Lillian and Dorothy, dancing and so many others. How Pauline loved them all and saw herself fortunate to be one of them.

Suddenly a chill washed over her. She wondered if sound would sweep these people away like a tidal surge in a storm. Who would survive? The answer came to her just as suddenly. All of them. They were that talented.

As if in a long shot from a great ballroom scene, they danced to the sweet strains of the music with an ethereal glow about them. Perhaps it was the champagne, Pauline thought, but she felt at that moment that these people were immortal.

Out of the throng of dancers, Lauren walked toward her in a black strapless evening gown. It startled Pauline. How did the woman get through such tight security?

"How long have you been here?" Pauline asked.
"All night."
"Really?"

"I served you a drink. I was one of the waitresses. You never even noticed."

"Really?" Her eyebrows knitted together in confusion.

"Thought I'd join the party."

The band fell silent, and an MGM producer dressed only in a diaper and a banner that read *1928* draped over his chest led Esther Ralston and the airily beautiful Lilian Gish up on the stage. The two women held hands.

"It's almost time," Gish announced. "Irving wanted us to say a few words so here goes. Our movies have developed into an art form every bit as compelling as painting, writing, or composing. In fact, we have produced a new art form, one without sound. Not just pantomime as critics have claimed, but something wonderfully expressive."

Ralston nodded her head in agreement, her blond hair bobbing, and added, "1927 has been the greatest year in the history of movies. People came out to see our work in record numbers. We are getting pretty good at this business, are we not, my friends? Let us make1928 as successful a year as this one has been."

Quickly, she glanced at her watch and at Gish. Together they took a deep breath and began counting. "Ten, nine, eight, seven, six, five, four, three, two, one. Happy New Year!"

The lights went out, the band blared, and the balloons fell from the ceiling. Throughout the room, couples were kissing.

Pauline turned to Lauren, put both hands on the other woman's cheeks, brought her face to her, and kissed her deeply on the lips. When the lights came back on, she released her.

She saw Lauren's surprise. "Don't worry," Pauline said. "I'm not that kind of gal. After everything that's happened, I just wanted someone to kiss tonight, and you were close."

Lauren's eyebrows lifted. "Well, in that case, that was the best kiss I've had in a long time. Don't tell Remy, but my toes are tingling."

Pauline laughed. They stared at the crowd, still kissing and cheering and shouting *Happy New Year*, then the actress said, "So, it's 1928. Thank God, things could hardly get worse."

CHAPTER FORTY-NINE: THE FATAL RING

Sunday, January 1, 1928, Southern Mexico

Just after dawn on the first day of 1928, Arty Pelosi drove Sorrentino's black Chrysler Imperial into a recently harvested sugarcane field near Puerto Los Llanitos in southern Mexico and drew to a stop. From the back seat, Sorrentino counted nine heavily armed Mexicans standing with Carlos Obregon in front of three dusty cars. Several wore bandoleers. They were armed with shotguns, rifles, and pistols.

El Jefe Carlos Obregon stood in front, broad shouldered and pot-bellied with a thick drooping mustache. He ran the distribution of bootleg liquor to Los Angeles from the safety of his deep-water port in Los Llanitos. For the last month and a half, Sorrentino had been negotiating with him for a piece of the business. It was all a sham leading to this moment, and Ben hoped the man hadn't figured that out yet.

Directly to his left, palm trees and rolling hills bordered the torn ground. A half mile away in a neighboring cane field, a controlled fire burned; smoke lifted into the sky.

Sitting next to Sorrentino, Dom Romano, one of his Chicago boys, said, "Odds ain't great, boss."

He lay his overcoat over his Thompson submachine guns. The morning had a chill to it, so the overcoat was not out of place. Obregon had insisted if Sorrentino wanted this meeting so badly, he would come with only two men. But at their feet, two armed men hugged the floor and one lay in the front passenger seat side, Sorrentino's hidden gunmen.

"The odds are what they are," Sorrentino said, unconcerned. In fact, the blood lust had risen inside him the moment they drove onto the cane field.

He, Arty, and Dom stepped from the car and moved to within twenty feet of Obregon. The Mexicans fanned out, faces taut, hands gripping tightly to trigger guards.

Obregon broke into a wide grin, a gold tooth glinting in the morning sun. "Amigo, it is good to see you again," he said, then frowned. "So soon though. I think we have talked too much already. Nothing else is to be said. You say you want to be my partner, but you don't offer a fair price. What is left for me to do?"

"There's always more to be said," Sorrentino remarked. "Talking is better than people dying over small matters. We don't want a war between us, Carlos. There's too much money to be made by everyone."

Obregon hooked his thumbs in his belt and laughed. There was nothing pleasant about his laugh. "So, you say, amigo. So you say. You should know. I hear of big gang war in the City of Angels."

Sorrentino spoke softly, "No more. The Colombini brothers are rotting in the ground."

Obregon's grin froze. In a swift motion, he drew his pistol and aimed it at Sorrentino. Unconcerned, Sorrentino shrugged, his palms up as if saying *bad way to treat a friend.*

At that moment, the side of Obregon's head exploded; skull bits and blood flew into the air.

In that stunned instant, Sorrentino and his two men flattened to the ground, drew their guns, and fired. In the Chrysler, the three men rose and opened up with their Thompsons, ripping the Mexicans apart. From the hills, the sniper picked men off in a rapid chain of kills. It was over in seconds. A few Mexicans staggered away, but the sniper quickly finished them.

Dom and Arty went about the field, firing into each man's head to make sure they were dead. In the distance by the line of palm trees, Sorrentino could see Jimmy Pelosi coming out of the hills and striding toward them, a sniper rifle slung over his shoulder.

Later that day at Obregon's Hacienda, now Sorrentino's hacienda, Benny met with a steady stream of dignitaries from Los Llanitos and the state of Michoacán. The chief of police, the alcalde of Los Llanitos, the captain of the local Federales, the harbor master, and captains from several ships that had been part of Obregon's network. They all came to pay homage to the new jefe and negotiate payment for the cooperation.

Sorrentino brought in Javier Vega, Obregon's former lawyer, to front the operation. Everyone would deal with him. But they all knew who was boss. By 5:00pm, the business was concluded, and the last of the dignitaries departed feeling both hopeful and frightened. Sorrentino's operation promised far more *mordidas,* bribe money, than in the past, but the American mob boss's reputation for ruthlessness and his merciless ambush of Obregon left no doubt what would happen to them should they become expendable.

On the veranda before dinner, Sorrentino stood alongside Pelosi, drinking Mexican beer from bottles and looking at the sea crashing onto the rocks far below. Pelosi still had specks of blood on his white shirt from the morning's work. Sorrentino now owned crates of the finest rum and scotch in warehouses twenty miles away on the docks of Los Llanitos. He controlled the ships that would be delivering the liquor to Los Angeles and San Francisco.

"This isn't bad at all, boss," Pelosi said, gesturing with his beer to take in the expanse of ocean. "We got a fucking fortress here."

"And far enough away from the Feds so nobody can touch us." Sorrentino took another drink of beer. "This is what success is, Jimmy. And there's much more to come. We are going to own it all. When the gambling is up and running in Hollywood, I'm going to buy Global Studio."

"I'll be a producer."

"You'll be able to fuck any actress you want."

Jimmy laughed "I'll slip into Los Llanitos. There's a little whore house with the sweetest…"

"That's for later. You're going back to Los Angeles tonight. The plan is ready now. There's no reason to wait." Lost in momentary thought, his eyes darkened. His tone was harsh. "I don't care what the fuck you have to do or who you have to kill, get me one of them. Send him down here to me. If she knows I have one of her damn kids, she'll sign anything you put in front of her."

Pelosi nodded.

Sorrentino spat into the sea far below. "When I'm done with that bitch, I'm going to pass her tight little ass off to you. You want an actress, you can start with her." He let several seconds pass before he lifted the beer bottle. "Power, my friend, is better than any damn piece of ass. Why? Because power gets you all the ass in the world."

He finished the beer and tossed the bottle into the ocean below.

CHAPTER FIFTY: THE END GAME

January 6, 1928, Los Angeles

It was time for the End Game. She would leave tonight. Time to delete Sorrentino and then go home where she belonged. Since New Year's, Lauren had made two trips down to Tijuana in the spacecraft to plan the gangster's end. If she could prevent Pauline's murder by killing Sorrentino, she could leave without any regrets. Well, at least without too many. She felt confident she had a good plan.

What determines a good plan? Matt asked.

One that allows me to escape. Then after a moment she added, *nothing is ever easy, but in this case, I have to put a round in Sorrentino, then make it back to the shuttle.*

Obviously, no one could follow us after that, Matt said.

Then, we travel into space to await the anomaly.

The AI's voice took on a tone sorrow. *You will not return to the Windsors?*

No.

That evening, three hours before she planned to leave, Lauren sat at the long dining room table with several film people and the Windsor family. Pauline had called an impromptu gathering to discuss the changes Zelinsky wanted for *Romeo and Juliet*, and asked them to stay for dinner afterwards.

Seated at the table now along with all the Windsor family were Michael Murray and his boyfriend, a handsome costume designer at Global; Clarence Martin, the director, and his wife Constance; and Francis Marion, the great scenarist who had penned the Shakespeare adaption; and Francis's husband, film cowboy Fred Thomson.

Assassin 13

They'd spent the last couple hours sketching out the final scene Zelinsky wanted added to the film, and Francis hastily wrote the four-page script. Ironically, she said the scene would work better without dialogue, but since Zelinsky wanted the audience to hear the actors talking, she gave them dialogue.

Lauren listened only half-heartedly to the talk. A great melancholy took control of her psyche. She had to admit leaving behind people she'd come to love, people she felt almost a family bond with, would be among the hardest things she'd ever done. But it had to be done. The compulsion and desire to complete her work in the 22nd century was just as strong as it had been when she left the Tin Can so long ago.

The sounds of the Windsor household, children giggling at the table and being shushed by Mrs. Windsor, the clink of dishes and friendly conversation, all of it cast her down through the dark memories of her own childhood to the last time she was happy. Her parents alive, sitting at a campfire with Lauren and Sybil and Sybil's family. Laughing and talking like these people tonight.

Then the darkness came. She saw herself placing a lovely bullet in the heart of the man who killed her father. Soon, when she returned to her own century, she would send her mother's murderers to hell. Then, she would be at peace.

Sitting beside her, Remy said to the group, "Everything is sound now. Everyone wants sound in their films, especially dialogue. Just like Zelinsky."

Martin said derisively, "It won't last. People will get their fill and cry out for their silent films."

Pauline gave a slight shake of the head. "I don't know. I hope you're right, Clarence."

Mrs. Windsor scoffed at the idea of talking pictures, "Yapping, yapping, yapping. People want to see their stars, not hear them."

"Here, here," Michael said.

Everyone ate and chatted with a joy as if this were their last night on earth. For Lauren, it was. Even now, her mind was dealing with the hyper-adrenaline rush that comes before an op, and at the same time, she felt the utter sorrow of leaving these people behind. She stared down the long table at them, trying to fix them in her memory, chisel them in hard stone there.

For when she returned to the 22nd century, they will have long been dust.

She noticed Russell talking pointedly with Francis Marion, desperately trying to impress her with his medical research work. She was pretty, and he was smitten with her, having fallen in love within the last hour. Unfortunately, she was married, but her husband, sitting on her other side, seemed unconcerned. Lauren smiled to herself. He fell in love like getting on and off a bicycle.

Beside him, Emmy struggled with a glass of milk, leaving a white mustache on her lip. She belched, then grinned up at everyone as if that had been a momentous occurrence. A loving, happy girl, too loving. She saw nothing but the good in people. A dangerous way for a female to be in any time, Lauren thought. So much like her mother.

"Say excuse me," Mrs. Windsor instructed the girl, ever the etiquette maven.

"Sorry." Emmy giggled.

For some reason, the pinch-faced woman caught Lauren's eye and scowled. Lauren nodded her approval. That ought to throw the old bat off.

Rolly was balancing his spoon on the edge of his soup bowl, piling little vegetables on each end to see which side toppled first. Ever vigilant, Mrs. Windsor caught him. Her sharp voice cut through the chatter, "Rolly Windsor, stop playing with your food."

"Yes, ma'am," the boy said but used the narrow end of the spoon to lift out the lentels.

It felt like an icepick was stabbing her heart. God, how she loved these kids. She never thought she'd ever feel that way again about anyone.

At the other end of the table, Pauline huddled with Michael and Martin, scripts out in front of them, a breach of etiquette almost too much for Mrs. Windsor to bear. Occasionally, she told her daughter to eat and, with a furrowed brow aimed at the two men, got them to eat as well.

"I have a silly voice," Michael wailed abruptly. "People will laugh when they hear me."

Pauline patted his shoulder. "Hardly, Michael. You have the smoothest, richest, manliest voice I've ever heard. Now, I have the voice and accent of a Swedish milkmaid."

Michael looked at her, astounded. "My God, Pauline, you have a sweet, beautiful voice with no accent at all."

She said a few words with a thick Swedish accent and everyone laughed.

"You sound like Garbo now," Martin said. "There's someone who will never make it if this sound madness continues."

At that moment, Lauren realized what part of Pauline would stick with her forever. People loved her. They loved her unconditionally. She was outgoing, always kind and friendly to everyone, no matter what station in life. To her family, her friends, and even people she met casually, she treated them the same. They all loved her for it. And so did Lauren.

She leaned over and kissed Remy on the cheek. He glanced at her with a curious smile. She patted his thigh under the table. "I'm glad I met you," she whispered to him.

A bit surprised, he said, "I'm glad I met you, too."

Later that evening, long after the meal was done, after the kids had gone to bed and the adults had talked well beyond midnight, Lauren and Remy lay naked in her room. They had just made love, and she nestled into the crook of his good arm. Their relationship had been rocky at first. He had learned what kind of person she was, revolted against it, then accepted her. No one had ever done that before, loved her like that, darkness and all. This man loved her despite knowing she was a lethal killer.

What is wrong with him, Matt asked rhetorically.

Butt out. "You love me, don't you?" she asked.

"I do."

"Why? You know I'm, well, different."

He laughed. "Honey, Pauline is different. Mary Pickford and Gloria Swanson are different. They are women who dominate an industry in a world where woman don't leave the house except for shopping and bridge on Tuesdays. You? There's no word that describes you. *Different* just doesn't do it."

Her hand caressed the side of his face. "But you love me anyway. You're crazy."

"I love you anyway, and I am crazy." He waited several seconds, then said, "Now it's your turn. You're supposed to tell me you love me. That's the way it goes."

She sighed and groaned as if in pain. Saying it meant actually admitting it to herself, and that made her vulnerable. "Yes, I do love you, Remy. I guess I'm just as crazy as you."

She lay in silence with him for another five minutes as if actually living in the comfort and security other people shared. Then the business part of her mind kicked in.

"I might be going away for a little while, just for a little while," she lied. She placed a hand on his mouth to stop him from speaking. "I cannot tell you how I know this. Sorrentino is going to murder Pauline, or attempt to do it. He will keep trying till he's successful. If I'm not here, you must protect her as long as he's alive."

He looked at her with a deep frown. "Going away?"

"Yes, for a little while."

An hour later, he had fallen asleep. Lauren slid quietly from the bed, dressed in her cargo pants, boots, and black blouse. She put on the leather flight jacket and strapped on her Glock. When she was ready, she stared down at Remy for several seconds, needing to kiss his cheek one last time, but didn't, not wanting to wake him. Then she slipped from the room.

CHAPTER FIFTY-ONE: GOING HOME

January 7, 1928, Tijuana, Mexico

In the darkness before dawn, the shuttle hovered five hundred feet above the Jockey Club race track in Tijuana. A full moon scudded in and out of black clouds, remnants of a storm that had run in from the sea. Lauren didn't like the glassy reflection below. The racetrack was flooded. It looked more like a lake.

"Take us down," she ordered Matt.

The AI navigated the craft into the hills that bordered the track to the east and set it down on an open plateau. Within fifteen minutes, Lauren had hiked down to the track, which was inundated with water, fit for boating instead of horseracing. Following the lantern lights, she made her way to the stables in the back. They were crowded with trainers and exercise boys attempting to keep the stalls dry with sandbags and bales of hay.

She found Top Outfit, Sorrentino's horse. A squat man in high boots stood at the stall door, directing the men inside to distribute more hay on the muddy ground.

"Excuse me," Lauren said. "Are you the trainer?"

He turned and eyed her suspiciously. "I am."

"I drove all the way down from Los Angeles to watch Top Outfit race today," she said. "Will the horses run?"

He pursed his lips in a grimace. "Does it look like we'll be running today?" When he saw her frown, he sighed. "I am sorry for your trip, ma'am. It's been raining for three days. You see, some fool built the Jockey Club race track on low ground, and when there's a bad rain, it floods. That's why the new track is being built on higher ground."

An enormous lump of coal lodged itself in her chest and ignited. For a moment, she couldn't breathe. "I'm a friend of Mr. Sorrentino. I was expecting to meet him here today. Is he still coming?"

The trainer shouted at one of the men inside the stall. "Careful with that damn shovel. Do you want to cripple the horse?" With a shake of the head, he turned back to Lauren. "Sorrentino? Are you kidding? He will not come just to see us clean the stall. The stakes race has been postponed till next Saturday. He'll be here then. Unless it rains again."

"Do you know where he is?"

"No idea."

"Do you know anyone who would?"

"Nope. He has any instructions for me, he calls my office."

As the dawn began to bleach into the eastern skies, Lauren slowly climbed back up the winding path to the plateau toward the ship, her mind in as violent a storm as had washed though Tijuana.

In 1928, she told herself, Ben Sorrentino murders Pauline Windsor. Even if Lauren stayed in this time, she might not be able to prevent it. And she would have failed both ways: her mother's killers would escape retribution and Pauline would be dead.

You're no help, she snapped at Matt.

I see no simple answer, he replied. *I see no complex answer. You are wrong no matter what you do.*

I'm going home. To my century.

She hurried into the spacecraft and lifted off just as the rising sun breached the horizon.

Clouds rushed by at great speed. They reached the thermosphere in less than a minute. In the widescreen FOV, she could see the dark curve of the earth framed by a sunlight glow through the haze of atmosphere. A packed field of stars sparkled beyond. Light raced across the landmass far below, opening the day.

A few minutes later, 250 miles above the earth, the shuttle settled into place, Matt said from inside the computer, "We are on site."

"The exact coordinates?"

"No, fifty miles' distance. Two seconds away. We must maintain a wide field of view in case the anomaly does not return at its last coordinates. When it returns, if it returns at all, it may not live longer than a few minutes, if that."

"That's enough time to get through."

"You are upset," Matt said.

"Of course, I'm upset."

Long ago, her ability to feel emotional pain had been destroyed. Now, it ransacked her psyche. As if fire scorched her blood.

Her last goodbye before flying down to Tijuana had been to Sybil, who would be born in the 22nd century and die early in the 20th. She was abandoning Pauline to her death, leaving the children unprotected.

If her mother were here, she'd know what to do. She'd be able to advise her.

"Would you like to watch a movie?" Matt asked. "We might be waiting minutes or we may be waiting more than forty hours. No way of computing."

"No, I do not want to watch a movie." But she did lay back and close her eyes.

Twenty hours passed. Nothing happened. Each tick of the clock went by more slowly than the previous.

Finally, Matt said, "Lauren, dare I ask you a question?"

"Are you registering activity from the anomaly?"

"No."

"Then, no, you cannot ask me a question."

"So, you are leaving them in the lurch. That's the phrase I believe. It was used most prominently in the 2066 film *Lost on Ganymede*. It fit the…"

"I told you I don't want to hear any of your questions."

"That was not a question. Merely a statement."

"Great. I know you don't want to return. Drop it. Do not speak until the anomaly appears."

"Lauren…"

"You are pushing me to a place you do not want me to go."

"It's the anomaly."

It burst on them out of nothing in all its brightness, a giant spider web stretched across the FOV. It grew brighter till it gleamed like gold and pulsed.

Though the readings indicated it nearly seventy miles away, it was an enormous circle a hundred miles in diameter. On the network of glowing strands blue sparks flashed everywhere.

"Shall we proceed through?" Matt asked her.

She hesitated giving the order. Everything in her soul cried out for blood, to avenge her mother. That pain, that desire for vengeance was as strong now as it had been. Anguish cut her like a razor through her flesh. For the first time in her life, she didn't know what to do.

"Shall we proceed?" Matt asked again.

She didn't answer.

In the next instant, the anomaly radiated a hundred times brighter and she would have been blinded had Matt not shifted the FOV to infrared.

"What is happening?" Lauren demanded.

"I cannot conclude without more data, but a reasonable hypothesis would be that the anomaly is dying. It only has seconds. You only have seconds to go through."

She could not lose this, the only opportunity to get home. "Mother, tell me what to do," she screamed.

The anomaly expanded to twice its size, flickering off and on like a light bulb with a short. Its spidery strands fell to a dead white, all color and life gone. And exploded.

There was no shock wave. The creature broke into particles of dust shooting in every direction, showering the spacecraft.

"We did not go through the anomaly," Matt said. "But it appears it went through us. Our clocks are askew. It is a reasonable assumption that we have gone through time."

CHAPTER FIFTY-TWO: TARGETING EMMY OF THE NEW MOON

January 9-11, 1928, Los Angeles

Monday morning, Pauline accompanied Rolly and Emmy to school with Tommy Corcoran driving, Rolly between them, Emmy in the backseat with Sergeant Knighton. Behind them, another car with Remy, Brady, and Beachum followed.

Emmy was talking a mile a minute about the book she was reading, *Emily of New Moon*, concerning Emily Starr, an orphan, and her remarkable friends. She called it *Emmy of the New Moon*. Knighton was nodding, enthralled. His tough veneer disappeared around the children.

Pauline thought of Lauren, wondering where she was. She had disappeared on Friday, but she had complete faith in her friend. She'd told no one where she was going, though Remy said she might not be back for a while. It had been Windsor's luck that had brought her into their lives. Otherwise, only God knows what would have happened to her children and herself.

Pauline was free for a few days while the studio attempted to jury-rig stage four into a sound stage. Filming Zelinsky's final scene for *Romeo and Juliet* would have to wait till then. Michael was absolutely terrified to speak. He knew his voice wouldn't pass muster, but she'd done Broadway, so using her voice was not exactly new to her.

When Corcoran turned onto Briar Summit Drive, Pauline felt a chill race down her spine. She studied the twisting road and the dry landscape and saw nothing untoward. Ahead, a Mercedes disappeared around a curve, the car of another parent. Nothing.

Abruptly, three Model-A Fords appeared ahead, approaching at a high rate of speed, driving in tandem like a fast-moving parade.

Corcoran placed his hand on his Army Colt. "What the hell?"

The lead car slammed its breaks and swung into their path. Pauline screamed. Corcoran swung the wheel to go around it but was clipped and driven onto the gravel shoulder. The second car blocked the way forward. Quickly, Corcoran shoved Rolly to the floor as gunfire erupted into the windows, shattering glass and sending shards flying. In the back Knighton threw himself over Emmy just as a bullet struck him on the side of the head, taking off much of his ear. He groaned and slumped over her, unconscious.

Behind them, Remy, Beachum, and Brady scrambled out of their car to return fire.

In the fog of the chaos, Pauline realized the gunmen were only firing into the back seat. With Rolly safe on the floor, she tried to climb over the seat to Emmy, but Corcoran pulled her back. "Stay down!"

Terror filled Rolly's eyes. Squeezing down over him, Pauline held him tight and prayed for Emmy. At that instant, the passenger door flew open. Corcoran tried to turn around, but a bullet pierced his temple. Blood burst from his forehead and he slumped over the steering wheel. The man yanked Rolly from under Pauline and took him up in his arms.

"No! Please!" she screamed and stared into the dead eyes of Jimmy Pelosi.

He smiled at her, the morning sun glinting off a gold tooth. "We'll be in touch."

"Mommy!" Rolly cried out as Pelosi ran with him to the nearest car. Now, gunfire ceased, no one wanting to hit the boy, and the three cars drove away.

Assassin 13

That's when Pauline heard Emmy moaning. Jumping into the backseat, she pulled her from beneath Knighton, saw the blood gushing from her arm and desperately tried to stop it with her hand.

Remy yanked open the door, Brady and Beachum immediately behind him. He saw Emmy's right forearm hanging loose, nearly torn off at the elbow, and bleeding profusely.

"Let go of the arm, Pauline," he yelled at her. "Let go. I need to stop the bleeding."

Working quickly, he tied a make-shift belt tourniquet on the girl's upper arm, shutting off the flow from the artery.

Remy waved Brady into the driver's seat. "Get us to the hospital. Run over anyone in the way."

***

Two hundred and fifty miles above the planet, Lauren stared out of the FOV at empty space. The anomaly was gone.

"What happened?" Lauren asked Matt.

"We have passed through time," Matt answered. "How far is unknown."

As soon as she asked it, she knew the answer. Her neurobots had no Internet access. "If we passed through time, it is not to the 22nd century."

"No, it is not," Matt said.

She threw her head back and screamed, "Fuck!"

She was forever cut off from her own century now. She had made that choice by hesitating. She would never find retribution. She would never drive the darkness from her soul.

"I detect no satellites. No ISS," Matt said.

She couldn't deal with it. It took several minutes before she asked, "When the hell are we?"

"I do not know. I have no data. I cannot detect TV or radio, but I might not be able to at some levels of development, that is if they do exist in this new time."

She decided to head back to earth. Where else was she to go? "Take us down."

Minutes later, on the glide path in, she saw some traffic below, cars and a few trucks similar to 1928. Matt finally picked up a radio station. Bessie Smith, a Blues singer Pauline liked. The 1920s still or the thirties. Had they jumped time? Matt said they had.

"Shut it off," Lauren snapped, and the radio went silent.

By the location of the sun, it was late-afternoon as they swept in over the Santa Monica Mountains and settled into the ravine. It looked the same, as if no time had passed at all. Sybil's grave in front of them, every rock, every dried brush in the same place, but then it all might look like this for many centuries to come.

After shutting down all systems and reluctantly allowing Matt back into her head, she left the ravine. Her motorcycle had a layer of dust on it, so some time had passed, but how much? Years? They had passed through the anomaly, a ghost of it. But they had gone through it, so were they in the 1930s? And by then, Pauline would be long dead, murdered by Sorrentino. If that were the case, then Lauren was lost, too. She would have failed in every respect.

An hour later, when she rode the cycle up the driveway of Pauline's home, she found out exactly what time it was from the newspapers on the front porch. The latest was dated January 11, 1928. Wednesday. In the dust of the dying anomaly, she'd been thrust forward just three days.

She could see no security about, but two cars were parked in front. She went in and found Brady and Remy in the living room. Brady sat, his head buried into his hands. Remy stood, his head bowed also. He glanced up when she came in, but said nothing. He looked as if he hadn't slept for days.

Mrs. Windsor entered the living room, carrying a small suitcase, and stopped abruptly when she saw Lauren.

"Something has happened. What?" Lauren asked.

Mrs. Windsor eyes blazed with fury. "For your information, while you were out getting drunk or catting around, Rolly has been kidnapped and poor Emmy lies right now on her death bed at the hospital. She is not expected to survive the night." The old woman jabbed a finger at Lauren. "And it's your fault. You only had one job, to protect those children. And you have failed miserably."

Stunned, Lauren took a step back as Mrs. Windsor pushed by her and out the door.

"Come on," Remy said as he and Brady followed.

On the way to the hospital, Lauren learned what had happened from Brady. Corcoran was dead, Sgt. Knighton wounded but not out of action, Emmy had an amputated arm. Blood poisoning had set in. And Rolly had been taken.

In the back seat, Remy was subdued, staring out the window. A stone-faced Mrs. Windsor rode in the back as well. She had come home to gather clothes for Pauline, who would not leave Emmy's side.

"Has anyone contacted Pauline about ransom for Rolly?" Lauren asked.

"No," Remy said. "But we know who took him. Sorrentino's man Jimmy Pelosi."

"Do you know where he is?"

Remy sighed and leaned back in the seat. "No. I've been trying to locate him, but Sorrentino's gone and so's Rolly. We don't know where they are."

"Don't you worry about Rolly," Mrs. Windsor said. "Pauline has taken care of it, no thanks to you. He will be all right."

"What does that mean?"

Remy said, "It means Sorrentino contacted Pauline yesterday through his lawyer and said he'd heard about what happened. He promised he would use his contacts to find Rolly and get him back, that is if she signed over her downtown property to him. She did yesterday afternoon."

A chill settled in the forward lobes of her brain.

Mrs. Windsor said, "See? I told you it's taken care of."

Remy shook his head. "All BS. Sorrentino took Rolly in the first place."

I know that," Mrs. Windsor snapped. "Now, he is giving him back. That's all that matters. I don't care what flimflam he plays at. Just so my grandson comes home."

Lauren said softly, "Pauline has signed Rolly's execution order."

The woman's lower lip quivered. "What are you talking about."

"Get this straight. When Sorrentino gets those documents, he must kill Rolly. If the boy lives, he can prove Sorrentino is behind this. That's the death penalty for him. Without Rolly, no one can prove anything."

"What about Pelosi?" Brady said. "We all saw him snatch Rolly."

Lauren gave a small shake of the head. "Sorrentino will claim he no longer works for him and no one can prove otherwise. Except Rolly."

Staring at Lauren, Mrs. Windsor's face went white. "You seem to know these people all too well. A person might think you were one of them."

Lauren knew Mrs. Windsor was frightened, and her voice softened. "Not exactly, but close. So, believe what I tell you. Once Sorrentino gets those papers in his hands, he can no longer afford to keep Rolly alive."

She thought Sorrentino would wait till he had the papers himself before eliminating his prize bargaining chip, but she couldn't be sure. The boy might already be dead.

At the hospital, Mrs. Windsor and Brady hurried inside. Lauren held Remy back. "You look tired."

"I am tired."

"We don't have time for you to rest. I need you to find Sorrentino. I don't know how you're going to do it, but it's our only chance to save Rolly."

He nodded. "I'll find him."

CHAPTER FIFTY-THREE: THE CABINET OF DR. CALIGARI

January 11, 1928, Los Angeles

In Emmy's hospital room, tears ran down Pauline's cheeks. She sat beside her daughter's bed, holding her left hand. The girl had no right hand. Her arm had been amputated at the elbow. A single table lamp cast a funereal light against the gray walls. The smell of rubbing alcohol and ether was overwhelming. A merciless sorrow burned through Pauline. She had been such a fool. She had brought all this on her daughter and son. Even if God forgave fools, she would never forgive herself.

She had not left her daughter's side since they'd come to the hospital more than fifty hours ago. Her dress was splotched with dried blood, the blood of her daughter and Tommy Corcoran and Sgt. Knighton. When people attempted to draw her away, she angrily refused.

Sergeant Knighton was sitting in a nearby chair, his arm in a sling, his head swathed in bandages to cover the raw area where his ear had been. His face looked drained.

He had sent the rest of the men to the lobby to wait out the vigil. They, too, had been devastated by the attack on Pauline and the children. The hospital administration was upset at so many men hanging around the halls and in the lobby, but no one dared tell them to leave.

A groan came from the bed, and Pauline glanced over, immediately hopeful, but Emmy remained in her coma. Pauline's heart lurched as it did every time she looked at her daughter. In sleep, Emmy's face was deathly pale. Her right arm had been amputated at the elbow and was swathed in white bandages. Blood drained through at the nub. She looked so small and frail, as if a broken flower.

At that moment, Dr. Wallace came in. "I'll see if her situation has changed."

He went to the bedside, rolled up the sleeve of Emmy's hospital gown, and placed a thermometer in her armpit. He was smoking a cigarette, exhaling to the side, away from his patient. "It will be a few minutes," he said to Pauline. "Her temperature will tell us if there's been any improvement."

In his three-piece gabardine suit, he appeared distinguished with gray hair and moustache adding to a sense of competence, one she didn't feel about him.

Suddenly, Pauline slid from the chair to her knees, her hands folded in prayer. She prayed for her daughter, pleading with God that He save her. Telling Him that Emmy was so young and did not deserve this fate. She searched her mind for anything to say to God that would move him. No words came. Just the Lord's condemnation.

"Please, take me instead. I'm the one who did this," she whispered.

When her mother, Brady, and Lauren came in, she was still asking over and over for God's help. She did not look up at them.

Mrs. Windsor set the small suitcase on the floor beside her and said quietly, "I brought you some clothes, Pauline. You're going to have to change out of that dress. It's been more than two days." She nodded toward Lauren. "And that woman has come back."

Pauline did not make any indication she had heard. Her hands squeezed together so tightly under her chin the knuckles were white. Her lips moved in silent prayer.

Lauren went to the foot of the bed and at sight of Emmy gave a long groan. Her eyes watered. "Damn it," she muttered.

Dr. Wallace glanced at her sharply, then, setting his cigarette on the bedside table, he withdrew the thermometer.

Pauline looked up at him expectantly. He frowned, slipping the thermometer into his pocket. After a few seconds, he said, "Up another degree. 105.6. It won't be long now."

At the words, Pauline flinched as if slapped. Lauren's voice shot out like a gunshot. "Who the fuck are you? Shut the hell up. She's not going to die."

Dr. Wallace took a half step back and stared at Lauren uncomprehendingly. Women did not talk that way and certainly not to him. Pauline gazed up, wiping tears from her eyes.

"Why are you standing there doing nothing?" Lauren demanded. "Give the girl antibiotics, for God's sake. A blood transfusion or something." Her teeth bared. "Do your damn job."

Taking another step back, Dr. Wallace blanched, then snapped the lapels of his coat. He turned to Pauline. "There is no call for talk like that. I am doing all I can. I have ordered morphine for your little girl. She will rest comfortably till the end. I assure you no doctor could do more."

Lauren's face twisted into an ugly mask. "You son of a bitch." She froze as if straining to listen to something far away. "What was that?" she said to no one in particular. Then, she looked accusingly at Dr. Wallace. Her voice held dismay. "You don't even have antibiotics?"

Dr. Wallace addressed Pauline. "I am sorry for the child's condition, but I tell you I will not stand here and be abused."

"You can do a blood transfusion, I assume," Lauren said.

He didn't speak till Pauline said, "Answer her, please."

"We can, Miss Windsor, but what's the point? That would do nothing to combat the infection. That's what's killing her. Besides, there is no storage of blood in this hospital. The nearest is ten miles away."

"My blood type is O negative," Lauren said. "Give her my blood."

"Out of the question," Dr. Wallace said. "A transfusion is a difficult procedure and will likely kill the girl outright. I am not going to allow my patient to spend the last hours of her life in such discomfort."

Lauren turned to Pauline. "We need to do something. Give her my blood, Pauline."

Pauline looked confused. When she didn't immediately dismiss this suggestion, Dr. Wallace said with astonishment. "You are not considering this claptrap, Miss Windsor? I will not be a part of it."

She had been praying for something, and she knew this was it. This had to be it. There was nothing else. Nothing else. Pauline rose from her knees and said forcefully, "Please, do as she says, Dr. Wallace."

He clasped his hands behind him and gazed at her with sadness. "I am sorry, Miss Windsor, but I am the physician in charge here. You must understand this. A doctor must first do no harm, and this most definitely will do harm. I will not take part in it nor will I condone it. I am removing all of you from this room except the mother." He glared at Lauren. "That includes you."

When no one moved, he started from the room.

Lauren said sharply, "Knighton, Brady."

The sergeant jumped to his feet, and he and Brady blocked the doctor's way. "Sit down, Doc," Knighton said. "You might be here a while."

Outside, at the rear of the hospital, Russell walked the grounds, lost in a confusion of sorrows. He blinked several times to keep his tears in check. It would do Pauline no good for him to show weakness. For nearly a half hour, he'd been treading the paths in the back garden, barely aware of where he was. He'd had to get out of that claustrophobic room. He could not stay one more second watching his niece die and bear witness to his sister's endless agony. It was why, when he graduated from medical school, he had gone into research instead of medical practice. He could not deal with so much pain.

Night had come and stars flooded the sky. He had not even been aware of it. Suddenly, he heard someone running toward him and turned around.

"Dr. Windsor," Captain Brady called, coming up to him. "Hurry, Doc. They need you in Emmy's room."

Russell struggled to get the words out. "Is Emmy gone?"

"No, no. They need you to do a blood transfusion."

"What?"

But Brady was already racing back toward the hospital.

Forty-five minutes later in Emmys' room, Russell arranged his instruments on a table by the bed. Transfusion needles with stopcock valves, paraffin coated rubber tubes to delay coagulation, a pint glass container also coated with paraffin, a glass tube for suction, and a glass tube for compression. All to draw blood from Lauren's cephalic vein at the elbow, and conduct it to the glass container, where it would be drawn out into more tubing and compressed into Emmy's same cephalic vein.

A direct transfusion from donor to patient had seldom been done since the Great War, but he had no time to spend hours preparing for an indirect transfusion. In the war, blood was often drained directly through one tube from donor to patient, hoping the blood did not coagulate before it reached the recipient.

Now they had the paraffin tubing, but still Russell thought this was doomed. Emmy was doomed. And he would be accused of quackery and likely go to jail. Worse yet, Emmy would be dead. He knew in his heart she was going to die anyway, but he could not deny Pauline this last hope.

Holding tightly to each other's hands, his mother and sister watched, tension etching their faces. He should tell them to leave, but knew they wouldn't go. Knighton and Brady stood near the door. Dr. Wallace sat back by the window, fuming.

In the chair next to Russell, Lauren placed her arm on the table top. "Let's get it done."

He said, "Another minute. Then I'll have it set up."

"If you go through with this abomination, Dr. Windsor," Dr. Wallace exclaimed indignantly, "I promise you, you will be a pariah in the medical community. You have not even taken precaution against further infection. This is hardly a sterile setting."

Uncertain about his ability to complete this procedure, Russell glanced over at him. "I've done what I can to sterilize my hands and the environment, Dr. Wallace. If this is going to work, it must be done now."

Knighton stepped over to Wallace and put a hand on his shoulder. "Quiet, Doc. I'll stuff a rag in your mouth if you don't shut up."

Dr. Wallace blanched.

Everything was finally set up. Russell stared at Lauren for second, then said, "I'm ready. Let's begin."

His hands shaking, he leaned toward her with the needle. She took his hand and steadied it. "You can't hurt me," she said.

He nodded. Then he inserted the needle into her vein. At once, blood began filling the glass container. Immediately, he inserted the second needle into Emmy's vein and turned the valve. Blood began flowing out of the glass and into his niece.

An hour after the transfusion, Emmy's temperature had dropped slightly. By nine o'clock it had come down a full degree. Everyone but Dr. Wallace cheered when Russell announced it.

"You know that it means nothing," Dr. Wallace said. He lit a cigarette and blew smoke into the air. "There are many reasons such a reading could occur. The prognosis is still the same."

Lauren strode over to him, snatched the cigarette from his mouth and flicked it out the open window. "This is a no-smoking zone as of now."

Knighton had placed all the men, including the old-timer Earp, in the hall outside Emmy's room. Only Pauline's people were allowed to come in or out. The night staff obviously knew something was wrong, but Russell kept explaining to them that Dr. Wallace did not want to be disturbed, and for now they went along with it.

By 11:00pm, Emmy's temperature had dropped below 104 degrees to 103.8. When Russell removed Emmy's bandages on her elbow and washed the stub, pus oozed from open wounds. He let it drain into a pan, then re-bandaged the arm. At midnight, the progress could not be denied by even Dr. Wallace, who finally deigned to examine her and seemed surprised when he found her temperature at 101.7.

With his stethoscope, he checked her chest. "Her heart beat is stronger," he said. "I don't understand this. How could this happen? I've never seen the like. Somehow, she is improving, but it can't be from just a blood transfusion. It can't."

Pauline and even Mrs. Windsor were crying now from relief and joy. Lauren felt her own eyes moisten. It had worked. She hadn't been sure it would.

Ever the great actress, Pauline convinced Dr. Wallace that Emmy's improvement was due to his fine care. She called him a miracle healer. He was no fool. He knew what was going on.

They had committed a crime by holding him here against his will while Dr. Windsor performed an unauthorized medical procedure. Yet, somehow, the girl was healing. This was one of the most famous people in the world standing before him. He thought about it a long time before saying to her, "Perhaps, a blood transfusion with my cold packs did do the trick. Yes, that is what happened." He fixed on Lauren. "Allow my nurses in."

Lauren nodded to Knighton, and two nurses were called in. Unabashedly, Dr. Wallace explained how he had brilliantly saved the girl's life with a transfusion and gave instructions for Emmy's continued care. Then, he announced he was tired and leaving for the night. Lauren let him go.

Two hours later, Remy returned to the hospital. He had found Sorrentino.

CHAPTER FIFTY-FOUR: WHAT THE HELL IS THAT?

January 12, 1928, Los Angeles and Los Llanitos

Concisely, Remy explained that he and the others had tracked down Sherman in a hotel room with his boyfriend, a recent law-graduate named Potter.

"Sherman didn't give it up, but the boyfriend did," he said to Lauren. "Sorrentino owns a large hacienda north of Puerto Los Llanitos in southern Mexico, and he is there now." His expression turned grave. "This Potter was scared. Scared of us and scared of Sorrentino, but he wanted no part in killing a child. He said Sorrentino is not going to let Rolly go."

"Are you sure he told the truth?" she asked.

"As much as I can be. He said Sorrentino doesn't trust anyone. He wants the documents you signed in his hand before he deals with Rolly."

"What did you do with Sherman and Potter?" Lauren asked.

"Took them to an airfield. They're locked in a hanger, and a few friends are watching them."

"I know Los Llanitos," Brady said. "I did some work for the Mexican government there. It's a big city. It takes a long while to get there from here by car."

By the speed of current automobiles, my calculation is thirty-six to forty hours depending on several variables, Matt said.

Lauren repeated his estimate aloud.

Brady nodded. "That's about right. If Pelosi left at three yesterday afternoon, he might be there in another hour." He sucked in his breath, realizing he had said it was too late.

"I can call together the Black Cats," Remy said hopefully. "We can fly some of us down there. If we can fly out by six this morning, we could make it by six at night."

Lauren said, "There's another way."

You're crazy, you know, Matt said, understanding what she intended

I know.

She stepped to the door and spoke to the men in the hall. "You boys ready to go to war?"

"Yes, ma'am," they shouted, bringing the floor nurse out from behind her desk shushing them.

"Good." Lauren said. "We're going to get Rolly back." She just wasn't sure it would be with him alive.

An hour later, among the brush and scrub oak of the Santa Monica Mountains, sixteen heavily armed men exited their cars and followed Lauren over the rocks into the bleak landscape. Two people were along she had not wanted. Wyatt Earp had slipped into one of the cars. She had left him with the six men who were guarding Emmy and Mrs. Windsor at the hospital.

The second person was Pauline. If she was destined to be killed by Sorrentino, she did not want to place her within a thousand miles of the gangster. But the actress had insisted, and she was paying the freight.

Overhead, the starscape spread across a brilliant, cloudless sky. A three-quarter moon hung just above the horizon, casting long shadows over the land. Sgt. Knighton, looking like a mummy with his head wrapped in white gauze, walked beside Lauren. "Whatever you have in mind, we are not going to reach southern Mexico in time to save Rolly."

"Have faith, Sergeant."

"I do. We all do. We're all here, aren't we?"

That gave her a strange sensation, one she didn't understand. Knighton, Remy, Brady, even Earp, and all these men had followed her into an isolated landscape when she said this was how they could save a boy thousands of miles away.

She understood now they felt something more than trust in her. Belief, maybe. As a result, what she felt was sudden depth of affection for all of them. It was odd for her. She didn't like it. She was leading them to a place where some may die. She preferred doing these type of things alone. Only she was at risk then.

The chance of several of these men being killed tonight is above 99%, Matt said.

I didn't need to know that.

She pointed to the sling on Knighton's arm. "I assume that will not be a problem?"

He tossed the sling away and flexed his hand and arm. "Not a bit."

Reaching the edge of the ravine, they saw the black mass below, the two long metallic pincers, the four antimatter ramjets in the moonlight, and stopped abruptly.

"What the hell is that?" Captain Brady muttered.

Beachum said, "Looks like a building of some kind."

Russell, who had come as the medic, said, "No, it's not a building. It's a...I don't know."

They all looked to Lauren, but she was already striding down the slope toward it, and they followed. Moments later, the sixteen men stopped before the odd structure and stared in bewilderment. They did not see Lauren disappear in through the cockpit hatch up front. A slit of brilliant light emerged in the side, then expanded to form a wide doorway with Lauren standing in it, backlit, hands on hips. "Come in, gentlemen. Your ride awaits you."

When she stepped aside, one after the other the men proceeded in as if entering a booby-trapped building.

"What is this?" Pauline asked.

"A flying machine," Lauren answered, then turned to the men. "Take a seat quickly. We need to get going. We'll be at Los

Llanitos in half an hour and we must be ready. Remy, you're up front with me."

Startling them, a thin blond woman with a hint of steel in her gaze suddenly appeared above the control panel. "Fasten your seat belts," she said in a raspy voice. "This is going to be a bumpy ride."

"Matt, get back in the computer," Lauren snapped. "And all of you sit down before you walk into a wall."

Confused, they stumbled to a seat, then she addressed them. "I'll make this simple. You're going to see some astonishing things. I'll explain what I can. Just remember we're all here to do one thing. Get Rolly back. Keep that in mind and deal with your disbelief."

She sat down beside Remy and heard them all gasp as the FOV screen spread open at 180 degrees in every direction. The ravine lay in front of them, the star-filled sky above.

The shuttle lifted off, and a couple men shrieked.

"What the hell..." Remy said, gripping the arms of the chair.

She heard mutterings and the shuffling of feet behind her as people tried to brace themselves or look for an avenue of escape. The spacecraft shot forward, gaining sonic speed in seconds. The nighttime lights of Los Angeles flashed passed beneath them in an instant.

Lauren glanced back at the men to see how they were dealing with technology that would seem like magic to them. They were the strongest and toughest group of men she had ever met, and they had terror in their eyes.

"This is just a flying machine," she said calmly. "Like Remy's."

"This is not like mine," he sputtered. For several seconds, he stared at her as if hoping to find answers to the impossible. After a moment, though still pale, he visibly relaxed. He leaned toward her. "Okay. We are flying. I can see that. And fast. Really fast. But no sensation of speed. I wouldn't spill my coffee."

"This craft has an inertia dampening system."

Remy looked blank. "A what?"

"An inertia damp...."

"Never mind," he said. "Are you the pilot?"

"No, Matt is the pilot."

"Matt?"

"He's inside the computer."

Utterly baffled, Remy nodded slowly, "I see."

She heard a couple men vomiting though it couldn't have been motion sickness. The others began shooting questions at her. She held up her hand to quiet them. "One at a time. I'll take questions for five minutes, then we must prepare."

"First, lady, who the hell are you?" Knighton said, then gestured, indicating the ship's interior. "And what is this thing?"

She called, "Matt, come out here."

Suddenly, the AI appeared above the panel in a tuxedo, startling them again. His face was painted white, his mouth thick with red lipstick. A movie character from some long forgotten future movie. His mouth split into a hellish grin. "Meine Damen und Herren, Mesdames et Messieurs, ladies and gentlemen, I give you that international sensation, Fraulein Sally Bowles...I mean, the famous, or I should say infamous, Malinche."

They stared at him, clearly without understanding. Brady muttered, "What?"

"Let's be a little less flamboyant," Lauren said to Matt. "This is tough enough on them as is."

Immediately, Matt morphed into a more acceptable apparition, a stern, gray-haired man in a military uniform, including a helmet with two stars on it and a pearl-handled Colt at the waist.

"I am sorry. I should be clearer. In our time, Lauren Ramirez is known as Malinche, the 22nd century's most feared assassin. She is master of the art of death. Yes, we are from the 22nd century. I will remain silent for three seconds while you attempt to comprehend what I have just told you."

She could not identify what stunned them the most, that she was an assassin or that she and Matt were from the future. Probably the latter. They already knew she was not a nun. Or maybe they didn't believe any of it.

She glanced at Pauline, who was staring back at her with an almost unfathomable look. Was that disappointment in her eyes? Disgust? Contempt? Usually good at reading other people, Lauren could not tell. It bothered her far more than she believed it could that she might have lost Pauline's friendship.

After three seconds, Matt continued, "This flying machine can travel at speeds in excess of fifty thousand miles an hour, though we are hardly producing that rate at the moment. We were stranded in this time when we passed through a time displacement anomaly. As for me, I am a sentient AI. That stands for artificial intelligence. I think that should make everything clear."

He went back into the computer.

"Is this a magician's trick?" Russell demanded, and several men nodded their agreement.

Lauren said, "I assure you it is not."

Then, taking them all in at a glance, she could see they still could not process everything. She fixed them with that cool gaze that could chill polar bears. "Now, we need to leave explanations behind. We can do science, or we can prepare for what's to come. In less than thirty minutes, you will be in a fight for your lives. Focus on that and on getting Rolly back." Her gesture encompassed the hull. On the view screen, occasional city lights flashed by below. "When the job is done, then you can try to figure all this out."

"You heard the lady," Knighton said. "Break into your two teams." When they did, he stepped up to her. "So, you're an assassin?"

Lauren responded, her eyes flat. "I am."

He grinned. "Son of a bitch."

CHAPTER FIFTY-FIVE: THE ICE WOMAN COMMETH

January 12, 1928, Las Llanitos, Mexico

Jimmy Pelosi arrived just before 4:00am. Already up, Sorrentino met him in the massive cathedral-like living room. A vast window took up the entire part of the house facing the sea. Light reflected off the glass, creating a mirror image of the twenty or so people in the room.

In various stages of wakefulness, his men had gathered, a few with suitcases. It would be a busy day. Some staying on here. Some traveling up to Los Angeles by car. Others taking passage with the freighter heading up to Long Beach, loaded with cases of rum and bourbon.

"You took your time," Sorrentino said to Pelosi. "You got it with you?"

"Yeah, boss, I got it." Pelosi handed Pauline's papers to Sorrentino. "Piece of cake. It's all over. We got the fucking place. Everything's set now."

Sorrentino grasped the papers like holy objects. "Yeah, everything's set now." He held the documents in the air and addressed the men. "See these? These are the future. These will make us all rich. There's nothing stopping us now."

Several more men had made their way into the big room from outside. They all cheered.

At that moment, Arty Pelosi led Rolly in by the hand. The boy was frightened, his eyes darting about the room at the men. After several days, he still wore his rumpled britches, coat, and tie.

Jimmy said, "The woman wasn't even around. She was gone who knows where? She won't be a problem."

Arty said to him, "We got a call last night from one of the hospital staff. He said she finally showed up."

"So what? She gets here in a day or two, I'll take care of her," Jimmy said. "I'm sure the boys will be glad to give her what she really needs."

They laughed.

Sorrentino looked from the documents to Rolly. "You say something, kid?"

Shrill with fright, Rolly said, "Boy, you guys are in big trouble now."

Arty snickered. "Yeah, kid, we're terrified."

Sorrentino went over to the boy and leaned down to his face. "Kid, here's some advice for you. Don't worry about dumb broads."

"She has a spaceship."

Not knowing what that meant, Sorrentino frowned, then said, "You scared of me, kid?"

"Not now."

Sorrentino could tell the boy was lying. He didn't like having to kill kids, but he had no choice. The boy could blow up his entire operation. "That's good, kid. That's real good." He turned to Arty. "Get it done."

***

As the minutes passed, Lauren grew more frustrated at their inability to find Sorrentino's seaside home. The spacecraft was ten thousand feet in the air, and Matt had directed the Infrared Imaging array down to the Mexican coastline. On the screen, magnified images of sleeping bodies in small homes flowed swiftly by like a stream of corpses.

She wondered if Sherman's boyfriend had lied. Everything rested on his information. If he had fooled Remy, then Rolly was dead. She hated that the boy's life depended on someone she could not trust or believe. But there was no other choice.

Standing beside her, Remy ran his hand through his hair, his face showing strain. Potter had said the hacienda was on the coast north of Los Llanitos, but that could be 100 yards to 100 miles. They were taking too long to find it.

The men had moved up front to watch the images with the same mixture of worry and tension that comes before a battle. All still looked on the technology with awe, Earp the most dumbfounded, still not accepting it. Pauline held back, sitting in a chair, her legs tucked under her, her arms wrapped about her as if cold. She stared out toward nothing.

Then, Remy saw it. "There," he shouted. "That's it."

Pauline shot a glance at the screen as Matt froze the scan in place. The outlines of a large structure appeared, bright blinding light spilling out, blocking any rendering of who was inside. Outside, the building was different. Lauren quickly counted twenty human images around the place. Guards. More had to be inside, but how many? She trusted her men in the fight, but she didn't want the numbers to make this suicidal.

"Why are the lights on?" Matt asked, his disembodied voice filling the hull. "It's not even 4:00am. Not the usual time for most organics to be awake. There must be some reason."

Brady whispered to Remy, "That guy gives me the creeps."

"Me, too."

"I heard that," Matt said. "I hear everything. I even know what you're thinking."

"He does not know what you're thinking," Lauren said, studying the screen. "Twenty outside, maybe ten or more inside."

"Thirty. That's not too bad, right boys?" Knighton said.

Several men nodded.

"Perhaps we should contact the local authorities," Russell suggested. "The more support we have, the better chance for success. After all…"

"No police," Lauren snapped.

"I'm afraid they're already down there," Brady said.

He directed Matt to wind back the images a quarter mile along the coastline to rows of sleeping men. They seemed to be in pairs, five pairs to a row. Four rows—forty men.

"They're in tents. Who are they?" Lauren asked.

"Looks like the Federales, ma'am," Brady said. "My guess, our friend Sorrentino made simpatico with the local comandante."

Knighton's face hardened "Sixty to seventy men. Damn."

Lauren nodded. She had sixteen including Russell and Earp. This was turning into that suicide mission.

"We stick to the plan," Lauren said. "I still go in first to locate Rolly. Only then will Matt bring you down. Once we get the boy onto the ship, you take off even if I'm not there."

Remy shook his head. "No. No need. We get Rolly and get out."

Her eyes grew cold as river ice. "I'm not going to let Sorrentino live out this day."

No one contradicted her.

Russell pointed at the screen. "What's that?" A small rectangular object just outside the hacienda, its front glowing brightly.

Lauren's heart sank. She knew instantly what it was. She should have seen it before. A car, and the glow was the heat from its engine. It could be someone from Los Llanitos just arrived, but she knew with certainty it was not. It was Pelosi, and that changed everything. He had gotten there much faster than anyone expected, and Rolly would soon be dead, if he wasn't already. Time was up. Long past up.

"The plan has changed," she announced suddenly. "That's Pelosi's car. We have to go in now. Surprise should give us an edge."

"Is that wise?" Russell said. "Surely, we should stay with the original plan. It may take a little longer but..."

"Tell that to Pauline at Rolly's funeral." Lauren snapped, and everyone glanced over to where Pauline sat.

She rose and came up to them to get a better look at the screen, then the actress said, "Get us down there, Matt. Now."

***

Inside Sorrentino's hacienda, Arty began to lead Rolly from the room. The boy stopped and stared out the massive front window into the blackness beyond. His eyes widened, his expression grew excited.

"She's coming," he shouted.

Curious, Arty followed his gaze and saw nothing at first except the men in the room reflected by the light, looking as well. Then, something in the night became more distinct. Distant amber lights rotated in the sky, growing in size and coming straight for the hacienda.

Sorrentino saw it too. "What the hell is that?"

Rolly burst out, "I told you she'd come. I told you. That's the spaceship. Now you're in for it."

The spinning lights approached at outrageous speed.

***

Inside the shuttle, the men lined up in their two teams at separate airlocks, weapons at the ready, Knighton leading one and Remy the other.

Angrily, Russell paced in front of the control panel. He had wanted to be on a team going in after Rolly. Lauren had forbidden it, forbidden him and Pauline to leave the shuttle, telling him his medical training could save lives tonight.

"Cut the lights," Lauren ordered.

The ship went dark.

Magnified on screen, they could see inside the living room. No Rolly. She searched the screen's infrared imagery outside the house. She saw figures of men running, but nothing resembling a small boy. She felt the first hint of panic. The bright lights of the hacienda rushed toward them.

Lauren commanded Matt, "Crash the building."

His voice came back mechanically, "Impact in five, four, three, two…"

The shuttle burst through the vast hacienda window, taking out part of a sidewall, sending bodies and debris inside the living room flying. The lights flickered and went out, casting them all into darkness. Matt bathed everything in infrared.

The airlocks opened, and Knighton shouted, "Over the top, boys!"

The men raced into a fusillade of gunfire.

CHAPTER FIFTY-SIX: THE BATTLE OF THE HACIENDA

January 12, 1928, Las Llanitos

Knighton's and Remy's teams surged into the firefight, finding cover behind toppled furniture. Bursts of Thompsons, handguns, and shotguns rumbled and flashed like a summer storm, including loud blasts of Wyatt Earp's long-barreled Colt.

The nose of the shuttle had penetrated the hacienda, leaving the airlock just outside on the patio. Lauren drew her Glock and waited in the darkness just outside, taking in everything, trying to get a sense of where Rolly might be. A stiff wind whipped in off the ocean, and amid the gunfire, she could hear the surf below crashing on the rocks.

Could Rolly still be in the house somewhere? Nothing resembling a small boy was picked up outside. If Sorrentino had already killed him, she'd unleash a hell upon him and his thugs never seen in this century.

A second later, three figures leapt over the stone railing and ducked into a crouch. They moved forward to come up behind Remy's team. In the moonlight, she recognized one of them, Arty Pelosi, and slunk back deeper in the shadows.

They hesitated, taking in the craft. "What the hell is that, Arty?" one muttered.

"How the hell should I know?" Pelosi shot back in a whisper. He carried a Thompson and the other two had handguns. "Shoot the fuckers."

When they lifted their weapons to fire, she shot. Arty first, then the other two, all in the head, all in less than a second. She wished she could have taken one of them alive, but that couldn't be done.

"Hello, Arty," she said, stepping over him.

In the living room, visibility was limited to amorphous shapes in the smoke. The gunfire from the gangsters was erratic. Even with Thompsons, they were no match for the controlled fire of the infantrymen. Any shape that poked up above the toppled furniture was shot down. The toll was devastating to the gangsters. Yet more of them rushed into the house.

In a crouch, Lauren darted over the debris and knelt beside Remy, crouching behind a shattered couch. He squinted at her. "At best, this is a stalemate. We're getting them now, but there's too many. They keep coming. We must find Rolly now."

"I need a prisoner."

"Then, get one fast."

She nodded and leapt out into no man's land.

The swift movement brought a volley of gunfire, and she went down. Crawling over broken glass, Lauren inched toward an overturned armchair, felt the sting of cuts and the warmth of her blood oozing from them.

Abruptly, a monstrous creature with snakes for hair, fangs for teeth, and yellow orbs for eyes appeared in the shuttle's front screen. A roar lifted above the gunfire. Beams of yellow light shot from its eyes, illuminating Sorrentino's men.

"Get out!" men cried. "Run!"

They tried but collided with the Federales rushing in, and all fell under the withering fire from the infantrymen. The Federales caught the panic that was spreading like a firestorm, and they, too, turned to run back out. The firefight had become pandemonium.

Bracing herself against the wall, Lauren fired at two fleeing men in quick succession, dropping each. Then, she saw Jimmy Pelosi. He was down a short hallway in front of French doors, aiming his gun at her. They fired at the same time. She felt the heat of his bullet sear her ear.

Her shot blew off his kneecap. She wanted him alive.

Assassin 13

He screamed and sank to the floor. An instant later, she jammed a knee into his chest, pinning him down.

"Where's the boy?" she demanded.

His face twisted in agony. "What boy?" he choked out.

He gripped his gun and tried to bring it up. She shot him in the hand, severing two fingers. He shrieked again.

Grabbing his hair, she jerked up his head. "Tell me where Rolly is. I'll get you medical assistance. You can survive this, Jimmy. I won't ask you again."

Through clenched teeth, he hissed, "Fuck you."

She put the barrel of the gun to his forehead as Remy rushed up beside her and gently pulled Lauren's gun arm back. Over the din of chaos, he spoke in a friendly voice, "We have your brother, Jimmy. He's in our flying machine right now with our medic. He'll be fine."

"Take me to him," Jimmy said. "The pain is killing me."

"We will. If you tell us where Rolly is, you can join your brother. You both can live. If not, I'm afraid you both die here. I guarantee you we will find someone with the answer, and he will get to live. You won't."

Christ, Lauren thought. He was giving him a Shakespearean monologue.

Then, as an explosion went off, Knighton dove into the short hallway and rolled to a kneeling position beside them. He fired his Army Colt back into the living room.

"That son of a bitch Brady," Knighton said. "He got ahold of several pineapples and brought them in a pack." At her puzzled look, he said, "Hand grenades. We got the bastards running."

She turned back to Pelosi. "Last chance."

He chuckled, winced, then groaned in pain. Sweat beads clung to his forehead. "What the hell, it's too fucking late anyway. You can't pin it on us cause you'll never find him.

Sorrentino took him. He's in the drink by now." He winced and groaned again, then focused back on Lauren. "I told you what I know. Now, do something about this fucking pain."

"Sure, Jimmy." Lauren jammed her gun to his forehead and pulled the trigger, obliterating the top of his head.

Remy jumped back in shock.

"Finish this, Remy," she ordered. "Knighton, you're with me."

While explosions from Brady's grenades shook the house, Lauren and Knighton raced through the French doors.

Outside, there was no one on this side of the house, but the commotion of the firefight spilling out in the front. Thirty feet away, a mangrove forest abutted the cliff's edge. About a hundred feet below, the surf crashed up on the rocks in a scene of reflected moonlight and sea spray. Ahead of them was a trail that split, one path continuing along the cliff edge through the mangrove trees and the other traversing down toward the sea. If Rolly was out here, he could be on either one of them.

Lauren said, "You take the top. Shoot anyone who gets in your way."

With a barely perceptible nod, Knighton sprinted off while she broke into a run down toward the sea. Moist, cool air rose from the ocean spray, covering the rocky path with a damp sheen. One slip would be a death tumble.

While not easing her pace, she assessed Rolly's situation. Sorrentino had to kill him, and he would have to do it far enough away from the hacienda so that the body would never wash up on a beach nearby. That would blow all his claims of innocence apart. Likely, Sorrentino would use a boat to take Rolly far out to sea. There, the boy would disappear forever.

That's when she saw it and knew she was right—the vague shape of a boat anchored near shore a half mile down along the coastline. She picked up her pace.

Assassin 13

After a quarter of a mile, the path reached sea level and flattened out. The surf burst over large boulders some twenty or thirty feet away, snaking through smaller rocks in toward her, rolling up over the path. High tide was coming in.

Each stride took her past crags and caves carved out over the eons by the water. Ahead, something was snagged on a rock and flapping in a gust of wind. When she snatched it up, she choked back a gasp. It was Rolly's suit jacket with the stickiness of fresh blood on the sleeve. Bile rose in her throat.

"Where are you, Rolly," she whispered.

That's when she heard a voice, made feint and indistinct by the roar of the surf. A man's voice, angry, demanding. It was Sorrentino.

She broke into a sprint.

***

Furious, Sorrentino stuck his head into the narrow crevice. It was too small for him to enter. In the darkness, he couldn't even see the brat. "I told you, kid. I'm just taking you down to a boat. I'm taking you back to your momma. That's all. For Christ's sake, don't you want to see your momma?"

"You're a liar," Rolly shouted at him. "You're a big fat liar. Lauren!" His scream echoed out of the crevice.

"She's not coming, boy. She's dead. Get that through your thick head."

Sorrentino considered firing into the small space; ricochets might get him, but he needed to be sure. The boat was waiting to take him back to Los Angeles where everything had finally fallen into place for him.

First, he had to finish the boy.

"Now, get your butt out here, Rolly." His voice echoed into the chamber. "Or I'm going to leave without you. I'm becoming a little impatient with all this crap."

There was no answer. He decided to give it another minute, then he'd empty his gun into the fissure and let the tide finish him. A wave of water swept in over his ankles and into the crevasse.

The boy screamed even louder. "Lauren!"

"I told you, kid, she ain't…"

As the water washed back out, he caught the sound of someone running on the path.

He froze.

***

Lauren heard Rolly's voice coming from inside the cliff itself and rushed to the small opening. She holstered the Glock and tried to squeeze in but couldn't. It was too narrow. "Rolly, are you okay?"

"Yeah."

"Stay where you are. I'll get you out."

"I can't move anyway. I'm stuck."

"I'm coming to get you."

When she turned to push in sideways, two things happened seemingly at once. She heard a gunshot muffled in the sound of the surf and something slammed into her back with the force of a sledge hammer. Instantly, she knew she'd been shot. The power of it drove her to her knees. A second shot burned into her thigh, and a third struck her head. Darkness swept in like a cut-to-black.

CHAPTER FIFTY-SEVEN: CHECKMATE

January 12, 1928, Las Llanitos

The hacienda had been cleared. Rolly was not inside. Outside, Windsor's Warriors pushed Sorrentino's men and the Federales farther into the mangrove trees. Brady pulled the pin on a grenade and drew his arm back to throw it when a bullet struck his chest. The grenade dropped from his hand and rolled next to Remy, who was aiming his Army Colt.

An infinite night closed in. Brady blinked, uncertain what was happening, then his head cleared for a moment. With his last strength he shoved Remy aside and fell on the grenade just as it went off.

***

WAKE UP. Lauren. WAKE UP.

Having no concept of elapsed time, she groped back to consciousness. She knew gunshot wounds, even ones to the extremities, were devastating and lethal. You did not shrug them off like in all of Matt's movies. Sometimes, adrenaline pumped seconds of strength into the body, but when that faded, the body went down and stayed down, and if you didn't receive immediate care, you bled out.

Like a shock wave, excruciating pain hit her body. Wincing, she burrowed her face into the damp sand and rocks of the path. She had been stupid. Concern for Rolly had stolen her edge.

Another wave of pain ratcheted up the agony tenfold as a small wall of water washed over her, then drained back out to sea.

Lauren drove the pain into a deep vault in her mind and banged an iron door shut on it. Then, as she always did when hurt, she assessed the damage to her body. Since the injection of nanobots years ago, that assessment had become clinical. Her neurobots drew data from the injured areas and gave her a precise reading.

A .32 caliber bullet had struck the upper left side of her back, cracking two ribs and gouging a tunnel at 45 degrees down her side to come around the front. The round now pressed against the skin of her lower abdomen.

The second round had punched through her thigh high up near the glute, missing the femoral artery and leaving a ragged exit wound. Striking the artery would have killed her before her nanobots could heal her.

The third had hit her head a glancing blow on the right side above the ear, cutting open her scalp along a three-inch groove. She bled profusely.

Lauren, you must do something, Matt said, his words frantic. *I hear someone just a few feet away approaching us. Get up! You must get up.*

She was severely damaged, but not mortally so. Her nanobots were shutting off the hemorrhaging and regenerating the cell tissue at a speed a hundredfold faster than normal. The blood flow from her wounds diminished. Extra adrenaline pumped into her.

In the moonlight, the shadow of a figure fell over her. She heard his laughter and knew it was Sorrentino. He flicked a cigarette lighter and lit a cigarette against the wind.

Out of the corner of her eye, she watched as he puffed several times on the cigarette, letting water wash over her, shifting her body, then flow back out. He holstered his revolver and snatched her Glock from its holster. He studied the weapon a moment and gave a low whistle.

He grabbed her shoulder and flipped her onto her back. He saw she was alive. "What the hell did you think you were going to do to me, toots? I'm not a priest. I'm Benny Sorrentino.

I've capped the toughest hoods around, and you think you can match me."

With a smirk, he stuck the gun in her face.

"What are you going to do?" she asked. "Talk me to death?"

With a quizzical look, he gave a grunt and pulled the trigger.

Nothing happened.

He jerked the trigger several more times, but the gun wouldn't fire.

Her left hand shot out and grabbed his gun wrist, jerking him down toward her. With her elbow, she popped a jab to the face, bursting his nose. Then, she swung her leg up around him and hurled him against the cliff face. The Glock bounced several feet away along the path.

Sorrentino reached for his revolver.

In one swift motion, Lauren sprang up and slammed her fist into his solar plexus. He bent double. The next punch took him down hard. Another wave of pain swept through her, stopping her for a moment. Gasping, he groped up to his feet. His right hook caught her in the jaw, staggering her back. Bright white sparks exploded in her head.

"Bitch," Sorrentino swore. "I'm going to tear you ass from limbs."

Like a bull, he charged, throwing another right hook. Stepping to the side, she deflected it and lifted a lightning kick to his nose as he passed. It exploded again with blood spray. He staggered a fraction of a second, enough time for her to drive her boot through the back of his left kneecap with such force it dislocated.

Then, she snapped off two savage punches to his jaw that dropped him to his knees. Spitting blood, he gazed up at her with a mixture of shock and black rage. She drove her boot into his chest, hurling him into the water.

Lauren grabbed the Glock.

With the oncoming wave, he struggled to the shore and pulled himself up. "I shot you. I know I shot you." His voice baffled, angry. When she aimed the Glock at him, he chuckled. "It won't fire."

"Oh, it will fire. You just have to be me."

He reached for his revolver. She pulled the trigger, exploding a canal through his chest. He tumbled back into the sea.

Exhaling, Lauren stared at the body being carried into the rocks by the retreating wave. Then, she heard Rolly's voice. "Lauren, get me out, please. The water comes up to my chest."

"I'm coming, honey."

A wave washed up over the path, leapt up the side of the cliff face, and rushed into the crag where Rolly was imprisoned. Soon the boy would be under water.

He screamed, "Lauren, hurry!"

The opening was slightly wider at the bottom. When the sea rushed out, leaving just a foot of water, she lay flat and wedged herself in, keeping her head up, crawling to within a couple feet of him before she could go no farther.

He asked in a tremulous voice, "Is Emmy…is Emmy…"

"Emmy is fine," she answered.

She reached her hand till it clasped onto his foot. His shoe was wedged in the rocks. Somehow it felt like the entire cliff held the boy in a vise grip. She struggled to pull him free, but his foot wouldn't budge. A new wave rushed in, burying her in it.

***

Brady lay in the hull of the shuttle, Pauline kneeling beside him. He was still alive, barely. She looked to Russell, who shook his head. Several men stood looking down at them. Earp, who looked as if he'd just come from a casual walk on the beach, said, "You did well, son. I'm proud to have stood beside you."

Brady gave a perceptible nod.

The battle was done, the gangsters and Federales driven off for now. But likely they'd be back. Remy had gone after Lauren and Knighton, who were searching for Rolly.

Her heart ached for Rolly, not knowing whether he was alive or dead. But she focused on Brady. He was staring at her. She held his hand.

He said something but she couldn't hear it. She leaned down to listen and he kissed her cheek. She rose up. Her eyes watered and she forced a smile. "You rogue."

Then she leaned down and kissed his lips.

He said, his voice barely audible, "If I have to die, looking at you, Pauline, is the way to go out."

"You're not going…" She didn't finish. His eyes glazed over and he was gone. Tears ran down her cheeks.

Moments later, one of the air locks slid open; Remy and the remaining men rushed in. At the rear, Lauren came in, carrying Rolly, who had one bare foot. Both were soaked. She set him down, and he ran into his mother's arms.

***

After the Battle at the Hacienda ended, four of Windsor's Warriors had been wounded and one killed. Captain Brady's body was brought back to Los Angeles where hundreds turned out for his funeral at Forest Lawn in Glendale. They sat in folding chairs on the green lawn, Pauline and her family up front with the Warriors. Their faces were stonily set in an attempt to hold back tears. Emmy was well enough to attend, nestling in her mother's arm and crying softly.

Brady, being a movie stunt pilot, brought out many from the movie industry. In the front row, Lauren sat alongside Remy, holding his hand. She didn't listen to the Lutheran pastor speaking in his soothing baritone. Instead, she gazed out at the immaculately manicured green lawn and the cloudless perfect sky, and listened to the nearby songbirds. Her heart felt squeezed like a rung-out rag. Captain Brady had been a man she could count on and did. He'd always proved his loyalty to Pauline, and his death hurt.

When the pastor finished, Pauline stood and faced the crowd. Her voice quavered as she spoke. "I have a few words to say. I've known Clyde Brady only a short time, but his friendship seemed like one born of years. He had survived the trenches of the Great War, then took up flying, never worrying about the odds. He wanted every moment of his life to count. It did. He gave his life for me and my children. A more unselfish act of friendship God has never seen."

The actress stepped up to the casket and placed a single white rose on it. "Thank you for my family," she said softly.

Captain Brady was lowered into the ground.

Remy sighed deeply, and Lauren squeezed his hand. While the pastor gave a final benediction, she glanced at the audience. Her friends. What a strange word for her. *Friends*. Indeed, she loved these people: Remy, the Windsors and Windsor's Warriors. Not since the Misfits had she so recklessly given her heart over to others. It made her feel strange and vulnerable, as if she were walking on a wire stretched between two biplanes at ten thousand feet.

Next to her, Rolly sniffled. Lauren shuddered. She had almost left him and Emmy to die. Lauren knew her mother would not blame her for failing.

Still, the hole in her soul that only vengeance could fill gaped wide and deep and would so for the rest of her life.

Without the anomaly, there was no way back. Yet, she would never stop searching for a way. She did not give up.

Nearly twelve years would pass before Lauren finally discovered the way back to the 22nd century, and she couldn't have been more shocked. It happened when she was in Atlanta, Georgia for the premiere of *Gone with the Wind*.

CHAPTER FIFTY-EIGHT: YOU CAN GO HOME AGAIN

December 15, 1939, Atlanta Georgia

In her suite at the Georgian Terrace Hotel in Atlanta, Lauren was rushing to get ready for the premiere of *Gone with the Wind*. She slid into her black evening gown and sat at the dresser to begin applying a light touch of makeup in the mirror. She needed very little.

A towel wrapped around his waist, Remy poked his head out of the bathroom. "Tell me again why we must arrive an hour and a half before the movie even starts?"

His hair was graying but the undamaged part of his body was still strong and fit. She liked that he kept himself in shape and didn't let himself grow to flab like many men in their forties. Surprising since he spent most of his time in an office now. In 1929, he had begun Grand Express Airlines, which now dominated the West Coast market.

She closed her compact and glanced over her shoulder at him. "We can't arrive after Gable or Leigh. That would be so gauche, don't you know."

"Well, if you'd gotten the role of Scarlett, we could be the last to arrive." He looked to the canopied bed, then back to her and raised his eyebrow in an exaggerated leer. "And then we could utilize the furniture for another hour."

She laughed as Remy ducked back into the bathroom. "You're so lecherous."

Like most actresses in Hollywood, Lauren took a screen test for the role of Scarlett O'Hara, but ended up playing one of her sisters instead.

As she applied her lipstick, she thought of how ironic it was that she was acting while Pauline had long since left the profession. Instead, after Lauren warned her and others about the 1929 stock market crash, Pauline ended her movie career and turned to business. She began buying real estate and investing in everything from hotels to Remy's airline. In those days, she was in a friendly competition with Mary Pickford, who had also retired from pictures.

Both had survived the coming of sound, but many hadn't. The motion picture world had altered, becoming an alien landscape. It had begun with *the Jazz Singer* in 1927, but the first half of the next year, many thought of sound as a temporary fad—that is till July 6. On that date, the movie *Lights of New York*, the first all talking movie, opened in New York.

It was an appallingly bad movie, perhaps the worst I've ever seen, Matt said, *with wooden acting and a plodding story.*

Yet, everywhere it played, lines stretched around the blocks. The situation was finally clear to all. Sound movies were here to stay, and silent movies were dead.

Panic swept Hollywood.

Actors and actresses who earned five to ten thousand dollars a week, many times the yearly wage of most Americans, feared that their dream lives would crumble. To make it worse, studios demanded that every one of them, no matter how big a star, take recorded voice test to see if they could fit into this new world.

When Pauline had taken her voice test, a stage hand burst out the door and screamed to everyone nearby, "Pauline Windsor has a voice! Pauline Windsor has a voice."

By the latter part of 1929, the studios were making only sound movies.

Sound brought down a few actors, like Pauline's friend Vilma Banky, whose thick Hungarian accent could not bridge the gap to talkies, and John Gilbert, whose voice, though decent enough, did not seem to match a romantic lover's. Both slipped out of the star firmament.

Assassin 13

The Hollywood landscape was changing for everyone, and soon new stars took the place of the old. A few silent film stars continued on as big as ever but most did not. Mary Pickford, Pauline, and Clara Bow, the reigning queens of Hollywood, found the new way of making pictures not to their liking. While at the very top, they all walked away from acting.

Lauren was one of those new stars. She had never reached the same heights as Pauline had but she had appeared in nearly thirty movies by 1939, mostly as the hero's love interest or the second female lead. Now, she was in Atlanta to attend the premiere of the most important movie of the sound era.

As she attached her diamond earrings, Remy called from the bathroom. "Look at all my gray hairs. I'm getting too damn old. Pretty soon you won't want to be seen with me anymore."

"Will you quit whining," she chided. "You look distinguished. More handsome than ever."

"How do you do it?"

"Do what?"

"You never seem to age. You look the same as the day I met you. What's your secret?"

Like the crack of lightning, light illuminated the darkness. Staring at herself in the mirror, she thought it couldn't be that simple. She studied her face closely. Since the day nanobots were injected into her body, she had not aged. She was nearing forty years old and looked the same as she did when she was twenty-three. The nanobot technology was preventing her from aging, or she was aging at such a slow rate that it was imperceivable.

Lauren leaned back in the dresser chair and sighed. She now knew how she would get back to her own time, but she was not sure she wanted to live for another two hundred years.

Assassin 13

CHAPTER FIFTY-NINE: A LONG JOURNEY HOME

September 5, 2116, The American River, California.

Erin Ramirez arose just before dawn, as the last stars were fading in the grayness of morning twilight, and knelt beside her thirteen-year-old daughter Lauren. As she often did, Erin intended to get in a quick run before the rest of the circus awakened, and last night, Lauren had pleaded to go with her. Because of the late summer heat, they had slept outside with her husband Hector beside their old Airstream camper.

"Wake up, mi hija," she whispered, gently shaking her. The girl groaned and turned away. Undisturbed, her husband Hector snored lightly on.

Erin's long red hair was damp with perspiration. She smoothed it back behind her ears and rubbed her temples. She knew the strain that the long summer had brought, going from town to town. It brought on another hammer and anvil headache. She stared down at her daughter, the girl's long black hair splayed out on the pillow, coppery skin, tall and angular for her age. So different from her in looks, taking after Hector, but so similar to her in attitude, aggressive and temperamental.

Nearby, a robin sang to her. Then she heard the sounds of the camp beginning to come awake, people rousing from their tents. They were the Misfits, a pitiful excuse for a circus. Three days ago, they had stopped here in the foothills of the High Sierras next to the American River, where, it was said, gold had been discovered sometime in the far distant past.

Erin loved the Misfits because they'd become her daughter's family, and so hers as well. They advertised themselves as a circus, but they weren't much of one, fifty people and an elephant named Ralph. They traveled in an old yellow school bus, several pickup trucks, campers, and a few wagons, all drawn by horses; no one could afford gas any more.

The first shards of sunlight glinted off the silver camper. Painted on its side were the images of herself, her husband, and Lauren, all in fierce combative poses. In large print were the words **Montezuma, the Irish Banshee, and Little Malinche. No holds barred fighting. Take on all comers. Win Big Money.**

Lauren was Little Malinche.

It was Hector and Lauren who made the money and barter that kept them alive and much of the circus going. Not Erin. No woman was brave enough to step in the Octagon against a world champion in judo, but Hector and Lauren were different. Everyone thought they could win against them. Hector was such a good actor he always seemed on the brink of defeat, and Lauren, a tall, skinny girl, seemed easy money for teenage boys.

As always, Erin felt both a sense of pride in her daughter, and guilt. A good mother would not use her daughter to fight other young people for money. But Lauren was a natural at it, she loved it, and if she didn't play the game, they wouldn't eat.

Alongside the American River, Erin stared down at her daughter. The girl had twelve fights last night, including one unusually tough one. She went to bed exhausted and a little bruised. Erin decided to let her sleep. She leaned down, gently kissing her daughter's forehead for the last time.

Pouring off the distant mountain peaks, the air was crystalline. A perfect day for a run. She drew on her shorts and T-shirt, and pinned her red hair back in a braid. Strapping on her old .44 Magnum in case of bears, Erin grabbed a canteen of water, set off westward alongside the river.

In the trees, the wind died down. A footpath hugged the river bank, and she kept to that, leaping over the occasional fallen tree. Her ponytail bounced as she ran, her stride long and graceful. She broke out of the trees, crossed an open field and back into the trees. Maybe two miles out and two miles back this morning, she thought. Too much to do today. Set up for a final show. Then, pack up and head south toward the small camps along the foothills. All the while pacifying her daughter for not waking her. She would hold a grudge all day about that.

Erin was aware that it was another irony in her life that she fought daily with her daughter who so desperately wanted to make her own decisions. Yet she couldn't love anyone more. The girl had a good heart and a strong moral instinct. She would always do the right thing. Thanks mostly to Hector.

At least two miles from the Misfits' encampment, she burst out of the woods into a field of tall grass, another tree line some thirty yards ahead. She stopped and took a drink from the canteen. Her T-shirt was soaked in sweat. To the left was a tall hill with yellow wild flowers. Two hunters wearing orange vests and carrying rifles slung over their shoulders were striding down the slope toward her. One of them waved. He was a lean man with a fake grin. The other was bald, no hat, and had disconcertingly intense, bulging eyes.

She felt a pulse of fear shoot through her.

The lean man called out, "Wait, please. Can you wait? We need help. I'm afraid we're lost."

Something told her he was lying, but she stopped, her hand resting on the Magnum. As they approached, she held up a hand. "Stop there. Don't come any closer."

Exchanging glances, they halted some fifteen feet away.

"If you actually need help," she said. "I'll do what I can. But if you step any closer, I will shoot without another warning."

The lean man's eyes went wide with surprise. "Whoa there, ma'am. We mean you no harm."

"Nevertheless. Stay where you are."

The bald man now grinned and began to take a step forward. She drew her Magnum and he stepped back.

"If you're lost, which I doubt," she said, gesturing to the water, "follow this back to town."

"Why, thank you. That's all we needed," the lean man said. Neither man moved, just continued to stare at her.

She did not want to turn her back on them. She glanced back at the tree line she'd just come out of. Her heart squeezed as if gripped by a fist. Two more men stood there, rifles aimed at her.

The bald man chuckled and the lean one said, "We saw you running from the hill. I said now that's a woman I got to meet." He indicated the magnum. "Drop that piece or my friends will drop you."

She dropped the gun to the grass. She felt the fear coursing through her blood along with the fury. She knew what they intended and doubted if she would survive. She was not going to let them touch her without fighting back.

All four closed in on her. She took a step toward the water, but stopped. She could not outrun the rifles.

The bald man grinned. "Love your hair, deary."

The lean man spoke to one of the other men, "Lad, introduce yourself to this woman. This weekend is your graduation celebration. This one's for you."

A young, broad-shouldered man about twenty came forward with a shuffling, hesitant gait. He was grinning though. His tongue shot around his lips. When he set his rifle on the ground, a gold medallion on a chain slipped out from the neck of his shirt. He stuffed it back in and stepped behind her.

The moment he reached around to grab her breast, she clutched his hand and flipped him instantly to the ground. She reached for her Magnum; the other three men lifted their rifles.

Assassin 13

The lean man eyed her darkly over the barrel of his weapon, then his lower jaw disappeared and blood erupted from where it had been. He pitched forward onto the grass. A gaping hole emerged in the bald man's chest and he collapsed while the third man turned to run. He got no more than two steps before the back of his head blew off, and he went face down onto the ground.

Erin felt the cold metal of a hand gun pressed to her temple. The young one had jumped up, and in the chaos, drawn a weapon. His arm slid around her waist to hold her against him, turning her to keep her between him and whoever was firing.

"I'll blow her head off," he shouted. "I swear I will. Show yourself."

A second later, a woman stepped from the tree line ahead, a gun in her left hand pointing casually to the ground. She was tall with raven black hair, about forty years of age. She wore black jeans, boots, and an old leather flight jacket.

"Who are you?" he shouted at the woman.

"I've waited four or five lifetimes to meet you, Eric."

"What the hell!" he shouted, his voice shrill. "How do you know my name?"

She gave a gentle laugh. "Don't worry. I'm not going to hurt you." She slipped the gun into the front of her belt. "That is, if you walk away now."

Eric hesitated, then aimed his gun at the woman. Instantly, Erin twisted his wrist down, causing him to scream, and the gun fell. Then she flipped him to the ground again.

When he scrambled for the weapon, the woman strode forward and pumped four quick bullets into him.

Reaching down, she yanked the medallion and chain from his neck. She retrieved the gold medallions from the other three and tossed them all in the creek. Next, she took one from around her own neck, stared at it for nearly a minute, then threw it in as well.

To Erin's utter surprise, the woman squatted on her haunches, buried her face in her hands, and cried.

After a couple minutes, Erin stepped over beside her. "I need to bring some people up here to bury the bodies."

"No, I'll take care of them."

The woman was so insistent, Erin decided not to argue. "We ought to leave. There may be more."

The woman rose, wiping her eyes, and nodded. "Yes, you're right. There are more."

Quickly, she carried the bodies to the river and tossed them in. Erin knew she should be appalled but felt they deserved nothing more. Something about the woman struck her as familiar, as if this was someone she met before, but in fact, she was sure she'd never seen her before.

When the woman finished with the bodies, she said, "Wait," and went back into the tree line. Moments later came the sound of an engine roaring to life, then the woman reappeared riding a motorcycle.

"Hop on," she said. "I'll take you back. We should get the Misfits moving south right away."

Erin climbed on behind her, and they started down the path.

"You should come with us," Erin said. "At least, till we get away from here."

"Not in my plans."

As they weaved slowly through the trees, Erin asked, "How did you know about the Misfits? Have you seen us before?"

"Yes, that's it. I've seen you before."

"I'm Erin Ramirez."

"Pauline Windsor."

Erin couldn't be sure but she thought Pauline said, "I know, Matt."

"Pauline, have we met before?"

"I told you I've seen the Misfits. You probably saw me then."

"Where did you see us?"

"Enough with the questions. You sound like my mother."

At that moment, they saw two figures running up the path toward them, Lauren about twenty yards ahead of Sybil, the little blond pixie.

Erin said, "Here's my daughter and her friend. Say nothing about what happened. I don't want to alarm them."

Lauren pulled up on the bike. Stopping, the two girls stared at the her.

Her young self said to Erin, "You were supposed to wake me. I wanted to run with you."

"You needed your sleep." She climbed off the motorcycle and put a hand on the woman's shoulder. "Girls, this is Pauline Windsor. Pauline, this is my daughter, Lauren. And this…" She gestured toward the little blond girl. "This is her friend Sybil. Pauline helped me run off some coyotes."

Young Lauren stuck out her hand. "Pleased to meet you, Pauline. Are you going to stay with us a while, become a Misfit maybe? Please say you will."

"That's an interesting idea. I'll have to think on it. Now you folks get on. Sybil, you in front with me. Lauren, squeeze in between your mom and me."

The two children climbed on, and Lauren headed the bike on down the path toward the Misfits and home.

THE END

ABOUT THE AUTHOR

Tom Reppert is an army veteran with a BA in English and History, as well as MAs in Creative Writing and Professional Writing. He spent twelve years in Africa and Asia teaching English Literature and Composition to international students. Previous writing includes two novels *The Far Journey*, and *the Captured Girl*. And now the publication of *Assassin 13*. Tom lives in Sandpoint, Idaho on idyllic Lake Pend Oreille. He can be reached at repptomauthor@gmail.com

EXCERPT FROM *THE FAR JOURNEY*
A Timeslip novel of Survival on the Oregon Trail
CHAPTER SIX

I was never so miserable in my life. I lay on a quilt inside a cramped, rickety covered wagon amid several old chests, assorted garage-sale junk and a single rocking chair. Wrapped in a sling, my left arm throbbed with intense pain at every bump, and the woman driving seemed to be hitting them on purpose. My hand tucked inside the sling felt numb and swollen.

A couple of hours before, a fierce-looking man with a long black beard and the eyes of a madman knelt over me with wooden slats set to splint the break. No meds. No doctor. Get me to a doctor! I had shouted, but no one paid any attention. Someone stuck a leather strap in my mouth to bite on, and a woman held my shoulders so I couldn't move.

Assassin 13

With a sickening snap, the man twisted my broken bones into place. I screamed, spitting out the leather onto his beard, cursing him and everyone else. In my life nothing, I mean nothing, ever hurt so much, ever. As he splinted me, I cried out, begging him to stop. They put me in this wagon—to wait for an ambulance to take me to a hospital, I thought, but then I heard a man outside say, "Henry, we can't wait any longer. We need to cover some miles yet today."

"She's a tough one. We're ready."

And with a jerk, the wagon moved forward.

I was scared, very scared. I didn't know what was happening. I couldn't remember how I had gotten here or anything that may have happened since I had passed out at the barbecue. On Thursday I had executed my run through the school auditorium, but when was that Thursday? For me to even be here, time completely lost to me must have passed. What was going on?

As the wagon hit another bump and pain shot through my arm, I called out to the woman driving. "God, lady, watch where you're going. Hey, you need to get me to a hospital. For Christ's sake, my arm is broken. I need a doctor. Please!"

She glanced back in at me, her face worried. "Oh, Libby honey, you know we're far from any hospital. Doc Pierce has fixed you up just fine. He says you'll be good as new."

"It hurts. Jesus! Don't you have any painkillers? At least let me use your cell phone so I can call my mother."

She gave me an expression of utter confusion that would have been comical if I wasn't hurting so much. "I know it hurts, dear, but in a couple of days it won't hurt so."

That was too much. I shouted, "You people are in big trouble. My parents are lawyers. They're going to sue your asses off. You won't have a penny left."

She sighed and went back to driving, soon singing about someone named Crazy Jane. Herself no doubt. Weird. Just freaking weird. I could not process what was happening to me. It was like tripping on bad drugs. I must have lost my memory, that much was clear.

At that moment, a man climbed in the back, grabbing a rope off a rung. "One of Captain Warren's calves got itself stuck in a mud hole," he said to me as if I cared. He had brown hair sticking out from under a battered, wide-brimmed hat. "You might start thinking about getting yourself up now. I hope you're not planning on sleeping all the way."

His face had such a hard, lock-jaw look I nearly flinched. Get up! Was the man crazy? I cut off a sharp reply because frankly the guy scared the piss out of me. This was one hard-ass bastard. I thought of a religious zealot at some commune. That might be it.

The wagon lurched sharply sending razors shooting through my arm. "Hey, you're deliberately hitting every freaking bump," I screamed at the woman.

"Do not talk to your mother that way," the man snapped. "What's gotten into you, Libby? I know you're hurt, but there's no call to take it out on your ma."

"My ma! What have you been sniffing, dude?" I shot back. "She's not my ma."

He had such a black look that I thought sure he would hit me. If I could have backed any farther away, I would have.

The woman said, "Henry, she's not herself."

"That's no reason to forget proper respect." He scowled down at me. "You show your ma respect, you hear me? No more of this squalling." He paused, his voice softening a bare fraction. "I know it hurts. Nothing we can do about that, Libby. Best you get out and walk. It will be easier on your arm."

"I'm not going anywhere," I insisted. "I'm sure not walking. Get me to a hospital."

We locked eyes for several seconds. "Suit yourself," he said with a shrug. "Bounce around in here, if that's what you want."

"If you would just get an ambulance out here," I pleaded, but he was gone.

"Honey, I know it's hard," the woman said. "But your pa's right. It would be easier on you if you would walk."

This was madness. My ma! My pa! These people had to be on something. But after a few moments in which my anger eased, I realized that, clearly, they were right. I couldn't take another bump. I had to get out of this wagon. Keeping my arm immobile, I scooted to the back and carefully climbed out.

Made in the USA
Columbia, SC
21 March 2018